Guardians

of

Sapphirus

Legends of Sapphirus Series

Book 1

Melissa G. Lewis

May the lights of Ryan shine upon you!

Princess Aurora Leigh

Guardians of Sapphirus
Book One

Published by:

LMR

San Francisco CA

Website: www.melissaglewis.com
Cover: Medieval Knight © by Diter
Chapter Dragon artwork © By draco77vector
Chapter interior dragon © Pixxart
Additional artwork layout & design © Rachel Dudley
Knight with Horse and Sword © LMR Copyrighted Logo

Published in the United States of America
Copyright © 2018 Melissa G. Lewis

ISBN-10: 172637209X
ISBN-13: 978-1726372091

DEDICATION
Part One

Dragon Throne is dedicated to my son, Nico Broos, for vowing to take care of me in the event of a zombie apocalypse. It's in writing now, buddy, you better not leave me behind!

Part Two

Legacy of Dra'khar is dedicated to Kyle Knies
I pledge to you the friendship code:
You cry, I cry
You fight, I'll fight with you
When you hurt, I hurt, too
You jump off a bridge
I will get in a paddle boat,
And save your butt – Because

I ♡ YOU

DRAGON THRONE

TABLE OF CONTENTS

Part I

LEGACY OF DRA'KHAR

Part II

Dear Readers,

As you read *Guardians of Sapphirus*, you will find that I wrote this story in third-person omniscient. Writing in third-person omniscient allows the reader to see and understand the story from more than one person's (or dragon's) mind. Because of this, you can see each of these characters' thoughts, feelings, reactions, and memories. This creates a stronger relationship and bond with many of the characters, and gives the story more depth.

Enjoy!

Melissa

P.S. Thank you for choosing to read *Guardians of Sapphirus*.

ACKNOWLEDGMENTS

First and foremost, I wish to extend my deepest gratitude to my daughter, Leanne. A thank you alone seems to pale into insignificance when you recognize the time and effort she put into this story. Without her added imagination, embellishments, and artistic brilliance this story could not have been told. Cheers to you, Leanne, for all you have done.

To Bryan Allinsmith, I want to express my utmost appreciation to you for taking the time in your busy, hectic schedule to read the story. Your invaluable advice and help was most appreciated.

Lynn Vance, you have put as much energy as I have into this story, hunting down errors, fixing misspelled words, and let's not forget your helpful editing notes—"what the . . ." and "huh?"—are two of my favorites. You are the best, Girlfriend.

Mike Kielkopf, I don't know what I would have done without your phenomenal editing skills. Your advice and fixes made the story shine. You're a great editor and proofreading pal!

If the story looks good, it's because of Lynn's eagle eye and Mike's remarkable editing talents. If you find a mistake, it's mine.

Part One

Dragon Throne
CHAPTER ONE

"C ap'n Wellsbough!" A voice resonated from the depths of the forest sending the birds to flight and a flurry of leaves and feathers to the ground. A lean, young lad materialized out of the shadows wearing a uniform of dappled leathers that blended into the woodland around him. His footfalls were barely audible as he made his way to his leader.

Captain Eralon Wellsbough turned from his conversation with a master knight of the king's guard. Mounted on his black stallion, Bladedancer, he towered imposingly over the approaching youth. He wore red and silver garb under a polished breastplate that was adorned with a finely etched, sinewy dragon, revealing his rank as captain. This same emblem waved proudly upon the banners of the Kingdom of Avala. Captain Wellsbough commanded the Elite Guardsmen of His Majesty King Lucian, and the men under his command were some of the best the realm had to offer.

"Aye Jhain," acknowledged the captain, "your report?"

Jhain, with eyes of turquoise and hair as jet as a moonless night, was fast approaching his eighteenth yearmark. His skills

1

were as honed and polished as the throwing knives he concealed in wrist sheaths under his sleeves. In a back-hanging baldric he carried a short sword, the weapon he chose to wield in battle. Though young and the newest recruit under the captain's command, Jhain was an excellent scout. Never had Eralon seen one so content on being a part of his group or so at ease in the elements.

"There be a camp in the forest, Cap'n. 'Tis certes o' what I saw," exclaimed the scout in a thick Liltian accent. "Nay yer normal band o' travelers or even poachers, fer they be armed ta the gills an' traveling with a dark-haired fella dressed as nobility."

"Sounds to be the ones we seek," Eralon replied. "We should move if we hope to catch them afore the light fails us." He hoped, for the sake of the people in Terra Leone, that this was the newly appointed steward, Danuvius Doral. "What is their location, Jhain?"

"They be about a league south o' here, a total o' eight wearing the colors o' Terra Leone. They dug a fire pit an' be constructing tents as I spied 'em. They're nay covering their tracks fer everything be out in the open. They dinna foresee us ta be about, that be sure."

"That may be," responded Eralon, his golden-brown eyes lost in thought. Jhain's description of the camp and its occupants seemed to fit. The captain tied his shoulder-length golden-brown hair with a leather band before speaking with the two men who had just joined their group. "Xyras, Bardric, you will ride with me," commanded Eralon. Upon hearing their affirming reply, he turned back to the scout and asked, "Where is your mount, Jhain?"

"I rode him hard. Me scout mate be walking him ta cool, then he will lead him ta the lake fer a drink. He'll take him back ta Terra Leone."

Nodding, Eralon addressed Keyon Nyquest, one of the master knights in the Elite Guardsmen. "See to it that Jhain gets a fresh mount and joins our group. Have the other guardsmen return to the fortress at Terra Leone. Eight Doral guards shall not be a problem for five of the king's men."

"Aye, Captain," answered Knight Master Nyquest, who smiled at Jhain and offered a hand to his brother-in-arms. "Good scouting, lad," complimented Keyon. Jhain nodded and accepted a hand up, settling himself on the horse behind the knight, and they left to do their captain's bidding.

Before Danuvius Doral's stewardship for the Fortress of Terra Leone, it had been managed by his brother, Ambassador Valen

Doral. The people within the fortress had described Valen as a noble of the highest caliber, as was his wife, Lady Mirah.

Then tragedy came to pass during the last harvest season. Lady Mirah departed this life while giving birth to their only son, and the babe only lived two days beyond. Valen's heart grew heavy from the burden of loss and he became withdrawn and secluded.

During the Festival of the Blue Moon, it seemed only fitting when Danuvius arrived for a visit to console his elder sibling. The entire populace of Terra Leone had welcomed Danuvius with glad tidings, as his presence had brought back a modicum of Valen's old vivacity. The two brothers had spent much of their time hunting, which was their most favored pastime.

Then a great misfortune struck the hearts of the people of Terra Leone once more. While out with his brother honing his falconry skills, Valen was thrown from his horse, struck his head upon a rock, and was knocked unconscious. He never awoke to see a new day dawn. The only comfort one could fathom now was that his lordship and his beloved family he had missed so immeasurably were holding court amongst the stars in the heavens.

The king had once believed Danuvius Doral to be a distinguished fellow who was loyally pledged to the Crown. He had told Eralon that Danuvius had previously performed a stipulated service for his country and, upon completion, he had been handsomely compensated with a plot of land. Therefore, the king had said he was not surprised when Danuvius made his claim of hereditary peerage as next of kin. Soon after, the king had appointed Valen's brother as temporary steward of Terra Leone. Danuvius might have been taken into consideration for ambassadorship of the fortress had things not taken a turn. The new steward's actions following his appointment had given the king time to reconsider Danuvius' virtues.

Within a relatively short time, the citizens of Terra Leone had displayed an overwhelming dissatisfaction under Danuvius' rule. The king had said that a change of leadership can often incite tension and squabbles. However, two full moons had come to pass under Danuvius' management, and the king's docket was laden with protests, complaints, and various charges against the new steward.

Disturbed by the growing complaints of neglect and the growing crime rate, King Lucian had then sent Eralon to investigate. While Danuvius had petitioned hereditary peerage in a timely manner, he had not—even once—appeared before the realm's Council of Nobles or the king since his appointment as steward. This made the situation all the more suspect. The steward was to return to Moorwyn Castle with Eralon. King Lucian would have an answer to each allegation promptly, or Danuvius' claim for ambassadorship would be deemed forfeit.

The faint pounding of hoofbeats alerted Eralon to Knight Master Keyon's return, followed by Jhain astride a sturdy destrier. They took their places next to Xyras and Bardric.

Eralon studied the faces of those before him. "Danuvius Doral shall be in custody afore the eve is out for the crimes against the good people caught within his tyrannical grip." He then waved the scout forward, "Lead on, Jhain."

Thus, the captain and his armsmen set forth upon their journey into the forest's obscurity.

Nestled within a grove of ancient trees, Eralon could clearly see the camp with its deep, roaring fire pit and hastily constructed tents. Tired horses were carelessly tethered to the thick branches of a nearby tree. Next to one dark charger, a large bush was draped with harness and trappings that displayed Terra Leone's lion emblem. Eralon recognized the spirited charger because he had stabled his own mount beside him on prior errands to the fortress.

There were seven guards who wore the gold-and-black garb of Terra Leone with an eighth man dressed richly. Not having met Danuvius Doral before, Eralon remained in the shadows and observed the elaborately garbed fellow closely, trying to divine his character before he approached.

A shock of dark-brown hair fell loosely in tattered lengths over the man's forehead above a wide nose and dark eyes. He was garbed in leather boots, black woolen pants and gloves, with ring mail over a richly patterned brocade doublet. Eralon recognized the bejeweled hilt and scabbard that hung from his waist as belonging to the late ambassador of Terra Leone. He was shouting orders and appeared nervous and agitated. This fellow seemed to lack the admirable traits that one would equate to a man of his station.

Leaving orders for his men to remain temporarily under the cover of the trees, Eralon rode alone into the meager campsite as if it were his own. All the guards of the House Doral were well-trained, so their hands immediately strayed to their steel at the sight of a rider, but they relaxed guardedly upon recognizing the king's symbol on his chest. Eralon had purposely left his helm tied next to his shield behind his saddle. He wanted them to get a good look at his face. If the Captain of the Elite Guardsmen, defender to the noble crown came to call, King Lucian meant to see his will done.

Danuvius was frowning deeply and staring into the shadows behind Eralon as if waiting for others to follow. Four of the fortress guards appeared tense, whispering amongst themselves, sharing a nervous look. The remaining three were grim-faced, so he could not read them as easily—probably loyalists sworn to the steward or devoted sell-swords. Though they wore the look of seasoned fighters, none of the Doral guards drew steel against him. Smart lads. Perhaps Danuvius would comply with the king's demands and submit peacefully.

Unwilling to venture into any of the steward's stratagems, Eralon reined in his horse at a safe distance to keep the encampments occupants in full view. As the captain's scrutiny met Danuvius' own, the steward's demeanor changed.

"Captain Sir Eralon Wellsbough, your reputation certainly precedes you," Danuvius spread his hands and offered a nod in greeting. "To what do I owe the honor of this visit?"

"I see that you don the late ambassador's attire, and you are carrying his sword and scabbard. Am I to assume that would make you the acting steward of Terra Leone?" Eralon's intonation offered little regard for the fellow. It was forbidden by law to dress above one's station, and Eralon was more than willing to add this transgression to the list of offenses brought against Danuvius Doral.

Danuvius' face snapped up to look directly into Eralon's golden-brown eyes. He did not reply readily, yet there was no mistaking the calculating look as he studied the captain.

"*Acting* Steward Danuvius Doral, at your service and behest," replied Danuvius as he gave the captain a mocking, over-exaggerated bow. "I wish you greetings, Captain Wellsbough. As you can see," Danuvius said, waving a hand to indicate the scanty camp, "we have been hunting, so I am afraid I did not receive word of your arrival. Forgive me for not providing you with a proper reception."

Eralon was not deceived by this little act. "Come now, you must deem me blind. Your horses are dressed for battle. You have no game on your fire. Is it customary to wear the ambassador's battle sword and garb on your hunts? I see no huntsmen here. The blameworthy have a propensity to flee when the law has cast a shadow upon them." Eralon continued as Danuvius' face flushed purple and his eyes turned cold. "I see a fellow who stands defiant of King Lucian's directives. You were ordered by royal decree from the king's messenger to come to Moorwyn Castle to defend your honor and properly claim stewardship. However, you did not send word of your intent to acquiesce, nor did you appear."

Eralon carried a copy of that same message in his saddlebags. Mayhap the fellow was ill of mind—or simply a cruel oppressor—but it truly mattered not. He would be dealt with swiftly in one fashion or another. "I pray you not continue with this pretense. Your tale is of spun air, and we both know it."

"Captain Wellsbough," the name flowed like a too-sweet port wine as a frown curled upon Danuvius' face. "The good people of Terra Leone are grief-stricken over my esteemed brother's death and reluctant to accept any fundamental changes. They cannot be left to their own strategies and movements in my absence."

Danuvius then glanced around as if something were amiss. He stepped closer to Eralon and, while speaking in low tones, he said, "I believe there are hidden schemes afoot. I deem the king and council are shrewd enough to see my rationale for remaining at Terra Leone in this time of crisis. I will not break a pledge I swore in my brother's name to uphold the laws of this fortress."

"I shall appoint a temporary custodian to sustain order here at Terra Leone and leave a contingent of the king's guards to look into your concerns during your absence," responded Eralon. "My presence here is to see our king's will be done." The captain tried to remain reasonable. "Yield to me, Danuvius, and come to Moorwyn Castle and comply with your king's bidding. Or, by declaration of the Crown, you will be stripped of your title and lands and your claim of ambassadorship to Terra Leone shall be deemed forfeit."

Danuvius looked shocked. "I assure you, Captain Wellsbough, there have been no crimes committed against the Crown. I need the citizens' allegiance, not disrespect. I will not become the mockery of Terra Leone!" Danuvius ran his fingers through his hair and took a deep breath. "Therefore, I must respectfully decline your escort and tend to Terra Leone as my role under stewardship demands. You have my pledge of honor that I shall strike out for the castle within a day or two, as decreed, when I have secured things to mine own liking here."

"You are disobeying the direct orders of King Lucian," Eralon warned, "and in so doing shall suffer further disgrace, proclaiming yourself a criminal. Do not force my hand, Danuvius."

Knight Master Keyon Nyquest chose that opportune moment to come forward. From the way Danuvius' guards scrambled in haste to defensive positions, Xyras, Bardric, and Jhain must have also made their presence known at Eralon's back.

At the sight of the king's guards, Danuvius' onyx eyes blazed, and he drew his brother's sword from its bedecked scabbard. Wan light ran down the sharp steel. Seven blades rasped from their sheaths following their acting steward's reaction.

Eralon sighed. The order had been given and disobeyed, and now with their blades drawn, honor demanded satisfaction for both his king and country. This fellow Danuvius was a reckless fool. Eralon had entertained hope that he would be a man of honor and fulfill his king's ruling peaceably. But it was not meant to be. With blades drawn, Captain Wellsbough was left with no choice but to follow the course Danuvius had hastily determined.

Captain Wellsbough was known for his ferocious skill with his sword *Dragon Fire*. Nevertheless, the king commanded his royal guards to never draw their swords unless a peaceful solution could not be reached and it became absolutely necessary. It seemed that time had come. As if of one mind, Captain Wellsbough and his men swung down from their mounts.

"You have awakened the dragons of the realm, the symbols of Avala, and you will taste their fire." Drawing *Dragon Fire*, Eralon saluted Danuvius, though he believed him to be of little honor.

Eralon's battle cry rose to the ears of his loyal armsmen. "For the Dragon Throne!"

With a cry of king and country, the pledge was quickly taken up by the rest of his men. "For our king and Avala!"

Clashes of steel echoed around the combatants as battles were joined. Blades deftly crossed with these traitors of the Crown, and the training in each of the king's loyal defenders was unmistakable. Though differing in stance and style, each man wielded his weapon of choice with absolute skill and proficiency.

Eralon witnessed two of the Doral guards stalking young Jhain, perhaps seeing him as the youngest and, therefore, the easiest kill. Alas, Eralon pitied them because Jhain's favorite entertainment was to fight multiple foes. Knight Master Nyquest took two of the sell-swords' blades against his bastard sword while Xyras and Bardric were battling back-to-back against the remaining three.

Eralon strode toward Danuvius because it was he who had drawn steel against the royal guards and, by representation, their king. Danuvius roared and drove his blade against Eralon's.

As Eralon and his men approached the fortress, he could see the citizenry through the trees. They were gathering, one by one, in the village square. Their eyes were fixed upon the edge of the Tall

Forest as if waiting for even the smallest crumb of comfort to lighten their hearts. The captain knew the citizens' hopes were on the Elite Guardsmen to deliver justice, for their fate was hanging in the balance.

When Captain Wellsbough and his guards emerged in the twilight with their prisoners in tow, hands bound and stumbling behind Knight Master Nyquest's destrier, a great sense of deliverance roared through the crowd. The alleviation of the distress that had enveloped their hearts could not be contained with the appearance of their champions. It was a glorious moment of thunderous triumph cascading from the people's hearts.

Torches of twisted tow dipped in wax ensconced Eralon's men in hallowed hues of gold and orange light, painting them in a heroic guise. The flickering flames cast a shimmering radiance upon polished silvered-steel helms, commanding the etchings of serpentine beasts to life. When Eralon ascended the steps of the raised platform in the village square, a great hush enveloped the crowd as he explained the series of events that had occurred.

"In a senseless confrontation," explained Eralon, "one that could have been settled peacefully and honorably, Danuvius drew his sword in defiance of the king and fell during battle into their camp's fire pit.

All eyes were on Eralon as he shook his head over the misfortune of a life lost in a senseless battle.

"Though we tried, he could not be saved, and his life came to a tragic end."

After Eralon finished his speech and left the village square, he knew great stories would spread like wildfire as to how Danuvius had met his demise. He could imagine the lore keepers spreading great tales of behemoths swooping down from the heavens in fulfillment of their roles as the great protectors of Avala. Tales of great fire-breathing dragons surely would provide the explanation for how Danuvius had died by fire.

But Eralon and the men who were there knew the truth. Even though they had all seen Danuvius fall into the fire pit, one fellow had cried "Dragon!" before fleeing in terror. Danuvius' remaining guards quickly threw down their arms and surrendered.

Although many of Danuvius' men were in custody and the situation was seemingly in hand, Eralon's instincts and training signaled to him that something was amiss, leaving him wary and on edge. The captain was unable to relax, even after he and the guardsmen had searched the perimeter of Terra Leone looking for something to explain his lurking discontent. He found naught to blame, nor could he lay his unease to rest.

Hence, Eralon set his men to the task of routing out any of Danuvius' remaining followers that the fortress denizens had deemed immediate threats. He decided to have the bulk of his squadron bring these villainous scoundrels back to Moorwyn Castle to stand trial for their crimes. He wanted their presence as far away from Terra Leone as possible. Under torchlight, he ordered the horse-drawn prison wagons to set out toward the castle. He refused to leave these disloyal traitors to fester unnoticed and become the root of future evils.

Eralon stood and watched as the last of the wagons pulled away. He had appointed twenty of his most trusted men to stay behind and keep a vigilant eye for any hidden intrigue. With all that had transpired, Eralon was pondering the disturbing possibility that Valen Doral's death was not an accident. Danuvius may have slain his own brother with malice aforethought.

The townsfolk had been charming in their merriment, inviting the king's guards to partake in their revelry. Their enthusiasm was infectious. Before Eralon allowed his men to join the celebration, he ordered them to remain watchful and alert. He reminded them that others could be lying in wait for the conquering wine to cloud their senses. As the king's guards, they were there for a purpose, and that was to protect the good people of Terra Leone. He knew that, just because the leader of the movement had fallen, there still could be hidden supporters who had not given up the cause. He warned them that, even with Danuvius gone, another power-hungry individual might step forward to seize control.

Tasks complete and worn to the bone, Eralon's next obligation was one he had made to himself, and that was a pledge to enjoy some solitude and rest. He longed for the quiet peace he felt when alone beneath the evening sky. He would leave the men under the leadership of Knight Master Nyquest, one he could count on to keep the peace in his stead.

Eralon departed through the back gates of Terra Leone and guided his stallion northwest over moonlit paths. The crystal azure of the full face of the moon was clearly visible, and he rode passionately toward his favorite retreat; it was a sanctuary he often visited after completing an assignment for his king and he was freed from his duties.

The captain reined in his mount having arrived at the shoreline of the Carillion Sea. He dismounted and walked his stallion to a comfortable, hidden cove where the tang of sea spray seasoned the night air and the brilliant stars added to its charm. The roar of the surf produced a calming effect, a result naught else could duplicate. He collected some dry driftwood and built a small fire inside a ring of sand-smoothed stones and crouched before its promised warmth. He suddenly found himself famished. He retrieved some bread and hard cheese from his knapsack, which he consumed heartily. He then fetched his waterskin to quench his thirst.

Sated, he opened another parcel and offered his trusty mount a handful of feed, but the black stallion turned his head away like a petulant child. Raising an eyebrow, Eralon had to conclude that Blade had been spoiled once again by Ristan, the stable master at Terra Leone.

"Pray tell Bladedancer, what indulgence did the stable master bestow upon you this time? Let me venture a guess . . . apples? I suspect you ate a tree-full." Eralon shook his head in amusement as the horse nodded as if in reply.

Eralon laid out his bed roll and, using his saddle to rest his head, he then pulled his cloak about him. As he began to relax, he readily released his thoughts to the sound of the waves crashing against the rocky shore and let the heat of the flames lull him to slumber.

CHAPTER TWO

P rincess Aurora Leigh felt a gentle breeze rustling through her long, golden hair as she opened the double doors to her portico at Morning Star Palace, located in the principality of Ghent. The perfume of night-blooming jasmine drew her out of her bedchamber and into her beloved sitting area.

A long, stone bench, made inviting by plump cushions, was placed between a matching pair of charming flower boxes. Gardenia and roses blended with other blossoms to fashion a richly aromatic bouquet.

She exhaled as she sat and allowed the evening breeze to sweep her into its embrace. The night displayed a full blue moon, and it was as dazzling as a sparkling sapphire surrounded by a multitude of brilliant, shimmering stars.

Long and ago Morning Star housed the first kings and queens in the country of Avala. Now it was home to King Lucian's younger brother's family: His Royal Highness Prince Dryden, Grand Duke of Ghent; Her Royal Highness Isa Dora, Grand Duchess of Ghent; and their daughter, Princess Aurora Leigh.

"Pray pardon, Your Highness," arose a voice from the portico entrance. "Your bath has been drawn." It was Aurora Leigh's handmaid, Murielle, who had been with Aurora Leigh since she was born.

"Gramercy, Murielle," answered Aurora Leigh, "I shall only be a moment."

Aurora Leigh gazed heavenward for one last look and caught sight of the fiery trail of an evanescent star. She felt a stir in her heart that told her this particular night would hold the mysteries of enchantment. This was a perfect moment to make her secret wish upon a star, and so she whispered:

"I beseech thee, O heavens above,
Hear my cry for true love
The keeper of my heart's key.
On swift wings guide him now,
For on this day I vow,
Once together, we ne'er shall part.
And with him I shall proclaim,
To be guardian of eternal flame
That burns in true love's heart."

A treasured dream, enshrined in the heart of a girl, made its way upon a shooting star to a remote shore where a weary captain of the guard lay sleeping.

ERALON was awakened from his slumber by what appeared to be the light of day. But when he focused his eyes, he found a bright, shooting star instead. It captivated his gaze as it streaked across the sky. What Eralon found odd was that the star's light trail did not fade in the star's path as had those he had seen before. He thought it had beckoned to him, as though it was lighting the way across the heavens and motioning for him to follow.

Though the position of the moon told him he still had a few more hours before sunrise, Eralon could no longer sleep. As he arose and broke camp, he kept his eye on the heavens and noted the tail of the star was still alight and showing the way to the east. Since he was headed northeast toward Moorwyn Castle, he saw no harm in pinpointing the star's direction. Filled with curiosity, he donned his armored breastplate, buckled his sword about his waist, and mounted his steed to follow the star's luminous trail.

As the light trail dimmed with the first signs of dawn, Eralon smiled. Nothing passed the time more quickly or shortened the distance of a journey so pleasantly than a curiosity that held one's attention. Eralon stopped at a stream to water his mount and looked out across the narrow ribbon of water. He spied an owl peering from a hollow in an old oak tree. He watched as she fluffed out her feathers for warmth and settled herself within. He thought it fascinating that her blinking, yellow eyes winked out in harmony with the shooting star's light trail.

Rolling up his sleeves, he knelt on one knee near the water's edge next to Bladedancer and splashed the cool, refreshing liquid against his face, neck, and hair. He was not far from Moorwyn Castle, but waking to this pre-dawn adventure had tired him. After tethering his horse to a sturdy branch, he sat with his back against the tree's cool bark. He closed his eyes, and drifted off to sleep while waiting for the rising sun to warm him.

A soft, honeyed voice sang to him upon the outskirts of his dreams. This mellifluous melody pulled him gently from his slumber. Upon opening his eyes, Eralon realized it was not a composition from his imaginings. A most glorious vision was before him, a fair maiden, picking herbs and wildflowers by morn's early light.

He noted she was dressed in attire that proclaimed her a noble. Her golden tresses framed her beautiful face, flowed down her back, and curved in tendrils about her narrow waist. Her skin was as flawless as fine porcelain. He could only see her profile now, but it was perfection. Head tilted toward the sun, her eyes closed, and her full lips parted into a smile. She was as lovely a woman as he could ever have imagined.

"Oh, do mine own eyes deceive?" whispered Eralon, "to tempt me with no reprieve, urging my deprived heart to yearn so?" He could not help but wonder if it was the shooting star that had led him to her.

She must have sensed his presence for the girl turned and met his eyes. She gasped and blinked. She let her gathered flowers fall as her fingers lost their grasp. Then she whispered aloud, ". . . the keeper of my heart's key." Her eyes grew wide, and her hand flew to her mouth as if trying to retrieve her traitorous words.

Come what may, Eralon wanted to believe she spoke from her heart. After all, he had been led to this lovely maiden by some unknown force. He rose and, as he drew nearer, the more familiar she felt, as if the pair had been in each other's company before. Her emerald eyes alone were enough to compel a man to give up his very soul, for her beauty was nonpareil. From where she came, he did not know. Surely, she was not traveling on her own?

The fair maiden bent down to gather the blossoms she had dropped and return them to her basket. Eralon was ready to offer assistance, but he thought she was, mayhap, feeling ill at ease. With a plan in mind, Eralon strolled along the water's edge to where he came upon a unique blossom, one that was about to have special meaning. He picked the everlasting flower and, retracing his steps, presented it to this most beauteous maiden.

"This particular bloom, normally overlooked, maintains its appearance and color when dried and tirelessly endures through time," declared Eralon. "An everlasting beauty, as is the one who stands before me."

PRINCESS AURORA LEIGH suddenly felt overwhelmed as her handsome captain drifted toward her. She had been in deep thought about Eralon and her secret wish upon a star. Then, suddenly, there he was, presenting her with a flower! His golden-brown hair was loose around his shoulders, and his eyes embraced hers.

Then she heedlessly backed away and felt a twinge of sadness envelope her as his hand holding the flower dropped to his side. She certainly was not accustomed to being so close to a gentleman, let alone by herself.

"I assure you, My Lady," Eralon avowed, "my intentions are purely honor bound."

Aurora Leigh knew at that moment he did not recognize her, for if he had, he would have addressed her as princess. On their last encounter, she had been but a child of ten yearmarks running about the castle. Her governess was on her trail, trying to cajole her into finishing her lessons. Eralon had the great misfortune of getting in her way, and she had given him a good, hard kick in the shin for his bad timing.

She wanted to hide in humiliation at that horrible memory. She forced herself to stand up straight and look into his golden-brown eyes. She took a deep breath and, steeling her voice, she said, "You have always presented yourself with honor and dedication to our family, Captain Wellsbough. His Majesty the King, my uncle, has always claimed that to be true of his champion of the throne."

"Your Highness," Eralon said as he formally bowed.

She could imagine the wheels spinning in his head as if looking for the words to recover from his blunder.

"It has been quite some time since last we were in each other's company. Might I inquire as to the whereabouts of your attendants?" he asked as he surveyed his surroundings. "Surely, they must be about."

It was then that Aurora Leigh realized she had wandered farther from Morning Star Palace than expected. She decided it was best to remain silent on the matter.

Eralon smiled and tried once again to present her with the everlasting blossom. Aurora Leigh's heart jumped and her emotions stirred at his gesture. He knew who she was, and he still wanted her to have the blossom. She managed a smile in return and held out her basket.

Eralon placed the flower inside her basket and broke the silence. "Your Highness, did I hear correctly when you uttered the words 'the keeper of my heart's key'? For then, truly, I believe in providence. For in the wee hours of this very morn, it was as if I were beckoned here by a star's burning trail of light."

Aurora Leigh gasped at his words and raised her hand to her face, and said, "By . . . star's burning light?"

She had wished upon that very star last eve! Aurora Leigh felt as if the secrets of her heart had been unveiled. She felt hot and could barely breathe, let alone reply. There were no words to express her discomfort. Her captain standing before her was too much to bear. She gathered her skirts and turned to flee from the champion of her dreams, for naught this day was what it seemed.

Aurora Leigh moved swiftly into the welcoming shelter of the trees, feeling Eralon's eyes like a tangible weight upon her back.

She welcomed the forest shadows closing in around her like an embrace, hiding her from Eralon's view. She noted he made no move to stop her departure, and she was unsure whether she should be surprised or disappointed.

She stopped running to catch her breath. She peered down at her basket and noted Eralon's everlasting flower atop her medicinal herbs and wildflowers. Was this wistfully conjured fantasy, or mere happenstance? Was her secret dream destined to come true? Disciplining herself for control of her wandering thoughts, she concentrated on returning to the palace and tried to let the fantasies playing in her head fade. She needed the comfort and safety of home to contemplate the day and ease her unsettled mind.

Aurora Leigh glanced at the sun and her surroundings. She

suddenly realized that, in her haste to depart, she had traveled south instead of north. She chastised herself for her error. Why had she run when the very opportunity that she had so urgently yearned for finally, and unexpectedly, presented itself? She felt a bewildering tangle of confusion from the day's events.

The forest had always been a pleasurable retreat with its scent of new growth and wildflowers, and she inhaled its freshness. It should only take her a few moments to settle herself, to find her intended course, and return to the path toward the palace. She turned and proceeded north to find the footpath to her estate.

As she looked about to navigate her course, she gave a startled gasp when a figure moved from the shadows to block her progress. Her surroundings suddenly seemed eerily quiet and still in his presence. She took note of this stranger's manner. He flashed a smile of straight white teeth and crossed his arms over his chest while he studied her up and down. Foreign angles and a scar on his chin gave the stranger the look of a seasoned fighter.

He was wearing ash-colored leather armor tooled with the symbol of a lion, and that caught her attention. The symbol belonged to a group of ruffians she had heard the palace guards talking about, a group that had been disbanded for causing a multitude of troubles. This was most definitely not the kind of company she should keep.

"Out in the woods alone, fair damsel?" asked the stranger as two other fellows materialized from the shadows, much to Aurora Leigh's great dismay.

"I cry your pardon, sirs," explained Aurora Leigh, putting on her bravest face. "I must take leave. My family is expecting me. My three brothers are on their way this very moment to escort me." She smiled politely and moved to brush past them, but one of the two newcomers startled her by grabbing her wrist.

"What do ya say, mates?" asked one of the newcomers, flashing a display of yellow, rotten teeth. "With an attractive lady, obviously gentry, we can fetch a sizeable prize."

Panic raced through Aurora Leigh as she realized what was about to transpire.

The first stranger she had encountered rolled his blue-grey eyes at his fellow's unsavory antics and said, "Come now, Thom. Let her go. Ya be scaring her."

Her shriek must have caught them by surprise, for it wiped the smile off Thom's face. She used that moment to break free from his grasp. These brigands were planning to abduct her, forcing her family to pay for her return.

"Nay, lit'l filly, me thinks ya be coming with me," said Thom, ignoring the first man's advice.

Thom and his companion started to move slowly in her direction and were taking up their positions to surround her, backing her into a tree. How she wished she had never left the captain's company. A twist of fate had devised a terrifying turnabout, for now she had gone from daydream to nightmare.

Suddenly, a way out of her plight appeared behind the three brigands—the unmistakable sound of a sword being drawn from its sheath spoke volumes. All three men turned in unison to look at the threat at their backs.

"As my sister has told you, she already has an escort."

Relief flooded Aurora Leigh, for Eralon seemed to her a golden benediction. The sunlight shone upon his armor as he stood in irrefutable confidence.

The lead brigand yelled to his cohorts, "Enough, Desh and Thom, ya lumpish, idle-headed, mammets! Look what ya gone an' done!"

Desh and Thom drew their weapons, and Thom shouted, "Bring yer weapon ta bear, Milord, the three o' us can take him!"

CAPTAIN WELLSBOUGH sprang into action upon the axe-wielding fellow closest to Aurora Leigh. The champion's blade whipped right with a backhand slash that bit into the leather armor of the short axe-wielder. The resulting hiss of pain and droplets of blood marring the tip of the captain's sword spoke for his strike. Eralon was already out of the way when Desh recovered enough to chop at him clumsily with his long battle-axe.

Eralon spun quickly, his blade slicing in a downward arc that forced Desh to catch the cutting edge between the axe blade and shaft. Eralon's unrelenting pressure on the odd angle of the axe caused the brigand's hands to tremble in their tenuous grip. Unable to give up leverage if he did not want to get cut, Desh found himself stuck in a position from which he could not extricate himself.

His fair-haired cohort, Thom, roared with rage and charged to Desh's aid. Eralon moved quickly to counter the threat. He shifted his weight, circled low, and forcefully kicked the axe-wielder's feet from under his already unsteady stance. Desh fell to his back on the leaf-littered ground with a thud.

Eralon then readied himself for the charging swordsman and stepped into his guard. His blade moved like a viper to open a slight gash upon Thom's cheek, and then Eralon stepped into the ready position as Thom staggered back.

From the corner of his eye, Eralon could see the flash of a sword coming from where he had last spotted the lead brigand. Feeling the threat drawing upon his back, Eralon continued his single-minded assault on the two combatants.

Eralon had the encounter well in hand. He saw the lead highwayman move into a position warranting Aurora Leigh's attention, and Eralon heard her gasp.

"Eralon!" spilled from Aurora Leigh's lips.

The silky sound of his given name spoken from that gorgeous mouth almost made him lose his concentration.

Almost.

But it did have a most peculiar effect on the three highwaymen. The lead brigand stopped in his tracks. Desh had just regained his feet and stared unblinking at the captain as if seeing him for the first time. Thom, the fair-haired swordsman was in position to strike—until he apparently realized who he was up against. His mouth moved, but no sound emerged.

Each studied the cut of Eralon's long hair, the intricate patterns engraved on his armor, the style of his sword stance. Eralon could almost see the wheels turning in their minds and could almost mark the moment they decided they were in way over their heads. It appeared that his reputation was at work. Eralon arched an eyebrow. Perhaps they would finally realize the futility of their endeavor and desist.

With a roar, the lead brigand thrust himself forward and whipped his sword across Eralon's in a startling move. Eralon was willing to wager that, of the three, this one had a little tutelage behind his stance and blade. Committed to the battle by his unexpected swing, Eralon wondered if the brigand fought to save his followers.

"Ya be a couple o' mangy fools, an' I'll aves no more o' it!" the leader bellowed, feet moving purposefully in intricate steps over the uneven ground as he squared off with Eralon.

"Aye Milord, if ya be determined," said Desh, clutching at his wound. "May yer path find ya good fortune." He turned and headed into the trees.

Thom only paused a moment longer. "Good fortune, Milord, 'twas an honor." He bowed his head and, in a foreign salute with fist pressed over heart, he trotted after his cohort and disappeared like a ghost fading into the trees.

"Ah, blast those blithering idiots!" whispered the lead brigand, though Eralon heard his words.

Eralon studied the one with whom he had crossed blades. He offered a lean look that belied his impressive strength. His muscles were more those of an archer than of a swordsman, and he all but flowed from one stance to another, his blade work intricate and adept. Clean-shaven, his russet hair was cut in a style unrecognized by Eralon, trimmed just past his shoulders all around, except for two longer lengths braided in front that held his hair off his coppery features. Hard, slightly tilted, blue-grey eyes marked him a Liltian with a hawkish profile striking enough to make him stand out in any crowd. A scar marring his chin line proved he had seen battle before.

Blade met blade as the combatant swung and parried, testing Eralon for weakness. Abruptly, the leather-clad fellow broke off and dashed around the nearest tree. He never strayed far from Princess Aurora Leigh, forcing the frustrated captain to pursue.

The wide-eyed princess looked frozen and frightened of the flashing swords. Eralon cursed softly under his breath. He needed to end this. Aurora Leigh had backed into a tree and was clutching her basket with white knuckles, the color drained from her face.

Eralon noted that, as they fought, the brigand's steps were still inching closer to the princess, confirming the fellow's motives. He must have been planning to hold Aurora Leigh hostage until he could get away or use the damsel as leverage to force Eralon to throw down his sword. But the brigand was unable to see clearly because of the anger consuming him, and he did not realize his plan was folly, for Eralon knew his intentions.

The captain needed an opening, so he decided to create one. Throwing himself at the highwayman in a brazen assault, he caught him by surprise and forced him further from the princess. The surprise grew as he was forced to give more and more ground to the captain's unrelenting attack.

Snarling, the brigand tried again to halt Eralon's advance. The man struck hard and fast, trying to create an opening of his own. Eralon's blade met his. Thrown off balance, the brigand was unable to parry the blade's second attempt, and Eralon's blade pierced the brigand's armor, slicing into his upper arm. The brigand staggered back from the pain and attempted to lift his sword, but Eralon knocked it aside and raised his for one last strike. Eyes closed in acceptance of his impending doom, the highwayman's body tensed. Seconds passed. Nothing happened. The defeated fellow opened one blue-grey eye with uncertainty only to see Eralon's blade inches from his skin.

"Yield!" Eralon's words were not a request. "Give over and you shall live."

The brigand had lost the contest, and it was understood what must be done. "I submit," he acknowledged with a slight accent. "A good, sharp dance, Cap'n Wellsbough," complimented the defeated man. His sword followed his promise by dropping heavily upon the forest floor.

"Aye," Eralon accepted the compliment, adding a brusque reprimand, "one that could have cost you your life, sir . . . ?"

"Treyven," he replied with a slight bow, "Treyven Fontacue o' Liltimer."

"Liltimer?" puzzled Eralon, for that country no longer existed. He looked down upon Treyven's chest and recognized the old, leather armor tooled with a lion, the symbol that had once decorated the flag of their country.

The fortress at Terra Leone was once Lionholm Castle and the surrounding lands had been known as the country of Liltimer. King Tridan, the country's ruler, had befallen a series of great tragedies, and he became suspicious, morose, and tyrannical.

King Lucian had enlightened Eralon as to how it all began. The Liltian king was riding home from Sunon, and his contingent of royal guards died in a mysterious battle, leaving the king the only survivor. Days later, the king showed up at Lionholm Castle unescorted. It was said that the tragedy that befell him was so horrendous that he refused to speak of it. Then, given that he was feeling poorly from his unfortunate encounter, he had sent his two eldest sons, the Princes Hayden and Blaine, out on a task in his stead, and they never returned home. The happenstance that seemed to plunge King Tridan into further despair was when his youngest son, merely a babe, had succumbed to a horrible accident.

The healers had believed that grief and sorrow had led King Tridan to madness. Ultimately, Tridan had lost his life in a confrontation with his former allies. It was widely believed that the Liltian king had instigated the conflict in an effort to end his misery, though that was only speculation.

With the last of her king's bloodline gone, Liltimer's queen had peacefully yielded her rule to Avala, believing King Lucian the best candidate to rule in her husband's stead. The queen herself had then succumbed to death shortly thereafter from what was believed to be a broken heart. An entire royal family destroyed by tragedy. Eralon shook his head at the thought of the horrible and heart-wrenching ordeal. He then scrutinized the man before him.

"What is one to make of your actions?" scolded Captain Wellsbough. "Former Liltian swordsman, have you no shame? Whatsoever the circumstance or the severity of the matter, attempting to spirit away helpless maidens is no way for you to behave."

Treyven's eyes held a look of defiance. "The misdeeds o' those from Avala be no better, marching Liltians off ta become serfs an' slaves fer the noble inclinations o' yer king an' country."

Princess Aurora Leigh gasped, and Eralon knew it was at the implication toward the king and her uncle. Eralon frowned in confusion at the anger burning through the Liltian's strained tone.

"I know not where you obtained such a notion. I assure you, Avala abhors the very concept of slavery, and I can personally guarantee you that we hold not to such practices."

Treyven's face was frozen momentarily and, looking perplexed, he asked, "Am I ta understand that ya shan't be taking me as yer slave?"

Eralon felt bewildered and more than a little disturbed by the Liltian's words. Where had he been taught such views?

"Treyven Fontacue," began Eralon, "regardless of where one originally hails from, you are treated as a free individual in Avala, subject to the king's laws, like any other. There are no segregated ideals in place in this country.

"Ponder this: If we held to slavery, why, pray tell, would our good King Lucian have granted Lionholm's former royal chamberlain, Valen Doral, the Fortress of Terra Leone? His appointment as ambassador was the start of making peace between our peoples. At the end of the Liltian king's reign, all were uneasy. Terra Leone was meant as a place where your countrymen could remain, where they could feel at home and secure if they could not feel as such living in other cities of the realm."

Eralon saw Treyven swallow hard at his words. Eralon could recognize sincere confusion and puzzlement in Treyven's expression.

"Come now," said Eralon, "as the captain of the guard, I would be aware of such unsavory practices if they were, indeed, transpiring right under my nose."

"Me band o' men an' I be camping in Sunon, near the southern border o' Avala fer two seasons," explained Treyven. "Danuvius himself came ta tell me about the king's wrongdoings."

"It was Danuvius who was causing the problems," said Eralon. "The new steward faced charges brought by the very people of Terra Leone you believe to be slaves. He refused to appear before his king. Danuvius lost his life drawing his sword against the king's directives. As a leader of men, I believe it would be in your best interest to stop the blame and seek the truth for yourself and the people who depend on you."

Treyven looked bewildered for a moment, and then he shook his head and said, "That I will. Pray, pardon me skewed philosophy, Cap'n, Milady, fer being led ta think elsewise." His eyes lowered momentarily, and he grimaced and clutched his wounded arm.

Eralon watched as Treyven gazed upon fingers stained red from blood soaking his leathers. He collapsed to his knees. The captain kicked the fellow's sword away from him and into the tall grass.

The brigand turned his attention to Aurora Leigh and said, "On me honor as a gentleman, I truly be repentant. I had just met up with Thom an' Desh this very day. They had told me they be in need o' coin fer food an' shelter. I make no excuse for their behavior, but I believe 'twas yer noble station that got kidnapping inta their heads. No harm woulda come ta ya, Milady."

He then addressed Eralon. "I be telling 'em they be frightening the lady an' ta desist, Cap'n Wellsbough. As their leader, I'll take full responsibility. Yea, verily, I be repentant fer their actions."

The fellow was a mystery. He acted the part of a ruffian and then offered what appeared to be responsibility and remorse for his follower's apparent schemes. Eralon had, at first, believed him daft or a liar, but it was possible that, perchance, he did possess some modicum of honor and found error in his ways. After all, the brigand had erroneously believed he was going to be taken as a slave and that fighting for his freedom was his best course.

Eralon offered a hand to Aurora Leigh, his sword point unwavering upon Treyven. "My Lady, what say you of this swordsman's fate?" Eralon suspected the Liltian was unaware of the royal blood flowing through her veins.

Aurora Leigh glided toward Eralon to take his proffered hand, widely skirting the fellow on his knees. "He did tell the others to stop scaring me, and he did not harm me, only frightened me—a little—and he is poverty struck and wounded." Her pretty face was clouded in concern.

Treyven's fate was set by the Princess of Morning Star's

misplaced sympathies. The captain whistled for his steed and the sleek, black stallion came trotting through the trees. He sheathed his sword and patted the horse's long nose as Bladedancer pushed against his hand. Eralon rummaged one-handed in a saddlebag to produce a thick, coiled strip of dressing.

"You were fortunate it was not your sword arm," Eralon told Treyven as he tossed him the bandage and then offered his hand to help Aurora Leigh to sit sidesaddle upon his horse.

Eralon turned to Treyven and said, "If you are a true representative of the people of the lost country of Liltimer, swordsman, prove so by your doings." Eralon was bound by the king and his royal family, and he had sworn to carry out their wishes. As the king's captain, he dutifully carried out Aurora Leigh's desires, though it was against his better judgment. "You are free to go."

The captain checked the straps and buckles adorning Bladedancer's light armor and handed Aurora Leigh the reins. "To not heed wisdom from this day's events would be folly. Spread the word of what transpired here and our conversation this day regarding your misconceptions of our goodly king." He then mounted his horse, adjusted the princess comfortably before him and, in effect, dismissed the Liltian.

"Mayhap I'ves fought too long fer a forgotten crusade," Treyven admitted as his voice rose louder. "I'll practice deeds that carry the weight o' tribute an' honor in me forefather's memory, an' pray thee, I ask exoneration."

There was a stretched silence from the captain of the guard. During this soundless instant Treyven spread empty hands and awaited their reply, hoping his unfeigned speech would garner their satisfaction.

"Sir," began Eralon, "I grant you pardon." His eyes hardened as he added, "But know this day you have walked a blade's edge. If lured to disobey Avala's laws in the future, reflect upon this day and quickly know better."

The captain then gently took the reins from Aurora Leigh, turned his horse and, with a quick glance over his shoulder, gave Treyven honors with a salute that befit their sword dance, and said, "Might it be under better circumstance when next we meet." Then he left the wounded fighter kneeling amongst the long grass and wild flowers poking through the fallen leaves.

Songs of wild birds filtered down from shady, moss-covered tree branches overhead as Bladedancer trotted north under Eralon's direction. He let the horse choose his own leisurely pace as they rode quietly through the forest.

Before their ride began, Aurora Leigh had twisted her mass of silky hair into a long ringlet and placed it over one shoulder. Sitting before him, Eralon enjoyed the comfortable weight of Aurora Leigh in his arms. He held his arms around her small frame in a protective circle to keep her from sliding about in her splendid raiment not meant for riding. The princess had been quiet and still as they rode, leaving Eralon to his own thoughts until she leaned forward.

He watched as Aurora Leigh ran her hand under her hairline at the base of her neck. Her hair unwound from its ringlet and tumbled around her back and shoulders in a golden curtain. He felt his heart leap when her long tresses slid like spun silk over the exposed skin of his wrists where he held the reins loosely before her.

Eralon suddenly realized the effect she had upon him. All this, mixed with the light scent of her hair, would have been enough to drive him out of his mind if he did not say something soon, so he cleared his throat and gallantly tried to recover his wits.

"Your Highness, if you would be so kind as to guide me toward your precise destination." He admonished himself for not thinking before he spoke. He most certainly knew where she was going; they were but a stone's throw from her palace.

"Where the sun rises upon the hillock before us are the medicinal gardens of Morning Star," she said. She motioned with a delicate nod in the direction of the dwellings ahead. "Yonder marks the edge of my destination. I need to take the slippery elm bark, honeysuckle flowers, and wintergreen leaves I found to the apothecary who needs them for the scullery maid's sore throat and cough. I fear that, in my eagerness to help, I traveled much farther than expected."

Eralon smiled at how grown up and formal she had become. She seemed to be taking the ordeal she had just gone through with great courage. "Very well, then. I shall see you delivered safely into the hands of the palace apothecary."

After being allowed entrance through the east gate, Eralon rode toward the medicinal gardens and dismounted. Placing his hands about her waist, he held her weight as she slowly slid down the saddle. He found himself captivated by her deep green eyes that magically held his own. Not until her feet lightly touched the ground did she release her captive, allowing Eralon to regain his senses. The powerful spell she held over him was broken when she looked away to stroke Bladedancer, thanking the stallion for the ride.

Eralon had to blink and settle his thoughts to regain his composure to speak. "You are safe and sound at journey's end, Princess."

"Mayhap the journey has just begun," she murmured softly into Bladedancer's ear, but not too softly for Eralon's ears.

Curious words, thought Eralon. He set it aside for later consideration. "I shall request an audience to speak with His Royal Highness Prince Dryden," Eralon continued, concerned for the princess. "Such a lovely rose should not be about by her lonesome, lest someone else try to pluck her. You are in need of accompaniment by one's attendants, and most assuredly when wandering the wood."

"Despite all that has transpired, your aim is yet to keep me safe, noble Captain." Aurora Leigh blushed as she said it.

Eralon noted she could not meet his eyes. He knew without a doubt that her royal family would never have let her leave the grounds without escort. She must have found one of Morning Star's secret escape routes.

"Truth be told, Captain Wellsbough, I have reached my majority and am deemed capable to manage my own affairs."

Eralon could not help the scowl on his face, warning her she most certainly would not make any headway using that line of defense.

"Prithee, Eralon," Aurora Leigh beseeched. Eralon noted she had uttered his given name, using a more familiar approach. "His Royal Highness Prince Dryden is away this day. I would hate to burden my royal mother with such news without his presence. She really does fret over me so." She gave Eralon a warm smile. "I believe those ruffians will talk and word will grow. Without doubt, news of your heroic deed shall surely spread quickly amongst those who might think to waylay anyone again."

At Eralon's silence, her eyes seemed to grow distant and her lovely smile weakened into a look of trepidation. Apparently, her words were not convincing, even unto herself, for her expression changed, and she appeared as if her world was tumbling down around her. She quickly turned away from Eralon, took a deep breath, and he saw her tremble as she exhaled. She gazed upon the ground, and he noted a tear had trickled down her cheek.

"I pray your understanding. I strayed from my path in my haste to depart, I knew not whither." Aurora Leigh's words were barely a whisper. She inhaled and glanced up at Eralon with her eyes glistening.

Eralon relented with a sigh, as he said, "As you will, Princess Aurora Leigh." His next words were spoken softly, yet firmly. "Upon your word of honor your attendants shall accompany you from this day forward when wandering from these grounds." He knew this was not the time to press the issue of an audience with all she had been through.

"You have my word, Captain Wellsbough," promised Aurora Leigh, curtsying in agreement, "and my deepest gratitude for your sublime deeds this day." And then she gave him a soft, sad smile.

"Know this, Your Highness. Fate, indeed, shall lend its hand and guide us to cross paths yet again," proclaimed Eralon, speaking from his heart, momentarily snared by her charms. He then regained his equanimity and attended to his duty as captain. "As you pledged," he reminded her, "accompanied by your attendants or family. Fare thee well, Princess Aurora Leigh."

Setting down her basket, she offered Eralon her hand. He took it with the back of his own and bowed formally. He was just straightening when her next movement caught him completely off guard. She closed her eyes, and he saw a wash of relief and sweet contentment smooth her delicate features. She threw her arms around him and tucked her head perfectly under his chin as if it had been crafted to fit there. Eralon was self-consciously aware of how rigidly he was standing, his arms held awkwardly out to his sides unsure of how to proceed or react to her sudden attentions. He then closed his eyes and allowed himself to relax and savor the moment with her lithe arms around him.

She must have realized her actions because she quickly disengaged from her familiarity as if her hands were on fire. The blush of her cheeks, burning marks of crimson on flawless skin the color of cream, only added to her innocent beauty. She picked up her basket and flitted away, not once looking back. She hurried along a pathway through the medicinal gardens toward the apothecary's workshop and dispensary.

The keepers watching the intricate wrought iron gates hastened to open them and admit the princess once they noticed her forthcoming arrival. She entered and disappeared into the workshop, the doorway quickly swallowing her graceful form.

Eralon smiled as he watched her disappear. She was innocence and delight, a portrait of feminine loveliness. He would, indeed, eagerly await their next encounter. Aye, he would meet with her again for he feared she would haunt his dreams.

AURORA LEIGH set her basket upon the floor of the apothecary's workshop. She took note of the everlasting blossom lying within the confines of her basket and pondered her captain's pledge. Now a symbol, to say the least, for this day had brought her champion, who fulfilled her most treasured dreams and saved her from what surely would have been her most horrible nightmare. She drew in a deep breath as she remembered how her arms had been draped comfortably around his neck and how safe she had felt within his protective embrace. Then, with a sigh, she leaned against the workshop door.

She bit her bottom lip in contemplation of the memory of her impetuous and impulsive behavior—but only for a moment—and then a smile enveloped her lips. A longing grew deep within, and she could not resist the urge to race to the window and watch as her captain rode out of sight. In her manner of blandiloquence, she uttered eloquent words:

"Once held safe within the haven of dreams,
Different now the certainty of thy touch seems
Merely thoughts before, its truth now burns bright,
When eyes gazed upon thee, ardor took flight
Swiftly thee came and as thou dost depart,
Such a longing grows deep within my heart
Evermore shall I be lost in its reverie,
Until next mine eyes catch sight of thee."

"Fare thee well, my champion of the throne."

CHAPTER THREE

E ralon rode through the sun-dappled shade along an avenue
of trees lost in the beauty of the day. Large, majestic
branches reached skyward forming a canopy of shifting emerald as
the leaves rustled softly in the caressing wind. Below, massive
trunks lined the main thoroughfare like steadfast sentinels that led
the way to the city of Kaleidos and her majestic Moorwyn Castle.
As he came into view of his destination, Eralon was surprised to
find the season of the sun's festivities in progress, having lost
count of the days he had been away from home.

Thrice a calendar yearmark, grand tents in bright colors were
pitched in a special area only a stone's throw beyond the city gates.
A few of the shopkeepers within the city of Kaleidos would shut
down their shops and join the outlanders who came from far and
wide to trade from the stalls at the fair, which could last for days
on end.

Making his way through the fair, Eralon surveyed many stalls
brimming with sunfruits and vegetables freshly picked from stalks
and vines. There were homespun wares of fine clothes and fabrics
as well as pottery, woodcrafts, and spices. The captain waved as he
passed Lore Keeper Windermere. The old storyteller was a regular
at the festival, who sang verses in honor of the heroic
achievements of champions and told stories of dragons and brave
fellows from faraway lands.

Eralon could hear the roaring crowds in the showground stands
where games and public contests were held. Knights in jousting
tournaments were the main attraction, but anyone could enter one

of many contests as long as they possessed armor, a horse, a sword, and a shield.

The scent of freshly-baked apple pies caught Eralon's attention, and he turned his head to absorb the aroma of the baker's stand. He espied a youngster running past, helping himself to a fresh roll on one of the baker's carts. Rolling pin in hand, the baker almost crashed into Bladedancer while in hot pursuit of the tiny thief.

Eralon dug into his satchel, gave the harried baker a smile, and said, "I would like to offer recompense, good baker, for your loss." Eralon held out his hand as he proffered the small, silver disk as payment. "I can understand the lad's desires for your baked goods, for I have enjoyed them myself."

"P-Pray pardon, Captain Wellsbough," stammered the baker. "I did not see your approach. My eyes were tracking the little urchin." He must have suddenly realized he was still holding his rolling pin in a threatening manner because, with a sheepish look, he dropped his arm. "Gramercy for the flattering remark and the coin," replied the baker, accepting Eralon's donation. "The little offender does, indeed, have good taste."

Eralon smiled and nodded in parting. He then continued along his path to the gates of the city.

In order to reach Moorwyn Castle, one first had to cross a drawbridge over a large moat and be allowed entrance through the main gateway to the city of Kaleidos. The gate was connected to a massive outer wall that was constructed around the entire city and castle.

As Eralon made his way over the drawbridge, the guards lifted the double portcullises. The heavy, grilled doors creaked as they rose slowly toward the gatehouse ceiling. The captain passed through the passageway and made his way through the merchant district.

Eralon rode Bladedancer along the cobbled streets as he watched craftsmen hard at work plying their skills. A thatcher was busily repairing a roof, and a candlestick maker was hanging his candles on a rack to dry. The blacksmith and his apprentice were toiling over the flames of their forge with hammer and anvil, shaping metal objects with heavy-handed blows. The result was a cacophony of city life far removed from the seashore and the lull of waves he had enjoyed late last eve.

He spotted Saunders, the village steward, conversing with the townsfolk. Saunders' job was to settle small squabbles, keep the peace, and serve as the village representative to His Majesty. Though still in conversation, Saunders waved at Eralon as he rode by.

A pleasant surprise greeted Eralon as he rode through the central market square. He noted a second well had been constructed to provide all who were living in Kaleidos with fresh water. It was only last season when the townsfolk had petitioned for a well, and it was just like King Lucian to fulfill his subjects' wishes in due haste.

Storage sheds and barns, along with groups of thatch-roofed cottages made of stone and brick, could be found clustered around freshly-plowed fields and pastures. A large lake supplied the castle and villagers with fresh fish. Upon the lake sat a watermill that was used for grinding grains, tanning leather, and processing cloth.

He next passed a variety of orchards and crops including nut trees, fruits, and a variety of vegetables. While some farmers raised these crops and reared livestock, others had dovecotes—buildings devoted to housing and raising doves. Thanks to the king and his ancestors' foresight, Kaleidos was grandly self-sufficient. It could provide all the food, water, shelter, and other daily requirements—including military protection—that the city residents needed.

Eralon could hear Hedge Warden Hadwyn blowing his horn in the distance. Hadwyn was responsible for all the animals, including making sure they did not stray too far. His other duties were to lead the sowing and gathering of crops and supervise the mending of the stone fencing around the hay meadows, making sure they were in good repair. Eralon could see a handful of villagers running through the fields. They were probably looking for old Bess, a milking cow, who was, no doubt, invading the cornfield again. The last time Eralon had talked to Hadwyn, they had yet to find the old girl's escape route.

Leaving the city, villages, and farmland behind, Eralon enjoyed a breathtaking view of Moorwyn Castle in the distance. It was an extraordinary sight, and if the castle was not enough to dazzle the senses, the mountains of Kaleidos Peak added to its beauty. To anyone viewing the stone stronghold it would seem magical indeed, for the builders had seamed the back of the castle to the mountain.

The uppermost reaches of the mountain's precipice were unscalable and sheer, but not with the usual jagged rock. These sleek mountain peaks were veined in a rare, crystalline stone. Beautiful to behold and slick as a mirror, the veins of crystals shimmered in the sunlight causing rainbows to dance in the reflected light, giving Moorwyn an otherworldly, radiant glow.

The castle's first line of protection was a water-filled moat that surrounded a lower circuit of outer walls. Within those walls stood a taller ring of defense that combined a supreme level of strength and fortitude. With the two rings of walls at different levels, archers on the higher inner walls could easily fire arrows over the lower outer walls at an enemy below. If a gatecrasher were to become trapped between the walls, it would almost certainly result in their capture or demise.

"Dragon's Row" was a line of dwellings built into the inside of the first ring of walls that served as housing for Eralon, the Elite Guardsmen, and stables for their horses. Beyond the next ring of higher walls was the inner ward. Located on the north side of the inner ward was the great hall and the castle's main well and kitchen. The king's kennels, stables, blacksmith, and a storehouse for threshed grain and animal feed occupied the eastern side. The western side of the inner ward housed the castle's gardens that included courtyard and labyrinth.

The soaring twin towers of Moorwyn Castle were built at the back of the stronghold, up against the mountains of Kaleidos. These two towers featured diamond mullion windows and tall, jutting spires. Elaborate stone carvings of dragons festooned these towers in grand splendor. The dragons' sinewy bodies were poised, ready to strike, giving the appearance that the castle was under their constant watch and protection. This was where His Majesty King Lucian made his home.

The king's personal quarters were located in the Royal Tower and included two private bed chambers—should His Majesty one day choose a queen—and a shared sitting room between them. Lucian also enjoyed a personal library and a private, fully-staffed kitchen. Between the two towers was an armory for the king's personal guard with attached withdrawing chamber.

In the adjacent tower, dubbed the Family Wing, there were three private bed chambers and a sitting room reserved for His Majesty's brother and family.

Moorwyn Castle and Kaleidos Peak had birthed many a tale. Even from a distance, Eralon could make out the images of great dragons displayed on banners as they snapped briskly in the breeze atop the towers of the castle. It was said that within the mountain's highest reaches dwelled the mythical dragons that had become the royal symbol of the king and folklore for the people.

The lore keepers painted appealing tales of these great behemoths who, along with their precious treasures, were said to be cleverly concealed deep within the caverns of Kaleidos Peak. Fearless warrior-dragons bided their time until they were truly needed, standing ready to protect the Kingdom of Avala. The lore keepers and elders loved to tell the young ones tales of how these mighty dragons magically knew the right moment to appear, saving Avala from certain destruction, and the children would sit in wide-eyed wonder. These stories had been passed down by way of oral tradition, from generation to generation.

As a boy with a wild imagination, Eralon and his wooden sword battled alongside many a make-believe dragon. He glanced at his helm hanging from Bladedancer's saddle with its dragon face etched into the metal. Examining the prominently decorated crest and the faceguard so intricately wrought by the smith to represent mythical dragon flames, Eralon could easily see how the kingdom's royal guards could very well be those "dragon protectors" the townspeople so fancied. Avala's warriors were known throughout the kingdom and beyond for their bravery in battle and their fierce loyalty. Consider the tales of dragons that had already begun to spread in Terra Leone from Eralon's encounter with Danuvius. It was no wonder the people drew upon the correlation.

As Eralon approached the castle's entrance, Bladedancer's ears perked and his hooves pawed impatiently until it was his turn to enter through the castle gates. Once on the other side the mighty steed advanced without urging, first to a trot and then to a gallop, his black mane flowing in the rush of wind. Eralon allowed his friend to keep his quick gait as the rhythm of hoofbeats carried them expectantly to the stable grounds.

Bladedancer spotted Eralon's squire and quickly headed in his direction. There the stallion approached and performed his routine behavior of nudging the smiling squire's arm impatiently, awaiting the removal of his armor. The captain slid down to help complete the task and, soon, the animal shook his head and neck vigorously, undeniably delighted to be without the articles. Eralon scratched behind Blade's silky ears and smiled in amusement while watching the horse close his eyes and lean into the motion. Bladedancer knew well enough that fresh food, water, and a good rubdown awaited him, and he was anxious for the pampering.

"Welcome back, Captain Wellsbough," greeted his good-natured squire, Calah. "Shall I have Blade made ready for another assignment?"

Eralon shook his head. "No, Calah, he has earned a much-needed rest. I will speak to the stable master to ready another, which may be upon the morrow."

"As you desire, captain," Calah replied. "I shall have your weapons cleaned, polished, and ready for your next journey." The lad took up Bladedancer's reins and followed Eralon to the stables.

Eralon had five grand horses from which to choose, depending on His Majesty's requirements. In addition to Bladedancer, Eralon owned a riding horse named Lightning. For royal hunts with his king, Wolf was his preferred mount. Eralon also had two personal packhorses he used for long journeys away from the castle. They were currently resting at the Terra Leone stables.

His two most prized possessions were Bladedancer and Lightning. Bladedancer was a noble black stallion who stood sixteen hands. Majestic and spirited, he had proven himself to have both the agility and strength needed in a mêlée. He displayed great vigor and was known to aggressively join in with tooth and hoof during battle. He was also Eralon's horse of choice for jousting; Eralon could not see himself bestride any other.

Then there was Lightning, who carried a name befitting its owner. Lightning was, indeed, a credit to her breed. This well-bred palfrey, though smaller, was equal in worth to Bladedancer. With her smooth amble and unparalleled long-distance speed, she was known to be the fastest horse in the Kingdom of Avala. A beautiful mount with a rich brown sheen, she featured a white star above her eyes and what appeared to be a white bolt of lightning striking down the middle of her face. She proudly carried Eralon during festivals and ceremonies.

With Bladedancer's needs well in hand, Eralon left the stable grounds with his rucksack, bedroll, and other personal packs slung over a shoulder. His first responsibility would be to check on the prisoners he had sent ahead of his arrival from Terra Leone to make certain there had not been any trouble with their transport. He would then check in with the royal guards, for Eralon had been gone from the castle on several assignments for more than a fortnight. Lastly, he intended to head toward the bathing rooms for a long soak before he met with His Majesty. He would utilize the relaxing routine to prepare mental notes, for he had much to discuss with his monarch.

His Majesty's great hall was spacious, twice as long as it was wide with ceilings that seemed to reach for the skies. The floors displayed several tapestries, gifts from a foreign monarch who had visited recently from across the Carillion Sea. Massive fireplaces stood in the four corners, each large enough for a man to stand within.

Each hearth had its own elaborate mantel displaying intricately fashioned candelabras, gemmed chalices, and hand-carved jade vases. Above each fireplace was King Lucian's coat of arms, a heraldic blazon identified as "Vair on a Chief Azure, a Silver Dragon Passant Guardant." In simple terms, it was made of fur that was used as the chief background, stained blue, and adorned with a silver colored dragon in profile, head facing the spectator, and standing with one front leg raised.

One wall of wide, mullioned windows spilled the afternoon sun throughout the room, haloing those present in a warm radiance. Stone benches were placed under these windows, and some of the guests were sitting and enjoying the view of the castle gardens. Hanging silk scrolls in radiant colors decorated the remaining walls.

With all the commotion in the room, Eralon surmised His Majesty had been entertaining. Self-effacing servants in silver and blue livery adorned with a silvery dragon embroidered on the left breast moved amongst the nobles. They offered golden goblets of wine upon shining trays to any of the throng of aristocracy who took notice of their presence. A balcony above the crowd was a screened minstrel's gallery where the soft, pleasing strains of flute and string drifted mellifluously to the throng below.

It was late afternoon before Eralon met with King Lucian. Eralon was advised that his monarch would meet him in the throne room where he was already engaged in a private appointment. Eralon strolled through the spacious passage, nodding to a few of those he recognized or who offered him a friendly smile. Most were familiar with the Captain of the Elite Guardsmen, while others were elbowed and whispered to until he had a clear path. Gilded doors at the end of the hall were hurriedly opened to admit him. The pike-wielding sentinels in their high-collared black and silvery-blue attire nodded solemnly as he passed. One of the door guardians bowed and turned to escort the captain from the antechamber and into the throne room.

He supposed that, to most, the throne room of a king would be a place of nervous tension, but to him it had always seemed a calming salve after a hard journey, a safe island in a tide of turbulent seas.

To Eralon's left, a lavish tapestry hung from ceiling to floor and covered the entire wall with scenes depicting the ancient history and mythology of Avala, including images of dragons fighting Avala's invaders. Upon the room's opposing stone wall was a bas-relief of an enormous dragon. It reared its huge, fire-breathing head high in the right corner, filled the wall's center with its massive, scaly body and outstretched wings while its massive tail curled around its hind legs at the wall's opposite edge.

Centered upon a broad dais against the farthest wall and under a high-set, stained-glass window sat the royal throne of King Lucian of Avala. The ornate chair was covered by a canopy and was richly upholstered in silver-blue velvet featuring pearlescent patterns reminiscent of reptilian scales. Two ominous, open-mouthed stone beasts flanked the throne. These white marble dragon pillars rose to the ceiling to guard the king. Their eyes stared in the direction of those called before His Majesty—be they friend or foe—in hard, steely-eyed silence. Eralon could see how the beasts could be quite daunting to anyone who stood before his king.

His Majesty was standing toward the back of the room where he was bathed in multicolored light from the stained-glass window, lost in deep conversation with a stately gentleman dressed in foreign attire. The sonorous voice of Eralon's escort sounded his arrival. Eralon respectfully dropped to one knee. He gave a bow of his head and placed his left hand upon his knee while the right rested comfortably on the hilt of his sword as he awaited his leave to speak. His escort, one exact pace to the right of Eralon, bowed regally to his king and the noble caller, and then he silently and quickly departed.

Upon Eralon's arrival, Lucian had nodded in his direction as he continued to speak in quiet tones. Eralon noticed the noble caller's regal bearing. He was tall, dressed in court attire, appearing about the same age as King Lucian. The noble gentleman looked tousled, as if he had just come in from the road. Perchance the foreigner was of noble descent from outland, for his monarch often entertained in order to form or strengthen alliances.

Their conversation ended, and King Lucian turned toward the patiently waiting captain. From the king's smile, Eralon concluded it had been a successful encounter.

King Lucian gazed in Eralon's direction and raised his voice to carry across the lengthy room. "Hail and well met, Captain Wellsbough. I suspect, by your presence, you have concluded your business?" And he motioned for his loyal servant to rise.

"Indeed, Your Majesty," Eralon said as he stood. "I arrive with considerable news and to dutifully report upon the circumstances at Terra Leone and its leadership under Danuvius Doral." Eralon went no further in his explanation, waiting for their meeting in private. Lucian's guest arched his brows in interest, but he remained silent.

"Splendid." King Lucian held up a hand to forestall their conversation.

Eralon watched as the king turned to his guest and spoke. "Duty calls, my friend. I do hope to have the pleasure of your company again. This time, let it not be so long between visits."

It seemed the tall stranger took the dismissal graciously. "Good King, you can count on it. I shall leave you to your meeting."

Lucian gave his guest a regal bow and the stranger, smiling, did the same, his cape flourishing artfully to accentuate the gesture. Eralon noted a slim crown adorning the gentleman's brow.

They were equals, for the king's guest was not simply any nobility from outland; he was a monarch. Eralon did not recognize this monarch, nor did he know from whence he hailed, but the captain had determined it was far and away. Since there was no indication of any welcoming royal fanfare, this particular meeting must have been held in secrecy. Lucian walked with his royal guest to the egress.

Upon his return, King Lucian bade Eralon to a pair of comfortable, high-back chairs and gestured at a pitcher and two goblets atop a low, oblong table. Eralon poured the apple wine into both cups. Taking one of the cups, the king settled his tall frame onto one of the seats and let out a sigh. He uncharacteristically crossed his dark, leather-tooled boots at the ankle upon the low table, leaned back into the luxurious upholstery, and took a long sip.

Even if Eralon had not known him as ruler, King Lucian's bearing would have announced it, but not from arrogance—it was something in the way he held himself and the manner in which he spoke. Eralon had seen him overlook a screaming, frenzied crowd and, in awe, watched as his presence and manner permeated the people until there was an expectant hush.

He motioned for Eralon to sit in the chair opposite. The captain lowered himself into the seat and waited for his leave to speak. The king studied Eralon for a moment with intense, cinnamon-hued eyes.

Avala's monarch wore a coat of deep red with silver and blue inserts running up the front, back, and sleeves. A simple gold crown embellished with garnets rested upon his brow and held back his long, dark hair. His soft, black breeches were tucked into the tops of high boots. Lowering his glass and placing it upon the table before him, Lucian tilted his head at Eralon and said,

"Prithee, Captain Wellsbough, do tell."

"Your suspicions of Danuvius' wrongdoings have been confirmed, Your Majesty. A wise course it was, undeniably, to send the Elite Guardsmen to Terra Leone. Danuvius had his own agenda, and it was not in accordance with your orders. When I confronted the temporary steward about his behavior and your desires, Danuvius lost his life by refusing to acquiesce to your authority. After speaking with the citizens of Terra Leone, I suspect Danuvius may have had something to do with Ambassador Valen Doral's untimely death."

Eralon could see Lucian was greatly disturbed by his words. It was not the first time His Majesty had dealt with greed and rivalry when it came to the question of hereditary peerage.

He nodded and said, "I was informed of the uprising by Knight Master Osualt upon his return with the prisoners. It was an ill-fated circumstance, but unavoidable. Valen would have been grief-stricken had he awakened to his brother's schemes. However, I must say I am surprised at this outcome. I had believed Danuvius Doral a capable fellow and a fine nobleman." Remaining composed, Lucian folded his hands across his lap. "We shall appoint a new temporary guardian of Terra Leone, one who has the best wishes of the kingdom and Terra Leone at heart. You will return to the fortress and supervise this appointment yourself, Eralon," commanded the king. "I want harmony restored to Valen's people."

"Your will be done, Your Majesty," vowed Eralon.

"There is another matter we must discuss, Eralon, one that can be carried out in tandem with our plans for Terra Leone."

Eralon shifted his position, leaning toward his monarch, his posture receptive and willing. "Pray tell, Your Majesty?"

Lucian sighed and his brow furrowed. "It has come to my attention that there is a large armed force of men marching upon our lands. From what I understand, they were first observed gathering in the southwestern borders of Avala. I have already received word from the kings of Avala's southern countries of Sunon and Vashires, and they have assured me they know nothing of this force on our lands. We have been advised this force carries more than enough arms to warrant attention. There has been no declaration of war, we know not from whence they came, and their intent is unknown. Nevertheless, if this force stays its present course, they will soon come upon the fortress at Terra Leone.

"I have surmised they will arrive there in less than a sennight. I believe it would be in our best interest to presume this a hostile force and take the necessary steps to safeguard our lands. Terra Leone will be our first concern. The fortress there needs to be fortified against any possible attack."

"Indeed, Your Majesty. I wonder . . ." considered Eralon. Contemplating what his king just told him, his mind instantly flashed back to his encounter with the Liltian in the wood and the man's strange beliefs. "There were three Liltians that I encountered near Morning Star this very morn," advised Eralon. "One held the peculiar notion that Avala was holding Liltians as slaves."

"Slavery in Avala?" scoffed Lucian. "Clearly this individual is a stranger to our realm."

"The Liltian told me that it was Danuvius Doral who started the rumor of slavery," advised Eralon. "Mayhap Danuvius had planned to align himself with a band of Liltian hirelings to stand against us, using the pretense of slavery as his ammunition."

Lucian then stood and bid Eralon rise. "I want you at my side while meeting with the realm's Council of Nobles, Eralon. There we shall discuss your findings and who we shall appoint as a temporary guardian for Terra Leone. You will need to prepare a contingent of Elite Guardsmen to fortify the fortress. Let us proceed." He gestured to the doors at the far end of the room and the council chambers beyond.

Eralon stood and accompanied his monarch to the council's assembly room.

With the sun hanging low, Eralon left King Lucian's council chamber with plans ingrained in his mind from the meeting. The captain knew the king trusted him implicitly, knowing he would do what was needed to get the job done to His Majesty's satisfaction.

Eralon's mind was teeming with tactical campaigns. Though he was weary, he knew he must put his monarch's plan in place before he could relax. Sleep would come later. There were orders to carry out, decisions to be made, and much to prepare before this mysterious army arrived. Eralon's lips formed a terse line as he organized his thoughts. Though he had left his twenty most trusted men behind at Terra Leone, now it seemed there might be a new danger heading in their direction. He wanted to get back to them as soon as possible.

As Eralon approached the guardsmens' stables, the path changed from familiar cobblestone to earth and straw. The scent of fresh hay and leather was pungent. Lines of stalls stretched across his vision. Droves of grooms crossed his path to the long rows of animals that were offered drinks, feed, and currycombing before being put to stall or saddled. It seemed chaotic to Eralon, but he knew the stable master kept the grounds well-maintained. The clomping sounds of destriers, rounceys, coursers, and palfreys stamping their hooves as they were led to and fro only added to the confusion in Eralon's mind. How the stablemen kept track of the owners of all the animals with nary a label on the stalls must have been a well-guarded secret. Mysteriously, the stable master appeared at Eralon's elbow, immediately recognizing that someone new must be fitted into his system.

He strolled alongside the captain, and in a friendly, casual tone asked, "An' what beastie will ya be wanting fer yer journey, Cap'n?" His voice, like his demeanor, was rough, but Eralon knew him to be a blunt fellow who was extraordinarily attentive to the horses in his care.

"Lightning, I believe, Sedgwick. Blade has just returned from a long undertaking and needs attending."

Sedgwick clasped his hands on his elbows, an instinctual move to cradle an old shoulder wound. He pursed his lips in careful consideration, and then he shook his shaggy head. "Very well then, I shall be getting the palfrey ready meself. Last time Bladedancer saw ya leave, I be left ta repairing the walls o' his stall. I dare say, he has a mighty kick an' be nay pleased ta be left behind. I shall 'aves yer squire stand ready ta brings Lightning out front upon yer beck 'n call. Best Blade not sees ya. Off with ya then." With the stable master's last word law in his domain, Eralon left for Dragon's Row, which housed the Elite Guardsmen.

As darkness approached, the encroaching shadows cast the landscape in a tenor of tired triumph. The activity around Dragon's Row was winding down, and everyone worked at a slower pace. While he walked, Eralon mentally mapped the briefing he intended for his fellows.

A master knight named Redwald Balderon had been chosen as the new temporary steward, and he would be leading a force of the king's guards to Terra Leone. Knight Master Balderon was raised by his uncle, the Duke of Hearne. The duke was well regarded for his leadership, diplomacy, and work ethic and had passed his knowledge along to his nephew. This made the master knight an ideal candidate to ensure the fortification of the fortress and secure the safety of its inhabitants. King Lucian wanted someone with a level head for any possible crisis and at least some understanding of tactical maneuvers, and Redwald Balderon was the best. Redwald and his regiment would need time to prepare.

They would arrive one day after Eralon.

Meanwhile, Eralon would put together a proposal to present to the master knight. Then, after a few hours of good, solid sleep, Eralon would head out as planned to Terra Leone and fulfill His Majesty's wishes. Once all was set in motion, Eralon would return to Moorwyn for further discussion with his monarch and the realm's Council of Nobles as to how to handle the approaching forces.

Eralon marched quickly and arrived at his private chambers in Dragon's Row. He was greeted immediately by Benton, his attendant, and Calah, his squire, who was holding a tray of steaming food.

Calah grinned and said, "Welcome home, Captain Wellsbough. I figured if Blade's hearty appetite was any indication, you must be equally as starved, so I took the liberty of having the cook prepare your meal. Shall you be eating at your desk in the library or take your repast in the dining area?"

"Gramercy, Calah." Eralon was thankful for Calah's keen foresight. "My desk would be ideal." Calah disappeared with the tray of food.

"I have a few things to go over with you regarding your household, Captain Wellsbough," his attendant Benton stated. "Firstly, your ordered garb has arrived from the tailor and your new boots from the cobbler." His attendant fixed his eyes upon Eralon's booted feet with a disapproving frown. "Not a moment too soon. Truthfully, your boots look to be worn through. Did you walk here from your last assignment?"

Eralon produced a smile for the old fellow who had been more like a father than an attendant, especially after Eralon's father had passed. "Gramercy, Benton. I know I can count on you to keep me well-groomed."

"And look at you—worn to the bone," Benton scolded. "Calah tells me you will be leaving yet again upon the morrow. I will prepare your travel packs with fresh food and clothing."

Calah emerged from the library at that moment, and Benton told him to take Eralon's packs to the kitchen. Calah took the packs from the captain's weary hands.

"Gramercy, Calah."

Eralon followed Benton into his library. Set out on his desk was an assortment of savory foods, steaming broth, and drink. Eralon had not realized how hungry he was until he sat to eat.

Before he had even touched his goblet to quench his thirst, Benton was at his side.

"Remember Captain Wellsbough, if you do not fill your stomach in the proper manner, the heavy foods will sink to the bottom and block your digestion. I will not have you eating like you are out in the wilderness." Benton continued his routine preaching on the proper method of food consumption. "Open your meal with your hot, sweetened milk and moist fruits. Follow with your delicious herbed vegetables, domestic fowl, and broth. Subsequently, close your meal with the aged cheese and spiced wine." Eralon raised his goblet of sweetened milk in gesture of respect.

Seemingly mollified, Benton left Eralon to eat his meal in peace.

CHAPTER FOUR

N aught had been amiss, and the eve had brought about a peaceful slumber for Aurora Leigh. However, within the darkness of the early morn, she was struck with an immense sense of dread. Her dreams had become so frightening that she bolted upright in her bed. She desperately gasped for air. Trembling, she rose and dressed in one of her favorite gowns, more for comfort than warmth, and placed a light circlet upon her brow, one of simple silver-worked flora, but it would serve to keep her hair back in the wind.

She opened a drawer in her bedside night table and removed a hidden panel. She reached for the treasure held secretly within its confines and left her bedchamber. This treasure had always provided comfort in times of need. Her velvet slipshoes whispered softly as she hastily traversed the wide sitting room and breathlessly threw open the double doors to the portico she so cherished.

A refreshing wind blew the delicate gossamer curtains of shimmering gold cloth that covered the doorway. The curtains billowed, dipping in waves of early morning shadows, surrounding her for a moment in a delicate golden cocoon. An opening appeared, releasing her from the chrysalis, and her wide eyes scanned the portico as if seeing it for the first time. The blue moon's glow covered the land with the majestic presence of a fairytale, and the stars still held their brightness. Nevertheless, the normally calm retreat with its breathtaking view failed to provide the comfort she so desperately sought.

Her dream had started peaceably enough with her captain riding out of the woodland and entering the outskirts of a town. But then things had taken on a darker turn. There was a dispute, and Eralon was suddenly outnumbered, bringing back the same anxious feelings she had suffered watching his fight with her would-be captors in the wood. In her dream, Eralon was on the winning side of one trial of swordsmanship against several foes. But then, without warning, additional enemies had emerged from nowhere. She spied the glint of an enemy's blade descending upon Eralon from behind in such a manner that she was sure he could not survive— and then her fear abruptly jolted her to consciousness.

Aurora Leigh placed the leather cord that was attached to her treasured keepsake around her neck to keep it close to her heart. Received as a gift in her youth, she kept it hidden from the castle staff lest they throw it out as a childish bauble. Its outer portion was carved from natural stone into what was called a "blessing disk," a sacred, circular stone with a centered hole. Intricately arranged upon the face of this blessing disk were sapphire cabochons placed between ancient pictorial symbols. A rare Allurealis crystal in the shape of a cylinder wand, with its pointed tip hanging down, rested within the stone ring. Winding around the polished hexagonal Allurealis wand was a silvery dragon.

A blessing stone with an Allurealis crystal was said to have mystical properties. It was believed that, if worn on your person, the blessing disk could protect you from harm. Aurora Leigh had never seen one quite like it, especially one with the dragon symbol of Avala.

". . . You will be sorely missed. Be good, Aurora Leigh, and remember . . . if you ever need me, you only need beckon." She could hear her childhood friend's voice in her mind, silky and strong, as if he stood before her now.

Aurora Leigh lowered herself to sit upon a stone bench to take in this recollection, though her hands still trembled from her upsetting nightmare. Taking deep breaths, she inhaled the fresh scent of blossoms that surrounded her. Strange though it seemed, the long unvisited memory of receiving the pendant she wore did bring her a modicum of the comfort she sought. Eagerly she delved into the memory, seeking to calm the accelerated pace of her heart. A warm wind stirred like a familiar caress, bringing with it the gentle phantoms from her past, and she readily surrendered to them. Her eyes closed, and she was again a small child at Morning Star Palace.

Young Aurora Leigh, Princess of Morning Star

Sunlight warmed a young child's fair skin, and the mystery of brook, stone statues, and flowers abloom enchanted her, drawing her further into the gardens to explore. A lazy, swirling breeze stirred the crowns of the trees, and she imagined it to be the sound of forest sprites whispering to one other. With a slender stick in her hand, the child was a magical princess strolling amongst her subjects and enjoying carefree adventures with her knights. With a bit of imagination, these knights were her castle attendants who never complained if one of them became tragically wounded in battle, for they would be restored to health with but a touch from their magical princess.

Aurora Leigh loved this part of the palace. It was the view from her bedchamber's balcony and neatly kept, but unlike some parts of the large grounds that were almost wholly sculpted with grace and geometric designs, this tiny corner was forest primeval. It even boasted a brook gurgling through it. When her parents were busy and shooed her outside, she would come here. She was safe in the gardens, and if one of the adults needed to see what mischief she was up to, she could easily be spotted from the portico or the balcony. But sometimes, when her games were through and when there was no one to feed her active mind, the young girl wandered to the brook and sat staring into the flowing channel until another notion for a game or daydream captivated her.

One exceptionally fine day, when the warm, sun-soaked grounds and playful winds could not rouse her from her lonesomeness, she had strolled along the water's bank only to find she was not alone. An adult was sitting casually beneath her favorite tree upon a bench that sat amongst the gnarled roots and grasses. He had dark hair, a regal look, and kind, cobalt-blue eyes. He displayed a most welcoming smile. Classic features and well-built, she imagined that elves would be dressed as he was in the greens and browns of the forest around him. The thought brought a trace of a smile to her lips, and young Aurora Leigh found herself curiously at ease with the stranger. His deep blue eyes regarded hers with a merry twinkle, and she approached him without hesitation, feeling as exuberant as if a best friend had come home suddenly to surprise her. Her desolate feelings of seclusion evaporated as quickly as a bubble in the brook.

"Greetings and well met, Aurora Leigh," the stranger said, his smile transforming his features into something most handsome to behold. "Is it not lovely here?"

"Indeed, Sir," Aurora Leigh replied, nodding, her eyes never leaving her visitor, as if she intended to memorize his graceful movements or the way his hair framed his face. She then spoke to him as her station as princess allowed. "How have you come to be at this very place, and how do know my name?"

His laughter and words were as merry as birdsong. "Pray pardon, Your Highness, for it was you who called out to touch my heart just the other day. Were you not sitting here lonesome, crying, wishing urgently aloud for companionship at times when the adults are busy with their politics and meetings?"

She blinked her suddenly damp eyes. That was entirely true. She had been weeping when last in the gardens, begging the heavens for a playmate, nearly inconsolable in her melancholy. In her youth, she did not think to question his motives or to ask how he had overheard her pleas. She merely accepted his heartfelt statements as fact and assumed her father had sent him. She ran over to where he sat and flung her arms about his shoulders, feeling the softness of his riding cloak beneath her cheek.

The wrinkle-free cape was as silky-smooth as a baby's skin. Streaks of a purple-hued thread ran through the fabric like the veins of leaves. His scent was that of nutmeg or cinnamon. Her companion did not seem to mind the sudden attention and, he patted a place for her to sit beside him on the bench.

As Aurora Leigh sat her place beside him, she noted that his earthy-colored riding clothes were fine indeed, embroidered throughout in a leaf pattern using the same colored thread as the cloth. She noted a slender crown upon his head, a crown that featured aged silver etched in a floral leaf design with a large, sparkling diamond imbedded in a silver colored metal that held a bluish tinge and graced the center of his forehead. Young Aurora Leigh stared in childish wonder.

"What an observant young lass you are, and where are my manners?" He unfolded his long frame to stand and broke the silence. "I, dear-heart, am the reigning Rex Imperator Kullipthius of the Oralian Empire, at thy most humble of service." He gave her the same sweeping bow she had seen some adults and servants give her parents, and a thrill of pleasure sparkled within her eyes. This was someone who treated her like an adult.

"I would be honored if you would call me Kulli."

And he wanted to be her friend! She wondered if an imperator was the monarch of a foreign land. From wherever he hailed, she definitely knew not, so that had to mean the land must be far distant. But, she pondered, if that were true, then why, pray tell, would he be here and not inside with her parents or holding audience with their good king?

Aurora Leigh asked as much, which brought yet another smile from her new acquaintance.

"I could indeed be at some function or another, but why on such a lovely day as this?" Kullipthius continued and gestured grandly to take in the grounds around them and the beautiful, clear sky. "Moreover, my family and yours have been friends for many a generation, though we have not had the pleasure of any recent visits to Morning Star. I assure you that I would rather be here to keep you company." He reached out and lightly touched her upon the nose, which made her laugh.

"Splendid, Kulli, it is an honor. We might—" Aurora Leigh suddenly cut her thoughts of play. Would an imperator enjoy playing by the stream, climbing trees, or picking flowers to make daisy chains for her valorous, tree-shaped knights? She had never asked royalty to participate in the things she enjoyed when out of doors. Only the palace guards ever dared participate when she invited them. Even when her nursemaid, Murielle, visited the grounds, she, too, watched but would never participate in the girl's fantasies of knights and dragons and damsels in distress. Murielle enjoyed other activities, like playing dress-up or teaching Aurora Leigh how to braid fresh-picked flowers into her hair.

The foreign imperator had looked thoughtful for a moment. Breaking the silence, he pointed to the large, leafy tree that typically was the hero in all of Aurora Leigh's stories. "That young fellow yonder has had his beloved spirited away by a nasty wizard. What do you deem necessary to remedy the situation?"

Imagination sparked the young girl. She jumped up, leaving behind all doubt. "Why, we must save her!"

Kulli grinned, picked up a slender stick and faced Aurora Leigh. "Then we must prepare. Make haste and gather your supplies, ere she is carried across the stream and all hope to pursue her is lost."

They were engaged in merriment and imagination for a time along the stream, and when the imperator bent over to prepare an imaginary spell upon the fictional wizard, Aurora Leigh stopped to gaze in green-eyed wonder at the amulet hanging from a leather cord around his neck. The sun was hitting it just so, and it had sent an array of colors to sparkle upon the stream and the trunks of the nearby trees.

"I have never seen such an amulet with a sparkling crystalline wand like that before!" exclaimed Aurora Leigh. "Of what is it made?"

"My amulet is called a blessing disk, and its hexagonal wand is made from a special crystal known as Allurealis," explained Kulli. "I was told that it holds magical properties. Have you heard the story of the 'Legend of Allurealis'?"

Eyes wide in wonderment, Aurora Leigh shook her head, never taking her eyes off the beautiful talisman. Hence, the imperator embarked upon the tale.

Legend of Allurealis

Long ago and quite far away, a heavenly star sat waiting for her moment to shine. The heavens bestowed upon her the name Allurealis. It was always understood that she was an extraordinary star, but so much time had passed that not a star in the heavens could remember why. She was the brightest star amongst her peers who dwelled within the Verona Croix Constellation.

Each and every day, she would watch most anxiously as the mighty Sawl, a great ball of burning fire, placed himself just so in her heavenly world. For you see, after a long day of burning bright, Sawl would hang his blue-jeweled moon back in the sky, light his bedside starry lights, and slowly drift off in heavy-eyed slumber.

How wonderful it felt to shine, for it warmed her through and through. And in the finest place a star could ever be. It just so happened that her favorite color was blue, and she could not keep her burning gaze off the sparkling, blue-jeweled moon.

Being the brightest of the evening stars, it was her exclusive job to dance for the inhabitants of the planet below her favorite moon. Allurealis displayed her beautiful colors of pink and green and a fleeting hint of yellow in a spin for every appreciative eye to see. Round and round her spinning halos of light swirled in cascading waves that made a waterfall of color.

One star-filled night, a winged messenger entered her universe and cried out to her.

"Salutations, Allurealis! You are quite an extraordinary star. I have come to assist you, for it is time for your children to be born."

All the stars listening in were envious indeed, for never had they heard of such a great honor bestowed upon one of their own.

"How many children will I have?" Allurealis asked eagerly.

"Why, thousands upon thousands," replied the winged messenger.

"How will I care for so many?"

The winged messenger smiled and said, "You are a very special star indeed, Allurealis, for your essence will be a part of each and every one."

The other stars in Allurealis' world were completely astonished and thought it a wondrous privilege.

"I am here to prepare you for your journey and their birth," the messenger said.

"Journey? But I will miss my blue-jeweled moon and the other stars. This is my favorite place to be in the whole universe." She went on to explain how she was not sure she was ready to leave her home in the Verona Croix Constellation. She reminded the messenger that it was also her duty to provide a colorful dance for the planet and its circling blue moon.

The messenger only smiled and said, "Allurealis, you have danced most admirably for the moon and the people on the planet below. Even though all appreciate your dance, we need you and your children for another special purpose. In fact, it is so astonishing I shall have to whisper it to you." And the winged being leaned forward to tell the tale.

Each and every star strained to hear this extraordinary purpose. A few almost fell from their perches in the heavens.

"That is so wonderful and exciting! I am ready, let us away!" exclaimed Allurealis.

With eyes shining bright, the winged messenger said, "As you wish: one, two, away!"

So swift was her departure that she flew out of sight before the other stars could bid her safe journey.

Allurealis was filled with joyful anticipation. She could feel the intensity, the heat, and the fire of the fall preparing her to be with each and every one of her children. As she shot past the blue-jeweled moon and headed for the nearby planet, Allurealis knew the time was nigh. She heard the faint whispers of her children crying out, "Mother Star, Mother Star! We are ready to be born. Will you stay with us?"

"With each and every one of you, my darlings," replied Allurealis.

Then, in one intense, explosive display, Allurealis and her children were brought to life anew. Each and every one of Allurealis' children was born as a precious starfire stone, cradled in the essence of their mother's shining starlight. As they fell from the sky, they displayed twinkling light trails in brilliant splendor, landing on the planet with the circling blue moon.

With a story that spectacular, how could Aurora Leigh not enjoy her new friend?

Her eyes grew large and bright as she said, "The children of Allurealis are the very starfire stones we use today for warmth and light for our homes and encampments."

"Aye, Aurora Leigh," responded Kulli. "They are indeed."

Thus, the games began. What followed was a wondrous time, full of enchantment and splendor. Aurora Leigh came to find Kulli did not care if the leaves they jumped into got caught in his hair or in the cuffs and hems of his magnificent garments. He did not even seem to mind if he got muddy as they built castles to defend or siege.

Whenever he appeared, he always brought with him a new game, puzzle, story, or adventure. His clothing changed in color, but he always wore the hues of the forest in its current season. But no matter what he wore, Kulli always retained his distinctive crown. When cold weather set in, he would wrap his cloak around them both and tell stories until she began to doze. Then he would send her to the palace with fond wishes and the promise of another day.

Days disappeared like mere moments, months like hours, but the child was no longer so young. She began to wonder at the knowing looks her parents exchanged whenever she mentioned her friend meeting her for the afternoon and the exceptional merriment they shared. Her royal mother expressed, in an odd tone, that he must be a "very fine friend indeed, this imperator." Her royal father was equally mysterious. He would smile in the way that all adults did when they indulged her daydreams.

Confused, Aurora Leigh tried her best to unravel the mystery of their reactions. Had they not noticed her graceful friend? Kulli had to arrive, after all, at the palace gates. How else would he be allowed in the gardens—they surely must have seen him at one point or another? Mayhap her parents were not experiencing enough sleep. After all, they retired much later than she. Something had to be responsible for their odd behavior, though she could not discern the answers she sought.

Unfortunately, she never found a chance to ask Kulli what he thought of this matter. Just as she had started to realize something was upsetting Kulli, he relayed the disheartening news that he had been called back to his empire.

The day had begun happily enough, but when the time to move indoors drew nigh, Kulli brought her to her favorite place, and he sat across from her, his dark blue eyes shadowed and his tone serious.

"Kulli, I do not want you to leave!" cried young Aurora Leigh, for whom the news was a bitter pill indeed. Her tears gathered as she heard the details. Her feelings were easy to read by the set of her mouth, the slump of her shoulders, and the tremor in her voice.

"I am afraid I must," Kullipthius stated sadly. His normally smiling countenance had turned morose and quiet. "I have grown quite fond of you, youngling, but time does pass ever so quickly. You are getting older by the day. Surely you understand my duties are important, and I cannot stay away evermore. My empire needs me as much as your kingdom needs its king, and my absence cannot continue, as much as you or I might wish it could."

"You must return soon!" demanded Princess Aurora Leigh, mimicking the same authority in her tone she had heard her parents use.

These words seemed to make Kullipthius even more serious. He tilted his head to study her, as if seeing her afresh. Though she tried valiantly to be brave, her friend could easily see her heart. His tone grew gentler still, as if she were as delicate as a gossamer-winged butterfly.

"Your cup looks so empty, youngling. Let us fill it with hope. And I know the very thing. You always love a good puzzle. If you resolve to find its solution, I shall bestow upon you a wondrous keepsake."

Aurora Leigh rubbed at eyes turning red from tears that she tried courageously to restrain, though she did manage a smile at this offer. She should have seen it coming, for he always tried to cheer her by keeping her mind occupied with mental challenges. And lo, she had never afore been given a gift from her imperial friend—aside from his company—and having his companionship was a gift in itself.

Apart from the dolls and dresses sent on her birthing day and odd and exotic festival or tournament souvenirs from her majestic uncle, she had no idea what a royal keepsake might be. Surely this gift must be something extraordinary. Indeed, her curious thoughts were helping distract her from the intruding sadness.

She took a deep breath and studied Kulli. He did not bat an eyelash or even halfheartedly wipe the tickling hair upon his brow, so intent was he on her face and reactions.

Finally, her curiosity got the better of her, and she asked, "What is your riddle?"

Kullipthius smiled grandly then, as if the clouds had lifted. The very forest around them lightened at his pleasurable expression.

"Splendid. Here is the riddle for you, Aurora Leigh. Solve it if you can— *'You must keep it after giving it.'*"

Aurora Leigh pondered thoughtfully, wanting desperately to solve this mystery if only to keep the smile a little longer upon her dear friend's lips. She chewed her bottom lip thoughtfully in concentration. "What must you keep after you give it?" She repeated the riddle, and when she thought she had found the answer, she replied, "One's pledge of honor and duty?"

"Indeed, Aurora Leigh. It seems I underestimated my young friend. This question now has two answers that work equally as well and with similar meaning. I shall make a mental note of it and present it to my council. They shall ponder that for days. Give the old boys something to do." With that, he gave her a little wink.

Oh, she was thrilled to have crafted another pleasing solution to a riddle—perchance even become the royal riddle solver. This gave Aurora Leigh added confidence and another quick answer, "A promise?"

"That is correct, youngling, a promise. Clever child. Then again, I believe we have always known that."

"Afore we go any further, I shall give you your keepsake." Kullipthius unfastened the clasp from the blessing disk he was wearing and placed it around Aurora Leigh's small neck.

Aurora Leigh gasped. That was the last thing she would have guessed. The pendant was something she had always admired. It was a lovely ornament of stone, cabochons, and crystal wand.

"For me?" asked Aurora Leigh excitedly. "O' Kulli, it is a most splendid keepsake, and I shall cherish it always. Is that lovely crystal one of the children of Allurealis?"

"Aye, little one," said Kullipthius. "I am delighted that you remembered the tale and will treasure your gift."

He bent down and pulled her forward to look directly into her eyes, and said, "The reason for the riddle and its answer is this: On my honor, I pledge you my word, that if you are truly in need of me, Aurora Leigh, I shall come." He leaned in closer and whispered in her ear, "I promise."

Aurora Leigh knew that he meant every word. And to seal the pledge, she gave her wondrous friend a heartfelt hug and a transcendent smile.

"Do you know the story of the 'Dragon in the Heavens'?" asked her ever-devoted entertainer.

Aurora Leigh shook her head.

Kulli sat upon the garden's stone bench, and Aurora Leigh took her customary place beside him. He pointed at the newly emerging stars and began.

Dragon in the Heavens

Long and ago, there was a mighty dragon that flew proudly over these lands. His scales held a bluish-grey sheen, marking him a platinum dragon. His name was Dra'khar, and he was recognized as The Great Protector.

One day, The Great Protector saw two ruby dragons that were carelessly breathing fire in the forestlands near his home. He tried speaking to these red-scaled dragons, but they did not appear to understand the importance of keeping the forestlands safe from fire. Though he and his flight had managed to chase the rubies away from the forest, he soon learned that they had not traveled far. They were now eyeing the humans hungrily from high atop the mountains of Kaleidos Peak. Fearing for the Sapphirians safety, The Great Protector and his flight screamed out their rage and charged. The moment the red dragons saw them coming, they fled with their great dragon tails tucked under their legs, flying in the direction of their desert homelands.

A most beauteous angel shining with light had seen what transpired. These particularly bright angels are wondrous heavenly beings who have passed from our world and shed their mortal bindings to fly free as spirits. They live in the celestial heavens and have grown to love unconditionally in what they describe as Divine Love. They watch over each and every one of us with compassion and devotion.

Not everyone can see these bright angels of light. However, The Great Protector was exceptional, for he had seen them from the time he was a hatchling.

So it was that the angel appeared before Dra'khar in all her splendor. She told him that she could see through to his heart, and she knew he was full of compassion. She proclaimed how wonderful it was that he cared for others—even his own enemies.

It was then that she told him about a dark and sinister beast lurking in their world, and explained how this foe was determined to rule over all of Sapphirus. She remarked how grand it would be for one such as him, to take a stand and defend all the natives of

Sapphirus.

The platinum dragon agreed, thinking how wonderful it would be to perform such an important task. He and his flight of dragons strived to live in peace and harmony amongst all the creatures that lived in their fair world, so he would do his best to find the perfect solution to tame the beast. Thrilled at such a prospect, he flew toward the mountains of Kaleidos Peak where he built his empire and made his position known.

The day finally arrived when the beast came to Kaleidos Peak to challenge Dra'khar. His armor was imposing and he beheld a strength that could not be matched, for he wielded a dark and powerful magic. The beast made many attempts to gain entrance into the dragon empire, but Dra'khar had blocked his way. Frustrated, the beast let out a horrific roar designed to intimidate The Great Protector, but Dra'khar stood his ground.

"You are the mighty beast who has come to challenge me?" asked Dra'khar, having had the opportunity to get a good look at his opponent's face. He was surprised at who stood before him. At one time, this creature had been his friend. "The dark magic you wield has clouded your mind with evil. You know I do not want to harm you. Let us work together and come up with a solution that will benefit us all. There is always a way to settle things peacefully."

There was a roar of laughter from the beast before he cried out, "This new magical power is impenetrable and I will use it if I must. On this I will not negotiate." The beast then uttered strange words, and his clawed appendages began to glow. They were thrumming and pulsing with a wicked green light.

"Though my magic is unstoppable, I am not unreasonable and will be more than happy to settle things peacefully," explained the beast. "If you get out of the way, you will not get hurt. If you choose not to comply, you will bring about your own demise." The beast appeared entirely pleased with his words. "I believe my solution is a sensible one." Staring directly into Dra'khar's green eyes, he demanded, "I recommend you listen."

Dra'khar was not easily intimidated. He continued to try to reason with the beast. "Why threaten me with brawn, might, and the power of dark magic when that same might can find peace within the power of your heart? And from that power, you can extend a peaceful outcome for the betterment of all."

"You have been provided with an answer for a peaceful solution," replied the beast. "I am losing my patience, Dra'khar."

"The mighty are those committed to improving themselves and

taking care of our world," Dra'khar explained in another attempt to reason with the beast. "Your dark magic will only cause death and destruction and serves no purpose."

The beast's eyes blazed and he looked as if he was losing all sense of control. "It is always the same with you, over and over again," the beast complained. "Enough talk! Get out of the way!"

Dra'khar declined to move, knowing full well that he was the last bastion between the innocent and weak and this unholy wielder of dark magic.

In retaliation, the beast leveled his magic arsenal at Dra'khar and flung arrow-like projectiles in devastating waves about the chamber.

As the arrows shot toward Dra'khar in rapid succession, Dra'khar used his draconic gift to protect himself by shooting bolts of lightning at the arrows, deflecting them from his body.

Unfortunately for the beast, he made an immense miscalculation with his aim. One of his own projectiles ricocheted off a rock wall and hurtled back at him, slamming hard into his magical, impenetrable armor on his chest, causing the beast to reel backward, inches from the cave's mouth. The creature regained his balance and steadied himself. He knew that he had to work fast. The deadly projectiles he had been shooting at Dra'khar also carried a disorientation spell, and he had no protection against it. The spell was beginning to exact its dizzying effect on the beast, so he conjured a healing spell. Then he summoned another poisonous bolt of green, gaseous light. It flashed quicker than the eye could see, heading straight for Dra'khar.

The Great Protector lifted his massive wings in defense and thrust them forward, sending out a concussive force to try and divert the evil bolt from striking him. The concussion slammed into the beast's chest.

Unbalanced from the disorientation spell, the impact sent the beast out of the cave and over the side of the mountain. Down he tumbled, bouncing off the jagged edges of Kaleidos Peak to the rocky depths below. Unfortunately, the beast had harvested the fruit of his own despicable behavior.

Sadly, the flight of the beast's green bolt was straight and true. It struck Dra'khar in the chest, and he collapsed to the cavern floor. The green bolt began pulsing, and Dra'khar knew he would tragically succumb to the poison that was mercilessly pumping into his blood. Even at that moment, he knew he would not have done anything differently. He had stood an unwavering sentinel, resolute in his selfless duty as protector, never faltering in his commitment to keep his dragon empire and the people of Sapphirus safe.

The angel of light appeared before her brave guardian. "You have been a wonderful guardian and leader of the dragons living in Kaleidos Peak, Dra'khar. Your son will lead by your example and will take superb care of the lands of Oralia and Sapphirus." She smiled ever so lovingly and held out her hand to him saying, "I have come to take you home."

Dra'khar noticed his pain was gone. He felt lighter, free. He looked upon the angel of light and said, "I have always wished to fly free amongst the stars in the heavens."

"I know a perfect place," said the angel of light. "Now that you are free from thy mortal bindings, you shall rise above the stars and soon find the perfect place as a child of the light within the celestial vault. No mortal mind can conceive of that which awaits the true children of the light."

Up, up, and away they went, disappearing from sight as they entered the skies' billowing white clouds on their way to the empyreal heavens.

Kullipthius momentarily paused from his narrative to examine the sky, pointed to the twinkling stars and said, "See that assemblage of stars? It is known as the Dra'khar Constellation. According to the legend, The Great Protector resides there amongst the stars in heaven's gentle embrace. One day he, too, will be someone's special angel, full of love and shining with light. Until then, he is in the heavens watching over our lands."

"Oh, Kulli, it was a most heartrending, yet bittersweet tale," said young Aurora Leigh. She delicately caressed the pendant that Kulli had given her and that hung low around her small neck. Her eyes were drawn to a tiny platinum dragon twined around the Allurealis crystal. "This blessing disk must be a rare treasure, for it is a part of the heavens—a dragon angel wrapped around a shooting star."

"Aye, so it is," agreed Kullipthius. "There is one more thing you need to know." He slipped behind her to adjust the amulet to her petite frame. His voice was soft as he said, "You are now guardian of this extraordinary treasure, Aurora Leigh. Take special care of this blessing disk for it is a cherished and magical heirloom. It will contact me if you are ever in need. Just call out my name while holding the blessing disk to the heavens." He finished the alteration and kissed the back of her head in a friendly gesture.

"You will be sorely missed. Be good, Aurora Leigh, and remember . . . if you ever need me, you only need beckon."

"Might I visit you? I would like—" Aurora Leigh turned and stared with wide eyes. Kulli had vanished like an apparition. There had been no rustle of leaves, no sound of his departure but the wisp of a breeze. She turned in a quick circle and peered anxiously into the trees, but she saw nothing. Her friend was gone.

CHAPTER FIVE

H er thoughts back in the present, Aurora Leigh opened her
eyes to gaze upon a peaceful landscape. She shook her head,
amused with her wandering notions, and pulled her childhood
keepsake from beneath the bodice of her blue and ivory paneled
gown.

Aurora Leigh kissed her pendant, drawing comfort from it like
she had so many times. No longer a child, she often questioned the
existence of Kullipthius with a critical eye. It was logical and likely
that he had been nothing more magical or royal than a dear friend
of her family—a spinner of tales and a bestower of joy—one who
took pity upon a lonely child and shared a welcomed time of play
and the power of imagination.

As a child, she had never tried to call upon her precious friend,
though she yearned for Kulli many times after his abrupt
departure, because she feared she would pull him from some
important task. As time passed, she grew to believe it all must have
been a concocted fairytale. Even so, she refused to let the
memories drift far from her heart.

Aurora Leigh took several minutes to ponder the exuberance
with which she, as a child, had embraced the lore keeper's tales of
dragons, knights, and adventures. Now she understood that those
narratives, which had once seemed so vivid and exciting, could
quickly turn into real fear when they played out in actuality. She
needed look no further than her own foiled kidnapping to see the
truth. How would that scene have played out had the brave
Captain Wellsbough not been so close at hand to save her? The

thought made her shiver. The bravado once held in innocence evaporated with age and experience upon the realization that there are sinister dangers in the world, upon recognizing people are flesh and blood, and upon knowing that no one is indestructible.

Sighing, Aurora Leigh turned her thoughts away from the days of yore to the perplexing emotions that had brought her to the portico in these dark, early hours.

Thoughts of her gallant, armor-clad captain brought an insistent flutter to her nerves. She knew that Eralon was in danger. It was obvious with said warning shrilling through every fiber of her being, screaming of coming peril. She desperately felt the need to warn him of impending danger. Thoughts of a looming, unknown menace descending upon her rescuer pounded at the forefront of her mind. Her heartbeat echoed loudly in her ears, and her breath quickened. She sought solace by clutching her pendant tightly, the trailing chain from the clasp glowing with pricks of waning moonlight.

The pendant was still warm to the touch after having been held against her skin, and she let herself muse for a magical moment that perhaps it was alive with the powers promised by her childhood friend.

She stood and removed the keepsake from around her neck, holding it before her eyes. Wordlessly, she implored the heavens for guidance and, after a prolonged silence during which she studied the skies, she thrust her pendant into the air in the direction of the constellation of the sleeping dragon.

"Prithee, beloved friend, Rex Imperator Kullipthius, I cry for your mercy. Let my words reach your Oralian Empire of Oralia. I implore you to arrive swiftly, for your help is requested this night."

The light breeze suddenly swelled and draped her hair across her vision in a golden swathe while it tugged tenaciously at her skirts. Aurora Leigh, feeling foolish, lowered her arms. She let out a breath she had unconsciously been holding, and a smile graced her lips. To think she had actually gone through with it. Although the love of her fondest memories all but flooded her portico, she had not really believed her efforts would come to fruition—did she? She called to a childhood memory, a ghost, yet she still stood alone and as lost as . . .

"In truth, Aurora Leigh, it is astounding how long it took for you to call upon me. As a youngling you were ever so impulsive."

The familiar voice broke through her thoughts. Aurora Leigh's eyes widened, and her heart quickened. She whirled about, praying with all her heart it was not her imagination.

Leaning easily against a marble pillar, dressed in the browns and greens of the forest, the imperator was unmistakable. Kulli moved fluidly toward Aurora Leigh, appearing not a trace older than her tender memories had always painted him. Still upon his brow sat the antique crown that was glowing with an innate light in the false dawn.

He spoke in that same magical tone that brought with it the memories of yesteryear. "I see that our time apart has blessed you rich in beauty, Aurora Leigh." His smile widened as he studied her shocked expression.

He came! Her thoughts kept singing blissfully, like magic, he came! She had called to him out of desperation, and he had come. Aurora Leigh found herself so overwhelmed by the abruptness of his appearance that she was unable to speak or move.

"Ah, I understand," Kulli said as he glided toward her. "You did not believe I would come." His memorable laughter stole some of the disbelief before he smiled and said, "I do not break my pledges. I gave you my word of honor."

Kulli drew to a graceful stop before her. He gave her the same polite and sweeping bow he had given her upon their first meeting. The familiar, warm twinkle in his cobalt eyes dispersed all apprehension.

"Oh, Kulli!" Aurora Leigh sighed, and she threw her arms around her long-absent childhood playmate, tears welling joyously. Only at the solid contact beneath her arms did she convince herself he was not a delusion born of childish dreams. She withdrew from the embrace to visually abolish her disbelief. "Time has bestowed great blessings upon you as well. You appear precisely as last I saw you."

"A natural peculiarity of my ancestry, Dear-heart." Kulli suddenly adopted a serious demeanor, and he said, "I sense from the troubled tone that brought me to you, this concerns a matter of import. I have not been denied so long this joyous reunion for mere trivialities and pleasantries now have I, Aurora Leigh?"

With that said, Aurora Leigh found herself explaining her trepidation in a rush of tumbled words as both took seats upon a stone bench on the portico.

After her narrative concluded, Kulli peered knowingly into Aurora Leigh's eyes. "Your fears are valid, for I feel it myself." He spoke as if he were able to see to her core.

"Answer this, youngling, a puzzle that will help you understand this rush of new feelings— 'To be gold is to be good, to be glass is to be fragile, to be stone is to be hardened, and to be cold is to be cruel.'"

Something within prompted her to speak. "A heart?" she asked, unsure of how she had arrived at the answer.

"Aye indeed, Aurora Leigh . . . a heart." Kulli smiled warmly at his young friend. "You have found your match in Eralon through your heart-bond that feels all things, including this present danger."

At the darkening of Aurora Leigh's cheeks, her beloved Kulli only grinned good-naturedly. "My dear, one does not become as ancient as I without understanding a bit about humanity."

"Oh, Kulli," said Aurora Leigh, smiling, "you are not ancient."

"One would think that almost two centuries would, indeed, be ancient by thy reckoning. But putting that aside, I promise I shall do everything in my power to find your Eralon. I dare say, there is naught in the Oralian Empire that I cannot find, if I truly wish it. We shall find his whereabouts and shed some light on these unsettled feelings that burden you so."

Relief flooded Aurora Leigh. To be in her dear friend's presence once again conjured feelings of grandeur. She felt strongly that, together, they could do anything and right the world. They would find Eralon and put her worries to rest. How that was to be accomplished, she was not yet sure, but she was sure that it could be done. Since her companion's sudden reappearance, everything felt magical and fresh, like she was viewing the world through new eyes.

Then, suddenly, the euphoria of his words mingled with fact and reason. Aurora Leigh wondered why he said he was almost two centuries old. And he seems to be able to read her every thought.

Kullipthius shook his head in amusement. "I can see I have much to explain. My family and yours have, indeed, been friends for a very long time. Before you and I became friends, Aurora Leigh, my last visit to these estates occurred long ago when I visited one of your ancestors."

As a questioning look of bewilderment etched her face, he continued. "Oralia is, indeed, my empire, but it is not as far distant as you might suspect. My people hold not to the boundaries on a map as yours do. Your kingdom and my empire share some of the same lands. However, my empire does not interfere with the politics of the Avalians or any part of the country of Sapphirus—unless it threatens us as a whole. I myself am a rarity, for I come into contact with your populace through choice more than most."

Aurora Leigh shook her head, mystified. "You are ageless?

Since your arrival, you have spoken in riddles and act as if you are living in a fairytale. Are you not flesh and blood like me?"

Kulli smiled. "I once knew a youngling who believed in magic and the lore keeper's tales. I believe that child is in there somewhere." Taking up her hand, he continued. "The time has come for me to reveal my true nature. Then you will understand. Fear not, Aurora Leigh, for you are dear to my heart. No harm shall befall you."

She knew this to be so, for he had been nothing but kind during her youth when they played in the gardens and throughout all their time together. She sensed no danger in the presence of her most precious childhood friend. Even so, unsure what to expect, Aurora Leigh watched as Kulli leapt from the second level portico and stood in the gardens under the open sky. She ran to the edge and held onto a marble pillar as she peered down at her childhood friend.

Tilting his face to the skies, his eyes closed, and he raised his arms to the heavens. As he stretched his arms, his tapering fingers lengthened further. His gorgeous cape unfurled as his back arched, the material moving as if alive. Then his cloak split neatly down the center at his back and turned into a pair of silvery wings that continued to grow, veined with lovely purple and blue hues. His angular features elongated, and his body expanded, quickly growing enormous. Any semblance to a human quickly faded, and Aurora Leigh found herself staring wide-eyed, her mouth agape in shock.

In the midst of the transformation, Aurora Leigh hid behind the pillar and almost fled, for her first thought was of fiends and monsters. She clutched her pendant tightly and understood exactly what it was she was viewing. The lore keeper's tales were true. Kulli was a dragon!

Then there was a flash of light. Aurora Leigh slowly peered over the side of the portico and Kulli was gone! She was frightened yet desperate to see him again. Where could he be? Had he really been there? Did he leave because she was frightened?

Wondering if he did indeed take flight, she looked to the skies, but could not find a dragon's dark silhouette in the light of the moon. She chided herself for not showing him her trust. Aurora Leigh had always believed there was something most magical about Kulli.

"Oh, Kulli," she whispered softly to herself, "I truly regret my childish reactions. I have missed you dreadfully." Tears welled in her eyes as remorse filled her heart. "Prithee, come back."

"I did not leave, Aurora Leigh," answered a voice from behind her.

She whirled around to find him standing next to the same pillar, where he had first appeared this night. "Forgive me," she cried, and ran into his arms.

Once again, Kulli was beneath her portico in his dragon form. Aurora Leigh was not worried any of the guards would see him, as the area around him was the wild, forested part of the palace where he and Aurora Leigh used to meet when she was a small child. His scales reflected a glossy, steel-blue hue in the moonlight. With the transformation complete, he stretched impressive wings and slowly moved his head to cast dragon eyes upon her. Aurora Leigh held her spot beside the column. Dipping his head to her level, he blinked his huge, cat-like eyes. His breath warmed her skin pleasantly. A glittering diamond was imbedded in the bluish-grey metal that adorned his forehead. He was resplendent.

Aurora Leigh reached out and cautiously touched the dragon's platinum-plated snout. She pulled her hand back slightly at the reality of the touch. But with amazement and childlike wonder written clearly on her features, she could not resist the urge to touch him again. The dragon's body looked and felt like armor. She took note of the beautiful rainbow colors shimmering upon the scales around his neck. She was surprised to feel how amazingly soft that area was. Knowing in her heart Kulli would never hurt her, she gathered her strength and resolve. She felt the need to give her most beautiful friend a hug in approval. Kullipthius returned the gesture by leaning into her embrace.

"A dragon can communicate their thoughts and ideas directly from one mind to another," explained Kulli. *"This form of communication is called Drahk."*

Aurora Leigh jumped at the direct transference of Kulli's thoughts as it entered her mind. Hearing with your mind and not your ears was not an unpleasant feeling, Aurora Leigh noticed. It was just a bit of a surprise to her senses, as she had never experienced it before. Actually, she thought it quite fascinating. She smiled up at Kulli and nodded her head.

"We are also capable of hearing thoughts," continued Kulli. He smiled and added, *"This is a secret my kind does not oft reveal. However, one whom I consider part of my family has called upon me in a time of great need. I shall carry you to Oralia. That is the only place where we can find the answers to calm your fears, Aurora Leigh. Flying is the fastest way to travel, after all, and we*

shall have you back to your estates afore you are missed."

Head swimming with all she had witnessed, Aurora Leigh reflected upon it in hazy wonder. All those times he had wrapped his cape about her, it had been his wings. She nodded at the dragon and smiled, her belief in the lore keeper's tales at once reinstated. Together they would find Eralon!

"Did you say fly?"

CHAPTER SIX

A urora Leigh relished every moment of the flight astride
Kulli's dragon form to her unknown destination. She seemed
to fit most splendidly in an area between his neck and shoulders
and felt wholly snug and secure, as if in a high-canted saddle.

Kulli's wings had beaten smoothly, yet forcefully, as they had
risen until the heavens appeared close enough to touch. She felt a
thrilling fearlessness that allowed her to enjoy the experience with
unfettered abandon. She could feel the chill of the rushing wind
while the heat of the dragon's racing blood proved counterpoint,
leaving her comfortable and warm as he moved with mastery on
the air currents.

The terrain rushed far beneath them in a turbulent blur as
Kaleidos Peak drew near. The mountain's sheer rock face was a
familiar and welcomed sight. It brought a sweet surge of childhood
memories as she recalled trips to her uncle's castle for holidays
and other celebrations. She beamed and turned her gaze to the
side, cheerfully certain that she would soon be flying above
Moorwyn Castle.

Moments later, as if anticipating her desires, two finger-like
spires of the castle's towers thrust into the unlit morning sky. As
they drew closer, Kullipthius veered to fly over the twin towers of
Moorwyn Castle. The view that Aurora Leigh saw before her was
breathtaking.

She was unsure how long they had traveled, and she found
herself disappointed when they began a looping, downward
descent. She cheered herself with thoughts of their quest to ensure

Eralon's wellbeing. Surely, surely, his situation could not be as dire as her dreams had painted it.

The dragon's powerful wings drove harder. Her gaze was drawn from the ground to what stood ahead. The rocky face of the mountain grew before them, but no entrance was in sight. She threw a hand before her as if that fragile barrier was enough to keep any danger at bay.

"All is well, Aurora Leigh," assured Kulli, obviously understanding her thoughts, and trying to calm her fears. *"It is a false impression. No harm will befall you."*

Kullipthius tucked his wings to his sides and dove through the craggy stone as if it were no obstruction. A moment of disorientation passed for Aurora Leigh, and when she found they were not dashed against the unforgiving rocks, she was able to breathe a sigh of relief.

Then sudden clarity hit Aurora Leigh. "Illusions," were what the lore keepers had called the false impression Kulli spoke of. They covered the outer sides of the peaks to keep intruders at bay and oblivious to the dragons' home. She was truly experiencing a lore keeper's fantasy tale.

The cave widened ahead and was veined with shimmering crystals. When they came upon them, they sped by as streaks of light to Aurora Leigh's vision. She observed a thick, lime-green moss that grew in patches along the cave's interior. The moss emitted a dispersive reflection of pale green that illuminated the cave's inner walls. She was surprised how clearly she could see.

Aurora Leigh watched as her childhood friend unfurled his beautiful, purple and blue veined wings to their full width. Kullipthius then began back-winging to reduce his speed while extending his fore and back legs to land gently upon the subterranean floor. The dragon lowered his head, and Aurora Leigh slipped from her silvery seat to the ground. Shielding her eyes at Kulli's warning, a bright light flashed behind her lids. When she opened her eyes, she found that Kulli had transformed back into the image of her fondest childhood memories.

"Welcome to my home," announced Kulli with a hospitable bow. "I must confess I never tire of its magnificence."

Aurora Leigh noted that the look upon Kulli's face held a grand sense of pride and fondness.

"This is the main entrance to the Empire of Oralia and the Crystal Palace," Kullipthius said, and then he motioned her forward. They walked side-by-side and embarked on a journey through the cave.

Aurora Leigh was stunned by the many glorious sights. She thought it remarkable that gold and silver veined the floors, and multicolored quartz crystals protruded from the cave's walls. The gateway leading into Oralia was extraordinary.

The cavern ended, and the mountain opened to the sky in grand splendor to reveal a majestic crown of fading stars. Kulli pointed into the distance to a churning waterfall that plunged over the side of the mountain. She watched the water tumble into a series of tiered rocky basins that cascaded in an elegant pattern to the crystal-clear lake below.

"You can walk along various paths around and under the falls," explained Kulli. "There you will find a large number of caves and grottos to explore."

"Its beauty is naught I could have ever imagined," professed Aurora Leigh. Her eyes were alight with wonder.

They continued along the path under the open sky until they came upon another cave on the opposite side of the mountain's deep crevasse. Two massive pillars were carved into each side of the cavern's maw and dominated the entrance. On the surface of the columns were natural cracks, and small plants were trying to live with remarkable patience and persistence.

After Aurora Leigh crossed the threshold, she turned to glance behind her. The early dawn, which was now crimsoning the skies, could be seen clearly beyond the yawning portal. She was speechless from the sight, but knew by Kulli's smile that he understood how honored and humbled she felt to be able to share this experience with him.

Aurora Leigh's gaze was next drawn to an area where water was dripping into a hollow. Making her way over, she saw what looked like a handful of lustrous pearls lying within a nucleus of sand. "Look at all these pearls. Where did you find such a treasure?"

"We call them cave pearls, youngling," explained Kulli, "one of the many extraordinary treasures found in these mountains. These formations are created in cave pools when certain minerals are slowly deposited around a grain of sand."

Aurora Leigh leaned over to feel them and found their polished texture peculiarly smooth.

"Come," Kullipthius said as he offered his arm in escort, and Aurora Leigh graciously accepted. "There is much more to behold."

He extended his other arm and pointed to a large, hourglass-shaped pillar that stood alone in the middle of the walkway. Aurora Leigh thought that it looked like it had been created by dripping candle wax falling from the ceiling.

"It began as a single drop of water rich in the land's raw minerals," explained Kullipthius. "Each single, subsequent drop falls upon the previous one and, eventually, these minerals build up. It is known as dripstone. With the passage of time, it can create many fanciful configurations, like the one you see before you, a magnificent, naturally-formed column stretching from ceiling to floor."

As they continued, the cave widened and Aurora Leigh noticed an area of what appeared to be miniature trees growing inside the caves. "Is that snow upon those trees, Kulli?"

Kullipthius grinned. "Move closer and they shall reveal their secrets."

As she drew near, she could see they were not trees at all. They were columns of stone and their "branches" were intricate crystals that were shaped in needlelike formations.

"The sight is likened to an indoor garden that will never wither," observed Aurora Leigh.

They continued talking and walking until their path emptied into a very wide, underground chamber. Aurora Leigh believed many dragons would fit comfortably into the space.

Kullipthius bid Aurora Leigh pause. She then watched as Kulli bent down to ladle his hand into standing water so clear Aurora Leigh had not realized it was there.

"We raise fish in these pure waters," Kullipthius explained, "and livestock in the Kaleidos Mountains for the empire's needs. We also have a wilderness area. It is stocked with birds and wild animals for those dragons that cannot transform and must rely on hunting for their food. Additionally, a small number of us trade and barter at the marketplace in the city of Kaleidos in our altered guise. Most importantly, we meet periodically with your uncle, the Supreme Ruler of Avala, to maintain peace and protect our shared interests and lands."

"His Majesty, Uncle Lucian?" asked Aurora Leigh. Then a realization came to mind. "Oh Kulli, the Avalians do not even realize at times they are bartering with Avala's great protectors? Can you imagine? Well, of course you can," said Aurora Leigh, self-conscious of her silly remark. "How utterly incredible," she whispered. She felt her face flush when she saw that Kullipthius was smiling at her ramblings.

Then came of a sudden a call likened to an exotic bird. Its mellifluous sound, lilting and alluring, drew Aurora Leigh's attention to the far left of the water's edge. There, lounging along the mossy shore of this glassy pool was a slender, glistening white dragon.

Aurora Leigh knew instinctively that this was a dragoness by the way she tilted her head to view those who approached and by the gracefulness of her movements. Whereas Kullipthius displayed a striking silvery shade, this sinuous dragon differed in that each scale held a pearly luster. Even the claws on each foot shone with a swirling of color, and her eyes were a bright violet-blue. Her wings, veined in the same royal hues as her eyes, were outstretched and curled in at the ends. Kullipthius smiled brightly as he ushered Aurora Leigh toward the magnificent creature.

"From one marvel to another," she said, and her heart fluttered at the sight of the dragon before her. "Oh Kulli, she is breathtaking."

The lustrous dragoness made soft, chirping sounds and approached, seemingly pleased by the admiring compliment. She lowered her head, and Aurora Leigh noted the dragoness displayed a large opal stone that graced her forehead, reflecting a rainbow of colors. Aurora Leigh smiled as she caught sight of her own reflection in the dragoness' blinking, violet orbs.

Kullipthius whistled. "Shield your eyes, Aurora Leigh. When we change our guise quickly there is a momentary flash of light. I wish to make introductions."

Even after Aurora Leigh opened her eyes, radiance still bathed the room, and from it stepped a slim, well-curved beauty.

Aurora Leigh felt her jaw drop, and she quickly moved to compose herself. The most stunning woman Aurora Leigh had ever seen approached from the exact spot that, only moments ago, the lustrous white dragon had stood.

Her skin was smooth, white, and almost seemed to glow from within while her eyes retained the same violet depth she had as a dragon. Not knowing otherwise, Aurora Leigh would have guessed she was about her own age, but there was an extraordinary presence and maturity about her.

The newly transformed woman stepped into the half-light, and Aurora Leigh saw the golden dress she wore take on a mystical glow as it swirled and shimmered with color. A delicate golden circlet held an intricate setting that surrounded the opal stone on her forehead. A gold and opal chain clasped a diaphanous trail of sheer, golden fabric that flowed down her slender shoulders, billowing in waves behind her, as she floated across the ground as magnificently as a great ship sails on a serene sea. Her pale blonde hair hung loose to frame her exquisite face and drape her curvaceous upper torso. As she approached, her eyes studied Aurora Leigh, and she inclined her head in welcome.

"May I present Her Imperial Majesty the Imperatrix Laliah, Supreme Dragoness of Oralia." Kulli's introduction seemed to overflow with pride. "My Empress, this is the Princess Aurora Leigh, daughter of Prince Dryden and, therefore, niece to King Lucian, Ruler of Avala."

Laliah's arms were at once around the princess, and she embraced her delicately and lovingly, as a mother would caress her child. Aurora Leigh felt safe and comforted, as if she had been acquainted with her for a very long time. Upon release of Aurora Leigh, Laliah's delicate hand trailed tenderly through Aurora Leigh's golden hair. "I bid you greetings, Princess Aurora Leigh," said the imperatrix. "I must say, it is indeed a pleasure to finally meet." She then turned to her mate. "She is such a delight, Kullipthius."

Aurora Leigh thought her voice exotic and sweet. She wondered wistfully what it would be like to hear such a voice sing, and this brought about a smile. The imperatrix then moved gracefully to Kullipthius' side to nuzzle her fair cheek against his outstretched hand in a soft, loving gesture.

Aurora Leigh immediately felt a fondness for this exquisite being. She was extremely welcoming and gracious. Then it dawned upon Aurora Leigh who she was to Kulli.

"She is your consort!"

Kulli's grin broadened. "Indeed, Aurora Leigh, Laliah is my mate."

"Your Imperial Majesty," said Aurora Leigh. She curtsied, and when she rose, she clasped her hands together while bowing her head in respect. "It is a privilege and an honor to make your acquaintance."

"As it is mine," replied the imperatrix. She gave Aurora Leigh a radiant smile.

"Aye," Kullipthius beamed. "Laliah is a wonder. She holds within the gift of healer, a most rare gift for dragons." Then his attention returned to Laliah. "My Empress, would you be so inclined as to direct us to Ra's whereabouts? He is expecting us."

Laliah dipped her head in response. "Aye, My Emperor, Ra informed me that he will be at the starfire globe preparing for your meeting."

She turned back to look upon Aurora Leigh. "Why, she is merely a nestling. You take care of this precious one or you shan't hear the end of it." Then she smiled.

Aurora Leigh knew she was scolding him good-naturedly, but there was an unmistakable current of counsel in her tone as well.

The imperatrix moved again to stand before Aurora Leigh and said, "I would very much like to have a longer visit when next we meet, Princess Aurora Leigh."

Aurora Leigh thought this marvelous. "It would be an honor, Your Imperial Majesty," and she curtsied once again.

"Excellent," said Laliah, and then kissed Aurora Leigh upon the forehead. "Until next we meet."

"Pray, My Emperor," Laliah held her hand out to her mate and said, "give Ra my fondest affection."

Kulli nuzzled the outstretched hand of his pale beauty adieu.

He then led Aurora Leigh deeper into the palace gardens. They walked alongside many natural pools where Aurora Leigh saw unusual fish and brightly colored plants unlike those she knew from home.

"We shall avoid the palace this time, Aurora Leigh," informed Kulli, "for it is our custom to offer formal introduction and ceremony to newcomers, and we do not have the time to tarry. We have a goal to accomplish, and we must get you back afore you are missed. Though Prince Dryden is aware of our existence, we do not want to cause him any concern over your absence. Upon your next visit, I shall show you the Crystal Palace of Oralia, and that is when we shall make formal introductions to my council."

"That would be a pleasure," said Aurora Leigh, and she gave her childhood companion a wide smile. Her attention then turned to the reason for this visit. "Kulli, this 'Ra' you speak of, is he going to be able to help us find Eralon?"

"Ra is Laliah's son," explained Kullipthius, "and I believe he is our best source of information."

"That would make him your son as well," said Aurora Leigh. "I am looking forward to meeting him."

"Aye, I adopted Ra Kor'el and proclaimed him Prince of Oralia when Laliah became my mate. He was but a nestling then. He possesses many wonderful gifts, amongst them the powers of a soothsayer, that is, one who foresees by rational, magical, or intuitive means. Ra is also what we call a 'land guardian.' He communicates with and works for the preservation and conservation of flora and fauna."

"Certes, he must be highly regarded here in Oralia, for there cannot be many who possess such qualities," said Aurora Leigh. She was looking forward to meeting Kulli's son. As a child, she had never thought to inquire about Kulli's life and family.

"Aye, youngling, Ra is unique. In truth, it has not always been easy for him. He had to earn his acceptance amongst dragonkind."

"This I do not understand," puzzled Aurora Leigh, "for he was decreed your son."

"Not all and sundry are accepting of things that are out of the ordinary," explained Kullipthius. "Some look upon differences as abnormal or evil and become fearful."

"Allow me to shed some light as to Ra's origins," continued Kullipthius. "Laliah has never revealed Ra's birth sire, and I have always respected her reasons. Even with the rumors of an unknown creature seen at night flying away from her lair—a being with the body of a man and dragon wings—I never questioned her. Such a being was unheard of, and if it were true, she had her reasons for keeping her secret. When Ra was born, his body partially displayed the human form, with the exception of the shape and color of the eyes, dragon-clawed hands, and scaled upper arms.

"When his uniqueness was discovered, my High Council of Dragon Lords brought it to my attention during a council meeting. They, of course, feared the unknown, thinking Ra's sire must be a dangerous threat because he had met with Laliah in secret and had passed through our elaborate security measures, thus gaining entrance into Oralia undetected. They believed Laliah to be a co-conspirator because she had not reported his intrusion into our empire. It was the council's wish that Laliah and the nestling be imprisoned for her refusal to reveal the perpetrator.

"Instead, I ruled they be relocated to Willow Glen, an uninhabited, comfortable area in the Tall Forest where dragons had made their home long and ago, even before the Dra'khar Dynasty. I believed that sparing them from prison was the proper course.

"Then, many decades later, Laliah returned to the empire asking for an audience. When she came before me, she explained that her son had many great gifts. One such gift was the rare endowment of perceiving what lies beyond the natural range of the senses. It was her intention to inform me that Ra Kor'el had foreseen a horrible fate for the Oralian Empire if we did not take steps to prevent it. In essence, Ra's forewarning saved the dragons of Oralia and the Avalians from ill-fortune.

"It was Imperial Advisor Vahl Zayne who petitioned for Ra and Laliah's reinstatement to the empire, citing passages from Oralia's ancient writings. Vahl Zayne is Oralia's historiographer, a scribe, and the official authority and keeper of Oralia's Ancient

Transcripts. He is in charge of tracing history, traditions, and lore. It seems it had been foretold, long and ago, that such a being as Ra would one day live amongst dragonkind and help save the dragons from impending doom. When they returned, Laliah and I fell in love, and she became my life mate. Thus, I am now honored to have Ra as my son."

Just then they happened upon a circular procession of tall, numinous columns of standing stones with intricate patterns carved by dragon claw. Within the ring's center was the largest, most powerful starfire stone Aurora Leigh had ever laid eyes upon.

This starfire globe appeared to be similar to the others she had seen before, as it held a slick and shiny transparent surface with pockets of iridescent crystals set within. However, this globe was the largest and brightest she had ever seen. It was surrounded with blue and white fire and hung without help of sconce or bracket. It cast an intense light into the ring of dark stones, resembling a miniature full moon.

There was a figure standing in the center of the circle. His head was tipped toward the globe, his eyes closed to the radiance bathing his face. His arms were spread wide at his sides, as if he were trying to embrace the illumination. The voluminous sleeves of his robes were hanging just beyond the tips of his fingers.

There was a soft chanting that Aurora Leigh could barely make out, like the susurrations of a thousand overlapping whispers. It was uncannily beautiful, although she could not see anyone except the three of them standing in the chamber.

As if sensing the newcomers' presence, his soft whispers immediately ceased, and Ra Kor'el turned toward them.

CHAPTER SEVEN

E ralon's gaze was captured by a crimson ribbon of dawn that decorated the horizon as he traveled the last leg of his journey to Terra Leone. He was pleased to be astride Lightning, as the palfrey was well rested and possessed a smooth, ambling gait that covered ground quickly. He did not want to leave his guards alone at the fortress for too long with the anticipated arrival of the force that was marching toward Terra Leone.

As Eralon rode, he found his company kept by the gossamer memories of the one he had come upon and rescued, she who had so captivated his attentions. Thoughts of a once willful royal adolescent turned beauteous princess brushed softly, yet insistently within his mind. Was it fortune that had brought their unexpected reunion? Was it fate that had sent the guiding light he had pursued?

The guards must have seen Eralon's arrival, for the large wooden doors of the fortress were open. As he drew closer, he saw the portcullis rise. He entered through the gates of Terra Leone and headed toward the stables. At first, Eralon noticed only the quiet of the early morn, but his instincts told him something was amiss. As he rode further, he glanced about the empty streets and saw more to add to the puzzle. Stalls in the market stood empty at an hour when merchants should have already set up shop. Farmers were early risers and should have begun offering their harvests for sale. Why was there no one about?

With no one at the stables to attend his horse, Eralon placed Lightning in one of the empty stalls equipped with a water trough.

He gave the palfrey some oats, hay, and a comforting pat. Eralon then took a long drink from his waterskin before heading out the stable's rear exit.

He began a systematic search from the back alleyways, slowly making his way toward Lionholm, the fortress manor. He remained hidden in the shadows and continued on silent footfalls, his sharp eyes alert for any movement. He took pause in his cautious exploration beneath the sign of a blacksmith's shop and stared in unsettled silence down the next street. From this vantage point the outlying streets had almost looked normal, save for the lack of citizenry. After checking the rooftops, Eralon dared a knock at the door of the smithy's abode. With no response, he tried to open the door, only to find it locked. His efforts elicited muffled sounds of a young girl crying and being comforted.

Glass crunched underfoot and pieces of broken furniture littered the walks around several merchant shops. When last at Terra Leone, the mood had been one of relief and freedom. He suddenly felt a great concern for the men he had left on guard. Surely they would have moved to stop any disaster . . . if they had been able.

Grim-faced, Eralon unsheathed his steel and walked warily through the fortress streets, his gaze scanning far and wide. He felt eyes upon him as he peered into every shop and examined every shadow the wan light did not touch. Exactly what had transpired in his absence from Terra Leone?

As he came upon the fortress courtyard, he spied a stain upon the ground. As he drew closer, his suspicions were confirmed. A large pool of half-dried blood darkened the dirt.

It was then that the mob that stalked him made their presence known. Eralon knew that he must have been marked before he had even entered the gates.

With the appearance of the hard-eyed multitude moving purposely toward Eralon, he worried even more for the fate of his men. One of the ruffians was wearing an ornately embroidered green and pale yellow doublet, one frequently worn by Knight Master Nyquest. This did not bode well. Eralon lowered his blade so they would not deem him an immediate threat.

The crowd parted, and the apparent leader of this motley crew stepped forward. He eyed Eralon dangerously as his cohorts spread out behind him and filled the street from side to side. They all held steel, poised for action like a pack of hunting dogs awaiting the command of their master.

Thus, the silence was broken, "Cap'n Wellsbough, how good o' ya ta come ta Terra Leone," said the leader. "Indeed, ya saved me the disruption o' an extended search."

Eralon noted the fellow's eyes held madness, and he wore a wicked smile. His body bounced to the rhythm of his low, rumbling laughter.

He was tall and athletic with hair silvered over that gave him a distinguished look, but his eyes displayed hate in their depths. Then recognition dawned upon Eralon. This grisly fellow was present when Danuvius and Eralon had their encounter in the wood. He had painted himself memorable in that instance by whispering in quiet undertones amongst his fellows when Eralon had first approached their camp. After Danuvius fell into the fire pit, this grisly fellow had been the one who fled and propagated the tale of a dragon in their midst.

Eralon could not recall the grisly face having been amongst those taken as prisoners. It seemed they had been wrong to neglect him, and that oversight would have to be remedied.

"This fortress lives by my rules alone, an' ya shan't spoil it. Me plans will nay be disrupted!"

"Your rules?" mocked Eralon. "Terra Leone is now under the rule of King Lucian, and I am here to appoint a temporary guardian. I mean to see it restored to good order. Danuvius fell for his beliefs; dare not make the same mistake."

Eralon's eyes took in his surroundings, weighing the odds, knowing he would have to retreat down an alleyway and bait them into approaching him a few at a time if he was going to have any chance of coming out of this intact.

"The king's marionette be a credulous fool," the leader chided contemptuously. "Must be embarrassing ta be taken by such a simple ruse. Know this, sirrah! For 'twas a devoted sellsword ya fought that day in the forest. He be the one who stumbled inta that fire pit. A loyal fella dressed as nobility so I could cleverly plan me moves without disruption." A dark fire burned in the madman's eyes as he said, "'Tis I, fool. I be Danuvius." The shouted din that rose from his fellows was nearly deafening.

Eralon gripped his blade tighter and thought back to when he confronted Danuvius. Now he understood what it was that had left him so wary and on edge after the foray in the wood. The man he assumed was Danuvius did not even have a Liltian accent! How daft to assume someone dressed in lavish attire would be Danuvius. Eralon cursed under his breath for being so blind.

"The capture o' Cap'n Wellsbough be letting the country know we be a force ta be reckoned with," continued Danuvius. "I'm gonna insist ya hand over yer blade."

Eralon dashed as quickly as he could toward a tight alleyway behind him, and he was followed by a rushing onslaught.

"I want him taken alive!" commanded Danuvius.

The charge of men rushed forward as powerfully as waves crashing against boulders. He held their line at a narrow alleyway's entrance, his sword a blur of action, the sounds of shrieking steel on steel ringing in his ears.

When the first lines of his combatants were down and the next cluster attempted to climb past their wounded fellows' sprawled forms, Eralon broke his stance and retreated. Force them to pursue and then pick them off as they came, he schemed.

Even after his methodical search, he was not fully familiar with the layout of the back streets and alleyways of Terra Leone. He only hoped he would not find himself caught in the open in one of the main streets where they might surround him.

Someone swung a crude club at him from a darkened doorway. Eralon ducked under the clumsy stroke and gashed the attacker's hand with his blade, causing him to howl in pain and drop the crude weapon. Darting down side lanes, sometimes through abandoned stores and houses, Eralon fought those who pursued him and let those who could limp or crawl away afterward do so.

But he had to keep moving.

AURORA LEIGH was awestruck. The radiant glow of the starfire globe illumined the unique and ethereally handsome features of Ra Kor'el. His long locks flowed in thick waves down to the center of his back, displaying the color of a strand of white pearls. His eyes were almond-shaped and a beautiful shade of violet. Most intriguing were his pupils, which were narrowed into vertical slits.

Ra wore a dark blue robe embroidered in golden threads of mystical symbols and patterns. He pushed back his long sleeves as he approached, and she saw that his fingers were tipped with dragon claws. He had small, delicate scales running up his forearms in lustrous shades of blues, and purples. He produced a warm smile with beautiful white teeth, and she noted his canine teeth were relatively longer and pointed. It was as if she had caught him in the middle of transforming from a dragon into a man. Although she found it peculiar, she could not deny there was something captivating about him.

Ra Kor'el bowed deeply. "Greetings, Imperial Father, I have been awaiting your arrival."

When his gaze turned to Aurora Leigh he produced a warm, welcoming smile. "It is a privilege to make your acquaintance, Princess Aurora Leigh. I must profess that you are, by far, even more beauteous in person than when viewed through the starfire globe."

"Gramercy, Your Highness," said Aurora Leigh. She curtsied to show her respect.

"I was never one for all these titles and formalities. Prithee, it would be an honor if you would but call me Ra," he said, smiling genuinely.

Aurora Leigh dipped her head in response, returned an appreciative smile, and said, "That is a wonderful name, Ra, and please call me Aurora Leigh."

"We are pleased to see the starfire globe made ready for viewing, Ra," Kullipthius said to his son, and added, "As you know, our task is of utmost importance."

"Aye," responded Ra, "I was just watching Captain Wellsbough enter the gates at Terra Leone."

"Captain Wellsbough? Oh, Kulli, he knows his whereabouts!" Aurora Leigh then turned to Ra Kor'el and asked, "Prithee, Ra, I must know; how does he fare?"

"Come, Aurora Leigh," beckoned Ra, "we shall see for ourselves."

RA KOR'EL met the princess midway and offered her his arm. As the trio advanced, Ra privately conveyed the current situation to his father. *The circumstances are not at their best at the moment, with the end result not what it may seem. She might be frightened. However, a vision showed me that her presence is essential while viewing the starfire globe. She is here for a reason, and whatever it is shall reveal itself in due course.*

"We cannot hide the truth if her presence is foreseen," Kullipthius advised. *"We must proceed as your gift suggests."*

When they entered the ring of stones, the inscriptions on the rocks smoldered with a faint turquoise light. Ra led Aurora Leigh and his father to stand before the starfire globe that hovered within the center of the ring, and then took his place, a sword's length away and to the left.

The globe grew brighter and expanded in size. Curling wisps of blue-edged fire licked at its outer edges. The chanting whispers began anew, and the blue fire blazed into a wall of flames. Colors undulated and swirled in the flames, forming fiery images that erupted to life.

Before them, the glitter of morning light was shining upon an armored breastplate and sword. Ra saw Aurora Leigh's eyes widen at the images that danced before her. He was intrigued by her reaction, for a human had never before displayed the ability to see within the flames.

Her voice trembled as she breathlessly exclaimed, "Oh, Kulli, I see Eralon!"

"It is as I suspected," Ra communicated. *"It seems she has the gift of sight."*

"Aye," Kullipthius answered aloud, seemingly to both Aurora Leigh's statement and Ra's mental announcement.

Eralon was fighting two swordsmen, and they saw a third fellow crouched nearby, cradling his wounded arm. One of the fighters shouted for reinforcements.

Aurora Leigh was staring at her sword-wielding hero. Sweat dampened Eralon's hair, and he appeared tired, although the cuts and deft movements of his blade remained sharp and exact.

"Kulli, I cry your mercy! I fear my dream is fast approaching reality! Is there naught that can be done?"

Ra was happy that his father took her hand in his to help calm her fears.

A hard-looking man with steel-colored eyes and a perpetual scowl was now matching moves with Eralon. Ra heard Aurora Leigh gasp as several more armsmen poured from another alley and advanced upon Eralon. She grew pale, and her breath quickened as she watched with tear-stained eyes.

"We must find a way to help him!" pleaded Aurora Leigh, as tears rolled down her fair cheeks, and she bit her bottom lip.

Too many opponents seemed set against Eralon. They watched as a man approached Eralon from behind. The fiend raised his blade to strike.

Horror painted her features as she screamed, "ERALON!"

Ra stared at the scene in the starfire globe with utter fascination. Eralon's eyes had widened in surprise at the sound of Aurora Leigh's voice. He spun around, saw his predicament, and then raised his sword just in time to catch a descending blade that had threatened to decapitate him. It was then that Ra realized the reason for his vision. Aurora Leigh had communicated a warning of imminent danger across the distance by calling out Eralon's name.

As Eralon dispatched the immediate threat, another fellow saw a perfect opportunity and, with the hilt of his blade in hand, slammed the side of Eralon's head with a mighty blow. Aurora Leigh's captain crumpled to the ground. Pale with eyes glazed over, Aurora Leigh stumbled into Kulli's arms and looked as if she were about to faint.

Ra opened a connection to Aurora Leigh's mind. He wanted to reassure her before the darkness stole her away. *"Worry not, Aurora Leigh. Your Eralon is alive, merely unconscious from the blow. Your warning saved him from certain death. Everything shall reveal itself, all in good time."*

AURORA LEIGH'S eyes shot open, and she jolted upright in bed. "It cannot be . . . no . . . Eralon!" It took a moment to realize it was a nightmare haunting her half-awakened state. Her breath was quick, and she must have been tossing and turning for her coverlet was twisted and shoved to the side. She tried to tell herself it was only nightmarish thoughts left over from the previous day's events. What had begun as a beautiful dream about her precious Kulli had turned into a nightmare. She could only remember bits and pieces of Eralon beset by foes, much conflict and swordplay, him being assaulted from behind, and then brought to a seedy dungeon and flung to the dusty, straw-covered floor. She placed her face in her hands as the memory assaulted her reasoning.

Her attendant and guards heard her cries and rushed into the bedchamber, interrupting Aurora Leigh's fuzzy thoughts.

"Your Highness!" cried Murielle, who was the first to enter, followed by four guards. They raced about the room checking behind curtains and everywhere else to see if there was any present danger. "We heard you cry out," Murielle said, and then she appeared to relax upon seeing only her troubled charge, hair disheveled from tossing in her sleep and her quilt twisted in a tight grip.

"Oh, Murielle, a nightmare it was!" cried Aurora Leigh, trying to reassure herself as well that it was only that.

"Shush now," Murielle advised in a maternal voice. "Let us soothe all your troubles away."

Satisfied that all was well, the guards bowed to Aurora Leigh and left the room, closing the double doors behind them.

Murielle had cared for Aurora Leigh since birth, and a welcome sight she was. Her handmaid's hair was pulled into a loose, greying bun. Little tresses had escaped the original knot and formed a soft halo around her face. Murielle moved to sit at the edge of the bed, offering outstretched arms and the welcoming shelter of a comforting embrace, and Aurora Leigh slipped readily within.

Murielle was silent and still until Aurora Leigh's trembling ceased. Tenderly tilting Aurora Leigh's face upward with gentle fingers, Murielle's soft smile upon her plump-cheeked face always seemed to banish away the most distressing emotions. When Aurora Leigh regained her composure, Murielle left her to open the curtains to let the morning light warm the bedchamber.

"You slept late this day, child," said Murielle. "We shall have you up and about and feeling grand in no time."

Murielle held a look of surprise on her face when Aurora Leigh threw back the covers and stood up from her bed. "Why, I see you have dressed and donned a beautiful amulet. I have not seen this amulet afore this day. Where did you acquire such a lovely trinket, child?"

"It was a gift," she answered distractedly. Aurora Leigh clutched her amulet and looked down only to see she was wearing the gown she had worn in what she had believed was a dream. "I could not sleep," began Aurora Leigh, speaking between thoughts, "and during the night" . . . *Was it possible?* . . . "I dressed to catch a breath of fresh air on the portico." *Was it real?*

Her memories surged to the forefront of her mind . . . Kulli . . . a dragon . . . flying . . . a magical viewing device. She had really been with her childhood friend in Oralia watching helplessly as Eralon faced impending doom. She remembered Ra had assured her that her warning had saved Eralon and that he would pull through, and Ra also had promised that things were not as they seemed. Aurora Leigh wanted to believe, with all her heart, that Ra was right.

CHAPTER EIGHT

S lowly regaining consciousness, Eralon opened his eyes and blinked a few times to clear his blurred vision. Not recognizing his surroundings, he sat up with a start and cursed at the vertigo that assailed him. While rubbing at his aching temples to help the dizziness pass, he tried to clear his muddled thoughts.

As his memory slowly returned, he recalled riding to Terra Leone . . . a mob of assailants . . . and Danuvius! Just thinking about that scoundrel made his head throb.

He ran his hand through the hair on the side of his head and found it to be matted with dried blood. Upon further inspection, he felt a large lump with a gash across its center.

Then a memory surfaced that made him pause. Had he heard Princess Aurora Leigh call out a warning? He had turned in the direction of her voice, just in time to block a descending blade. It had saved his life. Alas, he must have been hit harder than he thought if he had imagined hearing her cry out his name.

Queasy and unstable, he leaned back against a stone wall and absorbed his surroundings.

The sound of dripping water echoed from somewhere nearby, adding to the dark mood of the dank room. From the meager illumination of a solitary window, he could see he was in a small rectangular room with an iron-strapped door. The dirt floor was cold with only a thin covering of straw, and he could feel the chill seeping through his bones. Aye indeed, he was definitely in Terra Leone's prison. He had seen it before, but not from the inside of a cell.

He took note that he had not been bound and still possessed his breastplate. He was puzzled until he realized his captors must have been so anxious to see him securely locked away as to not care if he retained his protection. But his dagger and blade were nowhere in sight.

Then a voice from the shadows startled Eralon.

"Relieved an' pleased I be ta see ya awake an' sitting up, Cap'n Wellsbough. Even if the situation we find ourselves thrust inta be an unpleasant one."

Eralon recognized the voice. He managed a smile into the shadows. The concern he felt for his missing companions lessened, and he called out in relief.

"Jhain."

"Indeed," replied the lithe scout. He materialized from a darkened corner and offered his captain a hand. He helped Eralon to the brightest spot in the cell where the sun slanted meagerly through the barred window. He then helped Eralon to sit on a wooden stool near the window.

"Here, let me 'aves a look at yer head," said Jhain. After inspecting the wound, Jhain reached into his shirt and pulled out a wineskin.

At Eralon's puzzled expression, Jhain said, "They nay did a thorough job o' searching me before they threw me in here." He smiled and offered the wineskin to his captain, who took a good long drink. Jhain took a drink himself, and then used the rest to clean Eralon's wound.

The captain closed his eyes for a moment and let the sun warm his face. Taking his mind off the pain in his head, Eralon used the time to organize his thoughts. Remembering Knight Master Balderon and a contingent of Elite Guardsmen were on their way to Terra Leone, he hoped they had not yet arrived and fallen into a similar predicament

"How stands the hour, Jhain? How long have I been out?"

"I'd say, 'tis mid-morning," replied Jhain. "Ya were out a little o'er a day, dazed an' muttering throughout the night."

After cleaning Eralon's injury, Jhain handed Eralon a hardened crust of bread and dented pewter mug of water before seating himself on the floor across from his captain. "I tried keeping ya from the damp by moving all the straw b'neath ya."

Throat still parched, Eralon nodded his head in appreciation and took a drink. He dreaded the answer to his next question. "Where are Knight Master Nyquest and the rest of the Elite Guardsmen I had left here under his command?"

The look on the scout's face was heartrending as he told the captain his story.

"After yer departure, there be story telling an' singing with much drink an' merriment through the night. The next thing we know we be surrounded with swords drawn at our throats. The foes holding the swords be dressed in civilians' clothing, so we dinna foresee the danger 'til 'twas upon us. Then, a large band o' ruffians appeared outa nowhere an' had us surrounded.

"Danuvius lives! Curse the miscreant ta the abyss! There be many o' them ta the few o' us. The townsfolk knew him ta be the real Danuvius. Some citizens tried ta stand with us against his tyranny—thirty at most. They be cramped in similar cells as us." Jhain sighed and said, "We lost Knight Master Nyquest. Danuvius had him killed as an example o' his might."

"He will be sorely missed," replied Eralon, who had been worried for Keyon since he had seen the cutthroat in the street adorned in his green and yellow doublet. The master knight was a good, honorable man, one who always tried to keep everyone's spirits up with a belly laugh that could be heard across the kingdom.

Eralon could see the grief etched into the scout's features. Jhain had looked up to Keyon and thought of him not only as a brother-in-arms, but as family. The captain placed his hand on Jhain's back. "You must remain strong, Jhain. Keyon would want it that way. The wicked shall not go unpunished." That earned him a smile.

"Yer words mean much, but I fear fer us all. Danuvius plans ta overthrow the king an' claim Avala as his own. The beslubbering maggot-pie has an armed force headed this way as we speak. The fella be brainsick, Cap'n. He be wanting us out o' the way, that be sure."

The scout rose and pressed himself up to the bars of the small opening almost blending with the dusky walls in his dark, scarred leathers. He pointed into the distance to the left. Backing away, he helped Eralon up to look out the small cell window.

Blinking his eyes to adjust to the light, Eralon managed a perfect view of a guard's muddy boots as the men stood at attention outside. Beyond the guard, Eralon could make out hastily raised scaffolding. So Danuvius meant for them to hang, did he?

"Fear not, Jhain," explain Eralon, "His Majesty has been kept well informed and summoned a legion of his own. Justice shall be served."

A familiar voice outside the prison walls jolted Eralon from his thoughts with a strangled start. Fie, it could not be! He pressed himself to the bars of the window, straining to catch the words, positive in his recollection. A cold ball of rage formed in the pit of his stomach at what he saw.

Danuvius stood outside, many yards away, yet the figure who walked next to him in conversation caused Eralon to grind his teeth. Treyven Fontacue! The bandit, with his long braids and angular features, was all too easy to recognize. Betrayal flooded Eralon's senses as he wrapped his fingers around the bars of the cell window in a white-knuckled grip. He should have realized a promise to right his wrongs would not stand long in the face of offered power or riches.

Eralon took in a steadying breath and moved away from the window as his thoughts ran gloom-hazed circles. Had he all but handed Danuvius his newest recruits and power by letting the bandit live? Whatever transpired, he would escape his cell and see that the Liltian brigand paid just as dearly as that vile Danuvius.

The royal guards riding toward the fortress could be of better assistance if they knew what had transpired. Eralon glanced over to Jhain, who was leaning against the back wall with his arms crossed, obviously lost in his own thoughts. But the sounds of booted steps in the corridor beyond their prison door roused them both. Jhain's hands automatically reached for the absent blade sheaths normally found on his forearms that would have held his favorite throwing knives. Jhain realized his error and gave his captain a sheepish shrug.

Those purposeful steps heading down the hall caused no restless stirring of the prison guards stationed outside their door. There was a quiet exchange of words, then sounds of a scuffle. A loud thud rattled the door that caused dust to settle from the ceiling of Eralon's cell. The tiny window in the door slid back with a dry, grating sound to reveal the face of someone Eralon least wished to behold.

"Interesting predicament we find ourselves in," said Treyven, grinning at the pair in the cell.

Eralon glared at Treyven. "I should have known not to trust a brigand who proclaims himself repentant. Your words mean nothing, proven this day by the company you keep."

Shock showed momentarily in his slightly tilted eyes before composure returned to the brigand's face. "Harsh words," replied Treyven, "fer yer liberator." He swung the door open wide and said, "Fer me word be me bond."

Eralon paused as he let the scarred man's words play in his mind. The more he saw the more credence was weighed in Treyven's favor. Beyond the opened door, the prison guards that had been stationed outside their cell were now slumped against the walls on either side of the door. If Eralon had needed further proof, his wrapped blade was held casually in Treyven's hand.

From the edges of his vision, Eralon saw Jhain slowly making his way toward Treyven. The captain looked over to Jhain and abruptly held up his hand for the scout to forestall his approach. Eralon wanted to hear exactly what it was that this brigand had to say.

Treyven eyed Jhain and then spoke to Eralon. "Firstling in mind be ta rally 'round this Danuvius fella in his fight against the king. We believed his lies 'bout the king holding our countryman as slaves. We be hirelings for a cause, an' he be paying well ta stand up an' fight ta free our Liltian families an' friends."

"But after I met ya in the woodlands, I spoke with the citizens o' Terra Leone, an' they confirmed yer story 'bout the murderous steward's lies. Imagine me surprise when I discovered Danuvius still lives. He be quick ta bragging his deception an' newfound joy with the successful capture o' the famous Cap'n Wellsbough. He also told me we're ta meet up with another large band o' Liltians."

"That would explain the reason for the approaching force marching through Avala," acknowledged Eralon.

The hireling continued as he offered Eralon his weapon. "I showed Danuvius me wounded arm made by this sword an' fabricated a story o' vengeance in kind before the hanging. Fain he was ta relinquish it."

After accepting the blade and explanation, Eralon made his apologies. "Pray, pardon my mistake, Treyven. I sorely misjudged you. You are indeed a man of honor." Treyven smiled and nodded.

Eralon and Treyven dragged the two unconscious prison guards into the tiny vacated cell and shut the door from the outside with a satisfying click. Jhain moved on silent feet to survey the dusty, shadowed hall and stood peering down its length for several heartbeats before returning. "It appears none be suspect o' our escape. Only three fellas watching over all the cells shan't be a problem."

"Might I propose we keep up with the deception that naught be amiss?" Treyven offered genially in the semi-darkness. "I can walk freely about the fortress with none the wiser an' get word ta me band here at the fortress with any plan ordered."

"Aye," agreed Jhain. "I rather me skin stay intact. The Elite

Guardsmen canna be far."

"We need to set the others free and make our way to inform Knight Master Balderon and his men of the present situation," said Eralon.

"Aye, Cap'n," replied Jhain. He then motioned for Eralon and Treyven to lean in close as he spoke in quiet tones. "I do 'aves me a most marvelous plan."

Surprise was in their best interest, and Eralon knew the scout was well-suited to any task he set his mind on. Nearly invisible in his dark leathers, Jhain nimbly darted from shadow to shadow between the flickering torches lining the prison walls. The captain kept to the shadows with Treyven trailing close behind, watching their backs.

Jhain soundlessly approached a prison guard from behind. As quick as a fox, Jhain wrapped his right arm around the prison guard's throat, grasping his own left bicep. Then he brought his left arm up and placed his hand behind the guard's head for leverage and squeezed. Within seconds, the guard went limp.

"I'ves got ta learn that one," whispered Treyven.

Eralon only smiled.

Jhain might have been weaponless at the start, but he did not remain so for long. There were manacles, shackles, leg irons, and chains hanging from hooks on a nearby wall. Jhain retrieved a pair of manacles to restrain the jailer he had rendered unconscious. Eralon and Treyven gathered the last of the fetters, ready to restrain anyone else who crossed their path. They continued to follow in the young scout's wake, keeping an eye out for the key to the cell doors as they went.

Having bound and gagged the last two guards, they continued quietly down the dimly lit hall to the weapons room. Treyven stood guard while Jhain followed Eralon into the room. They found their weapons piled on a long trestle table. Eralon replaced his sword in its sheath and was relieved to find his dagger still attached to his belt. It was a gift from his father, the late Captain Xavian Wellsbough. He waited for Jhain to quickly place his knives in their sheaths under his shirtsleeves and helped him fasten his baldric and short sword upon his back.

Unable to find the keys to the cells, the three men whispered their plans to check the guardroom. Eralon told the men inside their cells to hold tight and remain quiet. Being unaware of the layout of the jailhouse and not knowing how many guards were on duty, they dared not wrench the cell doors open yet for fear of detection. They were concerned the noise would send one of the prison guards out an unknown back exit to warn any other guards of their escape.

Eralon paused outside the guardroom. Hushed words of nervous anticipation and caution filtered from the cells at his back. Peeping through the rusting bars on the guardroom door, Eralon noted four prison guards having a conversation while lounging in chairs, feet propped upon a low table. And resting on that table was the instrument of freedom for his men. A lit candle stood in a sconce on the wall above the table. The wax was marked to show the changing of the hours and the sentinels. Rapidly the candle burned, approaching the next mark, and the liberators exchanged knowing looks in the darkness indicating they had to move quickly. Eralon had an idea, and with a quick exchange of whispered words, the trio took their positions.

Treyven's voice broke the silence with a cry. "Guards! I be in need o' yer assistance!"

As expected, the prison guards rushed to help. The door opened, and the guards crowded through the narrow space to view the trouble. From the doorway, the prison guards could see that the scout Jhain had somehow escaped from his cell. He had acquired his weapons and some chains whose links were presently wrapped around Treyven's neck.

Jhain's voice seemed to shake with rage, his teeth bared as he growled out at the guards, "Come closer an' his death be imminent!"

"Do as you are bid," ordered Treyven, feigning distress.

The prison guards paused and eyed each other, giving Eralon the opportunity he was waiting for. He pushed with all his might from where he stood behind the opened guardroom door and knocked the men back. They tripped over each other, and two crumpled to the floor.

Since the guards were unprepared for the sneak attack, Eralon had gained the upper hand quickly, knocking out the two guards who were still standing before the other two could regain their feet. Jhain and Treyven took care of the other two, and the keys were secured in mere moments.

With all the prison guards locked away, the newly freed men followed Treyven and Eralon to the guardroom where they all pressed inside. Eralon noted a few of the farmers who had joined the cause greeted Treyven with fist over heart.

"Jhain, make haste to the outskirts of the fortress to warn Redwald and his guardsmen of what has occurred and then join us as planned. The men and I will lie in wait for the replacement guards and lock them away with the others. Take heed of your surroundings, and safe journey."

Jhain nodded to his captain, raced down the corridor, and was soon out of sight.

"I best take leave," Treyven advised Eralon. "I must speak ta me brothers regarding our change o' commitment an' pass the word o' new commands."

Eralon nodded. "Stay safe, my friend."

TREYVEN departed through the front door of the prison and combed the streets, searching for one of his number. Spotting his second-in-command, a skilled archer named Illuis, he hurried to where the man was fletching. Dressed in the dappled brown and green leathers that helped him blend into the wilderness, the forest-stalker stood up from his work and smiled at his leader.

A rumbling voice, accented as Treyven's own, met his ears with warmth. "Milord, relieved I be ta sees ya in good health. We just arrived this hour, an' all be accounted fer. What o' Desh an' Thom? Be they not with ya?"

"Nay, Illuis, an' they shan't be joining us," Treyven smiled and clasped Illuis' shoulder in a friendly gesture. "Hark Illuis, I need a word with ya. I need ya ta gather our brothers. 'Tis imperative we find a place ta speak in private without Danuvius' men overhearing our campaign. It seems he be a traitor. Many things 'aves I ta tell ya since last we spoke, an' in need o' discretion. Know ya a good place ta assemble?"

Illuis' dark eyes held Treyven's with intent and interest. "Yea, worry not, Milord. There's an abandoned inn called the Scarlet Guardian with room aplenty fer us all ta gather comfortably."

"Aye, that'll be grand," said Treyven. "Ya be a true brother, Illuis. I shall take my leave an' inform Danuvius o' our intent ta stay at the abandoned inn, an' none shall be the wiser. Now, I need ya ta pass word ta all our brothers. Make haste. We shall meet as soon as all can be gathered."

Danuvius had granted Treyven's request to stay at the abandoned inn. In truth, the steward had believed it a worthy suggestion. He wanted Treyven and his armsmen to stand ready and available to act when the time came to meet up with the other band of Liltian mercenaries.

As Treyven approached the Scarlet Guardian, he noticed Illuis standing guard at the entryway surveying those who entered with a critical eye. Treyven nodded to his trusted second-in-command as he passed through the portal of the shadowy interior. Once inside, Treyven paused a moment to look upon his gathered men.

His brethren-in-arms were broken and torn from almost two decades of struggling, and now they were caught up in a deluded cause.

They turned to him as their leader for guidance, and he decided at that moment that he would not allow their torment and anguish any longer. They would once again live their lives with honor.

In spite of everything, it was still their country, and they would achieve the respect and dignity that they all deserved. He would see to it.

As soon as every man was accounted for, Illuis bolted the door shut and nodded to his lord. Treyven leapt atop the nearest tavern table and held up his hand to quiet the crowd. He was passionately seeking, through his simple words, to touch the hearts of these men he called brothers. These fine people had been led astray, and now Treyven sought to show them a new path that would return them to a time of duty and honor.

Thus, he began:

"Good den, all me brethren," and Treyven gave the salute with fist over heart. "I bring ye tidings, both good an' ta the contrary. But in the end, these tidings shall bestow great joy upon us all. That, me brothers, be what we must fight fer." Treyven waited patiently for the cheers of his men and the murmuring that followed to diminish before continuing.

"Abide we must by our forefather's creed, an affirmation o' belief an' faith. This oath be sworn by the knights o' Liltimer:

"As we be sworn knights brave an' true,
Whose life rides a path of decency an' honor,
Ta rectify the wrongs o' mortal misdeeds,
Ta speak neither slander upon another, nor pay heed ta it,
Ta honor our word as our bond,
An' walk a path o' virtue fer as long as we shall live."

A grand hush fell over the men in the tavern from a creed never declared from their own lips, but one felt and sworn by their forefathers. Treyven's voice lowered in volume, but not in force.

"We'ves all been led astray by Danuvius Doral's treacherous words an' conniving tongue. There be no slavery in Avala. The fanciful story o' Avala's monarch holding our people as serfs an' slaves be untrue. Me own beliefs o' slavery in Avala be torn-asunder when I be wounded in battle by Cap'n Wellsbough an' set free.

"I propose, from this day forward, we pour our spirit in ta doing what be right. Not only fer our friends an' family, but fer anyone who canna break free o' the evils flouting the face o' righteousness. This creed shall lead us ta rectitude.

"Hence, me brothers, me foregone conclusion be somber indeed. Our dire actions, whilst meant with good intention, be caused by a bold-faced lie. Heated past the point o' reason, vexed with a monarch's decision made long an' ago, mourning the loss o' land an' a strong people we can still feel in our hearts an' souls.

"Hear ye, me brothers! We canna see the simple truth. Fer a kingdom be not the sum o' her lands, 'tis solely in the hearts an' minds o' her common people, an' as long as one o' us breathes, Liltian's be a part o' this land. We should care not the colors o' its banner. There be many o' us here that 'aves friends an' family born under the Avala banner. We call 'em our brothers, our children, an' our wives. Be we blind ta this truth? Look at the faces in this room an' tell me I be wrong. Do ye see not the unity here that has endured even after all the time that has passed? I see it in the eyes o' all me brothers, an' I believe in our credo. 'Tis why we shan't follow this traitorous Danuvius, fer his ideals be not our own. This selfish madman wants ta rule our land, our families, so we must join with the good Cap'n Wellsbough an' his men in this fight ta rid our land o' this menace."

"I cast me lot with Lord Treyven, fer his words be true," bellowed a voice from the back of the crowd. Illuis pushed his way to the front while the men began speaking amongst themselves in quiet tones. He navigated the obstacle course of tables and people, and he marched boldly to Treyven and gave salute. His voice rang clear in the taproom of the Scarlet Guardian, and silence descended immediately when they realized Illuis had the floor.

"Thy forthright speech has opened mine eyes, Milord." Then he turned to face his fellows, his dark braids swinging, eyes hardened, with hands on hips in a posture of defiance and in a rumbling voice heard by all. "Who be this Danuvius fella ta tell us his ideals rule supreme? Be we bunches o' packhorses, brought ta the whips an' forced ta blindly follow? Take away the shutters from thine eyes an' clearly see, me brothers. Worse off we be if his schemes be allowed ta go unpunished. Enough o' this, says I. Shall we tolerate this injustice paraded right beneath our noses, o' actively seek ta stop this madman an' cleanse our lands o' this threat?" The archer held his bow high with one hand and pulled his blade from its sheath with the other. "I say we show this man the strength we represent. Lord Treyven always 'aves our best interests in mind, an' would nay speak false. Who stands with Lord Treyven an' me in this?" asked Illuis of his brethren-in-arms. "Speak ye now, me brothers!"

This time the answer was clear and deafening. Some raised their swords and cheered, some nodded their heads, and others gave Treyven their answer with fist over heart. Most importantly, Treyven saw a new light shining in the depths of their eyes,

Treyven leapt off the table and saluted Illuis with fist over heart and a cordial bow of his head to reward his loyalty and passion. "Gra'mercy, Illuis."

Illuis smiled and returned the salute. Treyven made his rounds to speak with his men, and all were in accord, for Illuis' and Treyven's speeches had made their way into the hearts of these fine people, his comrades.

"Gather 'round, me brothers. We 'aves much ta discuss, fer this day we shall embark on our new future." His brethren-in-arms crowded closer, and Treyven's heart was light.

CHAPTER NINE

J hain made his way to the backdoor of the Terra Leone prison. His assignment was to reach Knight Master Balderon and his contingent of guards before they blindly walked into a situation akin to what his brothers-in-arms had experienced. He knew it was imperative that he make it to the front gates of the fortress without compromising the others' positions. He needed to move quickly and with stealth to cover the distance without being seen.

The jailhouse door was massive, bolted with an iron latch, standing like a sentinel between Jhain and his freedom. More than ready to set to his task, he curled his fingers around the door's latch and pulled. Cursing the mechanism as it screeched on protesting hinges, he slid the bar from the hollowed hole in the wall of the doorframe. He pulled the heavy door open and found it to be made of two layers of wood. The planks ran vertically on the front layer and horizontally on the back, and they were held together by iron studs strengthened with iron bands.

Hoping to leave unnoticed, Jhain scanned the immediate area through the small gap of the opened door. He let out a silent breath when he discovered it was clear. Jhain closed the door behind him and darted into the nearest alleyway. He was wearing a prison guard's coat over his dark leathers. If spotted on his journey, Jhain hoped none would look too closely because the coat was too large for his frame.

Jhain was moving with slinking grace from shadowed doorframe to shrouded passageway. Unfortunately, taking care not to be seen, he had only covered a short distance. Since time was vital, he decided to take to the rooftops.

He evaluated the buildings that surrounded him and found one suitable to scale. His fingers eagerly sought niches in the wall, and he pulled himself upward with quick, surging motions as effortlessly as if he were climbing a staircase. Reaching the top, Jhain crept to the opposite edge and judged the next building's distance. He backed off a few paces, and then he sprinted toward his destination. He jumped across the gap, landed, rolled head over heels and into a crouch on the other roof. On he continued, keeping to the flattest rooftops, avoiding decorative tiles or thatched roofs that would be slippery or that might cave under his weight.

Jhain finally came into view of the fortress's main entrance. He found a shadowed place behind a tailor's rooftop sign so as not to be seen by the gate's watchtower.

Before he had left the prison, Treyven had agreed to meet him at the Iron Forge, a blacksmith's workshop situated several streets east of the main gates. He had assured Jhain that the smithy was his friend and could be trusted. Treyven would fetch Jhain a horse and one of his men's unused uniforms so he could pass as a sellsword and ride freely through the gates. Looking east, Jhain saw smoke rolling thickly into the sky and knew it to be from the blacksmith's forge. He made his way to the opposing side of the building.

Halfway down the uneven wall, he heard voices and paused. Not wanting to be spotted, he pressed himself up against the building and wondered whether he should climb back to the rooftops. Jhain remained alert and silent, trying to divine the speakers' whereabouts. He scanned the area and caught a fleeting glimpse of movement in the trees.

Someone had built a cleverly concealed lookout in the branches of a giant oak that overlooked the main gate and road. From Jhain's position he could see that the lookout was large enough to hold four men with plenty of room to move around. It was to Jhain's advantage that the guards were watching the road and had not seen him on the roof.

Silently, Jhain dropped into a crouched position upon the ground near the side of the building and hid behind a large bush. Laughter drew his attention, and Jhain's heartbeat quickened. He noticed the flash of a vibrantly-colored fabric in a familiar hue that had been easy to spot through the foliage, one he instantly recognized. He clenched his teeth in anger, knowing he had spotted Keyon's murderer.

The memory of Keyon's demise flared, burning in the pit of his stomach and assaulting his mind like the licking flames of a ravenous fire. Jhain fought against the memory, but he found he was helpless to pry himself from its iron embrace.

Jhain's Memories

Jhain and his brethren had been ambushed mere moments after a steely-eyed man had joined the revelry. At the new arrival's unanticipated command, a band of mercenaries, posing as civilians amongst the citizens and king's guards, showed their true intentions. Jhain and his brethren were outnumbered, surrounded, and restrained before the king's men could even bring their weapons to bear. Jhain struggled against his captors as they divested him of his weapons and forced him to the ground with a swift, hard strike to the back of his knees.

This man with icy, unforgiving eyes was referred to as "the field marshal" by his underlings. With a hand on his sword, he paced before the kneeling line of prisoners, made a gloating victory speech and presented his leader. The Elite Guardsmen's heads were forced to bow with their hands bound tightly behind their backs. It was then they learned that Danuvius still lived.

After Danuvius' ceremonious arrival and introduction, he sat proudly atop his horse and observed his prized catch with a cruel smile. The false steward's eyes appeared as an eerie glow in the flickering lamplight. Jhain wished he could do more than spit on the ground at the sight of him.

The scout noticed the field marshal was making his way toward him and seemed to be addressing himself rather than his unwilling audience.

"Danuvius said ta show ya all what it means ta go against him an' teach ya a lesson o' his power an' might. But who ta pick?" He stopped in front of the youngest member of the troop.

When Jhain realized the blackguard stood before him, he froze in his stealthy actions of trying to free his hands from their bindings. Eyes grey as the toss of a stormy sea took in Jhain's features. The field marshal reached down, clutched the young scout's shirt, and pulled him to his feet. He then propelled him into the waiting and eager grasp of two of his cohorts who were standing nearby.

Standing before Jhain, the field marshal stared into the scout's turquoise eyes, trying to read his blank features. "Perchance ya be savvy enough ta see the error o' yer ways. Do ya see that Danuvius has the right ta use his own fortress as he sees fit? Our soon ta be ambassador has only just begun ta shows these people their mistakes. If it's fear that'll teach 'em obedience an' respect, so be it. Ya seem like a smart young fella. Show 'em all how smart ya be. Join Danuvius' forces and live! What say ye, lad?"

Having been addressed so matter-of-factly, Jhain almost laughed. He had worked so hard to achieve the ideals of Avala and to be accepted as one of the king's scouts that this was a bitter slap in the face. It was tempting to pretend submission, possibly winning his freedom and gaining an opportunity to free the others from Danuvius' shadow. Should he take such a chance? The loyalty in his heart and the trusting eyes of those he considered friend and family would not permit him to yield to that course. He would rather die for his beliefs than lose the respect of his peers. He had no family, save the men under Eralon's command. He refused to betray their trust and that of his king, even for a moment.

"Me thinks the new steward be possessed by madness, wanting ta torment," stated Jhain. "He seeks ta rule by fear an' bully us inta doing his bid. He'll be put down like a cur fer his crimes."

The field marshal delivered a tight-fisted blow to the side of Jhain's head. Spots flashed before Jhain's dazed eyes. A punch to his gut followed. The force of the blow caused him to lose his breath. Dizziness and nausea caused him to sag in the grip of the men holding him. They picked him up by the seat of his pants and threw him forward, face first. He hit the ground so hard he could taste the earth. Jhain was dazed and motionless, but the sound of a blade being drawn snapped him to his senses.

"Show your true strength upon a man and not a boy, you flap-mouthed coward!"

Jhain recognized the voice. Using all the strength he could muster, Jhain turned his head in the direction of Keyon Nyquest.

All eyes had swiveled to the golden-haired man in the green and yellow doublet. Jhain watched as the field marshal advanced toward his savior.

He could not command his voice to speak. *"Nay Keyon,"* thought Jhain in a silent plea. *"I pray thee, not fer me."*

Knight Master Nyquest had been like his brother since he had joined the ranks of Eralon's men. He was amongst the first to accept Jhain as one of their number.

"Ya 'aves something ta say?" asked the field marshal as he towered over Keyon's kneeling form.

Keyon had held his stare and refused to be intimidated.

Danuvius' voice had risen in volume to carry to all who were present. He nodded to his minion and said, "He shall do."

The field marshal smiled and bowed to his leader. "Aye, Excellency."

He turned back to Keyon and gave him a dark, superior smirk. He moved behind him and cut the bindings from Keyon's wrists and grabbed a fistful of the doublet he wore. "I do appreciate a splendid garment when I sees one," said the field marshal. "Take it off."

Keyon had barely finished removing the garment when it was jerked roughly out of his hands. Keyon knelt passively, which only served to further aggravate his tormentor. Perhaps he had believed his doublet a small price to pay for the life of his friend. Keyon glanced at Jhain to give him an encouraging nod.

The field marshal did not notice the exchange because he was busy admiring the doublet. He put it on and then moved into a position behind Keyon.

No one anticipated the steely-eyed man's next move. A blurring sword stroke was followed by the statement, "Nay, it wouldna do ta 'aves blood on such a fine garment."

Keyon's body jolted. A gasp escaped from his lips. He glanced down at the sword tip protruding from his chest. The field marshal put his boot on Keyon's back and, using it as leverage, kicked him over as he pulled his sword free. The ground darkened beneath the master knight with a growing pool of blood.

"Keyon!" Jhain's scream escaped as a hoarse whisper.

Others in the group sat stunned at the sight of Keyon's limp body. One kneeling man, Jeffries, bowed his head and prayed.

Adrenaline achieved what physical strength had failed to accomplish just moment's prior. Jhain sat up and strained to his feet, his arms still in their bindings. Denial flared as his mind struggled with what he had just witnessed.

The scout stumbled toward Keyon's prone form, suddenly oblivious to his surroundings. He dropped to his knees at his friend's side. Tears welled at the corners of Jhain's eyes, blurring his vision and obscuring the horrific sight. There was naught he could do. His closest friend, his brother, had already departed this existence for a better one.

The dark-haired marshal stood behind Keyon's motionless, bloodied figure, laughing breathlessly along with Danuvius, as if at some supreme joke. Stomping over to Jhain, he jerked him to his feet by his hair and snarled, "Still thinks the steward o' Terra Leone nay be deserving respect? Still hold ta those beliefs? Verily, this lit'l example will bring all the king's guards ta their senses."

Jhain's voice was lost and small. "I'd say 'twas yer mistake, ya dog-hearted mammet," said Jhain through gritted teeth. "Ya soon be wishing that be me lying there an' not me brother."

"Then ya shall hang," the field marshal retorted.

Danuvius gave the order, and the prisoners were gathered and herded toward the cell house, led by the assassin wearing Keyon's doublet.

Shaken from the memories and his brother-in-arm's demise, Jhain's heart was bent on vengeance. He could not let the field marshal get away with slaying Keyon in cold blood and wearing his doublet as a trophy.

Jhain was determined to make him pay. He moved toward the base of the trees and noticed two horses tied to some low branches. The horses appeared content and continued to eat the grass as he approached. It seemed safe to assume that, since there were two horses, only two riders lingered above. Jhain knew if he took care of the two men on the platform, he could use one of the horses to ride out through the fortress gates. Above and beyond his plans for escape, he could not live with his conscience if he did not act on this opportunity to see justice done for his slain brother.

Jhain climbed the tree and peered through the narrow hatchway that served as the entrance to the lookout. Unaware of his presence, the two men continued their discussion. The guard directly in front of Jhain was in a perfect position, blocking the view of the vile field marshal who had taken Keyon's life. He weighed his choices, noting their weapons were within reach, but not in hand.

He did not want the innocent guard involved, but there was the possibility that the man would get away to raise an alarm, and that was unacceptable. He quietly made his way through the hatchway and stood up. Looking through the opening toward the ground, he shouted as if he were conversing with someone below. "Aye, Sir! I'll tell 'em!"

The scrape of a foot told Jhain that the innocent one had moved toward him, buying into his ploy.

Perfect.

While the guard approached, Jhain slowly removed a chain from around his waist and whirled it in his hands. He turned quickly and slipped it over the approaching fellow's head and tightened it around his neck. He pulled the chain with his left hand, allowing the chain to conveniently turn the guard around to face the field marshal. Keeping a firm grip on the chain for control, Jhain allowed the field marshal the opportunity to see his face.

Recognition dawned, and the steely-eyed man smiled dangerously while slowly rising to his feet. "Ya just made a big mistake," said the marshal in a deep, menacing voice.

"Nay fiend, 'twas yer mistake," retorted Jhain. He then lowered the unconscious guard to the platform's plank flooring and took a wide step to his right, drawing his dagger.

The steely-eyed man sneered and drew his sword. "Know ya be fighting Field Marshal Eldred Whitlock, soon ta be second-in-command ta Danuvius Doral. I shall be by his side fer the moment o' glory ta watch yer monarch's demise."

"Ya be going nowhere," replied Jhain. "Ya brought about yer own demise the minute ya took Keyon's life."

Eldred ignored the threat and smirked. "Keyon, ya say? The man ordered killed ta subdue all ye traitors? His doublet be a fine prize." He taunted Jhain by running a grimy hand down the fabric of the doublet. "I'ves killed fer less, lad."

Jhain took a deep, calming breath. He knew Eldred was trying to provoke him, but he did not take the bait.

The field marshal savagely kicked his stool aside and then lunged at Jhain. A sidestep saved the scout's life, but the tip of Eldred's blade slashed the scout's side. The cut was only a flesh wound. Eldred slashed at him again, but Jhain ducked and turned as he slipped to the other side of the platform.

Eldred laughed contemptuously. "In o'er yer head me thinks. Poor lit'l lad! Ya shoulda run home ta yer ma whilst ya had the chance." The marshal hooked his foot under his comrade's weapon lying on the ground and kicked it toward Jhain.

"Lookie here, I'll even offer ya a better weapon, if ya think yer man enough ta wield it."

"I prefer the dagger," said Jhain through clenched teeth, watching his opponent warily as the sword clattered past him. The dagger was Jhain's weapon of choice in close fighting, but he had his own sword upon his back, and wrist sheaths full of steel if needed.

Eldred swung his weapon wildly, and the scout ducked in time to hear it whoosh past his head. He drew a blade from each of his wrist sheaths and tossed them both as he performed a tuck and roll. The blades found their mark on the left side of Eldred's sword arm and leg.

Eldred plucked the blades from his body, and the blood started flowing freely. Eldred clenched his teeth, threw down his sword, and pulled out his own dagger.

"Too bad ya 'aves none ta save ya from the predicament you're in now, boy! I'll be adding yer dagger ta me collection."

"Ya talk too much," replied Jhain coldly. He threw himself at Eldred's exposed side, his dagger flashing as his opponent blocked his strike. Jhain lunged again, and the tip of Eldred's sword caught Jhain's arm mid-sweep. Jhain staggered back and clutched at his wounded arm, over-exaggerating the shallow cut, hoping his opponent would take the bait.

Eldred moved in eagerly to take advantage of his feigned opportunity, and Jhain expertly changed direction, ducking and turning from Eldred's swing and escaping the blackguard's range. Eldred lifted his blade to strike as he turned toward Jhain. The scout saw his opening, so he raised his leg and planted his boot right between the blackguard's legs. Eldred flew backward, cracking his head on the thick tree trunk and crumpled to his knees. Jhain then punched him in the face, forcing him to fall on his back. The scout kicked the sword out of Eldred's hand and reach.

Jhain held his own weapon at Eldred's exposed throat and growled, "The almighty Eldred not feeling so almighty now, ay?"

Eldred was on the ground, dazed and moaning. The fight was over, outdone by what Eldred had deemed a "lit'l lad."

"I be taking Knight Master Nyquest's doublet with me," said Jhain. Then he added, "Would'na do ta 'aves blood on it now, would it?" Jhain rolled Eldred from side to side to remove Keyon's doublet.

Jhain waited until his opponent regained consciousness. The scout's blade moved to hover above his opponents' chest, inches from his heart. When Eldred's eyes seemed to focus on Jhain, his heart rate increased. A terrified look overwhelmed the blackguard's features, and sweat beaded on his forehead and upper lip. With dagger in hand, Jhain raised his arm to strike.

Wind rushed over the lookout's platform, throwing the leaves of the tree into a wild dance. Screams echoed through the trees—and then there was silence.

Jhain had not killed the arrogant man who lived by his sword, but he made sure he had broken his spirit by delivering the blackguard a fate worse than death. By slicing into the tendons in both of Eldred's hands, Jhain had ensured he would never swing a sword again. To a man like Eldred, this was a fate worse than death.

The scout stripped off the borrowed guard's coat and began the task of tearing the fabric into strips to make bindings. He bandaged Eldred's hands and bound and gagged both of the men on the platform. Jhain took up a jug of wine from a table which had miraculously survived the fight. He took a long swallow before dousing his two flesh wounds with the liquid. He then picked up Keyon's doublet and hurried down to the base of the tree. He felt free, unburdened, and surprisingly light, for justice had been served. Death would have been too easy a sentence for Eldred.

Jhain made it to the Iron Forge where he found Treyven with three men and five horses. As Jhain approached, they greeted each other with fist over heart. Treyven handed Jhain a Liltian overcoat and the reins to one of the horses. Jhain adjusted the horse's saddle and stirrups and put Keyon's coat in one of the saddlebags.

"Me brethren-in-arms relieved Danuvius' men at the gate without a hitch," explained Treyven. The men nodded to Jhain in acknowledgement. "They'll ride with ya ta the gatehouse. I need ta get back ta me brothers at the Scarlet Guardian fer a meeting. I'll advise 'em all about Danuvius' treachery."

Jhain nodded and pointed to the large tree he had just left. "There be two men left bound an' gagged up in that lookout."

"We'll be sure ta take care o' 'em," said one of Treyven's men-in-arms.

"I'll be back with the Elite Guardsmen," replied Jhain.

"Safe journey," said Treyven. Jhain nodded and flipped the narrow leather reins in proper position around the horse's neck and mounted.

With no one left to ring the alarm or tell the tale of Jhain's escape, Jhain and Treyven's men made the short distance to the front fortress gate. Treyven's brothers-in-arms dismounted casually and unlatched the heavy wooden doors. They then grabbed the winch to crank open the iron gates for the scout. Jhain urged his horse forward and left the fortress at a gallop.

It was mid-afternoon when Jhain spotted the king's guards in the distance. Recognizing the man in the lead, Jhain's spirits rose.

Knight Master Redwald Balderon was about as well liked as Captain Wellsbough. He was a wondrous tactician and friendly toward his troops. He would understand Eralon's plans and do what must be done without question. Jhain called out to the approaching master knight and was hailed in return. He reined in his horse next to Knight Master Balderon and began his tale. He saw a fire burning in Redwald's eyes as he spoke.

"Danuvius exudes evil enough to cast a shadow upon the darkest night," growled the master knight.

He turned to the man at his side. "Henson, you and Darius ride through the ranks and advise the men as to what lies ahead."

Signaling all his guards onward, he bellowed, "Forward men! Let us away and ruffle some foul feathers!"

Jhain rode alongside Knight Master Balderon as they made their way through the cobbled streets of Terra Leone with over a hundred men riding in formation behind him. The lead horseman flew Avala's swallow-tailed guidon. The added show of prancing horses wearing the silver and blue of Avala was to let the villagers of Terra Leone know that King Lucian's presence was with them, and he would no longer tolerate the suffering they had endured. Jhain thought it unfortunate that the citizens were so afraid they had locked themselves away in their houses and shops, leaving the streets barren. Though curtains twitched as they peeped through their windows, none came out to greet them.

Under Jhain's direction, they were riding past the Scarlet Guardian to alert Treyven that the Elite Guardsmen had arrived. Jhain knew Danuvius would come to regret his actions, and the Elite Guardsmen were about to march boldly to meet with the despicable steward and deliver the first lesson.

CHAPTER TEN

D anuvius lounged in an ornately carved high-back chair before the fireplace in Lionholm. His feet propped on a nearby table, he stared raptly into the flames. With curtains drawn, the fire cast a sunset glow over the room. He was lost in his thoughts and did not seem to notice the heat.

He knew he had the perfect bartering tool now that Eralon was in his clutches and under lock and key. With an army under his own beck and call, King Lucian would have to listen to his demands. He wondered hungrily how he should slay Lucian and the Council of Nobles after his victory. Perchance he would choose a public spectacle. What a wondrous, devious plan. He smiled wolfishly at his own cleverness.

With the strong show of force at Terra Leone and the additional force he had been building in secret, he would secure Avala's attention and respect with a heavy gauntlet-clad fist. His plan to become the new sovereign of the entire continent of Sapphirus was coming to fruition.

Then the elaborate wooden doors to his office crashed open and a household servant hastened into the room. His face was reddened from running, and it took him a long, gasping minute to catch his breath.

Vexed at the unannounced disruption, Danuvius' face turned an ugly scarlet as he rose to tower over the man. "What be the meaning o' this outburst? It best be noteworthy," he snarled in a thunderous voice that threatened retribution as he made his way to his desk.

"Excellency," the servant panted, "the king's guards have arrived. We had no forewarning. We count nigh a hundred men riding to the manor as we speak."

Danuvius clenched his fists tightly; a thick comma of dark hair slipped into his line of vision that he did nothing to clear.

"We'ves watchmen posted at the front gates o' the fortress!" cried Danuvius, his face painted red with fury. "I shoulda known o' their presence before they set foot onta me lands! Where be Field Marshal Eldred Whitlock?"

In one fell swoop, Danuvius knocked everything off his desk. He raised his foot and kicked his large oak desk onto its side. He clenched his fists and ground his teeth as he stared at the servant before him.

The man stumbled backward as if he had been struck, and he cowered on the floor, hands up as if beseeching mercy. "Excellency, I pray thee," cried the servant, cringing in fear. "I know not, for no one has seen him."

Danuvius wanted nothing more than to relieve his anger by tearing the cowering man apart. He was pounding toward him to do just that when he suddenly realized he did not have the time to tarry. The king's guards were at his doorstep. He needed to calm himself and remedy the situation. He closed his eyes and took a few deep breaths.

He would have to show the king's leader of these wretched guards that he did not need their assistance, and a show of his numbers would help drive the point home. A plan of action formulated in his mind, and he donned a wicked smile at his cleverness.

"Tell the sentinel outside the manor gates ta gather all the Terra Leone guards an' ta meet me at the new construction site near the town's square. You'll find Treyven an' his hirelings at the Scarlet Guardian. 'Aves him meet us at the new hostelry with his men."

"Aye, Excellency, I shall see to it at once." His servant picked himself off the floor and rushed from the room, sliding on one of the opulent carpets in his haste to depart.

Valen Doral had started construction on a large portion of land that was on the west side of Lionholm Manor. Since Terra Leone was growing, Danuvius' deceased brother had plans underway for a tailor shop, an apothecary, and a new hostelry to replace the crumbling Scarlet Guardian.

After Valen's death, Danuvius had ordered the workers to build a secret passageway beneath the new inn. This new underground pathway now joined an existing tunnel that had been built long ago when the ambassador's manor was the Lionholm Castle of Liltimer. With the passage complete, the inn would provide an underground route that ran under Lionholm and ended at the manor's personal stables. The back of the stable house was situated against the fortress wall with a secret exit. If anything went wrong during his meeting with the king's guards, Danuvius had his plan for escape.

The immediate force under Danuvius' command assembled quickly before the construction area. They stood at attention, ready to greet the king's guards. Danuvius hoped to convince the unwanted gatecrashers to leave without bloodshed, for an attack on Lucian's men now would draw attention he could ill afford.

Treyven's bands of men were on their way to add to his numbers, and together, they would easily be enough to quash this small contingent of Lucian's armsmen. But that blasted Eldred was still missing!

Danuvius could hear the clatter of horseshoes prancing on the cobblestone pathway even before he could see them. With twelve of his most trusted men at his side, Danuvius stepped forward in preparation to greet them.

The master knight in the lead had the air of a braggart, his reddish hair and large mustache shining in the sunlight. He and his stallion were dressed in royal finery, and he sat purposely afore his men. Avala's guidon snapped crisply behind him in the afternoon wind. He looked like one leading a procession at tournament time, though his flag stated otherwise, and this did much to further aggravate Danuvius' foul mood.

The braggart held up his hand to bring his men to a halt in front of Danuvius and his contingent of foot soldiers. Danuvius watched him as he surveyed the numbers assembled before him with nonchalance and tilted his head in greeting.

"I am Knight Master Redwald Balderon, leader of these fine men and representative of His Majesty King Lucian of Avala. Could you be so kind as to inform me of Captain Sir Eralon Wellsbough's whereabouts? His Elite Guardsmen have arrived to assist in the appointment of a temporary custodian for Terra Leone, as so ordered by our most gracious king."

It was obvious Redwald Balderon was used to getting his way. His hazel eyes were sharp and suggested he had seen so much that little could surprise him.

Danuvius tried to cover his sneer with a smile as he spoke. "I be the one left in charge here," he proclaimed, "handpicked by Cap'n

Wellsbough himself. There be no need o' yer extended assistance." Danuvius could not stifle the cold tone that tinged his declaration.

"Be that so?" scoffed the master knight. "I do believe the king's orders say otherwise, sir. Pray, pardon my lack of addressing you by your title or name, since you appear to have left your manners elsewhere. Now, where can I house my men for the duration of our stay?" An amused smile flitted across Redwald's features.

Danuvius' anger grew toward the arrogant windbag. Then, from the corner of his eye, he glimpsed a most welcomed sight. Treyven had arrived with his hirelings. They had poured in from the direction of the Scarlet Guardian with Treyven in the lead, and his men flanked Redwald's guards. Treyven's face was impassive as he nodded at Danuvius. With Treyven's men, Danuvius knew he had a better chance of winning if it came to a fight with the master knight and his guardsmen.

Feeling surer of his position and power, Danuvius said, "Captain Wellsbough be seeing ta matters elsewhere at the moment, and be due ta return upon the morrow. He asked me ta tell ya ta advise King Lucian that all is well."

"I think not!" A familiar voice from the crowd caused him to jerk his head around with incredulity.

Fie! His eyes sought the face to match the voice and came to rest upon the features of none other than Captain Eralon Wellsbough.

Shock and confusion engulfed Danuvius' visage as he wondered how the captain had escaped.

Eralon approached, blade in hand, with the rest of his once captive men behind him, adding to the numbers opposing Danuvius' force. Now Danuvius was forced to step up his schedule and occupation of the surrounding lands, but that could not be helped. Danuvius watched as Knight Master Balderon nodded once in welcome to his disheveled captain.

Eralon turned as he spoke so everyone present could hear his words. "I want to invite all the guards of Terra Leone to join our ranks. It's not too late to see err in your ways. You had been deceived by Danuvius' false accusations of our goodly king holding Liltians as slaves. The Elite Guardsmen are here to set things straight."

Danuvius watched as the Terra Leone guards made their way to stand with Captain Wellsbough and his men. He knew they would all stand by Eralon. Curse all the guards in Lucian's employ! Danuvius saw some of the citizens emerge from their homes to stand shoulder-to-shoulder with Eralon and Redwald's men, grain scythes and knives in hand—and in the case of the smithy, with naught but a hammer that somehow looked as deadly as any blade in those muscled arms.

Danuvius had to think quickly. Eralon's forces were gaining the upper hand. An idea struck, and he said, "The commander of the Elite Guardsmen lies fer his monarch! Treyven Fontacue, let's show these interlopers an' all o' Avala what it means ta stand against me!"

Some merriment twinkled in the depths of Treyven's exotic, blue-grey eyes, but his voice was level and menacing. "Give it up, Danuvius. I know Cap'n Wellsbough's words hold truth, an' as proof, we'ves joined his ranks. Yer pitiful numbers dinna exceed the forces o' the king."

Dumbfounded momentarily by Treyven's words, it suddenly all came together with compelling clarity in Danuvius' mind. Eralon had his own weapon in hand, which had last been in Treyven's possession. Who else but the brigand would have had the opportunity to free the prisoners? All his careful preparation for Eralon's demise had come crashing down.

It was time for Danuvius to put his backup plan into effect. He nodded at his archers and raised his sword. "Then ye all shall die!" bellowed Danuvius.

Twenty-five of Danuvius' loyal archers stepped forward to let loose their arrows. All the king's men raised their shields in defense while the citizenry hastened to take cover from the deadly rain of projectiles. As the steward of Terra Leone's archers were nocking their next arrows, Danuvius and his handpicked men rapidly made their way to the recently built hostelry's underground tunnel for their escape.

Entering the inn, Danuvius took a moment to watch through one of the building's unfinished windows as the remainder of his forces behind the archers ran forward with the next volley of arrows. He knew those he had left behind would be forced to protect themselves and provide the distraction he needed. An evil smile grew as he led the twelve men who had followed him down the secret passageway to their freedom.

ERALON fought boldly alongside his guardsmen as the two factions of fighters came together with fierceness, their ringing cries echoing through Terra Leone, washing over those present and sweeping all into a frenzy of action. Combatants charged each other, pitting their might against those perceived as the enemy. The horsemen behind the master knight moved up to form a rough line with their leader just as Danuvius' men fell upon them. The mounts reared and pranced in a deadly dance, their body armor dully reflecting the horror on the faces of those who feared they would be trampled under thundering hooves.

Men fought and struggled, triumphed or perished as they were caught up in the carnage like leaves in a windstorm. The air was charged with outrage and anger, the crash of steel on steel accenting the shrieks and moans of the wounded.

Eralon had thrown himself straight into the ranks of Danuvius' forces and relentlessly sought out the steward so he could bring him to justice. His eyes scanned the fortress grounds, but somehow the coward had vanished.

Luckily, Treyven's prior wound was not to his sword arm. Eralon was surprised to see him hold back Danuvius' remaining meager forces, never letting his injury keep him from his place. The king's guards fought side-by-side with the Liltians, who stood out in their strapped armor of ash-colored leather that featured a proud lion upon their chests. They had easily eliminated Danuvius' small force of mail-clad guards and had captured those who elected to drop their weapons and surrender.

With the majority of the fighting dissipated, Eralon glanced about and spotted his scout, covered in dust, marching toward him.

"Jhain, find Treyven and meet me in Lionholm Manor."

The scout nodded. "Aye, Cap'n."

Redwald dismounted and made his way to Eralon's side.

"Have a few men search Lionholm to see if Danuvius lies hidden within," commanded Eralon. "Likewise, send out your scouts to see if it's possible Danuvius got away and left a trail outside the gates. Then send a messenger to advise King Lucian that Danuvius still lives. Let the king know I shall return to the castle as soon as I can. Lastly, meet me in Lionholm's drawing room to see if we can divine Danuvius' intentions from any clues left therein."

"I shall see to it at once, Captain Wellsbough," said Redwald, and he set to his task.

TREYVEN was seeing to his wounded fellows when his attention was suddenly drawn to a large assemblage of his brothers. They were crowded around a figure lying on the ground. His heart was in his throat as he made his way to the crowd.

His brothers parted before him, and his heart all but stopped as he spied his trusted second-in-command, Illuis, lying breathless with one hand clutched around an arrow lodged in his upper torso. Someone had used his coat to prop Illuis' head against the stony support of the courtyard well.

As Treyven knelt before the man with braided hair, a hush fell over the others. It was as if a blanketing mist had come rolling in, blocking everything from Treyven's senses except for Illuis. With a heavy heart, he placed his hand on the archer's arm and squeezed it lightly.

"Milord Treyven," Illuis whispered as he struggled to breathe. "You've done the right thing siding with Cap'n Wellsbough. I wish I could fight by yer side."

"Hush, Illuis. Ya must rest." Treyven knew his friend was in trouble.

Illuis looked into Treyven's eyes. "Remember our credo . . . protect our lands . . . a chance ta right the Liltian name . . . me family . . . tells 'em . . . I love 'em . . . ." With that, the wounded archer clenched his fist and placed it over his heart as his last breath left his body.

Treyven closed his eyes and gave a final valediction for his loyal friend. When he opened his eyes, he lingered a moment to muster the strength to offer his Liltian brethren a strong, capable leader. "Lucas, choose three of our brothers and take the wounded to Terra Leone's healers. Set up a funeral pyre for those we've lost and fetch their families so our brethren can be properly mourned.

I shall take me place with Cap'n Wellsbough as Illuis requested."

"Aye, Milord," replied Lucas, and he set to task.

Treyven searched through the mass of faces that surrounded him to find the man Illuis wanted following in his footsteps. "Alban!" he called out, spotting him in the crowd.

Alban made his way to Treyven. "Aye, Milord Treyven," he replied, standing at attention before his lord with fist over heart.

"You are now the next in command, handpicked by Illuis himself, chosen ta lead our brothers in my absence. After meeting with Cap'n Wellsbough, I will return with further instructions. We shall pay tribute ta our lost brothers by honoring Illuis with his last request. This be our chance ta right the Liltian name fer our families. Let not his words go unheeded."

"Aye, Milord," responded Alban, and he then turned to his gathered clan. "Brothers, ye all heard Lord Treyven's orders!"

Treyven felt a presence at his back. He turned to face Jhain, who was looking at Illuis and seemed to be reflecting upon his own personal suffering.

Jhain looked up at Treyven and placed a hand on his back. "The Cap'n sent me here ta retrieve ya. We rounded up Danuvius' forces an' 'aves the battle in hand. We must away, me friend."

Jhain looked solemn when he continued. "I, too, lost one o' me own brethren here, by the command o' that vile Danuvius. I meself am o' Liltian blood. Together we'll join Eralon an' end this madness. 'Tis fer our lost brothers we shall find peace in their name an' fer their honor."

Each man looked upon the other and gave fist over heart, a salute to their Liltian brotherhood.

"Ya be right, Liltian brother," said Treyven with a newfound determination. "Let us away an' join Cap'n Wellsbough."

ERALON looked up as Jhain and Treyven entered Lionholm's stuffy drawing room, where a fire was burning itself out in the hearth. It was uncomfortably warm within the office. Redwald was wiping his brow with a handkerchief and handing a curling parchment to his captain as Jhain and Treyven approached. "Take a look at this."

Eralon placed the terrain map on the desk and the four men studied it. The captain tapped the parchment thoughtfully and spoke of its contents. "There are brief annotations on positioning troops for combat and a sketch of the area directly outside of Kaleidos. This confirms Danuvius' objective to try to take the Moorwyn Throne." His eyes burned as he turned his attention to Redwald. "Redwald, you must question those captured and ferret out the details of Danuvius' plan. If we know his movements afore they are carried out, we shall be one step ahead and prevent this atrocity."

"As you command, Captain," said Redwald.

Eralon then turned to Treyven. "Do you know of these stratagems?"

Treyven traced his finger over the red lines and arrows on the parchment. Tiny notations on the map spoke of a northeastern route through the Tall Forest and then, off the terrain map, to an uncharted destination.

"I canna elaborate on any landmarks, time, o' dates he planned ta attack. He kept his arrangements largely ta himself. Although, I know we be planning ta meet up with what he called a 'secret army' he had assembled. He declared it an invincible army that King Lucian's forces canna defeat. Last I heard, he be planning a meeting with us all gathered in the forest." Treyven looked thoughtful for a moment. "In truth, I know not if the secret army an' the Liltian mercenaries be one an' the same."

Treyven turned to Eralon and said, "Ya 'aves me brothers an' me at yer disposal down ta the last. Command us as ya would yer own; I vouch me men's allegiance."

Eralon's spirits rose upon hearing Treyven's words. He was grateful for the proffered help.

"Your offer is accepted and appreciated, Treyven. We can arrange a meeting with Knight Master Balderon and your second-in-command. Then you, Jhain, and I shall make haste back to the castle and tell King Lucian of all we have discovered here."

Treyven nodded and displayed fist over heart to the captain.

"I will take this map and show it to our king," Eralon said as he folded the terrain map and placed it in his hip pouch.

"Before you take leave, Captain," said Redwald, "I have a missive from His Majesty." He produced a parchment from his breast pocket that was sealed in wax with the king's signet ring.

Eralon broke the seal and scanned the document. "Knight Master Balderon, as decreed by our king, you have been appointed temporary steward and sworn protector of the Fortress of Terra

Leone. In conversation with His Majesty, I endorsed you as worthy of regard for this position, Redwald. I have complete faith and confidence that you are the best man for the position."

"I accept the honor bestowed upon me, Captain Wellsbough, and pledge an oath to the Crown of the Kingdom of Avala to provide my best service as guardian of Terra Leone. I will not let you or King Lucian down, Captain. This I swear."

"Excellent," Eralon said, and then he smiled and nodded. "Jhain, find Lionholm's herald and direct him to make the arrangements for a proper introduction of Knight Master Balderon as the new temporary steward of Terra Leone."

"As ya request, Cap'n," replied Jhain, and he set about to accomplish his captain's request.

"We shall leave you to attend to your duties to strengthen and fortify the fortress and re-establish order. Once you have questioned the prisoners send a missive to King Lucian to let him know all that you have gleaned. Fare thee well, Steward Balderon, and felicitations on your new assignment."

"Gramercy, Captain Wellsbough."

"Good Fortune, Steward Balderon," echoed Treyven displaying the fist over heart salute.

"Aye, good providence upon you as well, Treyven," replied Redwald with a smile.

Then Captain Wellsbough and Treyven took their leave through the elaborate manor doors.

CHAPTER ELEVEN

W ithin the darkest reaches of the Tall Forest, a cloaked figure stood transfixed watching a small, glowing orb make its way through the woodland beneath a midnight sky. Its incandescent light pierced the blackness, leaving eerie shadows in its wake.

The light abruptly stilled, as if in contemplation of its path, only to begin again in the spectator's direction. It bobbed and weaved its way through the trees, settling itself in an abrupt motion just within a hand's-breadth of the shrouded figure's face.

The orb then began to pulsate like a beating heart, illuminating the darkness in a brilliant display. As if blinded by its power, the observer lifted a scaled and clawed hand to shelter his cat-like eyes whose pupils had narrowed into vertical slits under the light's intensity.

Of a sudden, a soft whisper was heard riding the currents of a gentle breeze, causing the leaves to rustle. Indistinguishable at first, these whispers seemed to bounce off the trees before coming together in audible clarity.

"It is as you feared," proclaimed a voice within the whispering wind. *"You must prepare for what is to come. Take heed these words, Land Guardian. The cause of this uprising is not Sapphirian-born."*

Ra Kor'el awoke from his dream with a start. "Not Sapphirian-born?" whispered Ra into the darkness. The premonitory dream definitely proclaimed who it was not. That very fact was a clue to the answers they sought. Ra threw the coverlet back from his bed and donned his night robe. He must advise his father at once.

KING LUCIAN ate an early supper and had retired to his library to consider all that had transpired over the course of the day. He sat at his desk studying his best terrain maps, scrolls, and charts. Now open before him was a large geographical representation of the continent of Sapphirus.

Sapphirus was surrounded by the Carillion Sea and was home to the countries of Avala, Sunon, and Vashires. Avala was located in the northern-most region of Sapphirus, occupying one-third of the continent. The mountains of Kaleidos, the country's highest peaks, were situated in Avala's northeastern region and were home to the Oralian Dragon Empire. The countries of Sunon and Vashires ran along Avala's southern borders, west and east respectively.

He recalled the details of Kullipthius' dragon scouts' reports, and with a warrior's eye, he attempted to divine the exact location of the army that marched through his country.

From high above, Oralia's dragon scouts had first spotted these invaders along Avala's southwestern seaboard. Kullipthius and Lucian had first wondered if the invading force had come from across the seas. But they had not found any foreign ships or evidence to support that theory along the country's seashore.

It was determined that the intruder's size and strength were not substantial enough to cause major concern in Avala. However, apprehension arose once it was noted that there was a swelling in the group's ranks and weapons as it proceeded in a northerly direction up the coast under the cover of the trees. They may have remained hidden were it not for keen dragon eyes.

Kullipthius had come to Moorwyn Castle to advise Lucian of his dragon scouts' findings. They decided they needed to determine who guided this force and why it was marching upon their joined lands. Once this was understood, the partnered monarchy could best dictate how to deal with the situation and try to find a peaceful solution to prevent any potential tribulations.

The two monarchs decided their first course of action would be to consult with their allies to determine if they knew of the force's intentions and origins. King Lucian had formed an alliance with these countries, and all were at peace. Therefore, one particular dragon scout was sent to the southern borderlands to speak directly to the rulers of Sunon and Vashires on behalf of the King of Avala. This dragon had conducted previous interactions with the foreign kings and was known to the two countries' rulers as King Lucian's liaison, Baltizar.

Upon landing, Baltizar shifted from dragon to human form, procured a horse, and made his way to question the rulers of each country. Neither realm claimed any knowledge of the force that had gathered. Their responses were deemed reliable, for Baltizar would have ferreted out any dishonesty or deception with his gift of truth. This dragon's keen inner perception could surmise in an instant if any falsehood was spoken.

Both countries had sent a communication with Baltizar advising King Lucian they would be taking the necessary precautions for the safety of their own countries, as King Lucian had recommended. In addition, they were prepared to offer assistance to Avala if deemed necessary.

If the armsmen kept to their current path, the first populated settlement they would come upon would be the fortress at Terra Leone. Lucian's orders to Eralon had placed a contingent of his guardsmen en route to help reinforce the fortress and protect the populace of Terra Leone. He would need to meet with his council soon to discuss the details and make further preparations.

A polite but firm knock reverberated through the embellished wood of the drawing room door, and Lucian bade the caller enter. Candlelight fell on the faces of two men Lucian easily recognized. Xyras and Bardric crossed the threshold, bowed in respect to their king, and were bid to rise.

Xyras was a Baron's son, a little mischievous at times but well-trained and trustworthy. Bardric was always watching after Xyras, and his record was above reproach. Bardric had grown up in the former country of Liltimer and had taken his Oath of Fealty to serve as a guardsman under the direction of Knight Master Redwald Balderon. Both Xyras and Bardric were good, reliable men. Something must have transpired to bring them to his door. Xyras, tall and auburn-haired, gave a sharp bow and began the tale. Lucian listened patiently, his frown deepening as the two spoke in turn.

"Danuvius lives?" The king rose from his chair with enough force to send it tumbling backward to clatter against the floor. Wrath clearly visible in his cinnamon-brown eyes, he continued.

"Valen's own brother is a corrupt traitor against the Moorwyn Throne!" He turned toward the fireplace as if to find calm in the flickering flames. "He would be devastated to learn of his brother's treachery and deceit transpiring within the walls of Terra Leone."

A devout man, Bardric winced as he retrieved the chair for his king and quietly prayed, "Prithee, Heavenly Majesty above. Send yer ministering angels ta comfort him when learning o' his brother's betrayal."

"Aye," Lucian responded, clasping his hands behind his back. With thoughts of his own brother, he turned to stare out a small window and into the night sky. Since Danuvius was the one spreading rumors of slavery in Avala, there was no accounting for what he would do next. This prompted Lucian to open the library doors. One guard turned immediately toward the king and bowed.

Lucian then decreed, "Fetch the master commander of the castle's garrison and the royal chamberlain and have them report to me at once."

"Without delay, Your Majesty," said the royal guard. He bowed and set about his task to accommodate his king's orders.

Lucian then turned and went to his writing desk and dipped quill in ink to pen a note to Knight Master Osualt. He removed the pot of melted wax from its burner and dripped some of its contents upon folded ribbon and parchment and sealed it with his gold signet ring. Placing this noble symbol of the dragon in the far left corner was, indeed, affirmation to his master knight that the contents were not only authentic but a matter of great and immediate importance.

King Lucian rose and, handing the document to Bardric, said, "I have further need of your services. I want you to take this missive to Knight Master Osualt. He will lead a contingent of knights to gather my brother's family and their personal attendants from Morning Star. The two of you will accompany him. You are to bring my family back to Moorwyn Castle for protection, leaving their garrison behind to protect their property. You are to speak of this to no one along the way and to constantly be on guard until my family is safely within these walls. Is that understood?"

"Your orders are exceedingly clear, Yer Majesty," said Bardric, standing proudly at attention. "Yer will be done. We shan't sleep 'til yer family be safe within Moorwyn."

As the two guards were departing, Commander Mason, the chief officer of the castle's garrison, and Gregor, the royal chamberlain, arrived. They bowed to their king.

"Walk with me," directed Lucian. They left the library and

headed toward the king's chambers. As they strolled, Lucian first addressed his chief officer. "Commander Mason, double the watches and be on the alert, both on and around the castle walls, including the outer gate and walls surrounding the city of Kaleidos. Keep every guard alert and on the lookout for any hidden intrigue. Upon first light, begin the task of fortifying the castle against any possible attack. I want every detail of the castle's defenses checked, from the state of the garrison's weaponry and ammunition to the soundness of Moorwyn's structure. Increase security at the castle's hidden rear entrance and front gate. I even want the depth of the water in the moat examined. It is best to be prepared."

"Consider it done, Your Majesty," replied Commander Mason. He bowed and turned to set about his tasks.

Gregor kept in step with his king as he headed for his private chambers. When they reached the king's solar, Lucian broke the silence.

"My family will be arriving upon the morrow, Gregor," advised Lucian. "We need to make ready their quarters in the Family Wing."

"I shall take care of it at once, Your Majesty," replied Gregor.

Lucian's creased brow softened, and a grin grew as he said, "Gregor, I believe we should notify the cook to prepare Aurora Leigh's sweet cakes or I shall not hear the end of it."

The king smiled in memory of a wee child tossing a sweet cake back at the server and ever so sweetly demanding, "Prithee, would you be so kind as to notify the kitchen that the king's niece likes her sweet cakes served warm? It would be ever so delightful if the kitchen could commit that to memory."

"Aye indeed, Your Majesty," agreed Gregor. "We would not have it any other way."

"I shall retire now, Gregor. No need for my attendant tonight. Double the guards at my solar door, and I wish to make it perfectly clear that I am not to be disturbed until my family has arrived."

"All shall be done as you require, Your Majesty," said Gregor. He bowed and made his way toward the family's quarters.

Lucian's solar guards bowed in greeting upon the arrival of their king and opened the elegantly carved doors to His Majesty's Great Chamber. Sleep was the last thing on Lucian's mind. He determined he needed guidance from another perspective and decided it best to make a call upon Imperator Kullipthius, Ruler of the Great Empire of Oralia.

Fortunately, since the empire had made its home in the

mountains of Kaleidos Peak, their very presence and due diligence had kept any opposition from a lone dragon or ungoverned clan at bay. Since the people of Sapphirus had never actually seen a dragon attack since times of yore, not much credence was placed on the rare claim of dragon sightings, so their existence remained shrouded in mystery and legend.

Lucian had known of the clandestine pact between Avala and Oralia long before his ascension to the throne. The then young crown prince was officially introduced to Kullipthius by his late father, King Sebasteen, when he reached the age of twelve yearmarks. Lucian's younger brother, Prince Dryden, was but a wee child at the time, Lucian being eight calendar yearmarks his senior.

King Sebasteen had taught Lucian to regard the dragons with respect, and he painted a colorful picture of just how frighteningly beautiful their empire could be. His father also explained to Lucian that not all in dragondom were of the same persuasion as the Oralian Empire. Any ungoverned flight could pose a potential problem for Avala and surrounding countries.

Thoughts of Lucian's father had him smiling. He had ruled the throne for six decades, longer than any king in the history of Avala. He had always been in exceptional health and quite fit, and Lucian had thought his beloved father would outlive him. It brought to mind a time when then King Sebasteen called for a formal meeting with both Crown Prince Lucian and Imperator Kullipthius.

Crown Prince Lucian's Memories

Crown Prince Lucian awoke at the break of dawn from a sharp rap upon his door. The crown prince rubbed the sleep from his eyes and sat up. "You may enter," he called out. He was too comfortable and warm to place his feet upon the cold flagstone below.

"I beg your pardon, Your Royal Highness," said the chamberlain, expressing his regrets for the early morning arousal. "His Majesty, King Sebasteen has requested you make all possible haste, for your presence is required in the throne room."

"Did the king elaborate as to the nature of this urgency, Gregor?" Prince Lucian questioned. He watched as his bathman, an attendant, and the keeper of the wardrobe entered the chamber to ready him for the meeting.

"I am sorry, Your Royal Highness," replied Gregor. "His

Majesty did not."

"Very well. Advise His Majesty I will make all possible haste to arrive in a timely manner."

Lucian sat up and moved to the edge of his bed and let his personal attendants carry on with what they did best. Dashing about his chambers they opened his curtains, rekindled the fire, drew his bath, and gathered appropriate attire. Next came the scrubbing, the plucking, the polishing, the preening and, voila—he found himself placed in front of his mirror bathed, combed, and dressed with servants awaiting his approval. A nod of his head was their clue to proceed, and they whisked him away down the hall and deposited him into the throne room. Lucian smiled at what had just occurred—all was accomplished before he was fully awake.

Lucian was surprised to find he was alone in the throne room. His father was not one to make grand entrances for the benefit of the crown prince. He was just about to fetch someone to determine if the royal chamberlain had been mistaken as to the location. Of a sudden, as if out of nowhere, the king appeared, scaring Lucian out of his wits. He knew not how it occurred, but there King Sebasteen was, wearing crisp blues and silver tones, an arrangement that made his father look rather stately. It would have been easy to mistake him for a much younger man if not for the stark slips of grey at his temples.

"Lucian my boy, excellent," said King Sebasteen. "Sorry to keep you waiting, but it would seem we lost track of time."

We? Lucian spun around to face his father who was advancing, unaccompanied, from a section of the chamber where there was no entryway.

"It was no trouble, Father," replied a perplexed prince. "I only arrived a moment ago. I apologize, but I arrive unaware of the reason for this meeting."

King Sebasteen laughed, and a smile touched the corners of his lips. "I fear that I was not forthcoming when I asked Gregor to fetch you this morn, but you shall understand all quite soon." He draped an arm around his son and said, "Come with me, my boy."

They made their way to the council chambers. The room was lacking its normal activity in these early hours, save for a stately individual seated at the head of the council's discussion table. The exotic and regal guest rose graciously as they approached, and the crown prince received a partial answer to the mysteries of the day. With the dragon imperator present, surely something significant was about to commence.

As royalty took their seats, the servants brought forward two platters of assorted breads, berries, cheeses, and spiced cider to break their morning fast. The king was the first to speak after the servants left, and they each had food and drink beside them.

"This is an indispensable treaty we must keep safe, my son," advised Sebasteen, speaking of the pact with the form-altering dragons. "Today marks a vital exchange regarding our agreement between the Kingdom of Avala and the Oralian Empire."

Lucian nodded and began to prepare mental notes while King Sebasteen reviewed the details of the aforesaid treaty. They were covering points Lucian had studied extensively as part of preparations for the crown being passed to his hands. But halfway through the meeting, events began taking a turn the crown prince had not expected.

"Henceforth," Kullipthius continued, "King Sebasteen and I have agreed that the time has come for you, Crown Prince Lucian, to join your majestic father in these matters. From this moment forward, you shall be privy to all dragon politics and meetings."

In his shocked state, Lucian stammered his gratitude, not remembering exactly how he had answered. It appeared it was something humble and gracious, for they both were smiling and nodding.

A whirlwind tour of the passageways within the castle followed. Lucian became privy to the shrouded accesses and their inner workings that linked Moorwyn Castle to Oralia. There was a scattering of portals and entryways spread throughout the castle and the immediate grounds. The most fascinating were the ones hidden in plain view, and cloaked in mystery. It was then Lucian realized how his father had seemingly appeared from nowhere in the throne room earlier that morn.

The tour concluded in King Sebasteen's personal chambers after they had finished showing Lucian how to find the hidden portal and gain entry. Kullipthius strode past them into the dark void beyond the portal's frame. The darkness of the passageway swallowed him from sight and senses. Then an eerie disturbance erupted in the air, causing the hairs on the back of Lucian's neck and forearms to stand on end. A streaking bolt of light was followed by a sharp crackling. Lucian uncovered his head, feeling a bit embarrassed for having reacted to the mere lighting of a torch that cast a flickering light upon Kullipthius in the passageway beyond.

Sebasteen's smile and reassuring voice bolstered the young prince's courage. "Go on," he said, as he patted his son's back. "I shall wait in my chambers for your return. This first step is only to see the tunnels and where they lead. The next time you enter the tunnels, we shall do it together."

Not wanting to disappoint his royal father for the honor given, Lucian courageously took his first step into the empire of the dragons.

Even though Kullipthius' torch showed the way, the crown prince placed one hand upon the smooth stone wall for reassurance. He cautiously made his way through the winding passage with the imperator. A glance behind him revealed no illumination or sign of where his father had once stood. Fear blended with excitement and, with his heart hammering in his chest, Lucian was filled with anticipation of the wonders that might lie beyond.

Finally, after what seemed an eon of traversing the depths of Kaleidos Peak, another faint illumination appeared ahead of them, and Lucian silently rejoiced. As they drew closer, Lucian could make out a sentry standing at attention in front of a doorway, the torchlight reflecting in his polished armor. His breastplate was extraordinary, festooned with precious stones and elaborately constructed with valued metals. His smile was welcoming, and he bowed deeply to his imperator.

"I would like to introduce you to Chief Romus."

Romus bowed deeply to the crown prince.

Lucian gave him a respectful bow in return, and asked. "Are you a dragon, Chief Romus?"

"I am, Your Royal Highness," Romus responded.

"Are you a Jeweled or Metallic dragon?"

"I am a Jeweled dragon. I am the chieftain of the Amber Quartz Dragon Clans here in Oralia."

I am curious," pondered Lucian, with a quizzical look on his face, "and I mean no disrespect, Chief Romus, but I was told by my royal father that the Jeweled and Metallic dragons living in Oralia have an identifying marker on their foreheads."

Romus gave the prince a smile, and his amber quartz crystal suddenly appeared on his forehead.

Lucian was taken aback by its sudden appearance and he felt his eyes grow wide.

Romus' smile broadened as he explained. "If anyone uninvited happens upon this portal we try our best to be as discreet as possible. We don't intentionally want to frighten anyone, or cause them any undue concern. Thus, we will wear a headdress to accompany our marker or, as I have done, render it invisible with my gift of influence."

"Remember, Crown Prince Lucian," said Kullipthius, joining the thread of conversation, "if you ever find the need to come down one of the castle's shrouded routes, there will always be a transformed dragon sentry standing here to greet you."

Lucian wondered what would occur if anyone with ill intentions mistakenly happened upon one of the shrouded routes.

"If someone mistakenly discovers one of the hidden portals within your castle, the sentries will direct them with their gift of influence, soothingly and resolutely back to their place of origin. All three of Romus' sons have this essential gift that also allows them to influence an interloper to forget they had found the portal or traversed the secret tunnels."

Even though his royal father had explained that the dragons could read minds, this was the first he had actually experienced it for himself . . . well, that he was aware of, at any rate.

King Sebasteen had told Lucian that dragons had special gifts, but knowing what the amber quartzes could accomplish with the gift of influence gave Lucian a newfound, healthy respect for the powerful inhabitants of Oralia. He turned and took in his surroundings. He then looked back the way they had come. He was surprised to see how many doors and entryways were leading back to the castle. "How do I find my way back, Imperial Majesty?" asked a perplexed crown prince.

"Upon your return," Kullipthius informed him, "Romus will guide you so you can return from whence you came."

"With memory intact, Your Imperial Majesty?" inquired Lucian courageously.

"Aye, Crown Prince Lucian, without doubt." Kullipthius reassured the youngling with a smile.

"Without doubt, indeed." the now King of Avala repeated aloud, smiling at reflections of times gone by. Lucian wished at this moment his father could have taken him to his first meeting with the dragon lords. Unfortunately, King Sebasteen passed from this mortal realm before he ever got the chance. In the twenty-seven yearmarks that followed, Lucian never had the opportunity to venture beyond the dragon empire's reception hall. The imperator had continued to visit the castle annually using the anniversary of Sebasteen's passing as a date of reunion. One would guess that, because a dragon could live a few hundred yearmarks, that indeed the twenty-seven that had passed would seem a short time for the inhabitants of Oralia.

There had only been one issue great enough that required Lucian to call upon the dragon alliance, and that council was held at Moorwyn. That was quite an opportune time for Prince Dryden, as it was his first opportunity to direct the castle in the king's absence.

Lucian went to his wardrobe and changed into attire more suitable for meeting with royalty. He wanted to follow the proper customs for a visit such as this. Deciding it better to be slightly overdressed for courtesy and warmth within Kaleidos Peak's tunnels, he added a coat of red and gold embroidery. Shaking off lingering traces of hesitation, Lucian focused on his knowledge of how this passage worked, took a deep breath and moved toward the back wall of his study.

This particular wall displayed a lovely, ancient tapestry that depicted men flying upon the backs of dragons. Lucian pulled the tapestry cautiously from its place and carefully folded the fragile, ancient material. Setting the bundle on a well-padded chair, he stared at the blank wall before him and wondered if where he was about to traverse would be covered in cob webbing or be as dark as the blackest of nights. He grabbed the nearest lighted torch to be able to see within the cavern's depths. Though the wall was but an illusion, it seemed as sturdy and solid as any.

Lucian closed his eyes so his senses would not protest, took a deep breath and, holding the torch before him, plunged through the back wall of his study. After several heartbeats, his hand finally brushed a solid surface, and he opened his eyes. Shadowed in the alcove was a heavy, iron-bound wooden door. Its purpose was not only for privacy but necessity in preventing the flow of air from the tunnel's passage and exposing its existence. Lucian grabbed the heavy ring set onto the door that acted as a handle and gave it a tug. Surprisingly, the door slid open quietly, and as he stepped through it shut of its own accord behind him. Lucian was thrilled that he had the foresight to bring the torch. Inside the darkened doorframe, the shadows seemed almost tangible, and he felt a presence in the tunnel's still passage.

Lucian took a tentative step into the silence, and as light bloomed against the dimness beyond the entry, he could make out a silhouette. There was a rustling of cloth as Kullipthius stepped out of the obscurity. The imperator smiled and nodded his head in greeting.

"Ah," said Lucian, returning the gesture of respect to Kullipthius. "I am pleased to see it is you on the other side of these walls."

"Well met, Lucian. I did not want to startle you by coming through this passage with no forewarning. My son, Ra Kor'el, foresaw the importance of stopping these interlopers. He knew you would be coming this way to see us. That is why I am here to greet you."

Kullipthius then tilted his head, and Lucian read concern in his eyes.

"Any army marching upon Avala will, indeed, affect both our lands," said Kullipthius. "In my meeting with Ra, we concluded that the dragon lords, specifically the five members of the High Council of Dragon Lords, must be convened. With the utmost swiftness and concern, these matters must be contemplated and discussed."

Lucian nodded. "A wise course, Kullipthius. I myself will arrange an assembly of my own council to discuss this potential threat. However, I entered the passage to request an audience with you first. Your perspective on this matter would be much appreciated."

"Our pact as allies and our friendship demand no less," said Kullipthius. "It seems the time has come for you to meet the dragon lords. Come, Lucian, let us away and plan for the defense of our lands."

The passageway was wide enough for them to walk side-by-side. The torch sufficiently illuminated the walls and ceiling of stone, banishing the oppressive feel of the dark caverns. Lucian surmised that the dragons, indeed, had a greater sight within the darkness, for Kullipthius had arrived at the passage without illumination.

Upon arriving at the entrance of the dragon empire, Lucian smiled. He was happy to see that it was the same guardian at the portal doors that he had met long ago when he was the crown prince. Lucian noted Chief Romus was dressed in his formal ceremonial garb as his station as chieftain allowed, unlike his usual uniform as guardian of the realm. He had seen Chief Romus in this same garb when he accompanied Kullipthius on a prior meeting at Moorwyn Castle. He offered Lucian a warm, welcoming smile.

"Hail, Your Imperial Majesty," Romus said as he gave a salute to the imperator. He then turned to the king and bowed his head in greeting. "I bid you greetings and welcome to our empire, King

Lucian."

King Lucian smiled and said, "Gramercy, Chief Romus. It is good to see you once again."

As Lucian entered the dragon empire, he noted the passageway widened considerably. Along the expanse of one stone wall were elaborately-carved, shallow, recessed alcoves filled with statuettes. Writings in scripts unknown to King Lucian were carved into the wall above each niche.

Kullipthius gave Lucian a tour that started with two statues of Dra'khar, one as a dragon and the other in his human guise. Kullipthius explained that he and his father were known as platinum dragons. Setting a diamond into the center of the raw metal that inherently graced a platinum dragon's forehead, was how they crowned his father Imperator of Oralia. Kullipthius explained that he had added the diamond to his own forehead in his father's honor and would carry on the tradition.

The next alcove held a statue of Lucian's royal grandfather, King Salvadorio, whom Lucian had never met. He was surprised to find how much his brother Dryden resembled him, and Kullipthius said as much. The next alcove held a statue of Kullipthius, who looked much like Dra'khar in both dragon and altered guise.

Lucian smiled when he reached the statue of King Sebasteen, for it was an extraordinary likeness. He could even discern the kindness in his eyes. He could not help but stare at his father's regal image, paying him silent tribute.

When he arrived at the alcove that held his reproduction, he was stunned. The regal attire he was wearing was some of the best he owned, down to his favorite boots. He had to admit that each statue was created by one with an exceptionally skilled hand. Never had he seen such excellence in craftsmanship. This silent, historical representation was one Lucian would be keen on studying at his leisure.

Pondering his own lineage made Lucian wonder how many dragon species there were.

Kullipthius answered his silent query. "There are several species of dragons in the Kingdom of Draconalia. At this time, two of these species are residing in the Oralian Empire: Metallic and Jeweled dragons. You can distinguish each by the identifying marker on the dragon's forehead, such as, a cluster of crystals on a Jeweled dragon, or—using me as an example for a Metallic dragon—platinum ore.

"There are exceptions to this rule: For instance, I have seen gold dragons manifest their markers as ornaments in their hair or on their wrists.

"Regardless of species, we all work together harmoniously. All bring their contributions to the integrated whole, sharing their way of life, peaceful solutions, and dragon gifts. It has not always been easy, but ultimately our diversity and collective talents have proven a superb combination that makes up for any conflicts.

"There are, however, certain clans outside Oralia that deplore our values and believe passionately they are the grandest of all dragonkind. Thus, they are misguided by vainglory and see themselves as the most important aspect of existence. The strength in our alliance here in Avala and Oralia is the very reason those particular dragons stay away from Sapphirus. Nonetheless, if any dragon were to choose differently and wanted to join our ranks, I would not deny his petition solely on past behavior. After all, everyone deserves a fair opportunity.

"We are a unique flight in the Oralian Empire, and we try to see potential in everyone. It is why we choose to be open to involvement with other species. We have discovered that compassion, not hate or fear, bring accord to most. We have learned from the mistakes of those who came before us, both good and to the contrary. We are constantly evolving, and while you might think this would bring a source of chaos to our existence, there are rules and order here. History and tradition play a central role in our lives, and like the statues that line these walls, are a constant reminder of who we are, how far we have come, and how far we have yet to go to achieve our goals."

"Aye, it would be a grand existence indeed if all species would be so inclined," Lucian confirmed. Then they spent a few moments admiring the stone figures around them, Kullipthius mentioning interesting facts about the various ruling officials and officers and what they had contributed during their time and the difficulties they had encountered. The very fact that he knew so much about the history of so many dragon species, as well as the history of human rulers and customs, was astonishing.

"I believe I inherited my majestic father's enthusiasm for history," said Lucian. "You can learn so much from the past."

Kullipthius nodded and smiled. "Imperial Advisor Vahl Zayne will treasure your inquisitiveness and interest in the past, Lucian. You might remember meeting Vahl Zayne during the confrontation with Liltimer. He is our Royal Archivist and Keeper of the Ancient Scriptures of Oralia. As such, he is in charge of tracking its history, traditions, and lore.

"We have, for the most part, an oral tradition when it comes to our history, but we do maintain written records for future generations. My knowledge is that of a nestling compared to Vahl Zayne's comprehension of times long and ago."

"Vahl Zayne is a sapphire, or frost dragon, if memory serves," said Lucian, thinking back to his first encounter with the blue dragon. "Observing his breath gift of frost personally was quite an extraordinary experience."

"Aye," replied Kullipthius, "he is the only frost dragon we have in our empire and his gift is rather unique."

He then led Lucian through a passageway that opened into a well illuminated, circular cavern. He advised Lucian that this was where meetings with the royal family had been held for the past three generations. Previously, the dragons had always met at Morning Star Palace where Dryden and his family now resided.

The spacious room was unlike anything Lucian had ever seen. Large, multicolored marble boulders were elaborately-carved in the shape of rectangular tables. Around those tables were high-back chairs boasting plump pillows. In the center of the room was an exquisite grey marble pulpit bedecked with the carving of a dragon and set with emerald cabochons for eyes. The walls were lined with polished diamonds, and four elaborately-carved white marble thrones stood regally in the front of the room.

Lucian noted three figures conversing on the other side of the room. Kullipthius began the introductions as they approached.

"King Lucian of Avala, might I present to you the Jewel of Kaleidos, Her Imperial Majesty Laliah, the Imperatrix of Oralia. She is a rare opal dragoness with dual gifts—healing and the breath of sleeping gas. And if I may be so bold as to say, she can tame even the fiercest of beasts if our meetings get out of hand."

Laliah smiled at her mate and then turned and nodded her head in greeting to Lucian.

"Your Imperial Majesty, it is an honor," said Lucian with a smile. He would have marked her of an age akin to Aurora Leigh, though he knew that dragons aged at a different pace. Looking at the fragile flower before him, he was suddenly seized with an overwhelming urge to protect her from all harm and smiled to himself thinking that, in actuality, she would make a better protector of him were the regal lady in her altered, scaled form.

Currently, she was of pale radiance, hair the color of sun-sparked sand, upswept and pinned in place. She wore a gauzy gown of lavender that matched her enticing, violet-blue eyes. She also wore a jade-colored scarf sashed about her hips and twin garlands of opals set on golden chains adorned her forehead and her neckline, both shining in opulent splendor.

"Greetings and well met, King Lucian," Laliah said as she extended her hand.

Lucian kissed the beautiful opal ring that gracefully adorned one slender finger.

"We met once before, Your Majesty," Laliah reminded Lucian. "I was at your father's bedside when he passed to the spirit realm. He lived a long and fruitful life. After your Queen Mother Anasofia's passing, you and your brother were always his main concern. He would be so proud to see all that you have accomplished."

"Gramercy, Imperatrix. You are most gracious. Words cannot express my gratitude for all you have done." Laliah's words brought peace to Lucian's heart.

Lucian remembered seeing a woman covered in gossamer shimmering cloth at King Sebasteen's bedside. He had thought she was a relative from his mother's side. The one thing he remembered and treasured most was that his father lived a substantially long life with Avala at peace. He had passed with a smile and with his sons at his side.

Kullipthius then politely steered Lucian's attention to an extraordinary figure, unique in appearance, who wore distinctive clothing made of fine white silk under a dark blue formal robe.

"King Lucian, I would like to introduce you to my son, His Highness Ra Kor'el. He is a soothsayer and guardian of the Tall Forest. His gift of foresight is a great blessing.

"His draconic gift is as unique as his foresight, for it is liken to a tether of blue light that can be used to strike like lightning. He can throw it out whip-like, and it can draw targets to his person as well as repel them. He can also wrap it about his quarry as if it were a length of rope, and hold them in place. He has worked tirelessly for the welfare of our empire and has earned the admiration and respect of Oralia. As the imperatrix's son and heir presumptive for the empire, his entitlement as Prince of the Oralian Empire is well deserved."

"Your Majesty," declared Ra, displaying a cordial bow. "It is a pleasure to make your acquaintance."

Ra's eyes held a lavender sheen around vertical pupils, and his long hair was a shimmering white cascade that fell to the center of his back. His dark blue silk robe was painstakingly embroidered with a high standard of craftsmanship that featured great detail in its foreign design.

He smiled warmly and said, "I am pleased to meet such a fine king as you, one who passionately believes in our alliance and is so devoted to maintaining it."

As Ra raised his hands to adjust his long, flowing robe, the king took note of sharp talons at the ends of his fingertips and small, scalloped scales covering what little he could see of the soothsayer's upper wrists.

Lucian was fascinated by Ra's uniqueness; it added to his mystique.

"The pleasure is mine, Your Highness," replied Lucian, and he meant it. His father had told him of the soothsayer of Oralia, and Lucian had been looking forward to meeting him.

It was then that the lean form of Vahl Zayne stepped forward and bowed before their majesties.

"Imperial Majesty," he said to Kullipthius and then turned his attention to their royal guest.

"King Lucian," said Vahl Zayne with a broad smile and a bow, "you are looking well. It is a pleasure to be in your company once more."

"It is good to see you again, Vahl Zayne," replied King Lucian.

The sapphire dragon was dressed richly with a swirling cloak of deep blue. Out of character for a dragon, though adding to his charm, Vahl Zayne wore a small pair of spectacles perched high upon his nose. His clean-shaven face was open and friendly with eyes that were the lightest shade of crystal blue Lucian ever bore witness to. His dark blond hair was tucked neatly behind ears that held the slightest hint of points at their tips. A leather band decorated his forehead and glittered with tiny inset sapphire stones. In the bands center was this Jeweled dragon's marker: A rough sapphire stone, in deep blue.

A great flash of light was detected coming from the entrance of the cavern. Three stately noblemen entered the room and made their way to their seats which faced the four thrones. Two he did not recognize, however, the third nobleman was Chief Romus. Lucian knew that Chief Romus was a member of the High Council of Dragon Lords, as he was the amber quartz dragons' high chief. Nine other dragon nobles followed, and they took their places in a grouping of seats on a raised platform.

Taking Laliah's arm, Kullipthius said to Lucian, "I shall turn introductions over to our Imperial Advisor Vahl Zayne so that he may escort you to your seat and present you to our council, as is customary, and officially begin our meeting of the dragon lords."

Kullipthius took his place upon the throne with Laliah on his left while Ra took his seat next to her. The blue dragon showed their royal guest to his place next to Ra and then made his way to an elaborately-carved podium to begin the session.

Vahl Zayne's voice boomed throughout the chamber, a surprising contrast to the quiet tones in which he had addressed Lucian so personably only moments before. "Regina Imperatrix, Your Highness Ra Kor'el, King Lucian of Avala, and Dragon Lords, let us first pay homage to Imperator Kullipthius, son of Dra'khar."

"Hail, Imperator Kullipthius, son of Dra'khar," echoed the council members.

"Our dragon council consists of sixteen members. This is our 904th session of the seven high council members of Oralia's dragon lords. The remaining nine dragon lords are present only to hear the details of our meeting.

"We are truly honored today to have as our guest and ally, His Majesty King Lucian, Ruler of Avala."

"Hail King Lucian, Ruler of Avala!"

"He is a great king, and more importantly, our ally who maintains the peace within our surrounding lands. His Majesty honors and respects our clandestine existence so that we may all live in peace and harmony here at Kaleidos Peak.

"Before we begin our meeting, I would like to present the three remaining high council members for the benefit of our guest, King Lucian.

"We will begin with Chief Romus. Since His Majesty has been officially introduced to the chieftain before, he is aware of his gift of influence and his status as High Chief of the Amber Quartz Dragon Clans. Therefore, it is unnecessary to delve further into formal introductions with the Jeweled dragon at this time."

The chieftain had remained standing during Vahl Zayne's introduction. Romus smiled, returned King Lucian's nod, and then took his seat.

"Next, I would like to present Chief Elder Var'ohk, our eldest and wisest dragon. He is an emerald water dragon. These Jeweled dragons build their lairs below the water line, constructing them to remain dry within. Water dragons are often sought out for their wise council, knowledge, and unique perception.

"Our chief elder has lived in the mountains of Kaleidos since the beginning of the Dra'khar Dynasty. He is our major domus, meaning chief of the house, who commands the Imperial Palace in the absence of our Imperial Majesties and His Highness Ra Kor'el.

"The major domus has the gift of demolition. He has the ability to create and launch a massive ball of fire and lightning a great distance. Upon impact, this projectile has the capability of exploding and shattering its target to fragments. This talent has helped in the mining, and construction of this very empire. He has assisted in the creation of our homes, tunnels, and this very room we are now occupying."

King Sebasteen had only told his son that he was astonished and amazed by the major domus' abilities, and now Lucian understood why.

"Your Majesty," Var'ohk acknowledged, and he bowed his head in respect to King Lucian, who reciprocated his greeting.

In his altered guise the major domus appeared older than the other Oralians in the room. He was of a medium build with greying hair cropped close to his scalp, and he wore a close-shaved beard with streaks of white at his temples. His deep blue-green eyes held a lustrous darkness, like a forest stream under the shade of a willow tree. An emerald was wrapped in golden filigree which decorated the circlet on his brow.

He dressed in unadorned, comfortable clothes that included deep browns and forest greens. His skin was a healthy tanned hue, and his face was weathered. Huntsmen in Lucian's employ often displayed this same appearance.

As Var'ohk took his seat Vahl Zayne continued.

"May I present Commander Blayz. You may remember seeing him during the conflict with Liltimer, but you were never officially introduced.

"Commander Blayz is responsible for the Imperial Champions including their training, and what they do or fail to do. He is also held accountable for our Imperial Captains' actions in the field of battle and how these dragons lead their missions.

"Our commander is a unique dragon. His mother, Et'opia, is a bronze, marking her a Metallic dragon. These dragons are known to be timid and loyal. His sire is a fire-breathing ruby dragon that hails from a place known as the Desertlands, a large, inhospitable wasteland across the Carillion Sea.

"When Blayz's sire found Et'opia preparing a nest, he attacked her and left her for dead. Rubies believe they stand supreme above all other dragon species, and nesting with any other variety of dragonkind would make them a disgrace amongst their brethren.

"Our imperator found Et'opia and the imperatrix healed her. When her nestling hatched, Their Imperial Majesties graciously participated in his upbringing. His gift is fire-breathing, and we are most honored to have him on our council."

The commander was unusually tall with black-brown hair and a ginger tone to his skin, marking his exotic heritage. His clothing was a deep brown, except for his vest, which was dyed in tones of amber and orange, and embroidered with vermillion flames and swirls. Though his mother was a bronze dragon, his identifying marker was a large ruby stone, marking him a Jeweled dragon.

Commander Blayz made a dramatic, sweeping gesture with his hand, and displayed a formal bow. "Your Majesty," boomed the deep voice of Commander Blayz. "It is good to see you again."

"Likewise," said Lucian in acknowledgement.

Vahl Zayne then rapped his knuckles upon the podium, the sound ringing about the chamber as he said, "With introductions concluded for those who will be speaking at this meeting, I now leave the floor to Imperator Kullipthius. Let the meeting commence."

CHAPTER TWELVE

Nature unleashed its fury with a relentless downpour as
Danuvius led his guards and personal servants through the
Tall Forest into uncharted territory. The twelve men who
accompanied him were as tired of his rants as they were the
slippery mud, and a dark layer of misery gripped them all like
sticky tree sap. The men flinched when Danuvius came to a
sudden stop, reined in his horse and barked out his orders,
screaming to be heard over the pounding rain.

"Ya weather-bitten mongrels!" cried Danuvius. "Set up me
tent!" He dismounted his horse and brandished his sword to
emphasize his haranguing. "I'll skewer the next good-fer-nothing,
boil-brained lout who whines about gusty winds!" He refused to
stay out in the hammering rainfall any longer. "Get a move on!"

Mud sucked at the hard soles of their boots as they tried to
carry out Danuvius' orders as quickly as possible. He poked the
nearest man in the back with the tip of his sword. The man arched
his back, lost his footing, and fell flat on his face in the mud.

"Get up!" Danuvius ordered as he gave the downed man a kick
to the ribs. "I will nay tolerate anyone lying down on the job!" He
continued his seething rage and prodding until the camp was
made ready to his exact specifications.

After a cold supper, everyone had tried to steer clear of their
leader, doing their very best to look occupied and unapproachable
whenever he had entered into their midst. Even now, as the
steward sat inside his tent counting his gold, he did not hear any
casual banter amongst the men. There were only ghostly echoes of

bitter agreement drifting through the encampment that the steward of Terra Leone was mad. Danuvius smirked. He liked the way they felt about him—money and fear kept them loyal.

Truth be told, Danuvius cared nothing for these men who had risked their lives and the king's wrath by helping him escape the mutinous trap and resultant battle at Terra Leone. Like weighty, cumbersome armor, the steward used them as protection from the king's guardsmen, thieves, and wild animals. Unbeknownst to them, their presence was tolerated for a much greater purpose that would reveal itself upon journey's end.

The next morn, Danuvius peered through the tent's canvas flap to see a new day dawn. He noted the clouds were parting and the rain had let up. He heard the two men guarding his tent talking, standing together in a small huddle. Their long-hooded mantles were soaked through and were heavy burdens that no longer offered protection from the damp morning air.

"Why are we out here?" One shivering man wondered aloud, pulling his mantle tighter about himself. "We are outside the Tall Forest and nearing the northern coast of Avala."

The second man looked around nervously and spoke in low tones through chattering teeth. "Where do you think the steward went when he left the camp last eve?" He exhaled his breath on his hands and rubbed them together vigorously. "As far as I know, there is nothing in these parts!"

Tired of listening to the guards' ramblings, Danuvius chose that moment to emerge from his shelter. He was dressed in his finest and shrouded in a warm, woolen cloak. He glared at the two guards who suddenly straightened their stance when they spied him. He raised his voice to carry across the site, but he offered no explanation. "Strike camp an' make ready. We be moving out on foot!"

As his retinue hurried about gathering their gear, Danuvius then pointed to the two fellows guarding his tent.

"Night guards!" shouted Danuvius.

The two guards stood at attention, awaiting their fate.

"Remain here an' watch over the horses an' supplies 'til our return. Make ready the evening meal, fer these men shall be hungry from carrying back the treasures that await us." Danuvius fabricated this story because he wanted them to have a reason to stay put and do as he bid.

It was noontide before the remaining ten men began their trek behind Danuvius' steady gait wending through uncharted territory. A chill wind blew from behind, pushing them forward through a meadow of tall, wet grass. They came upon an unkempt, overgrown path, and Danuvius took it without hesitation.

The forest was eerily silent. Neither songbird nor any other living forest creature was in evidence. The path wound down a steep incline, and Danuvius slid the last few feet to level ground and waited for each man to follow suit. The men traced their leader's steps in a ragged line, clutching at rocks and roots—anything that presented itself as a handhold. The steward then led them to an overhang of jagged rock that offered shelter from the wind. The men looked out of breath and exhausted from Danuvius' relentless pace, and seemed happy for a place to rest.

"Wait here," he commanded, the first words they had heard him utter since they had left that morning.

Danuvius was aware that the men were watching as he approached three waist-high standing stones located before a dark cavern. The smooth stones stood approximately five feet apart to form a triangle. It was within the triangle's center that the steward positioned himself. Swirls of wind and curling mist drifted around him, and he shivered. He glanced over at the stillness of the foreboding cave's mouth, some five and thirty paces from where his men were standing.

Danuvius' lips curled into a feral grin as he pulled a dark, swathed bundle from his cloak. He removed its contents and let the black silk wrapping drop to the damp ground.

Foreign words grated from his throat: "Laqueus statim, laqueus statim, laqueus statim!"

The large crystal in Danuvius' hand pulsed once with a blinding crimson light before it shattered into ten pieces, equal to the number of men who accompanied him. The shards of crystal melted into a puddle of red liquid in his palm. It then flowed off the sides of his hand and burrowed into the ground.

Sounds of shock and terror rose from those behind him, but Danuvius did not bother looking back. He knew the result of his incantation. The men who had followed him here found their feet were effectively stuck to the ground, as if rooted in place. After all, it would not do to have them fleeing.

"Silence!" snapped Danuvius, never turning to look upon the faces of those who served him. "Lest ya favor the alternative o' becoming the main course in an elaborate feast."

The ground quaked and a few of the men tried to escape by tugging at their thighs, but their legs refused to budge. A thunderous roar shook the trees and startled large, black carrion crows off their branches and into flight.

Fire blasted from the murky entrance of the fissure and from the billowing smoke, a large, horned reptilian head emerged. A rough ruby stone that adored his brow almost seemed to glow in the morning light. His huge claws, each roughly the length of a forearm, gouged the earth, and the green eyes of a mighty red dragon narrowed at the sight of Danuvius.

Four armored servants followed in the red beast's wake. Dressed in intricate, immaculate armor, each carried a wicked spear. They remained at the cave's mouth, heads bowed submissively, awaiting their orders. One looked to be in better favor of the monster, for he held his head proudly and wore a large stone pendant around his neck. Danuvius recognized him instantly, for he was his chief rival for the dragon's amity.

Danuvius immediately dropped to his knees. He tilted his head up to the creature, the black hood falling back from his features. His eyes were obediently set upon the red behemoth as he said, "Master Flayre."

The red dragon before him was, indeed, a frightening monstrosity, the largest Danuvius had ever glimpsed. This dragon was not only formidable due to his bulk, but many of his large blood-red scales possessed a different arcane engraving. Each scale had been painstakingly carved with ancient characters, each containing its own magical significance that could be evoked for protection or tapped for offense. With the duty of being head vassal for Flayre, Danuvius himself had helped the dragon invoke and carve some of the spells. Though treated as a slave and ordered to labor for his dragon master's wishes, the position he held was not without its reward. Flayre held his service with promises of freedom. He was allowed to freely travel throughout the territory to carry out the red's wishes and served as the eyes and ears for his master in exchange for his continued existence. For you see, Flayre literally held his life in his talons.

There was no preamble; there were no pleasantries. *What has brought you to me?* The dragon's booming thoughts invaded Danuvius' mind and sent a shiver up his spine.

Danuvius bowed his head submissively. "I'ves brought ya an offering o' me most loyal men, Lord an' Master, ta serves ya, fer their service be impeccable. There be two guards an' twelve horses' fer yer bidding left back at our camp."

"Excellent. I accept your offering. You have served me well." The red seemed pleased. *"Guards!"* Drahk assaulted the minds of all who were present. *"See to it these prisoners are taken to the*

holding pen."

The man with the stone pendant nodded, and he led the guards to the trembling captives. He lifted the stone pendant that hung around his neck and touched it to a flat, circular stone just outside the sheltered overhang of rock, thus freeing the captives from the dark magic that tethered them to the ground.

The four servants then herded the ten terrified prisoners to the cave's entrance. One horror-struck man started to panic. Danuvius saw his comrades try to hold him in place and calm him, but it was of no use. He was frantic beyond the point of reason, and he started to scream. He pushed his companions out of his way, stumbling and darting, working his way past the spear wielder's attempts to detain him, and began running for his life.

Danuvius ducked as the red dragon stepped over him. Surprisingly quick for such a large dragon, Flayre grabbed the panic-stricken fellow with a razor-sharp claw, threw him in the air with ease, and swallowed him whole.

Steam plumed from the dragon's nostrils, and he licked his tongue across his sharp teeth. Flayre then turned and looked upon the other prisoners, as if daring them to try an escape. He stared at the men as a wildcat would stare at its prey. The rest of the men ran into the cave without further prompting. The four servants followed in their wake. Danuvius was thrilled that his master had found his offering suitable.

Now for the bitter pill: "Lord Master Flayre, Lucian's forces came ta the fortress. Some o' the mercenaries hired with the gold ya supplied turned a traitorous coat. Terra Leone an' me own lands aves been taken from me."

"Your loss is of no consequence to me. You are not even a dragon! You are a shape-shifting slave! You've taken the form of the Liltian called Danuvius Doral and have allowed the influence of his memories to take over your reptilian senses. You need only complete your assignment and not jump at shadows. Dare not show me such weakness in the future, Scale, or you will suffer the consequences."

"As ya command, Lord an' Master," replied Scale. How he hated it when Flayre made him cower. "It shan't happen again."

Scale had to forcefully remind himself that his present appearance was that of the former Danuvius Doral. He had to remain strong and keep to his reptilian senses for his chance to escape. Even though Flayre's magic was fierce, cunning, and powerful, he was not invincible. Scale would lie in wait and formulate a plan to destroy the wretched red dragon.

FLAYRE growled through clenched teeth in utter irritation. It was fortunate Scale was so obedient and useful. If Flayre had not invested so much time in training this slave, he would have killed him where he stood for losing precious gold.

The creature before him was known as a *Monstrum,* an Old World reptilian species that was thought extinct—until Flayre raided his father's hidden treasure trove and discovered two nests of Monstrum eggs.

Flayre also found a scroll lying next to the nests. When he unrolled the parchment, he had discovered that these large eggs once belonged to a dark wizard. This magician had cast a spell to hold all seven eggs in a dormant state for later use.

But the greatest treasure lying amongst the old wizard's belongings was a leather-bound tome called *The Dark Arts*. The knowledge held within the book's confines was everything one required to gain a masterful understanding of black magic.

Once Flayre became experienced in wielding dark magic, he had tested his skill on the dormant eggs and, with only one failure, he had successfully brought four of the Monstrum eggs to life.

Thrice the size of a large horse, these creatures were viciously cruel. With three rows of needle-sharp teeth, a voracious appetite, and a deadly venomous stinger at the end of their tails, they were perilous. Once their prey was stung and consumed, Monstrum had the uncanny ability to alter their physique into an exact duplicate of their victim, thus the nickname "chameleon." Once transformed, they could imitate their victim's characteristics, because they also acquired their intelligence and a lifetime of memories. Adding this to a Monstrum's inherent cruelty, deadly venom, and insatiable appetite, they were recognized as dangerous predators.

Under Flayre's directives, Scale had been ordered to kill Ambassador Valen Doral and make it look like an accident. Then he was to kill his brother Danuvius and assume his identity.

Flayre had assured Scale that once he had finished his assignment at Terra Leone, Scale and his mate Sauria would be set free, and the remaining clutch of eggs that were his brethren would then be revived.

As soon as Scale had returned from his assignment, Flayre cast an evil enchantment over him. Flayre smiled at the memory of Scale's realization that he had been deceived. He was told that his life would forever be held in Danuvius' form if he did not continue to do as he was bid. To further assure Scale's obedience, Flayre had his red dragon slaves take Sauria and the remaining dormant Monstrum eggs to a secret and secure location. If Scale failed, Flayre vowed he would kill Sauria, and the remaining eggs would never be revived.

"Let us retire to my lair. We have much to discuss," urged Flayre as he peered around suspiciously. *"The trees have ears."*

There was something disturbing in the air, and he felt the need to escape. He turned and made his way down the passageway to his lair. His thoughts were on that half-breed whelp, Ra Kor'el. The soothsayer could cause massive problems if he even caught a tiny whiff of what was being planned.

The best step Flayre had taken to guard his secrets was to meet with his warlords in caves lined with lead. Through his magical study, Flayre had learned this dense, malleable, bluish-grey metal helped keep mystical scrying and spells contained. With that and his own body covered in magical protection, it kept Kullipthius' infernal prophesying son from discovering his actions and whereabouts.

After Flayre had betrayed and killed Dra'khar, he killed his own father, Py'ro. He then took over his father's position as High Chief of the Ruby Dragon Clans and ruled over the Desertlands. At first, he had gathered a few rubies who eagerly followed him because they hated and feared the Oralian Empire. But he knew he needed all the assistance he could find if he wanted to defeat the largest dragon empire ever to exist.

More often than not, ruby dragons preferred to remain solitary creatures, content to focus on petty goals for their individual treasure hordes and lands. So, in order to ensure the assistance of other red dragons, he had to resort to drastic measures. Flayre found that dark magic was a great means of persuasion. When that did not work, he used his dragon gift of flash fire, an intense flame that burned flesh and charred bones until naught was left but ashes. Thus, through dark magic, broken promises and scorching threats, Flayre had a large force of obedient ruby dragons under his control.

His plans were so close to completion he could almost taste the blood of his enemies, almost hear the cries of the vanquished.

When the time came, Kullipthius and Ra would be turned to ashes, and that lovely morsel, Laliah, would be forced to become his slave. Then the humans would be forced into serfdom and bred within their cities as food and workers for their dragon overlords.

Caught in his own musings, Flayre suddenly realized his vassal was not following him. He looked back and saw that he was still standing at the cavern's entryway stammering apologies for his lack of insight. With ferocity evident in his eyes and smoke escaping from his nostrils, Flayre turned and headed back toward the cave's entryway.

Scale backed away from the cave's entrance as Flayre approached him. "Prithee, Master," pleaded Scale with fear in his eyes, clearly recognizing Flayre's anger. "I can be more useful ta ya if able ta change ta me own form. I'ves no skills fer slaughter in this body. With no claws or venom, these weak bodies be subject ta every chill an' slight they happen upon."

Flayre snaked a clawed forearm forward, snatching Scale up by his cloak only to dangle him helplessly before his dragon maw. The chameleon gave an involuntary yelp of surprise and then obediently went limp. The ruby's mouth opened wide to display teeth the size of daggers.

"*Hark now, you sniveling half-wit! I shall take you to your encampment. You and the two remaining guards will take the twelve horses and supplies to join the force that is marching upon Avala's borders. We shall locate the army from the skies so you will know your course. You want your freedom and that of your mate's? Do not bother me again with your petulant ramblings, and finish your assignment. I want no more mistakes. I want results!*"

He shook the terrified vassal like a ragdoll, and threatened, "*Dare not speak another word in my presence, Scale, unless it is to proclaim our victory.*"

Struggling to contain his dragon fury, Flayre had to invoke every ounce of his willpower not to crush the puny reptile in his grasp. The giant ruby leapt up into the damp cloud filled sky, flapped his monstrous wings, and carried the trembling life form away.

CHAPTER THIRTEEN

R a Kor'el noticed he was feeling lightheaded. He attributed it to his lack of sleep. The meeting with the Avalian King had gone long into the night, and then reconvened early this morn. He rubbed at his temples and realized he was no longer able to concentrate on the debate between Commander Blayz and Chief Elder Var'ohk. He blinked his eyes a few times and noted his visual world was shifting as the images around him turned muddled and fuzzy.

Ra knew from experience that he was receiving a vision, right in the midst of an important meeting. Normally, he had enough warning to be able to erect his mental screens and then take his leave to his private chambers. But this time, it seemed, that was not going to be possible.

The room felt bitterly cold. Ra attempted to stand, but he swayed while everything tilted drastically. Ra fell to his chair and, using Drahk, he called out to his mother. He did not want to alarm anyone, especially their royal Avalian guest. He could make out her words, but could not move or respond.

"There is no need for alarm, King Lucian," Ra heard his mother say. "Ra has many gifts. One is soothsaying, which allows him the ability to have visions. He also can hear sounds and voices outside the natural range of hearing. Whatever vision has brought Ra to this condition must be significant indeed for it to strike with such intensity. Ra has not experienced such a reaction since he was but a nestling, and that particular vision saved our empire from destruction."

"Is there anything I can do?" King Lucian asked.

"Nay, all we can do now is stand watch," replied his mother. "But pray, take heed. He is guided by his vision and instinct, and he may lash out. His claws are as sharp as any dragon's, and our current forms do not hold much protection against them. If you don't mind, Your Majesty, I would like to trade seats with you, and I will watch over him. This position will give me the space and freedom to change into a dragon if I must."

With his mother having the situation well in hand, Ra allowed his dragon gift to kick into full force, and the chamber around him disappeared.

Ra's Vision

The soothsayer's vision was misty, as if he were viewing a world through light-distorted vapors. Images swam before his dazzled eyes and spun away quickly. After a moment, everything sorted itself and the unsteadiness and confusion passed.

Ra found himself gazing upon a cave in a wooded region. Before him were three stone pillars carved with magical, draconic glyphs. Ra was well-versed in a multitude of languages and hieroglyphics, but these particular symbols proved foreign, and Ra sensed evil intent.

A man in noble attire approached a triangle of three stone pillars. While the man remained composed, his eyes captured Ra's attention, as he seemed twisted somehow. His aura was tightly wrapped in dark ribbons, as if something evil were waiting to escape.

Standing behind the nobleman, Ra noted a dozen or so indistinct men huddled under an overhang of rock who appeared anxious and fearful. It was often thus; the most vital of details standing out starkly, while other images, less crucial although noteworthy, were hazy and ill-defined.

A nearly blinding beacon of magical power suddenly seized Ra. It seemed to be coming from the glyphs on the stone pillars. He winced from the bright red bursts of light his mystic vision showed him. A cavern's maw came into focus and was suddenly alive with movement. From the shadows a colossal winged figure emerged.

Flayre! Ra seethed in outrage as his gut told him it was so. This desert dragon was a notorious figure in Oralia's history. He knew his supposition was accurate from the sheer number of evil, magical runes and spells that encircled the red dragon's body like a second skin.

Ra's attention was next drawn to strands of dark magic that surrounded all the trees in the area. These strands adhered to the branches and trunks of the tall sentinels like the sticky silk of a spider's web, holding them in a dormant state. The soothsayer now understood why the trees had not advised him of Flayre's arrival in Sapphirus.

The mysterious noble then dropped to his knees before Flayre. Through his gifts, Ra knew the noble's performance was not out of worship or respect, but of fear and hatred.

They conversed, seemingly undisturbed by anything around them. Then it became clear why the other men were in the presence of a dragon. He watched as Flayre brutally murdered and devoured one who panicked and tried to flee. Ra shuddered in horror.

Ra felt the sudden familiarity of his mother's healing gift comforting him. Ra surmised she must have sensed his dismay. Once soothed, Ra focused his attention on Flayre.

Ra noted multiple forms of protection from magical divination surrounding the vile behemoth's body. He could easily detect the spells glowing on Flayre's scales that were used to keep magical senses from finding the ruby's location. But Flayre seemingly underestimated Ra's unique talents.

The soothsayer's gift was not the usual magic Flayre assumed others used. Ra did not need elaborate potions, spells, ceremonies, or runes. His was an innate gift from nature, a magic that he had been born with. It was a unique ability, one scarcely heard of throughout the chronicles of dragon history. An exceedingly rare talent as natural to him as breathing.

"Lord Master Flayre," the noble's thoughts were reflecting tones of reluctance. He ran his hands down the edges of the dark cloak he wore, mayhap a sign of his nervousness. *"Lucian's forces came ta the fortress. Some o' the mercenaries hired with the gold ya supplied turned a traitorous coat. Terra Leone an' me own lands aves been taken from me."*

Ra knew the king would have a vested interest in this. Avala and Oralia had to be alerted that the forces marching toward them were at the behest of the mad dragon, Flayre. With all this new evidence, Ra knew for certain that the dream he had revealing the cause of the uprising as "not Sapphirian-born" was about Flayre. This changed things drastically. This Desertlands dragon was cunning and cruel. He had some deeper intentions, verily, and would never help humans in any endeavor, much less aid in overthrowing a monarchy, unless it abetted his own selfish needs.

Flayre seemed to be lost in his own thoughts as the noble continued with his apologies and ramblings, but the rest of the dialog was suddenly indecipherable and lost to the soothsayer. The red's magic saw to that. Ra caught sight of a dark repulsion spell etched into the red's hide as it pulsed with light. Flayre appeared oblivious when this spell was activated. Ra watched as a green light began to glow fiercely. A disruptive jolt erupted from the spell, and a tremendous force broke Ra's connection to the scene.

His mind began to spin helplessly. He was unable to stop the motion, feeling frustrated and alarmed at the loss of control. He tried in vain to halt the process, but he found he could not concentrate.

An earthy presence manifested itself within his besieged mind. It was strong and welcoming, offering him shelter from the mental storm he was caught in. He was relieved by the comfort and strength and he mentally relayed his gratitude.

"Gramercy, Sani."

Sani responded by enveloping Ra in a soothing blanket of serenity that seemed to have the same effect one could achieve on a casual morning stroll through the Tall Forest: Where the dappled sun warms your skin, and the call of a purple feathered wookatah lulls you into a sense of tranquility as her hauntingly beautiful birdsong fills the air.

Lovingly hailed as the "Ancient One" by the denizens living within the Tall Forest, Sani was the oldest and grandest living forest being, an evergreen tree hailed by the lore keepers and described as having a natural power that enabled this tree to live eternally. The legends attributed Sani with phenomenal intelligence, great wisdom, and keen foresight, for Sani was said to be one of the first living entities on the planet.

During Ra's exile from the Oralian Empire, Sani had become his mentor and guide. He taught Ra how to use his unique abilities to communicate with nature, which Sani referred to as "defero."

Sani had explained that defero was an ancient tradition from the Old World used to communicate between the visible and spiritual worlds of nature. By achieving this core wisdom from the deep past, Ra opened a doorway of communication with flora and fauna and therefore, he was bestowed the honor and title of Land Guardian of the Tall Forest.

Using defero, Sani now helped Ra to settle his vertigo. Ra quickly recovered from his struggle against the magical protection spell that—unbeknownst to Flayre—had been unleashed upon the land guardian.

Sani appeared in Ra's vision, merrily shifting the leaves and branches of his upper crown. This was the formal greeting of The Ancient One, and Ra was eternally grateful for the help. Ra knew that it had taken tremendous effort on The Ancient One's part to aid him as he did.

Ra's vision suddenly shifted, and his mind was whisked to a different part of the forest where his thoughts were suddenly assaulted by many beings.

The sentinel trees in the Tall Forest were conversing, sending their distress down into the earth and rustling their leaves in indignation. Their anger was directed at raiders who had invaded the southwestern side of the forest. There were far more interlopers than the woodland had ever seen.

These two-footed creatures had come into their domain and trampled many young saplings as they made their journey through the forest lands. The trees wailed with the wind when the raiders used torches and were careless with their flames. The trees were in despair and suffered great anxiety over the axes and swords the raiders carried, knowing that they had cut and slashed without regard to their smaller brethren's fate as they built their campfires.

Each tree held its own great power, but these aggressive and armored, weapon-brandishing raiders with their short lifespans only had one thing on their minds, and that was warfare. They seemed unfeeling toward the great natural magic that flowed within the forest.

As land guardian, Ra respected the reality that trees were living beings and that improper pruning or cutting could permanently damage or kill them. He knew something had to be done. The system of life naturally thriving within the Tall Forest had been disrupted. The presence of these raiders was causing havoc amongst the native inhabitants that thrived within the great circle of being.

Spreading throughout the forest like wildfire, the information one tree gathered was transferred to the next, each forest sentinel adding its own flavor of thought and sensation to the notification it received and, thereafter, passing it along to the next tree. Within seconds, the magical maelstrom passed from his view, traveling to the heart of the forest. Ra felt a tingle as the magic swooped past. He knew the information the trees had gathered was being passed on to Sani.

The land guardian understood he would have to make the physical trip to see his guide and friend if he hoped to gather all the details of the mad dragon's plot and the trees' distress caused by the approaching forces. With the sensation of waking slowly from sleep, Ra emerged from his trance.

Ra felt his mother's healing touch upon his arm as reassuring warmth spread throughout his being. He was grateful for his mother's curative abilities, for it always seemed to set him right. With his dizziness now subsiding, he saw his father and Lucian arrive at his side to help him to his feet.

Ra paused a moment, closing his thoughts to the council's mind-probing inquiries. Though drained from his vision, there were many points to consider before he revealed the outcome of his visual perceptions to the dragon council. Their reaction would be one of dragon rage.

The Sacred Acts were the supreme laws and the moral foundation of those who dwell in the Oralian Empire. Flayre had committed many acts of betrayal against the Sacred Acts. The study of the black magic arts was crime enough, but the most horrific violation was the murder of men and dragons, including Kullipthius' beloved sire, Dra'khar.

"I know the dragon council has many questions," Ra explained. "However, as you are well aware, the imperator is the only one who has the authority to answer them."

Ra's weary gaze locked with his father's. "I have just been shown some valuable information regarding the armed men who are marching through the Tall Forest."

Kullipthius' eyes narrowed, and Ra knew it was in anticipation of his news and the growing tension in the room.

"Prithee, Father," Ra implored, "might I have a private moment?" Ra did not relish this announcement, but due to the nature of his gift, it was a burden for his shoulders alone, and a message best delivered discreetly. Excusing himself from his royal guest's company, Kullipthius led his son to the next chamber reserved for personal consultation.

Ra studied Kullipthius for a short moment. How, pray tell, does one express such harrowing news to the only father he had ever known and loved, realizing the impact it was sure to deliver to an already aching heart?

"This new vision confirms these forces marching upon our lands were not instigated by the people of Sapphirus. It is dragon born and instigated by ancient treachery."

Kullipthius' gaze held a glassy, far-off countenance, and Ra knew his father understood. Lightning crackled around Kullipthius' hands as he clenched them into tight fists. His father's body slowly began to sway and tremble, and his voice broke as it whispered, "Flayre."

Looking into his father's mind, Ra could see that his long-buried memories were now as fresh as yestereve, and rushing to the forefront of his mind. Ra knew that it took his father's entire strength and willpower not to succumb to the grief and fury that licked around his ever-rational mind. Kullipthius' mind was open to Ra, and the soothsayer observed the frustration mount as Kullipthius mentally examined his reign and knew the reappearance of this terrible menace could tear down his empire. Kullipthius' sizeable reserve nearly caved to the more primal side of his instincts.

Ra knew that Flayre had been a trusted and valuable confidant of the dragon council until the black arts stole his loyalty with the temptation of promised dark power. Every dragon in Oralia had reason to loathe this power-hungry abomination, though none more than Dra'khar's own son.

Being so young when it transpired, Kullipthius had then masked his emotional wounds. He had immediately become the new ruling Imperator of Oralia, never having had the chance to properly mourn Dra'khar's death. Subsequently, his empire and people became an all-encompassing, ever-important, and most welcomed distraction.

Now, with his past thrust so abruptly before him, anguish and resentment burst from the careful dam of his control. Ra had never seen his father so emotionally distraught. With fists clenched, Kullipthius' draconic gift of lightning charged the air without warning like a crackling tempest threatening destruction.

LALIAH was sitting within the council chambers, when she felt a disturbance that heightened her senses. Her gifts bloomed in response to the startling peril that presented itself in the surge of power that crackled through the air. Though her mate and son were beyond her line of sight, they were not out of range of her draconic senses. As her alarm heightened, she raced from the council chambers, not even bothering to excuse herself. She wanted to reach him before he lost himself to his suffering. She burst into the room, and her violet-blue eyes drank in the scene.

Kullipthius stood with eyes closed, his breath coming quickly. Laliah could sense him fighting against the growing tide of power his raging emotions had summoned. It was unheard of for her mate to be in such an agitated state. The news Ra had dispensed must have been something wretched indeed.

Within the blink of an eye, she conjured a healing and protection spell around Ra and herself and was at Kullipthius' side with her hands placed at his temples. She closed her eyes and sent her powers to cool and sooth his fuming mind. His grief was tangible, and his heartache enveloped her. Laliah's tears of sorrow gushed because of the unbearable anguish she saw emanating from her mate.

After a long moment, Laliah could feel Kulli's gut-wrenching pain mercifully begin to subside. His cobalt-blue eyes fell gratefully upon her face, and then a small grin appeared on his face when he lifted his eyes to her hair.

She reached up to find that her hair had become a wild halo from the lightning effects in the air. Laliah's cheeks blushed as she smiled back at Kullipthius. It was worth the discomfiture she felt just to see the smile on her emperor's face.

He took Laliah's small hands and entwined his fingers comfortingly with hers in gratitude. They bowed to touch foreheads in loving mental communication, and a lull of peace presented itself.

"Prithee, Ra," said Laliah in a composed voice, "your father has conveyed to me his wishes. Have Vahl Zayne escort the dragon lords to the training grounds, and then ask Lucian to meet with us here. The king should not be subjected to our anger. After our meeting, you will return and explain the situation to our dragon lords and let them properly vent. Remind them of their vows of silence."

RA KOR'EL exited the chamber, and he let out a relieved breath to relax his tense muscles before he rejoined the dragon lords. He paused to smooth his ruffled, silvery-white mane and robes with his clawed fingers. Though the soothsayer had known his safety was assured through both his farsighted talents and the reassuring bond of his mother's presence and healing abilities, he wished he did not have to deliver such news or bring about such vehemence and sorrow upon his father's heart.

Ra also knew he had to present his newfound information to Lucian. A nobleman was in Flayre's employ and must be wicked, indeed, to ally with this treacherous red dragon. Flayre was as infamous as he was cruel. Perhaps Lucian could offer some additional insights.

Ra entered the councilors' assembly room and was immediately surrounded by concerned faces. The commander and chief elder stood together, united in their apprehension, opposing viewpoints from moments passed now forgotten.

It was the imperial advisor who approached Ra as he entered the chamber. Vahl Zane pushed his spectacles higher on his nose and tilted his head slightly.

"What news, Your Highness?" His words were quiet, and worry showed plainly in his eyes.

Ra spoke quietly and calmly knowing all ears were bent to his every word. "My imperial family and I regret our abrupt departure, and I have come to carry out our Imperial Majesty's wishes. He asks that we take our usual allotted time for recess, and then we will meet at the training grounds where I shall make plain the details of my vision. Thereafter, all members of the High Council of Dragon Lords will be called. Prithee, Vahl Zayne, advise the dragon lords of my father's wishes, and I shall soon follow."

"As you wish, Your Highness," replied Vahl Zayne, and bowing respectfully he made his way to the dragon lords.

Ra turned to the king and said, "King Lucian, might I have a word?" Ra could sense unease in the king, though outwardly he did little to reveal his mood. Lucian's cinnamon-brown eyes were intensely focused on Ra's own. "I wanted to speak with you about the circumstances I foresaw in my vision. I could only receive bits and pieces, however, I do know there was a Sapphirian nobleman plotting and speaking of the army that threatens our lands. He spoke of a fortress lost that belonged to him, and I was curious if this held any meaning to you?"

Lucian's eyes hardened as he spoke. "Aye, indeed, his name is Danuvius. I received news of Danuvius' connection to this army from Captain Wellsbough and mentioned my suspicions to the imperator earlier this eve."

"If you would be so kind," said Ra, "I will take you to my imperial mother and father where we can discuss the details of my vision."

Ra led King Lucian to his mother and father. The chamber was awash with every possible shade of grey and blue, including the natural stone upon the floor. Elaborate carvings were etched in intricate designs upon the stone walls. The natural curves of the stones were accentuated by the complex workings of dragon imagination and polished fiercely to a high shine. The lantern lights were glowing softly, though everything seemed as clear as if it was brilliantly lit. It was like being outside in bright sunlight, though not straining on the eyes.

They crossed the distance to the far side of the space where Ra discovered his father looking pale from fatigue, lounging on a sumptuous mound of downy pillows. Laliah sat beside him, deep concentration showing on her features. She was drawing designs on his bare forearm with her fingertips, which left visible trails of intricate patterns of light along his skin.

"Sit, my friend, so that we may discuss Ra's findings during his vision. I am sure you have many questions." Kullipthius gestured graciously to another heap of plump pillows, and Lucian took his cue, sinking comfortably against them.

Ra took his position across from his mother. He folded his clawed hands upon his lap and instantly seemed to adopt an air of peace. His mother radiated an aura of tranquil serenity and Ra could see that Lucian was being soothed in it as well.

"I do regret the disruptions and the meeting's abrupt ending," Kullipthius apologized. "With all that has transpired, along with unfamiliar customs and procedures, I am sure this day has proven understandably unsettling and confusing."

"I was most concerned for you and your family," replied Lucian, "and I must admit I am relieved to see everyone in good spirits."

"Gramercy for your concern, Lucian, however you need not worry," said Ra. "My mother's healing effects are filling our inner wellsprings as we speak, placing us in a contented state of health and wellbeing. All is well, I assure you." Ra gave the king an encouraging smile.

"We are all friends, here," said Kullipthius. "All of us here have a great respect for you, Lucian. I do hope you feel welcomed in Oralia."

"Most welcomed," said Lucian.

"Through my soothsaying gifts," explained Ra, "we now have no doubt that this strife and concern of the approaching force has been caused by dragon claw. This enemy's treachery runs deep, and his schemes are far-reaching. Dragons are most patient and can lie in wait for decades because of their lengthy lifespans. That is why dragon scouts patrol our borders constantly to prevent any dragons—rogue or otherwise—from entering our lands.

"The ruby dragon named Flayre is the one instigating this force. Even though we know it is the Liltians marching toward Terra Leone, they are unaware of who is behind the curtain pulling the strings. We are most distressed by this new information. Our biggest concern is that he is a practitioner of black magic."

"Although the news of this treacherous dragon concerns me greatly," said Lucian, concern written clearly on his features, "I have the utmost confidence in the dragon empire's stratagems and capabilities. I hope you know I will do whatever I can in support."

"We will work together on this, Lucian. You have my word," pledged Kullipthius.

"I do have some information that may be of use," said Lucian. "Eralon came upon a brigand who believed that, by my decree, their kindred are being held hostage and used as slave laborers." Lucian also explained the story of how Danuvius had taken over Terra Leone, possibly killing his own brother before escaping.

Laliah frowned. "That sounds like one of Flayre's schemes. Long and ago, this red dragon was known for spreading such rumors and causing much treachery. I would wager Flayre had gathered shape-shifting dragons to pose as Liltians to motivate these unsuspecting forces into action."

"It seems this treachery is aimed at both our lands, Kullipthius," said Lucian. "Mayhap it is he who wants the populace of Sapphirus as slaves for himself and his ruby dragon followers."

Kullipthius nodded his head in agreement. "Since we now know part of Flayre's schemes and that Danuvius is working at his side, we can direct our efforts accordingly."

"I must warn you there is something in Danuvius' appearance that is not right," advised Ra, "though as of yet, I am unable to determine what it is. Nevertheless, he is definitely under a dark magic spell."

"Since Lucian's captain has dealt with this Danuvius firsthand," added Laliah, "we should question Eralon and see what other information can be gleaned for our cause."

"My thought as well, dear-heart," said Kullipthius.

"I agree, Laliah," said Lucian. "I shall make the arrangements for us to meet with the captain."

Ra faced the king and his royal family with intense, cat-like eyes. "From all the information I have obtained regarding this matter, there is one thing of which I am certain; Flayre does not know that Oralia and Avala are on to his schemes. That gives us a great advantage."

Lucian picked up on this thought, his eyes glowing with realization. "This will make him certain in his actions, falsely secure in his hopes for victory, and prone to miscalculations we can exploit."

"Aye, precisely," said Kullipthius. "I believe we should make it a priority to locate these armed mercenaries. We must learn where and when they plan to launch their assaults so we can take action and stop this before things get out of control."

"Do you have a plan, Kullipthius?" asked Lucian.

"I propose we send our dragon scouts who can alter into the human form to enter the mercenaries' encampment. They can hide in plain sight, so to speak, to scavenge for clues as to the reasons for this puzzling crusade. That way, we can collect valuable information to determine our best options."

"An excellent tactic," said Ra.

Lucian nodded. "Mayhap we could come up with a way to have the dragon scouts send these Liltian mercenaries to the safety of Terra Leone to keep them away from Flayre and his plans."

"Brilliant," replied Ra. Laliah and Kullipthius agreed.

"If it pleases Your Majesties," added Ra, "I have a suggestion to go along with our plans. We could take a small band of our own, mayhap three or four representatives from both Oralia and Avala, and make camp within the Tall Forest where I can speak to The Ancient One directly.

"Sani stands in the middle of the Tall Forest, giving us a better advantage to act, if necessary. He has a direct link to all the trees of the forest and can keep us abreast of the force's position at all times. After the scouts collect their information, they can meet us where Sani stands."

"Agreed," said Lucian

"I concur," said Kullipthius.

Laliah spoke next. "I am glad for your forethought, Ra. I believe we must concentrate on Flayre's involvement. There may be other dangers we have yet to discover, since he is not only a danger to Oralia but to all the inhabitants of Sapphirus."

"Aye, My Empress," said Kullipthius. "We should ready the Imperial Champions for any possible attack on our lands."

"We should place them on constant alert while patrolling our borders," added Laliah. "We cannot have Flayre or those under his wing, flying over the city of Kaleidos or any other populated settlements."

"We will double the watches and send our dragon champions and scouts to protect our borders," said Kullipthius.

"The season's festival outside the city of Kaleidos' gates is due to end upon the morrow," said King Lucian. "I will send the Elite Guardsmen out to hurry along any stragglers."

"Would you like me to send a few of our amber quartz dragons to aid your guards?" asked Kullipthius. "With their gift of influence they could make sure the festival participants leave in a timely manner, and take the appropriate routes to assure their safety."

"Gramercy, that would be most appreciated, Kullipthius," said Lucian.

"With our agreement established, Lucian, we should allow you to take your leave to meet with your council, and I will advise the dragon lords of our plans. I will send word by messenger when we are ready to meet with our group that will be going to where Sani stands."

As everyone rose to leave, Ra turned to speak to Lucian. "Might I offer additional insight?"

"Aye, certainly, Ra," responded Lucian.

"Firstly, I want to apologize for calling you away from your family when they arrived at Moorwyn Castle this morning. We kept you so busy that you did not get a chance to visit with them."

"No apology is necessary, Ra," said Lucian. "Dryden is aware I must answer when duty calls."

"In addition, your captain will arrive at the castle this day with two traveling companions. It has been brought to my awareness that this trio will be vital to our plans. My intuition tells me that all three can be trusted, and they should not be overlooked as part of our defensive force."

"I know my captain can be trusted," said Lucian. "I have complete faith in my captain's loyalty and your intuition, Ra. Consider it done."

CHAPTER FOURTEEN

W ith every fragment of his being, Scale wished he was in his own reptilian body. He was dangling from Flayre's sharp-edged claws in Danuvius' frail form. Scale tightened his grip around the ruby dragon's piercing talons as they tore into his shoulders. The red beast back-winged harshly, which caused the surrounding greenery to whip about in a turbulent frenzy as they arrived at their destination. Scale closed his eyes to block out as much of the dust and debris from the wind-stirred terrain as possible.

"Incidentally, the last time I was in the Desertlands, it came to my attention that your mate, Sauria, was expecting," advised Flayre. *"I allowed her to change to her chameleon form so she could care for her hatchlings once they are born. She is now caged with a healthy clutch of eggs and all are doing well. Congratulations."*

"I am to be a father?" asked Scale aloud, wondering if he should be pleased or fearful of Flayre's intended purpose in sharing this news. "When can I visit them?"

"Your mind should be on completing your assignment, Scale. If my instructions are not followed to the letter, you will never see your family again! Is that understood?"

At the same time that Flayre's departing snarl of threatening words screamed into his mind, Scale found himself in a heart-pounding, free-falling descent.

The evil dragon had not given any thought, or perhaps he had, about where he would land, because Flayre had dropped him into a large, muddy pond. Soaked and sputtering, Scale vowed that the ruby would pay if he harmed his new family.

He flailed upon the murky bank until he finally pulled himself onto dry land and took note of his location. He was not far from where he had left the two guards to tend the horses and the camp. He noted that the screen of trees would have concealed Flayre's approach and departure.

Danuvius' body was much too confining and slow, and he had not the weapons of tooth, claw, and venom he was accustomed to. How he longed for his natural state. He wanted to drive his fangs and talons into the red tyrant's hide, end Flayre's worthless existence, and become blessedly free from the red's black magic spell.

Scale looked at his sopping, ruined finery and sighed. Flayre's claws had caused nasty rents and punctures in his shoulder, and there was blood covering the elaborate material. Then an idea came to mind. Perhaps he should use Flayre's cruelty to his advantage. He needed to spin a tale for the two guards he had left at camp, and his appearance would help him look the part of a wounded survivor. Though the wounds caused him little harm, the blood stains on his clothes offered an appropriately gory testimony. He had a knack for healing quickly, even in Danuvius' form, and his wounds would mend themselves before the day was out.

He bent down to study his image in a rain puddle and tried on a miserable and desperate countenance. "Alas, the others put forth their best efforts when the king's men attacked us!" He applauded himself for his superb performance and wolfishly smiled at his reflection in the unclean water.

He rose and headed for the outline of the trees that were surrounding the tents, wondering if he would be able to see his younglings hatch or his mate, ever again.

Thoughts of his mate halted at the crisp snap of the twig that now rested uncomfortably underfoot. Scale seethed as he surveyed the tattered remnants of what was once his camp. His elaborate tent was gone. His warhorse and armor were counted amongst the finer things missing. His clothing was ransacked, the best taken. He found his large travel chest overturned in the mud with nothing left but filth. His brother's ornate sword was missing as was what remained of the strongbox of coin Flayre had given him to hire the sell-swords and mercenaries. They must have absconded with their newly acquired treasures upon horseback. He was sure they had set the remaining horses free because saddles and bridles were lying haphazardly about.

Resentment and hot rage consumed him, and his screams echoed through the trees. In a fit, he lost all restraint. He grabbed the nearest items and flung them viciously, cursing the absent men for their filching. He should hunt them both down for pilfering his fine garments and ruining his belongings.

Scale exhaled noisily in exasperation and mentally took a step back from his anger, dropping the empty scabbard he clutched in white knuckles. He had to forcibly remind himself that he was not Danuvius. He took a panting yet steadying breath.

Scale had spent far too long in Danuvius' form and persona. It was truly overwhelming at times. Scale wondered if it was this imprisoning enchantment that caused him to feel this Liltian's personality so strongly. It was likened to being forced to lie in one position too long or wearing clothes three sizes too small, your body unable to stretch out in full. Life as Danuvius was cramped and crowded and claustrophobic, his true potential straining against these hated bonds that enslaved him. And all the while Danuvius' memories whispered, seduced, and provoked his senses. Flayre was going to die a slow and painful death once Scale escaped his magical bindings.

He looked again at the pitiable hodgepodge remnants of base camp and pounded at his head while trying to think rationally. Had the two men he had tried to deceive with promises of riches caught on that something was amiss? When he had taken their comrades-in-arms on a march to the reviled ruby's lair, had they suspected they would never return, or were they simply common, petty thieves? At the end of his considerations, he had to concede that it truly mattered naught. He was stuck in the present situation, and he did not dare return to the caves and hope for understanding. This would just be another failure heaped upon Scale, even though there had been nothing he could have done to foresee or prevent it.

He came upon a packed rucksack half-buried under the remains of a smashed crate. There had once been the finest vintage wines contained within that crate, along with wine goblets and matching decanter. Mourning the broken crystal, he opened the rucksack. He was elated to discover clothing of about his size, even though it lightly smelled of wine and was slightly damp on the hem of the leggings from where the top of the pack had come untied. He quickly changed out of his mud-ruined garb. He had to roll the sleeves of the brown tunic to his elbows and belt the middle to help the scavenged clothing fit properly. The boots in the pack were well-crafted but too large around the upper calf, so he rolled the bottom of his pants up to his calf to help keep the boots from sliding down.

Just then he smelled something burning and glanced at the fire pit. The cooking pot had fallen off its tripod and spilled half the food into the mud. What little food that remained in the pot was burned beyond recognition, for it had fallen atop the hot cinders. His stomach growled. He dumped out the rest of the contents of the knapsack and counted two rations of dried and salted meat, cheese and a skin of water. At least he would not starve to death. He would forage for other sustenance while making his tedious journey through the wilderness.

He knew how to hunt with the supreme perfection of a reptile. Hunting with hawk, arrow, or snare was uncomfortably foreign to him. He understood the "how" of the process through the memories of Danuvius, and he even pulled the feats off masterfully when he was in Terra Leone, but he did not have the patience or the gear necessary to accomplish the act had he been so inclined. He was about to go off on another bruising rant against those who had done this to him when, of a sudden, he heard a soft whinny. He looked up and spied a lone, unsaddled grey horse in the distance. His grin was toothy. Perhaps his recent string of unfortunate circumstances was about to change after all.

CHAPTER FIFTEEN

"Truthfully, mine eyes are blessed by your very visage!" said Lucian. He was pleased to see his family safely within Moorwyn Castle's walls.

"Oh, Uncle Lucian!" Aurora Leigh ran to Lucian's open arms and was grandly embraced. "It has been ages. Pray tell, where have you been hiding yourself? I have missed you dreadfully."

Lucian beamed with delight. "My favorite niece," he stated with pride. He always doted over Aurora Leigh. He could not have loved her more if she were his own daughter.

"Truth be told, I am your only niece and I want you all to myself."

"Behave, Aurora Leigh," scolded Lucian's sister-in-law, Isa Dora, in her usual good-natured tone, "and mind your manners, dear."

The Duchess of Ghent then smiled at Lucian and curtsied. "We were most pleased to receive your invitation, Lucian. It has been quite some time since last Aurora Leigh and I visited the castle."

"Isa Dora, you look the picture of health. Given the chance, I would give you a proper reception. However, it seems this young maiden here has captured my attentions with quite a strong grip."

"She takes after her mother," laughed Prince Dryden.

"Dryden!" exclaimed Isa Dora, blushing. "Honestly, Lucian these two are the reason I carry this fan!" With her feather and jewel-encrusted fan fluttering, Isa Dora tried her best to pout, but could not help joining in the family's laughter.

"Let loose your grip upon my brother, Aurora Leigh," said

Dryden with a smile. "He needs a good, hearty greeting." Aurora Leigh did as she was bid while Dryden and Lucian grabbed one another's right wrists and touched opposing shoulders to deliver a good, old-fashioned slap-on-the-back welcome.

"Dryden, it is good to see you again, and I am pleased you could make it here so quickly. Let us break our fast, and then you can return to your quarters and rest. I know you could not have slept well last night with all that traveling."

The king smiled at his sister-in-law and said, "Isa Dora, what say you and Aurora Leigh meet us in the tower's dining chamber for our morning meal? The kitchen is expecting you. Dryden and I have business to discuss and will meet you there before long."

"Did you inform Cookie we were coming?" asked Aurora Leigh, using the nickname she had given the king's personal cook. "Did she make my favorite sweet cakes?"

"I am sure that, as you approach my quarters, you will be able to identify a sweet aroma coming from the baking ovens." No further prompting was needed. Lucian smiled as he watched mother and daughter stroll away arm in arm.

Lucian then turned to speak to his younger sibling. "I regret I had to roust you from your warm bed in the middle of the night, Dryden. I have received new information since our last meeting regarding the mystery of the approaching armsmen. I am going to be away from the castle for a time, and I will need you here to make sure things are running smoothly. Come, let us walk and I will explain."

Lucian draped an arm over his brother's shoulders. He explained the gravity of the situation, telling Dryden that he would be leaving soon with the dragons to take care of the force marching upon their lands with whatever means and measures that entailed.

"Kullipthius and I decided it best to take to the Tall Forest whereupon we shall gather information deemed necessary to stop this force from causing any further concern. We will take a small force only, teamed with the necessary Avalians and Oralians, to take care of this situation as swiftly and peacefully as possible."

Dryden knew the inhabitants of Oralia well, and Lucian watched as concern washed over his brother's features. If might was called for, it did not need to be pointed out that things had taken a turn for the worse since they had last met.

"Ra deemed it necessary that Eralon and two others could be trusted to join our ranks," continued Lucian. "You will be left in charge here at Moorwyn to take care of the castle and her people and all the realm's dealings during my absence. Gregor will be at your disposal, and Knight Master Osualt will be left in charge of the guardsmen."

Dryden nodded and said, "You have my allegiance, my brother. I shall take care of everything while you are away."

Lucian gave his brother a nod. He was confident and trusting with the monarchy resting in his brother's capable hands. "There is one more important directive, and this one comes from my heart," continued the king. "We do not know what the outcome of this situation will be. I must insist you take the usual precautions and urge you and the family to stay within the safety of the castle walls until everything is resolved."

"I will do whatever it takes to keep things in order here, including the safety of our family," reassured Prince Dryden. "You can count on it."

"I have always been able to count on you, brother."

Breaking fast with his family had always been a most pleasant affair for Lucian. It was times like these that made him realize how much he treasured having family around. Aurora Leigh's laughter and innocence, Isa Dora's gentle demeanor, and his brother's companionship had been sorely missed. He made a mental note to invite them to the castle more frequently.

They had just finished when a messenger arrived with a missive from Oralia. It stated all was ready and that Kullipthius was awaiting his arrival. Lucian excused himself, and Dryden gave him a knowing nod.

Lucian made his way back to his private chambers. He bathed and his master of the wardrobe brought him fresh attire. Once dressed and alone, he scrubbed a tired hand down his face as he studied himself before a looking glass. A knock at the door dragged him from his private musings. A royal guard crossed the threshold and bowed. The king bid him speak.

"Captain Wellsbough and two companions are requesting an audience, Your Majesty."

"Very well, you may usher them to the throne room," replied Lucian.

It seemed the time had come for Eralon to be introduced to the dragon empire, just as his father had been before him, the previous Captain of the King's Elite Guardsmen, Xavian Wellsbough. Only this time, two more would join the ranks of the privileged few. Ra's revelations had proved accurate once again. It was a rare gift indeed, having a soothsayer such as Ra Kor'el around.

Cape billowing regally behind him as he entered the throne room, Lucian ascended the platform to assume his throne and receive his guests. Lucian then bid his captain and travel-worn companions to rise.

"I bid you greetings and well met, Captain Wellsbough, and to you as well, Scout Jhain." He recognized Jhain, of course, with his easy demeanor, significant talents, and the mystique of his background. He had always stood apart from Eralon's men in the king's eyes. But it was the stranger standing at his captain's right elbow, with head bowed, that drew his notice. Something about the foreigner and the way he dressed in the old Liltian uniforms screamed of unknown importance, and this insistence would not leave Lucian's awareness. With certainty, he would have the mystery solved before passing any pertinent and confidential information unto his captain. Eye on the unfamiliar guest, the king remarked, "I see we have a visitor, Captain Wellsbough."

"Your Majesty," Eralon said as he acknowledged his king with a bow of his head. He then gestured to the tall, dark stranger. "May I introduce Treyven Fontacue, formerly from Liltimer and here because of his own good judgment and my approval, for he has much to tell regarding Danuvius Doral."

The king was taken by surprise when he heard the Liltian's name. Lucian studied the fellow before him. The man held the hard-edged look of a soldier, and Lucian surmised that he had seen and endured much.

Lucian smiled and nodded, as he asked, "Fontacue is it? Any relation to the healer in Grennan Village named Arland Fontacue?"

A look of puzzlement crossed Treyven's features and he responded, "Aye, Yer Majesty, that would be me father."

"I came across your father when the Elite Guardsmen and I were traveling to Sunon to visit King Doros," explained King Lucian. "A band of thieves surprised us on our travels when they emerged from the dense underbrush that bordered both sides of the road. Using the element of surprise, the thieves believed that they had us captured. Nevertheless, it was not long before Eralon and his guards had the matter well in hand, and it was over with very quickly. Unfortunately, I received a flesh wound from a stray arrow. Grennan Village was nearby and your father tended my wound."

Lucian had more to tell Treyven; it had to do with a promise he had made long ago. Certes Ra, crafty dragon and clever soothsayer that he was, had to have known something of Treyven accompanying Eralon this day. For the time being, Lucian told himself, this promise would have to be placed on hold until the right opportunity presented itself.

"Treyven Fontacue, I bid you welcome to Moorwyn Castle. If you have our captain's approval, you most certainly have mine."

"Gra'mercy, Yer Majesty," Treyven said, and then he displayed the fist over heart salute and bow, as was customary of Liltians.

Course clear, Lucian rose and crossed the distance to stand before the trio. "We have a task to perform. On our way, we can have that conversation about Danuvius Doral."

Lucian beckoned them follow to the furthest corner of the throne room. Little did those who followed know that they would soon embark on a journey that few have ever traveled.

King Lucian's burning torch was the only source of illumination pressing back the darkness as the foursome made their way through the long, winding passageway within the mountains of Kaleidos. As he walked before the group, Lucian felt a small, private smile grace his lips in the memory of Eralon's perplexity, as indicated by the infamous raised eyebrow, when he discovered the shrouded doorway back in the throne room.

Eralon was so much like his father, Xavian, knowing his place, remaining the king's ever-noble confidant able to conceal a look of surprise, a gasp, concern, dread, or laughter. Whatever the occasion, Eralon and his late father had always presented themselves as honorable, worthy advocates for the throne. However, Lucian knew them both to be so much more. He knew them as his friends.

As they traveled, Lucian turned his head toward Treyven and said, "Tell me, Treyven, of Danuvius' plans and what you know of these approaching forces."

Treyven was quick to reply. "Guards from Terra Leone found me band an' me in a settlement on the northwestern coast o' Sunon. They be bearing an urgent message from Danuvius asking if we be willing ta fight fer the Liltians. He said he be paying handsomely. In the missive, he asked me ta meet with him at a place near our settlement.

"When I met with Danuvius, he had Liltians with him ta corroborate his story. He said many o' our people be missing around the country an' taken as slaves ta yer castle. The Liltians themselves spoke o' their brethren disappearing from their homes leaving many a family bereft with young'uns unable ta fend fer themselves. He had heard that I be a leader o' men, an' he invited me ta lead a band o' armsmen ta the castle, fer he knew many would follow. He also mentioned a 'secret army' he was assembling that could nay be defeated.

"After talking ta Cap'n Wellsbough in the wood an' checking with me brethren in Terra Leone, I knew who the traitor truly be. Now me brethren-in-arms remain at Terra Leone ta stand with Knight Master Balderon, an' I told 'em ta follow his orders."

Eralon confirmed Treyven's information and then held out a folded map to Lucian. "I believe the red markings on the map indicate Danuvius' intended path and targets," concluded Eralon.

Lucian paused in the passageway to study the map. He handed Eralon the torch and unfolded the map. Under the flickering torchlight he noted a red line of arrows heading north from Sunon to the Fortress of Terra Leone, then east through the Tall Forest on a secluded path to Moorwyn Castle. Both the fortress and castle were circled in red.

Lucian agreed with Eralon's conclusion. He folded the map and tucked the parchment into an inner pocket of his surcoat. He took back the torch and they resumed their journey. "I want the three of you to join me in a meeting so we can discuss this and prepare for any difficulties that may arise. The more information we have, the better off we shall be. That is where we are headed now."

After a goodly distance, comparable to a leisurely walk within the twists and turns of his castle's labyrinth, Lucian saw a gentle glow seeping bravely through the obscurity ahead. He led his small group closer to the luminous source.

The trio followed Lucian across a threshold and into a huge receiving area with its ceiling heights lost to the shadows beyond the torchlight. This large, circular chamber was the meeting place for other passages that emptied into this one vast chamber lined with doors and portals. The cavern walls were filled with fist-sized chunks of gold. Lucian's torchlight bounced off the surfaces of the gold, and amber light buttered the walls and faces of those who passed its glory.

The king led them to a recessed area displaying an extravagant feast on a long, stone table that was placed in the center of the room. Plate after plate was arranged atop its polished surface, holding enough food and decanters of wine to serve a king and his court.

Large stone benches were carved into the rock walls, and someone had taken the time to decorate the offered seating with a multitude of plump pillows. Lucian placed his torch in a holder above the seating area.

Lucian noticed Chief Romus standing at formal attention dressed in the rich colors of his sophisticated uniform as guardian of the realm. He was so still, he gave the impression he was a part of the curious surroundings and was, at first, overlooked by the new guests. Lucian had to admit the man certainly looked a part of his element. His features were appealing with amber, wolf-like eyes, bright and sharp. He was tall and broad-shouldered with a sun-kissed skin tone. His blond hair was spiky and held a tawny hue. A silken headband enveloped a cluster of amber quartz crystals, marking him a Jeweled dragon.

It was quite unfortunate that the chieftain's particular type of dragon belonged to one of those groups whose numbers were so dangerously low that they were endangered. Lucian recalled from a long conversation with Kullipthius that Romus was of royal descent who hailed from a land far and away called the Desertlands. Dragon history was extensive indeed, and with the gathering of the varied draconic types here in the empire, it was difficult for Lucian to truly determine or understand their rankings.

It was a pity that the vast majority of the reclusive reds could not get along with other species of dragons, for the original desert homelands of the ruby and amber quartz dragons were one and the same. While living in the Desertlands, the amber quartzes were nomadic, preferring peace to fighting over land which, in their beliefs, belonged to none.

It took many ruby dragons to overwhelm even one amber quartz. This is because the amber quartz dragons' gift of influence kept the ruby dragons at bay. But that fact did not stop the red behemoths from ambushing the amber quartzes and doing whatever it took to try to wipe them from existence in a mad bid to keep all of the desert sands for themselves. Their hatred and rivalry seemed boundless. Nevertheless, Chief Romus was kind and patient, though fierce when necessary. He enjoyed his self-chosen post and made the perfect guardian of, quite literally, anything.

Lucian marched straight toward Romus to bring the others' attention to him, bowed his head in greeting for the benefit of his companions, hoping to set them at ease. "Greetings and well met, Chief Romus."

"Hail and well met, King Lucian." Romus bowed formally to the visiting ruler and gave a nod to His Majesty's guests. "I was advised by our imperator to be expecting you. I pray your pardon while I announce your arrival."

By the startled look on his companions' faces, Lucian surmised they had missed the guardian's appearance due to his unique gift of influence. Jhain, in particular, was looking the most ruffled, for he was unaccustomed to being taken unaware. He was glancing around and scratching absently at the back of his head, an act he was often seen performing when contemplating unfamiliar territory while scouting. Lucian smiled upon seeing the behavior.

Romus turned from his position to rap upon a door to his left. A wooden window set high in the middle of the door opened inward, and a pair of inquisitive eyes with bushy-brows came into view. The eyes peered at Romus for a moment, scanned those standing behind him, and without a word spoken, the window shut.

Returning to the king and his guests, Romus said, "His Imperial Majesty shall arrive momentarily. While you wait, we have prepared a feast for your enjoyment."

Romus returned to his formal position next to the entrance and stood at attention.

The table's centerpiece held an arrangement of large colorful feathers, violets, and green branches tied together with vines of honeysuckle. Around this showpiece was a loin of veal, civet of hare, two enormous meat pies, and two chickens glazed in egg yolks and sprinkled with spices.

Four mouthwatering sweet dishes, one placed at each of the table's four corners, were displayed upon gilt-rimmed serving dishes. There was a platter of creamy white cheese cut into slices and topped with fresh strawberries, a tray full of almond cream tarts, a bowl of figs covered in sauce and pomegranate seeds and, lastly, a serving pot of apricots stewed in a sweet wine medley. With a tantalizing aroma seeping from each dish, who could resist?

The trio followed Lucian to the table. The king chose a decanter containing an amber liquid with the aroma of a sweet-spiced cider. A bouquet of apples, pears, and cinnamon filled his senses as he poured the beverage into four goblets. The king raised his chalice and nodded to his companions to join him in a toast.

"To adventure," he stated with a knowing smile. They returned his gesture, and each downed their drinks before setting about to fill their plates.

Soon after their meal, the door swung open and Romus announced, "His Imperial Majesty Kullipthius, Imperator of the Oralian Empire." Romus then turned to bow before the figure who stepped from the shadows to greet them.

The imperator was lavishly attired in rich layers of the finest silk. His blue underlayment had long, fitted sleeves and was worn under a white silken over-robe that hung shorter in front and draped to the knee in back. A wide, black leather panel belted his garments in place. The panel was embroidered with a silvery dragon and adorned with emerald cabochon eyes. His form-fitting black breeches were neatly tucked into black leather, knee-high boots ornately festooned with gold embellishments along the outer side of each boot. Over his attire the imperator wore a black silken mantle, patterned and luxuriantly embroidered with a thin thread of gold, set with precious stones and tiny, colorful, freshwater pearls. Upon his head he wore a black silk diadem, a diamond encased in platinum at its center. The silken fabric was decorated in the same opulent manner to match his cloak and boots. There was something in Kullipthius' appearance and mannerisms that marked him a ruler that Lucian knew his three companions could not miss.

CHAPTER SIXTEEN

K ullipthius knew the three men who had accompanied Lucian
were trustworthy from previous talks with Lucian and his
own investigations. However, it was the young scout Jhain who
had drawn his attention.

Jhain was a master in wilderness survival and exhibited an
innate sense of things. The lad took pride in knowing he could
quickly gauge his environment to ascertain danger. With a
heightened awareness, he noticed even the most minuscule
details, and Kullipthius knew the wheels in his head where
churning at full capacity.

The minute the imperator stepped into the secret passageway,
Kullipthius heard Jhain's mind start to assess his surroundings.

The scout's mind was filled with probing questions: What was
the reason for the secrecy of the passageway? Why is there a need
for someone standing guard at these doors? What would await
them on the other side?

Kullipthius knew the answers to these questions would come
soon enough when they crossed the threshold into his dragon
empire.

Kullipthius smiled at Lucian as they each nodded their heads in
a greeting. Following propriety, the others dropped to one knee in
respect and curiosity, wondering exactly who this ruler was,
meeting them in the caves of Kaleidos Peak.

"You may rise," began Kullipthius. "I bid you welcome, King
Lucian and guests." He watched as his three new guests rose. The
imperator could not help but hear Jhain's continuing thoughts.

"The hairs on the back o' me neck are responding ta this monarch as if he be a fierce Vashirian desert cat ready ta pounce," thought Jhain. *"It be best ta remain wary of me surroundings, for no matter how prettily wrapped in ribbons this package may be, something is screaming at me ta remain alert."*

Kullipthius smiled to himself, bemused by Jhain's descriptive thoughts.

The imperator looked upon Jhain and his two travel companions and said, "Verily, it is a delight to have all of you here, for only a few are ever received beyond these doorways, outside of those whom reside within. As King Lucian can attest, your arrival has been anticipated. Providing you hold to the warranted rules, a pact both your king's ancestors and mine had agreed upon, you shall be allowed passage within our halls.

"Once admitted, you will be in the Oralian Empire and under our laws." He smiled and continued, "Lucian has vouched for the three of you, so we shall move on without hesitation."

Kullipthius then turned to the young scout who stood a little straighter under the scrutiny of the imperator's intense gaze. "Scout Jhain, long have we marked you."

Jhain arched his brows at the comment.

The imperator then paused and gave Jhain a smile. "Pray pardon, the inference was not intended to come across as a desert cat would taunt his prey. The empire considers you a fine, accomplished woodsman and a gifted scout, displaying a keen awareness. You are a fine defensive combatant for one of your age and rank, and you follow the laws of the land.

"Make no mistake: If any of you deviate from your oath, swift and sure punishment will be forthcoming. So I ask you, Jhain Velendris, will you uphold your honor and swear under agreement with your king and me that you will never reveal the existence of my empire's whereabouts, its inhabitants, our shrouded passageways and tunnels to and from Moorwyn, or what lies beyond this door?"

Jhain appeared flabbergasted. At the mention of his full given name, his youthful face contorted into utter bewilderment. It was times like these Kullipthius enjoyed having highly reliable sources—and being able to listen in on someone's thoughts always helped. Lucian had once confessed to him that even the best informants in his employ had not been able to glean any knowledge or history of the scout.

"As a desert cat would his prey? Wait one moment," pondered Jhain, as he remembered using that same comparison. *"It canna*

be possible. 'Twas if he be reading me mind."

Kullipthius watched as Jhain shook his head and smiled at his bemused wonderings. Then he looked into the imperator's eyes for a moment.

"Nay," he thought dismissing it. *"But there is something about this imperator; I just canna put me finger on it . . . yet."* A lock of ink-dark hair fell in front of his eyes as he made a courtly bow.

"I, Jhain Velendris, will uphold Yer Majesties' agreement upon me honor, I do so swear."

Kullipthius turned to Eralon and continued. "Captain Eralon Wellsbough, I understand swearing an oath without fully comprehending what it is you are swearing to is vexing and warrants some trepidation. Nevertheless, I must make the request. Your esteemed father, Captain Xavian Wellsbough, took this very same vow I offer you. He was a good man, Eralon, and upheld his agreement impeccably. I would be grateful this day if you would swear under agreement with your king and me to the same rules I explained to Jhain Velendris."

Kullipthius watched Eralon look over to his king, who gave him a nod. Then he bowed his head to Kullipthius as he answered truthfully, "I do so swear, Your Majesties."

Kullipthius smiled and looked upon the last member of King Lucian's entourage.

"Treyven Fontacue of the former country of Liltimer, you are known by your fellow brethren-in-arms as a hireling for any noble cause to help your countrymen. I do know that if you swear an oath, your word is your bond. What say you of the aforementioned pledge?"

Treyven gave pledge with fist over heart and said, "On me honor, I do so swear."

Kullipthius looked pleased. "Our agreement has been so sealed."

A youth chose this moment to move hesitantly from the shadows of a doorway and make his way over to Kullipthius' side in the reception hall. The imperator then introduced Andro as the youngest son of Chief Romus, who was there for the changing of the guard.

Of Chief Romus' three sons, Andro was the most sociable. His features favored his sire's, aristocratic and appealing, and though by all appearances to the newcomers he was young, his eyes held the same ancient wisdom of other dragons. He may have been considered a "nestling" by the dragons at fifteen yearmarks, yet he was easily double his age in maturity, for dragons mature at a different rate.

Kullipthius watched Romus' eyes turn prideful upon seeing his offspring. He moved to his boy and welcomed him, placing his calloused hand carefully against the boy's cheek. The dragons were always openly affectionate. Andro's lips quirked into a wide smile, and he suddenly seemed more at ease in his sire's presence. They bowed to one another, and Andro took up the spear from Romus, and stood guard in his father's place.

As they crossed from kingdom to dragondom, Kullipthius provided each of his guests with a burning torch for their safety while traversing the mountain's dark chambers. As they made their trek through the caves, their light source dappled the walls in orange and yellow waves.

Kullipthius watched the faces of his followers as they took in the precious crystals and gold that decorated the cavern walls, and the fanciful formations that dropped like icicles from above. They stared in awe at the various rock formations that sprouted from the floor like plump toadstools. When they came to a place where stairs were cut into the side of the cavern, they followed Kullipthius up its steep side.

After the incline leveled out, the light of day shone ahead, and Kullipthius and company placed their extinguished torches in the sconces that lined the wall. They noticed tree roots clinging to the rocky walls as they moved out of the cave's mouth and followed a winding, open-air path. They continued their journey until they came upon a wide, open space overlooking a rocky crag. The view from the edge seemed to stretch forever as it revealed a marvelous, unspoiled vista. The air was crisp and cool with a teasing wind smoothly tugging garments and ruffling hair. It was a breathtaking perspective that sparked the sensation of being on top of the world. Kullipthius knew they were all captivated by their surroundings. Since their arrival upon the summit, not a word had been spoken as they drank in the vision before them.

A breeze originated west of their stance and brought the sweet aroma of floralberries. The wild floralberry patch, with its curling leaves and dainty, lavender-colored flowers, sprang from under an outcropping of jagged rock, and a vast field of the vegetation flooded the sloping hillside in a sea of purple. This colorful sight fluttered and rippled in the wind like ocean waves. While delectable by the handful, the rich display of the fruit's promised harvest would have been a vintner's delight. The floralberry was not plentiful because it was so difficult to cultivate, and yet if aged just right, it made for a fine wine indeed.

To the north, a hidden inlet was fed from the sparkling blue waters of the Carillion Sea. Within the cove many small islands rose up in the distant waters.

"The inlet below is known to us as Serenity Bay," said Kullipthius. "There are numerous hollowed-out limestone islands that boast caverns and grottos where many of the inhabitants of Oralia make their homes. These islands within the bay are linked closely, despite their variation in size, to form a natural barrier that keeps the bay, and Oralia, concealed from the rest of the world."

Kullipthius then pointed to the east. "The mountains rising above the clouds are the highest peaks of Kaleidos." They gazed at a massive waterfall that tumbled from the clouds into a large lake. "Our empire first originated in a valley at the base of that great waterfall."

As Kullipthius was giving his guests their visual tour, three young men had emerged from the path and were making their way toward them.

"King Lucian, may I present to you our Oralian scouts Swift, Kayne, and Talin." The three bowed before the king, and Lucian bid them rise.

"Swift, Kayne, and Talin, may I present the king's traveling companions, Captain Eralon Wellsbough, Jhain Velendris, and Treyven Fontacue."

They all graciously acknowledged the scouts. Kullipthius watched as Jhain studied them with intense interest, sizing them up against the scouts in Lucian's employ.

"These three Oralian scouts will infiltrate the force marching upon our lands and will later meet us with their findings. I will need to cut formal introductions short, I'm afraid, so we can begin preparations for our assignment."

As they were talking amongst themselves, Kullipthius heard Laliah's voice enter into his thoughts.

"My Emperor, I apologize for the intrusion, but might I have a word?" asked the imperatrix.

The imperator excused himself for a moment, to give his mate his full attention. *"Certainly, My Empress, how may I be of assistance?"*

"My healing abilities are calling out to be used on the one who is called Treyven Fontacue. He has a serious wound that will soon turn into an infection with fever if not healed. Might you come to the gardens at the palace after you are finished?"

"Aye, of course, My Empress," replied Kullipthius.

After speaking with Laliah, Kullipthius turned back to his guests and overheard the end of Treyven's conversation.

". . . Even the view be a visual work o' art." Treyven motioned to the steep landscape before them. "With such beauty all around, if I dinna know better, I would think I be dreaming."

Treyven then looked over at Kullipthius. "If I had nay been made privy ta all that I'ves seen here before me this day, I would'na guessed that anyone, let alone an entire empire, coulda survive in the mountains o' Kaleidos Peak."

"Our empire has been here long before Moorwyn Castle was built, and the pledge of peace that was made between our empire and Avala has withstood the test of time. You have my solemn oath that those who reside within the continent of Sapphirus will continue to enjoy peace, security, and protection from the Oralian Empire."

Lucian then added to Kullipthius' declaration. "I have known the imperator since I was a lad, and I know this to be true. There are no secrets between us, and we will stand by one another through any altercation. Oralians respect our way of life, and they, in turn, can rely on me to honor their privacy and clandestine existence."

Kullipthius expounded on Lucian's words. "It is truth that we have a great respect for one another. However, we rely upon you to understand that there are things here in Oralia that must be kept private, lest the knowledge fall into the wrong hands, become misconstrued, and cause panic.

"The captain could, perhaps, appreciate my line of reasoning. You do not give up your stratagems to just anyone for these very reasons, do you agree Captain Wellsbough? There is a chance it could be used against you, or for the wrong purpose. Likewise, one may know an accomplished scout, for example, the best in his class, one held in high esteem for his accomplishments and perfect tracking record. However, they may know nothing of his experiences or life's challenges, as things could be misinterpreted, when in fact, his history is what made him the fine young man he is today."

Kullipthius nodded to the Oralian scouts who were standing quietly and attentively at their imperator's side. At his unvoiced command, the three men took off at a sprint, heading straight for the sheer, deadly edge of the summit.

"There are few who can perceive what has been so carefully hidden in plain sight," explained Kullipthius.

Kullipthius watched Jhain, Eralon, and Treyven stare in

shocked silence as the three scouts leapt over the side of the summit, disappearing from sight. Jhain managed a small strangled sound, his eyes wide. His distress was emulated by Eralon and Treyven, who stood with mouths agape, staring hard at the place where the scouts had disappeared over the edge of the cliff. They glanced at one another and then at King Lucian, who appeared unruffled, even relaxed.

Kullipthius gave no evidence of anything untoward as he continued his conversation. "Once you open yourself up to all that is life around you, with its endless possibilities, you realize that your perception of things may not always be accurate."

A blast of wind rushed up from the verge, unsettling attire, stirring up dust, and whipping the leaves of the berry bushes about. Then, a goodly distance from the summit's edge, three monstrous heads appeared above the rim of the rocky crag.

Beasts known only in fantasy as the subject of lore keepers' tales were staring at the king's men. Teeth gleamed, claws flashed, and great wings stirred the air around the mountaintop as three dragons wheeled and spiraled in the sky before them, making the observers' clothing and hair dance with each gust. The undulating bands of color that saturated their scales in hues of honey, amber, and brown made for a dazzling motif, mimicking their rough topaz stones atop their foreheads.

Kullipthius had intentionally not revealed the coming change to Lucian's men. It was imperative for both monarchs to bear frank witness to their reactions, courage, and steadfastness. What he saw pleased him.

All three men were understandably shocked. Eralon had reacted as any good captain should to a possible threat against his monarch. He had protectively stepped before his king at the first appearance of the transformed scouts, but he was rapidly adjusting. His posture was alert, and his dark eyes tracked the tumbling creatures before him. Treyven looked dazed, but then again, he had just had his tidy understanding of the world turned on its ear. His eyes leapt from one dragon to the others and then to Lucian and Kullipthius. His mind was rapidly assimilating the sight and putting the pieces together.

Jhain was, perhaps, the most accepting, and Kullipthius knew the reasons. He had already figured out while at the entrance to the empire that there was something untamed and exceptional about the Oralians. His earlier wandering thoughts had allowed him to grab tight to the reality before him and accept it.

Kullipthius watched as Jhain's face transformed into a glow of childlike wonderment. Jhain turned to his captain and nudged him softly with his elbow. With a touch of humor behind his words, Jhain declared, "Delighted ta see they survived the fall."

This comment seemed to turn the tide. Eralon and Treyven laughed aloud, pulling sanity from the calmer reaction of their teammate. With a bemused grin, Eralon turned to his king and raised an eyebrow.

Lucian laughed and said, "I offer no apologies for the coarse surprise, but we had to see how you would handle the change without warning. Though their true forms can be intimidating when seen for the first time, they are—without doubt—extraordinary, are they not?"

"Undeniably, Your Majesty," Eralon replied.

Kullipthius smiled and said, "Before you ask, I want you to know that all who dwell in the Oralian Empire, including myself, are the creatures of your lore keepers' legends, and we are, indeed, your allies."

King Lucian explained the task before them. "The three of you have been chosen to join us in a clandestine undertaking for your kingdom and Kullipthius' empire. These dragon scouts before you will approach the Liltian force in their human forms and pose as fellow mercenaries. They will learn of their intentions and let us know their findings."

Lucian looked over to Treyven. "That is where we will need your help, Treyven. Since the Liltians will be looking to you as their leader, we would like you to send them a missive, directing them to meet you at the fortress for further instructions.

"With the help of the imperator and his empire, we will put a stop to any unscrupulous deeds Danuvius has in mind or any troubles that may come about."

The dragon scouts had just landed with their heads facing the summit. It was then that Kullipthius revealed another shocking surprise. "It is time for your flight lessons."

He let that sink in a moment while the king and his companions watched three Oralian guardians approach the dragons. The dragons' backs were fitted with thickly-cushioned pads, vaguely resembling a horse's saddle, complete with cinching straps and clever stirrups.

"As you can see, the Oralian guardians have placed cushions in front of the scouts' wings. This is for your protection against the protruding spikes running down these topaz dragons' necks and backs," explained Kullipthius. "However, you will be riding bareback on the dragons that will be carrying you to our encampment in the Tall Forest."

They all followed Kullipthius over to the topaz dragons near the summit's edge. Kullipthius brought them over to the dragon scout, Talin, who lowered his neck on Kullipthius' silent command.

"The two curved spikes that are sitting side-by-side in front of the cushion are where you will hold on for further support. However, it is best to wear gloves for a firmer grip." One Oralian guardian approached and handed Jhain, Eralon, and Treyven each a pair of fingerless gloves.

"We will all meet here at the summit two days hence," Kullipthius further instructed. "Your goodly king will be happy to fill you in on all the details. There will be other dragons that will be joining us in the forest. We will go over all the details of our assignment for everyone at that time."

"We also have the ability to transmit our thoughts." The imperator's words filled their minds to prove this point. He wanted to give them a moment to adjust to hearing his thoughts before he continued.

"You can think or speak out loud to the dragons at any point, and they will be able to understand you," he said verbally, before he continued again in Drahk.

"Are there any questions before you leave for your flight lessons?"

"Merely a comment, Yer Imperial Majesty," thought Jhain.

The scout was smiling when Kullipthius looked at him.

"I'ves upgraded me unfortunate comparison o' a desert cat ta dragon ally."

Imperator Kullipthius returned Jhain's smile.

CHAPTER SEVENTEEN

K ing Lucian led his three companions back along the passage to Moorwyn Castle to prepare for their journey to the Tall Forest. They had just left the Crystal Palace's gardens and had met the imperatrix. Treyven seemed baffled and astonished with the healing the imperatrix had provided. While walking back to the castle, he was rotating his arm and smiling.

Though Lucian could only speculate on the others' thoughts, he knew they would be full of questions soon enough. Their minds must be spinning with all they had done and seen this day. It would take time to acclimate to this new reality they found themselves thrust into. Jhain could be counted on to start a conversation soon with pointed questions, and the others would be wringing out the accounts of everything they had seen and done while in the presence of their newly-discovered allies.

As if on cue, Jhain said, "I dinna believe I 'aves 'ere had such an exhilarating experience. Ta think only moments ago, we be on the back o' dragons in flight. Indeed, 'twas most invigorating."

"Aye," agreed Treyven. "It be likened ta a day o' miracles. Even me upper arm be completely healed by Her Imperial Majesty without even a mark left at the site o' the wound." The others nodded in agreement, each expressing their thoughts in turn.

Even Lucian had to admit it had been quite an experience. "I, too, am in awe of the day's account. However, it is important to keep in mind our pact with our allies. We must be very careful not to speak of this again after we leave this passageway. This is a long-kept secret we are privy to. After our task is complete, we will get together and drink fine ale and share our tales. Agreed?"

All were in accord.

Lucian spared a glance upon Treyven Fontacue. He debated heavily with himself for a moment, then he decided more information was due Treyven, for he was a good man, one who passionately and purposefully sought to defend a fallen kingdom and her people.

"You were but a child during the collapse of Liltimer, Treyven, and you have relied solely on secondhand information concerning the country's tragic downfall. I would be happy to give you a personal account from someone who was there to witness the events firsthand."

Lucian found that he suddenly had everyone's undivided attention. Treyven and Jhain were interested in the events that led to the fall of their former homeland, and unbeknownst to Eralon, who believed he knew all the facts, he was about to learn the truth of his father's fate.

"I was also privy to speak with the Liltian Queen after King Tridan's fall, and I heard her account of the incident in her own words just before her untimely end. Valen Doral was also most forthcoming in offering his recount of the tragedy."

"I'd be most obliged fer that information, Yer Majesty, fer 'twould mean a great deal," admitted Treyven. "I'd prefer hearing the truth."

"So be it."

The King's Tale

The lands of Liltimer once flourished under the rule of King Tridan. The Liltians had great respect and admiration for their ruler, and even those in the neighboring countries held King Tridan Leone and his lovely Queen Mariselle in high esteem.

While Liltimer shared its boundaries with Avala to the north, east, and south, the country's entire western border ran along the coast of the Carillion Sea.

As you are aware, the western coastline of our continent of Sapphirus features dramatic cliffs and jagged rocks that rise to dizzying heights. There is only one area along the entire western coast where a sailing vessel can dock, and that is the thriving fishing village of Bocca di Leone.

What you may not know, is that the village and dock was constructed and named after the king by the Liltians, as it was the original idea of King Tridan Leone himself.

Liltimer had long and ago joined in the signing of a treaty to uphold the peace with its neighboring countries of Avala, Sunon, and Vashires. On each anniversary of the signing of the treaty, a grand festival was celebrated when the kings and courts of all four countries would come together.

During that fateful time in question, the merriment and tourneys were hosted in Avala. The citizenry turned out en masse, and as I recall, it was Tridan who insisted on sponsoring the combat, jousting, and archery tournaments, bolstering the prize for the winners with coin from his own coffers. He had long been an enthusiast of the tourney stands. During the festivities, the Liltian monarch was full of joy and laughter, coaxing everyone to partake in the revelry.

What happened after he left the festival and our borders came directly from Queen Mariselle and Ambassador Valen Doral.

The queen had gone ahead of her husband, returning home to their three young sons, while King Tridan had made a necessary detour to the Kingdom of Sunon. For some unknown reason, he did not return home in a timely manner and, just when the royal court was beginning to worry, he turned up at the gates of Lionholm Castle on foot looking haggard and worn. He arrived alone, without pack or horse, his contingent of guards alarmingly absent. Worry tipping dangerously into the realm of alarm, Queen Mariselle tried to gently question her exhausted spouse about his trip and his missing escorts, but she was met with stony silence. Tridan retired directly to his room and locked himself away behind his thick chamber doors without so much as a cursory greeting to his loving wife or children.

None of the missing men turned up in the days that followed, and so it was assumed that the king had undergone some terrible ordeal. His men must have given their lives for his safety, and his silence was his means of dealing with the blow. Perhaps, they reasoned, given time, their once-loving king would speak to someone and shed some light upon the mystery.

Conversely, the silence and solitude stretched on, and for a sennight King Tridan remained locked within his bedchambers, not even letting his goodly wife enter, determined to remain undisturbed. On the eighth day he finally emerged looking surprisingly better, and he broke his fast and silence by going straight to the kitchen to demand food, which he ate ravenously. The kitchen staff was astounded by his appetite and stunned by his curious behavior.

Queen Mariselle and Lionholm Castle's royal steward, Valen Doral, hastened into the kitchen thrilled with the reappearance of Tridan. Valen had long held favor with the monarchs, having been the king's confidant and friend for many yearmarks. Both he and the queen had spent many sleepless nights worrying about their king, and they hoped to inquire into his wellbeing.

But when they tried, they were dumbstruck by his behavior. He turned wild, angry eyes upon them and growled low in his throat like an untamed beast. Mariselle promptly sent the scullery maid to fetch the healers. Tridan's words were utter nonsense. He proclaimed disjointed rants about the necessity for power and control and displayed a sudden, newfound suspicion and distrust for the surrounding kingdoms he had called allies.

Observing their king's behavior from the kitchen's threshold, the healers believed that whatever mysterious tragedy had befallen the king, it had driven him to the brink of madness. In addition, they noted a large contusion upon Tridan's head and thought it possible this injury had disoriented him and was the cause for his delusions. They expressed their concerns to Queen Mariselle and told her it was imperative they treat his injuries immediately.

Queen Mariselle approached King Tridan and asked him to go with the healers for examination and care. He promptly called for his most loyal castle guards, and when they arrived, he attacked the friendly relationship between Mariselle and Valen, citing wild charges of adultery. Valen and Mariselle could not believe their ears. Valen was happily married, the union blessed by Tridan himself. No one could doubt Mariselle loved her husband, always putting him and their three beloved children before her own needs.

Over Mariselle's protests, Tridan ordered Valen thrown in prison, and when she objected, he ordered her and their youngest son, his own namesake, locked away in her chambers. Nothing he did seemed to make sense. The Lionholm staff became frightened, for any little thing could arouse his wrath. He became preoccupied with everything, as if viewing commonplace items for the first time while ranting and raving that everyone was against him.

Believing his former allies were now dangerous enemies, he called an emergency council meeting. He tried to convince his advisors that they must wage a full-scale war across multiple fronts, attacking Sunonites, Vashirians, and Avalians before those countries could muster their armies. Tridan could not be swayed from his campaign, even when reminded of the peace treaties he himself had helped pen, or the good times he had shared with his neighbors at tourneys and feasts. If anyone dared mention his poor, sweet queen or Valen Doral, they were immediately silenced.

Tridan's advisors tried their best to stall, hoping that time would erase his paranoia, telling their king they would debate the best course of action and decide how things should be handled. But agitated and extremely impatient with the slow-moving proceedings, King Tridan summoned his two eldest sons, Princes Hayden and Blaine, aged fourteen and sixteen yearmarks respectively, to a closed meeting in his chambers. They talked long into the night, emerging at the break of dawn.

Mariselle watched from her window as her boys, dressed for war, rode away with a contingent of guards. Weakened from scanty food and drink, Mariselle pounded ineffectually on her chamber doors, sobbing and demanding her husband call her children back to at least allow her to bid them a proper farewell, but he coldly ignored her desires.

Days later, when he finally did come to speak with her, it was to bluntly inform her that both princes had been sent on a task for their father. The distraught queen fell into further despair. Her only consolation was being in the company of their youngest son. The babe prince had not yet reached his second yearmark and clung to his fragile mother like a lifeline.

Soon this small comfort was ripped from her as well, for Tridan demanded their youngest. Mariselle refused and clutched tightly to her son, arguing that he had taken everything from her already. She wailed and said that if he truly loved her, he would let her keep the child. When Tridan finally seemed to relent she relaxed, and that was when he acted, trying to snatch the prince from her arms. In the ensuing struggle, the boy fell and struck his head upon a bedside table.

Mariselle picked up the tiny, limp form and cradled him in her arms. Tridan was furious, insisting it was her burden to bear. He taunted her viciously by proclaiming she had killed their son.

He stormed from the chambers in a rage, shouting that Mariselle would be left to die in her chambers, informing the staff that she was not to be fed or cared for because she had murdered their small son. She begged once more at the doors of her opulent prison, grief-stricken and sick for release. None were allowed to call on her, with the exclusion of the queen's attendant, and only then to remove the child's body from the chambers. The staff members were all so fearful of the king's fury and beleaguered by his wrath that they dared issue no protest.

Fortunately, one dared to stand against the king's decrees, and that was Lord Bromwell, Liltimer's Marshal of the Royal Liltian Court in charge of military affairs. Lord Bromwell was Mariselle's only sibling, though not in line for the throne because it was the king's bloodline who ruled the country. Lord Bromwell looked so much like his sister, having her coloring and features, that they might have been twins.

Unable to see his sister while she was under strict house arrest, the marshal freed Valen Doral, who was bruised from the chains that bound him and weak from his stay in prison. Under cover of night, they both traveled to Avala, taking their well-founded fears to Moorwyn Castle.

Avala was suitably stunned to hear the terrible news and, of course, offered its assistance to free Mariselle and procure proper care for Tridan. Valen and Sir Bromwell were advised to stay safely hidden in Avala. Lord Bromwell refused, for he was determined to see the queen freed from her prison.

Meanwhile, a meeting was held at Moorwyn, with the dragon realm in attendance, to discuss the looming threat of war. Under the wise council of Imperator Kullipthius of Oralia, a small garrison would travel to speak with Liltimer's leader. The group consisted of Imperator Kullipthius, Chief Romus, Vahl Zayne, Captain Xavian Wellsbough, Lord Bromwell and me. The queen's brother could not be dissuaded from going and held no knowledge of the existence of the dragon realm. We let him join us for we knew he would surely follow us anyway had we tried to leave him behind. We decided that we could deal with any untoward consequences later, should that be necessary. Within two days, a meeting with King Tridan was arranged on neutral ground and under a banner of peace.

As soon as we arrived, Tridan had us surrounded in an ambush attempt. He was, of course, furious with his marshal for alerting his enemies. He had brought a small army, and if not for Chief Romus' abilities, we would have had a terrible fight on our hands. With the staggering power of his influence, Romus sent the Liltian army trickling back to the castle and their awaiting families. So busy was King Tridan, gloating and raving over his imminent victory, that he did not notice his men departing under Chief Romus' suggestive power.

As the King of Avala and head of the party, I tried to reason with Tridan, for I was intent on a peaceful resolution. My goodwill was thrown back in my face as he screamed out fantastical atrocities I supposedly had perpetrated.

Once Tridan discovered that he stood alone amongst his would-be enemies, he was unable to restrain the darkness lurking within. He slid from his horse and stomped toward us with sword drawn. Captain Xavian Wellsbough, ever my loyal friend, placed his horse in my path to shield me, and our dragon allies formed a line of defense to block Tridan's advance. None of us understood exactly what it was we faced.

With a speed that blurred our vision, Tridan suddenly hurtled himself into the air. We all looked around, but no one could see where he had gone. Of a sudden, he reappeared in his original spot. The only evidence of his actions was the blood dripping from his sword.

Xavian turned to check on my wellbeing, and I watched as he clutched at his torso and looked down. He pulled his hand away from his chest and found his fingers and palm stained red. His body slowly collapsed over the side of his horse. My captain and my friend had been struck down, passing from this world in only a few short heartbeats. It was then we knew that Tridan was something more than what he had presented himself to be.

Kullipthius and the others rushed the false king. However, he was just as fast—if not faster—than the dragons in our group. The false king dodged and struck repeatedly, keeping multiple attackers busy. It was frightening to behold—the streaking blurs of fighters around us with only brief moments caught in time to reveal their whereabouts as each blocked and struck, whirled and fought.

Lord Bromwell disengaged me gently from Xavian's limp form and helped me to my feet. To this day, I do not remember dismounting or rushing to Xavian's side, for I fear I was in shock. Lord Bromwell saw my distress and stood before me, blade at the ready, intent on protecting me.

Finally, Kullipthius called out, "Enough!"

That word jolted me out of my traumatized state. The mêlée halted, and everyone was breathing raggedly and heavily from the tension-filled encounter.

Then Kullipthius faced the Liltian usurper and demanded, "Show yourself! What manner of creature are you? You are not King Tridan."

The imposter appeared pleased and pompous, and instead of answering, he showed us his true essence. He seemed to explode from within, and when the light and dust cleared, there stood in his place a fierce, slithering reptile.

The beast before us had a wicked, wedge-shaped head with a cavernous maw that contained several rows of impossibly sharp teeth. It hissed in warning. Its hate-filled, yellow eyes took in our positions, and its forked tongue flicked out to test the particles in the air and catch our scent.

The dragons had understood immediately what it was we faced, although they had thought them extinct for almost two centuries. They believed the creature that stood before them had to be the last of his kind.

I will attempt to explain what this creature was so you will understand precisely what it was we were up against.

These fierce reptiles were known as Monstrum, meaning monster. The dragons had nicknamed them chameleons for their abilities of transformation. They were a malign and violent predator and, though flightless, were capable of deft and deadly combat.

The chameleon's scales were more like plates of armor than typical scales, similar to an insect, and they were streaked like agate. Their plates shimmered with varying veins of color, and they could transform to whatever shade, shape, or texture the beast craved, a blank slate waiting to be filled. Their bodies were about half the size of a dragon in height and width, and they were stocky with a short neck and bony spines projecting from the back of their heads. They possessed thick, muscular limbs with four splayed digits on each foot that ended in sharp, deadly claws.

If that were not enough to frighten even the bravest of knights, the most perilous part of these creatures was their segmented tail that could bend and strike at will. The ends of their tails held a soft, bulb-like, venomous sac with a stinger at its tip. The sac contained a deadly toxin and a sharp, curved, and hollowed point that delivered the venom to its victim.

Their transformation abilities allowed them to retain the memories and appearance of whatever they killed and consumed, thus making them furtive, devious hunters. They had the ability to mimic the looks, mannerisms, vocal inflections, and movements of their prey. This would not be such a great problem if the chameleons themselves were not vicious creatures by nature. They lived for strife and war, glorying in battle and bloodshed, longing to be at the top of the food chain.

Kullipthius and Romus altered to dragon form and spread out, moving to flank the striking beast while Vahl Zayne stood guard over Lord Bromwell and me. The platinum and amber quartz struck as one, causing the smaller chameleon to back toward the tree line.

Vahl Zayne spoke directly into the minds of his fellow dragons as they fought, startling Lord Bromwell to no end. Not only was it the marshal's first encounter with dragons, but hearing someone else's thoughts can be overwhelming if one is not prepared for it.

The sapphire dragon relayed what information he could about the chameleon. He advised them to strike at the back of its neck plates so as to subdue him. Also, he told them to beware of its jaws which were connected by ligaments. Their jaws had the ability to stretch and consume the bulkiest of prey.

The cocky chameleon smirked. He spoke in Drahk and he told the dragons, "Go ahead and confer and conspire against me as you will. Know I hold the measure of you all. It is only a matter of time before I feast and add your memories and likeness to my repertoire." Though the monster communicated in Drahk, we heard it in Tridan's Liltian accent.

The sapphire dragon then shed the vestiges of his humanity in a blinding light and turned toward us in his towering, dragon form. He explained that he had orders from the imperator to hold himself in reserve, observe and watch until He could find any vulnerability and then pounce on the chameleon.

With that, Vahl Zayne turned back to the battle, keen eyes watching for any weakness he could exploit, Ice and rime spread in spider web patterns about his claws where they touched the earth.

While Kullipthius kept the beast busy, Romus barreled into the chameleon's side, tumbling them both into a tangle of limbs, claws, and flashing teeth. The chieftain tried to use his gift of influence, but it had no effect. When it easily flung Romus away, it knew little triumph, for Kullipthius pounced upon the chameleon's back, clawing and tearing at the nape of its neck in a frantic effort to dislodge the plates protecting it. The beast's tail struck at the platinum dragon, but Kullipthius leapt clear in a lightning motion, the strike falling far short of its goal. They harassed and harried the beast as hunting hounds would a fox, keeping it on its toes so it was unable to do more than defend itself.

Lord Bromwell watched the assault in much the same manner as Vahl Zayne, his eyes intent and burning darkly as if awaiting his chance to subdue the masquerading chameleon.

The two Oralian dragons tussled for dominance over the nimble chameleon, but it managed to evade them. Standing on the sidelines, we could tell that Romus and Kullipthius intended to capture or incapacitate the beast if they could, rather than kill it, but it had no discernible handicap and was out for blood, making their objective that much more challenging.

So keenly drawn in by the struggle, Vahl Zayne and I did not realize our trio was minus one until Kullipthius was thrown bodily against a nearby tree. The imperator was momentarily dazed from the collision that left the blameless tree broken in two. Romus leapt forward to protect his sovereign, and the chameleon bit down on Romus' hind leg in a retaliatory strike. That was when the frost dragon and I spied the errant member of our triad. Lord Bromwell had been screened from our sight by an outcropping of rock near the splintered trunk and the battle.

The chameleon arched its tail high while the amber quartz was trying valiantly to recover. The venomous stinger hovered over Romus. So focused on its victim, the chameleon took little note of its surroundings, and we watched with unvoiced trepidation as Lord Bromwell ran to Romus' aid. He leapt high and his sword struck true, shearing the hazardous tip from the chameleon's tail. The beast screamed in an unholy octave.

With the chameleon's flesh severed, the descending tail tumbled and the sharp tip raked the marshal's right shoulder with enough force to inject vile venom under his skin. Lord Bromwell crumpled heavily to the ground with a howl of agony.

Vahl Zayne took advantage while the insidious creature was preoccupied with its pain. Something vital must have been slashed, for the chameleon was bleeding heavily. Kullipthius carried the wounded man a safe distance from the flailing monster. A freezing stream of Vahl Zayne's breath caught the chameleon off guard as it tried to gather itself to pounce, and it was soon enclosed in a thick coating of ice and frost.

Vahl Zayne had hoped he was in time to stop the chameleon's blood loss, for he could sense the monster's life-force fading. There was a vivid flash of radiance, and the blue dragon reverted to his human form. He placed his hand regretfully on the block of solid ice that surrounded the chameleon. He looked at the beast with a sigh, and through their Drahk connection he told him: "You would not listen to reason. You were a dangerous threat to my friends and to the world at large. I wish it could have ended differently."

Romus reverted to his two-legged form and limped to Lord Bromwell's side. Romus knelt next to the wounded marshal and took stock of his injury, gripping the man's hand tightly and thanking him profusely for his life. The skin around Bromwell's shoulder wound was already inflamed, his blood circulating the vile toxins. Vahl Zayne offered to rush the wounded man back to Oralia and place him in Laliah's capable hands in an attempt to save his life. All agreed, and Vahl Zayne shifted to a dragon and carried the barely conscious marshal back toward Kaleidos Peak.

As the remaining group watched, the blue dragon's form diminished over the horizon.

Though they had tried to stop both the blood loss and the chameleon's unrelenting assault with the sapphire's gift of ice and frost, the beast had lost too much blood.

Kullipthius explained that it would be ill-fated for the body to be discovered, so with a nod from Kullipthius, Romus strode purposefully to the monster. On his right hand, his fingers had elongated into wicked claws. With a strike that carried the size and bulk the amber quartz truly was, he shattered the creature's ice-covered remains to pieces with a single blow. The mighty dragon Blayz was summoned from Oralia to his imperator's side, and he applied his gift of fire to burn the chameleon to ash. Once it was done, the dragons intoned a quiet benediction, and then Romus announced, "And so it is done."

Kullipthius was highly concerned with the discovery of the evil chameleon. If a lone beast had done this much damage to one kingdom in such a relatively short time, what would an unchecked nest do? They later searched the continent of Sapphirus and beyond, and thankfully, they never discovered any others.

Long and ago, when the Dra'khar Dynasty was in its infancy, I was told the dragons had tried to help these fierce creatures, hoping there was something that could be done to assist the reptiles in learning to live a peaceful existence. Unfortunately, it was not meant to be, and they perished from sight because of their own insidious behavior and violence toward themselves and others. The dragon empire had thought all Monstrum were extinct, but our sudden conflict with this one proved just how unsubstantial those beliefs were.

Our grim findings, of course, explained what had truly happened to the King of Liltimer. It seemed King Tridan and his escorts had, indeed, been attacked during their trip home from Sunon, but by something far worse than Liltimer could have imagined. Now we were tasked with freeing Queen Mariselle and informing her of her husband's fate.

When we did arrive at Lionholm Castle, we were greeted with unfortunate tidings. Mariselle was so weak as to be bedridden. She was most fragile and thin, deteriorated passed the point of repair from being improperly fed and cared for. She was devastated that the two older princes, Haden and Blaine, had yet to return home, and she told us of the babe Prince Tridan's tragic accident. When I spoke with her, she was under no delusions of her fate, and the healers confirmed our worst suspicions.

With all haste and while her strength permitted, we explained to her what had happened with the king and discussed what would become of her people and country. She was understandably grief-stricken when we presented her with the truth behind her husband's mysterious malady, but she smiled sadly and said her faith was justified in the end, for she knew Tridan would never have acted so cruelly.

Queen Mariselle wanted to entrust the kingdom of Liltimer and her people to me, to have it absorbed under Avala's banner, for there were no others known in Tridan's bloodline, his heirs all taken from her by the evil chameleon's mad whims. Their country was nestled along Avala's southern seaboard, and she said she had always admired the way I dealt succinctly, yet benevolently, with any crisis. She had gazed upon me fondly and declared that I was the perfect candidate to help her torn-asunder kingdom become whole. She believed I would treat her people properly in the face of the many blows they had suffered.

Thus, with Valen Doral back at Lionholm, he made a formal announcement to her people while she sat upon her throne. With the queen's assurance that Valen spoke the truth, he told those present that King Tridan had succumbed in a conflict he instigated while suffering from mental anguish and grief. She also nodded confirmation as he explained that the other kingdoms had kept to their treaties and never wanted war or the Liltian lands, as Tridan had so mistakenly believed. She concluded the speech with her request that the kingdom of Liltimer be placed into Avala's capable hands. It was her belief that this would best serve all involved. She wished them peace and joy under their new banner, and then she collapsed.

After her death, the kingdom of Liltimer did, indeed, come under the rule of Avala's flag. There were, of course, the unbelievers, those who lived on the farthest outskirts of the country who were not present to bear witness to the false king's foul atrocities, and it's from those folks that the rumors started to spread that Avala had coveted the power and lands of Liltimer. But those outbursts were few, and the bulk of the people lived peacefully enough under Avala's governance. I set up Lionholm as the fortress manor, which became home to Valen Doral. He became the ambassador for Liltimer's people, and until his untimely death, he helped me keep the peace and provided a welcomed retreat for those who wished to feel closer to the true Liltimer of old.

"I hope I have cleared up any misconceptions any of you may have had regarding these events," said King Lucian. "Now you know the true circumstances concerning the tragic end of King Tridan's rule. It is regrettable that we cannot let the citizenry know the truth of King Tridan's fate."

The king then glanced at Eralon and said, "Or the exact circumstances that led to Captain Xavian Wellsbough's untimely death."

"My father died protecting his king, a task and risk I now assume in his place," responded Eralon.

They exchanged a silent moment, and then the king said, "Ah, we have arrived at journey's end. There is more I wish to tell you, Treyven. However, let us save it for another day, shall we?"

"Aye, Yer Majesty, that would be grand," replied Treyven.

"Everyone keep in mind Prince Dryden is the only other person aware of the dragon realm. Avala's Council of Nobles knows not of the imperator's secrets. The imperator is only known as our ally whose ancestors came from across the seas long and ago and made a pact with our forefathers. My council of lords believes he protects the eastern seaboard of Avala where his empire exists on the far side of the Kaleidos mountain range. They understand the Oralians to be a reclusive empire, desiring a clandestine existence known only to the king and council of Avala."

They soon arrived at the entrance to Lucian's chamber, where they extinguished their torch in the cave's passageway before proceeding. The king then escorted the men through his private quarters to the exit.

"Ready your things and prepare for our assignment," said King Lucian. "Jhain, find Treyven accommodations in Dragon's Row and make sure he has all the essentials he needs for our journey. Now, we must all make haste, for lost time is never found."

Part Two

Legacy of Dra'khar
CHAPTER EIGHTEEN

K ing Lucian of Avala sat in front of his private chamber's fireplace, staring into the dwindling flames, mentally going over the last several days. An approaching force was invading his lands under the leadership of a corrupt steward from Terra Leone named Danuvius. Once believed to be deceased, Danuvius seemed to have miraculously risen from the dead and was in league with a ruthless ruby dragon who wielded dark magic. That evil red dragon was hell-bent on crushing the entire dragon empire and ruling over all humankind. Lucian sighed. He thanked the heavenly stars that good fortune had provided an ally in Imperator Kullipthius.

"And what could be better than our alliance and friendship," commented Kullipthius, aforesaid ruler of the dragon empire who stood in his human form before the fire, his arm resting casually on the mantle.

Lucian smiled and shook his head. "At least with your ability to read my mind, I do not have to repeat the perils that are afflicting the entire continent of Sapphirus. Avala and Oralia have been living in peace for so long that it is difficult to fathom all we have learned over the course of the last sennight."

"Even with the few struggles we have encountered, we have always emerged victorious, my friend," said the imperator. "I believe this matter will be no different."

"That is a comment you have made before, Kullipthius, and I must say, I have yet to be disappointed," responded Lucian sincerely. "In truth, it is the dark magic that has me unsettled."

"I concur," said the imperator as he picked up the hearth's poker to stir the fire back to life.

Lucian did not have to be a mind reader to know what the dragon ruler was thinking while stoking the flames. The ruby beast had used dark magic long ago to murder Kullipthius' father, Dra'khar, and Lucian could see the grief in his friend's eyes.

"We have found that the spells, incantations, and rituals in *The Dark Arts* tome tend to exacerbate natural feelings of fear, distrust, and suspicion and often cause the user to commit foolhardy and irrational errors," advised the imperator. Then he gently replaced the poker in its stand and turned to face Lucian. "I believe we can use that to our advantage. Moreover, the dragons in my empire have their own special gifts and talents that I fully intend to draw upon.

"And speaking of special talents, this day I am going to meet with a dragon that I hope will join us in our fight; then I must take Ra, along with our pavilions and supplies, to the Tall Forest. There Ra will begin the necessary preparations for our encampment. The area we have in mind is centrally located—the perfect place for monitoring the environment. More importantly, we will be able to react quickly to any event that would require our immediate attention.

"Our assemblage of dragons and humans will be joining Ra upon the morrow. When all is ready, I will send Chief Romus through the secret passageway that connects our two realms. He will collect you, Captain Eralon Wellsbough, Scout Jhain Velendris, and Treyven Fontacue. Then we will meet in Oralia at first light."

CHAPTER NINTEEN

T he dragons' Ancient Transcripts chronicled an enchanted region located in a wonderland of flora and fauna called Nirvana Kai. It was there, nestled in a lush valley below the highest reaches of the eastern slopes of Kaleidos Peak, that the mighty dragons of the Dra'khar Dynasty had made their first home.

From the mountain's uppermost peak, the melting snow had once trickled down craggy inclines and crisscrossed into murmuring rivulets that gurgled gently along rocky streambeds. Natural channels of stone had guided these streams of icy water to tumble over the sides of the mountain in three cascades. It was said that the rising wisps of spray from the waterfalls generated a misty haze so thick that it hid the mountaintop from view. When seen from below, it gave the illusion that the waterfalls descended from the clouds into what was then known as the Crystalline River.

Long and ago, Nirvana Kai had been the perfect paradise. At the mountain's base, the river's cool, clear water had been surrounded by lush woodlands that housed a plethora of exotic birds and wildlife. Peaceful and serene, this area had displayed a breathtaking magnificence beyond description, and its locale had provided a wondrously safe haven for the dragons that lived within.

One would think such a locale would forever render refuge for it was lovingly cradled in the arms of an opal dragoness known as Haelan, Mother of Nature and Healer of the Planet. Haelan was the beloved grandmother to Imperatrix Laliah who was Imperator Kullipthius' mate. Haelan's exceptional efforts had kept the dragon lair lush and flourishing for all to enjoy. But then an unprecedented cataclysm shattered the serenity that was once Nirvana Kai.

When reading about the great groundshake that had struck Nirvana Kai, one could surely sense the devastation and desolation from the descriptions in the pages of the Ancient Transcripts. Woe the day when not even the grande dame of nature could prevent the grievous effects of such a natural disaster, one that had left its merciless mark in dragon history.

The groundshake had begun with a great trembling deep beneath the mountain below the eastern slopes of Kaleidos Peak. As the earth shifted, cracks expanded into deep crevices that weakened Kaleidos Peak's three great waterfalls. Soil and rocks careened down the steep slopes to generate a catastrophic landslide. The addition of water turned the landslide into a massive mudflow that uprooted trees, destroyed natural caves, and killed many of Nirvana Kai's dragon inhabitants.

While Haelan had been working her healing restorations at the heart of the devastation, the mountainside collapsed and buried the Mother of Nature under mudspate and rubble. It was heartbreaking for all who lived through it.

But from all the devastation, one natural creation was born. The once winding river rose and spread through the valley to become what is now lovingly hailed as Lake Haelan. A midair inspection shortly after dawn offers an incredible view of the water's intense, sapphire-blue hue at its calmest. It is a time when the lake's mirror images of the surrounding landscape are inconceivably perfect in a fitting tribute to the Mother of Nature, for she gave her very life in an attempt to save Nirvana Kai.

Yet, to this day the dragons of Oralia believe that Haelan still performs her restorative magic. As evidence, they point to Lake Haelan's northern shoreline and its abundance of medicinal plants and herbs that contain great curative properties. The dragons believe the Mother of Nature is the sole reason for Nirvana Kai's slow, steady restoration, and that it is she who is helping to heal the land with new vegetation and the return of wildlife.

The dragons of Oralia regularly perform an aerial assessment of the area. They recently found that many of the natural caves that were once believed to be destroyed were sturdy enough to be restored. Plans were devised to remove the unstable rock and complete all necessary repairs. Until the work is complete, Nirvana Kai has been deemed unsafe for habitation—except for one mighty beast, and that particular dragon became the topic of great debate between the dragon lords and Imperator Kullipthius.

Kullipthius had announced to his dragon council that he would be visiting the lone dragon living in Nirvana Kai. With Flayre instigating a war between the Liltians and Avala and coercing his red dragon clans into exposing dragondom to the world, Kullipthius deemed the trip necessary. His news was met with trepidation for their ruler. But with valid points argued and the wise counsel of Imperial Advisor Vahl Zayne, Kullipthius found himself preparing for the expedition with a promise to his council that he would take his son, Ra Kor'el, as his traveling companion.

Upon landing in Nirvana Kai, Kullipthius transformed into his human guise to tread the narrow mountain passageways next to his son, and they quickly came upon an ancient trail that sloped into a deep ravine.

"My intuition has not hinted at any extreme danger with this dragon," explained Ra, the empire's soothsayer. "This particular breed has lived in the wild for many centuries. Remember that he is not accustomed to our way of life, and our words and actions might be misinterpreted. Be observant. You may be surprised at what knowledge you can glean from him."

"Gramercy Ra," acknowledged Kullipthius, who had been waiting for his son's valuable insight all morning. "Your words are well-received and greatly appreciated, as always."

Kullipthius traversed the remainder of his journey alone as he navigated the steep slope with careful, deliberate steps. As soon as he had made it safely to the bottom of the ravine, he turned back to look up at his son.

Ra was sitting on the ground in his usual posture—back straight, legs crossed and hands clasped in front of him—for a period of quiet meditation. His son had already tapped two starfire stones together to light them, and was warming his palms over his roughly made fire pit. These stones emitted as much heat and light as any encampment fire, though they were not hot to the touch. Ra then turned toward his father and they waved their farewells.

Kullipthius soon came upon the discarded bones of native wildlife. He observed fresh markings of tooth and claw on the side of a rock and tracked dragon prints to the entrance of a large cave. Upon entering, Kullipthius knew instinctively that Ra's words of caution would surely apply. Heightening his senses, he proceeded cautiously into its depths to find his intended objective—an amethyst dragon.

Discovery of the Amethyst Dragon

A few moons past, Kullipthius and his entourage had been exploring, reveling in the feel of the wind beneath their wings and the warmth of the sun on their backs. They had been investigating the uncharted wilderness of Avala's southeastern countryside and mapping the terrain for future expeditions.

Battle cries echoed through the air from the east, and an agonized wail followed, drawing the attention of the imperator and his attendants. The treetop's branches and leaves swayed under the collective strokes of monstrous wings as the Oralian dragons made their way toward the sounds of conflict.

Kullipthius and his flight came upon great beasts that tumbled and fought before them under the clear morning sky. Even from a distance, the color of the attackers had been readily apparent—stark claret against the brilliant blue horizon. There was no known provocation. Regardless, it was one-sided domination by the ruby dragons. Pride and prejudice drove them into battle, and safety in numbers spurred them on, saturating their thoughts with murderous intent.

On this day, these particular reds were attacking a lone dragon from all sides. It hardly seemed a fair fight. If the imperator and his entourage had not come along, the ten-against-one odds would have yielded a slaughter.

Enraged at the senseless brutality, Kullipthius had screamed his rage. His mate, Laliah, on point beside him, had trumpeted her own fury and had charged toward the mêlée with Kullipthius at her side.

The injured dragon had been slowly driven groundward by the weight of two reds clinging to his back. They were using tooth and claw to rip at his wings. The other attackers had been circling overhead, awaiting their turn in the assault. Kullipthius had watched as Commander Blayz, the leader of Oralia's dragon warriors, charged the attackers. Blayz's reddish-bronze scales had glittered brightly in the sun as he rammed one of the reds, which had sent the beast crashing into three others; the hit was a testament to Blayz's power and strength. Not much coaxing was needed after that. The reds had quickly scattered, taking to their own injured wings in the direction of their home across the sea.

Heeding the call to her healing gift's insistence, Laliah had been the first to land near the injured dragon. Her slender form and shimmering white scales offered a somber contrast to the still, dark form that had been stretched out before her in the grass. A flash of light emanated, and in her altered, human form she cautiously made her way to the injured dragon and placed her healing touch upon him.

Taking guidance from Laliah's intuitive and heartfelt insistence, Kullipthius and the others in the rescue party landed, and they quietly stepped forward to view their hard-won prize. Upon closer inspection, they realized the behemoth before them possessed a purple hue of the deepest dusk that marked him as a biped dragon known as an amethyst.

This particular species had been reviled and feared by many a dragon, all because of the tale of one legendary dragon that had lived long and ago. That legendary dragon had been dubbed "Dark Shadow." He was well-known by all dragonkind for his sinister past. But because of this lone dragon's evil reputation, all amethysts were feared. Long ago, rogue dragons had banded together and senselessly murdered amethyst dragons in their homes as they slept. It was not known if the amethysts were now on the edge of extinction, or living a clandestine existence.

Even with the warning from his beloved, Kullipthius was unprepared for the devastation wrought upon the purple dragon. One hindlimb rested at an awkward angle, and his scales wore a bloody red mask. Kullipthius had worried that the wounded dragon would lash out at his mate, either from pain or from misunderstanding her intentions. Thus, he had launched his dragon senses in hopes of learning more.

The first strong sensory impression Kullipthius received from the amethyst dragon was that of surprise. The amethyst was unaccustomed to dragons coming to his aid or providing a healer to mend his torn flesh and broken bones. The imperator had sensed no danger or malice directed toward his rescuers, but as a precaution he had asked Chief Romus, an amber quartz dragon, to stand ready to apply his gift of influence if they needed to keep their patient calm.

Bones from the amethyst's rib cage protruded from the nasty gash in his side. Patches of scales and strips of flesh hung in wet ribbons from shoulder to flank, and the amethyst had lost a vast amount of blood.

Kullipthius also noticed anatomical differences in the dragon. The vast majority of dragons had two hind legs, two forelegs, and a set of wings. But the amethyst's unique anatomy revealed only two hind legs and a set of wings.

Each wing consisted of bones similar to a human arm, but

much longer, that ran to the tip of the wing. In the center joint of both wings was a wrist with a clawed finger and thumb that was used for eating, climbing, and walking in semblance to a four-legged gait.

The purple dragon had been submissive to Laliah's ministrations. Truthfully, in his debilitated state, there was little he could have done in opposition, even if he had so desired. When his broken bones were reset, the amethyst's only reaction had been a great shudder that had run the entirety of his large frame. His only other movement had been a slight nod or shake of his head in response to Laliah's inquiries. Though it gave them little insight into the stranger, it was better than fighting every inch of the way. Throughout the rest of the healing process, the purple-hued dragon remained still and silent, the intense agony undeniable in his faintly glowing eyes.

Blayz thought like a warrior, not a healer, and had been all for putting the pitiful victim out of his misery, but Laliah would have none of that. Though the wounded dragon posed an unknown risk, Laliah had pledged she would do whatever it took to save the rare dragon. Kullipthius believed if the purple dragon lived, gaining an ally from one of these rare and beautiful creatures would be advantageous for both parties.

They decided to set up camp in the forest until the patient was well enough to move. Kullipthius had made arrangements for Romus to fly back to Oralia to retrieve a rope stretcher in order to carry the wounded dragon back to their home in Kaleidos Peak. He had also directed Romus to inform Ra of their whereabouts, and ask his soothsaying son what insight he may have on the amethyst dragon.

Advisor Vahl Zayne, the keeper of Oralia's Ancient Transcripts, had been fascinated by the appearance of a member of the scarce and endangered species. While Laliah had worked her healing gift, Vahl Zayne explained what he had learned from the Ancient Transcripts of one amethyst in particular.

Dating back to the earliest annals of dragon history, Vahl Zayne had imparted some fascinating information that painted a dark tale indeed. It did not say all purple dragons were of the same nature, yet it did tell of one of the cruelest and maddest of dragons, the beast known only as Dark Shadow. It had been written that its brutality was great against those deemed of a lower station, and it held its enemies in thrall with its cruelty.

This dreadful dragon harbored the powerful breath gift of paralyzing gas and had used it as a weapon of destruction. It was whispered that Dark Shadow had often done much to torment his enemies before releasing them into death. Akin to a spider, he would weave his web of evil by ensnaring his enemies with the dark vapors of his breath weapon, the effects ever-draining of life energy. Once the process of paralysis had been complete, the captive was rendered helpless, yet it remained aware of all that transpired. It was then that Dark Shadow would administer his wrath upon the powerless victim and gain information by torturing and devouring them ever so slowly, bite by agonizing bite.

After Vahl Zayne had told his tale, Blayz had become anxious and feared for the empire's safety, while having the amethyst in their midst. Kullipthius and the others had to convince Blayz that you should not judge one dragon by the character of another. The imperator had pointed out that Blayz himself had once been misjudged for his own heritage.

Kullipthius assured Blayz he had been observing the amethyst dragon's intentions and character since they had rescued him, and he would continue to do so until he was satisfied that the injured dragon was not a threat to the empire.

Laliah was determined that her patient would survive his encounter with the reds. For three days, the opal dragoness refused to move from the amethyst's side while she fought to save his life. Kullipthius had been concerned for his mate because she had been healing as rapidly as her gifts allowed, but the process had been lengthy and energy-draining to the healer. So extensive were the wounds inflicted on the purple dragon that Laliah had not slept but for restorative naps required to renew her healing gifts.

On the morn of the fourth day, Kullipthius noted some of the wounds had turned pink with new skin. He had watched as Laliah leaned close to the injured dragon, placed her hand against the smooth scales on its snout, and murmured encouragement. Kullipthius knew his mate had done all she could. Only time would tell if her patient would survive.

On the next eve, the purple dragon's pain had finally diminished enough that he was able to fall into a peaceful slumber. Laliah was pleased with her charge's progress and believed the patient would pull through. Even so, she had said that he needed many sessions over time to help speed the recovery of his grievous wounds.

Though Kullipthius had known little about the amethyst, he believed the wounded dragon held immense power, and wondered at the questions that nagged him.

Why did the amethyst not try to be a more worthy adversary in its fight with the reds? Could he, in truth, be a docile creature even when provoked? Could it, perhaps, have been the acts of a cruel ruler that painted the entirety of their species in such a ferociously negative light? They had been so long hidden that it would be unfair to judge them all on the actions of one.

But the one thing that had pleased Kullipthius the most was that Laliah had successfully enticed the purple dragon to reveal his name: Shayde. Giving them his name had showed them his trust, and that made Kullipthius feel better.

Skittering stones brought Kullipthius' back to the present, drawing his attention to his immediate right in the dark cave he had just entered. Loose rocks scattered from the movement of massive claws that glittered in the shifting shadows at the rear of the cave.

Mentally projected thoughts slithered forth from the depths of the cavern. "Tell me your will, Your Imperial Majesty. It has been some time since your last visit."

Kullipthius wondered if there was an underlying note of loneliness in the dragon's greeting. He wanted to be heedful, yet respectful, in Shayde's presence. There were many aspects to consider. For example, showing signs of weakness to a predator was an invitation to become its prey. According to legend, of all the predators in dragondom, amethysts were amongst the greatest. Still, legends and myths have been known to be inconsistent with the truth. Kullipthius only need look at his own empire's clandestine existence and reputation to know that to be true.

Kullipthius did not even know the most basic information about Shayde: his age, the location of his hunting territory, or the type of environment he lived in. Could he shift his outward appearance? Did he have an aversion to the presence of the human form?

With those thoughts in mind, he decided it was best to speak with Shayde dragon to dragon because it heightened his senses. He wanted Shayde to be at ease while in the Oralian Empire and, above all, to feel valued and respected. He checked the chamber and noted the ceiling soared to dark stone far overhead. A light then encompassed Kullipthius' body during the change, and it brought a slight groan from the shadows of the cave.

"Apologies and peace, Shayde," professed Kullipthius, expressing his sincerity in a calm and soothing manner so as not to offend. *"I should have forewarned you of the forthcoming illumination from my changing form."* His thoughts and feelings showed the truth, and he knew Shayde would sense that. An uneasy silence followed, and Kullipthius stared into the darkness unflinching, his gaze filled with the massive form before him.

The dragon's scales were so dark that they glittered as black as obsidian. Shayde uncurled from the darkest corner, and vaporous shadows could be seen pluming from his nostrils and jaws. One piece of the puzzle is solved, Kullipthius thought, but without opening his mind to the other dragon. Shayde did, indeed, have a gift of one of the various gaseous forms.

The purple dragon's eyes glowed with an evanescent light. Pound for pound, he would prove himself a worthy opponent. From Kullipthius' own experience with the dragon, he believed the beast would not attack without provocation.

Laliah had acquired further data about this particular species during her healing sessions. Shayde had told Laliah that the dragon known as Dark Shadow had acquired his infamous name and reputation from using dark magic. The use of *The Dark Arts* affected one's mind, causing addiction and mental instability. Flayre was an example of this, and Kullipthius knew the user of dark magic should not be considered as representation of any one particular species. Laliah had also learned that amethysts followed honorable principles. Their customs were so deep-rooted that it would be unheard of for them to break tradition.

When Kullipthius accompanied Laliah on one of her healing sessions, the behemoth had declared he wanted to remain at Kaleidos Peak and join their empire. He also explained he would fulfill an amethyst custom and uphold his responsibility to the imperator.

Not even Vahl Zayne—an erudite historian—had realized exactly what that meant, or what it meant to have saved the life of an amethyst. It had required research through many obscure, crumbling records before they could fathom the motives of the dark dragon. Amethyst Law, they discovered, demanded lifetime protection of one's savior. This fact made for an uneasy situation. Kullipthius would rather Shayde remain at Kaleidos Peak because he wanted to, not because he felt obligated.

Kullipthius observed Shayde as he stepped into the light of the cave's entrance. He had two wicked-looking horns atop his skull that pointed straight at Kullipthius as he dipped his head in respect. Just behind the amethyst crystals that adorned the dragon's forehead, a double ridged crest ran the full length of his spine, coming to an end right before the tip of his tail. Small protrusions of hard bone and scale also sat in the curving ridges above his eyes, serving as a form of protection in that vulnerable area. Shayde's claws were currently dug into the solid stone flooring of the chamber, proof of their strength and sharpness. He recalled Ra's advice to tread carefully and opened his mind to Shayde.

"Upon our last visit," began Kullipthius, *"you advised me that Her Imperial Majesty's healing skills had produced positive results. I have come to ask if you are well enough to travel. Since you have expressed your desire to live in the Oralian Empire, I must inquire if your injuries have healed and, if so, ask for your help with a dire situation."*

Kullipthius had learned from his mate that it was important to speak straight to the point with Shayde, for the imperator's every word would be weighed gravely. Trust understandably came hard for an amethyst that was reviled and feared on sight because of one insane ancestor.

Shayde's horned head stretched out before Kullipthius, his gaze unblinking. His eyes narrowed, swirling with pricks of the faintest light. He stepped toward a ray of light slanting into the cave's mouth and unfurled his wings to their fullest length. *"See for yourself, Your Imperial Majesty."*

Kullipthius never realized how massive this dragon's wingspan truly was until that moment, and the color was breathtaking. In the gleam of the cave's entrance, Shayde's wings glowed, swirling and undulating in shades of violet, purple, and black. It was hypnotic.

For as grievous as the amethyst's wounds had been, Kullipthius was pleased to see his speedy recovery. The only remaining visible signs of trauma were the bandages about Shayde's wrists and small tears in his wings. In the next phase of Laliah's healing regimen, she would focus on his wrists because they supported the movements necessary for flight. According to Laliah, the most debilitating damage that was left from the attack was inside his wrists. The last step would be to repair the tears on the wing membrane. Kullipthius was empathetic. As a youngling, he had suffered a painful tear in his left wing, and he vividly recalled how frustrated he had been at being grounded.

"No need for concern, Imperator Kullipthius. The pain is now

manageable. Save for my wrists, I have recovered to full strength. I can feel the healing effects within, and I am growing stronger by the day. I have tested my wings, and they are strong enough for short flights and gliding. As for my full power in flight, that will come with the imperatrix's next healing. Please inform the imperatrix that her last healing has produced great results, and I am ready for our final curative session. I am in her debt, as well as yours." Undercurrents of gratitude wound through the dragon's thoughts. *"What is your bidding, Your Imperial Majesty, and how may I be of service?"*

Kullipthius made his way back up the rock-strewn path to the upper reaches of the ravine where he caught sight of his son awaiting his return.

"I trust all went well?" Ra's expression told Kullipthius he had already gleaned the answer.

"Aye, Shayde has agreed to help us in our endeavors. During this visit, I learned he has a cloaking ability that I found most intriguing. He has the ability to deflect the light around an object to render it virtually invisible. I do not understand the details of how it works, even after he gave me a firsthand demonstration. As Shayde covered himself in magic, his image rippled and distorted. Right before my eyes, his dragon form blended with the shadows and colors of the cavern walls as he disappeared from sight. The gift of invisibility is a fascinating talent, indeed."

"That is remarkable," Ra replied.

"I will send your mother to finish the healing this day. I am reluctant to accept Shayde's help unless his wings have regained their full flight capability. He also believes his wrist muscles will be restored to good health upon your mother's next visit. I shall counsel with Laliah after the healing and gather her recommendations."

Father and son strode side-by-side. Kullipthius ran a hand through his hair and reflected upon the conversation he had shared with the amethyst. "Shayde was adamant to have Amethyst Law observed, so he promises a lifetime of protection. I told him he would have the same rights and privileges as everyone in Oralia, and that we all looked out for one another. He considered me for a long while, and I feared he would be offended. Instead, Shayde made a request."

"What request would that be, Father?"

"Shayde requested that he be allowed to retrieve his mate and bring her to Oralia. He wishes to apply for full citizenship with our empire, and I am pleased. The species is at such a fragile stage. I told him to encourage others to apply for citizenship as well. Doing so would allow them to thrive in an environment where they would neither be hunted nor feared. Additionally, they could help in the restoration of their new home in Nirvana Kai."

Ra grinned, and Kullipthius saw a touch of mischievousness in his bright eyes. "He will settle in nicely once Dusk, his mate, arrives," he said with certainty.

Though Kullipthius knew his son held the gift of soothsaying, he was always astonished by his perceptive abilities. He released a low, deep-chested laugh. "Ra Kor'el," he jested, "spying already?"

"Verily, I am only looking out for the empire's interests," said Ra, returning a smile.

"And that you do quite well, my son."

By then they had reached the point to take flight, and Kullipthius changed into a dragon.

"Have you made ready your gear for our journey to where Sani stands?" inquired Kullipthius.

"All is in order. I will start setting up camp and have things under way when you and the others arrive."

"Excellent idea, Ra. We will drop the gear as we fly over our camping grounds."

"I have not been there in a long while," said Ra. "I would like to explore the area where mother and I once lived. I have many fond memories I would like to revisit."

"As you wish," replied Kullipthius, knowing how much his son loved the forest. *"It would be best to leave in these early morning hours. That area in the forest is dense, and you have a small trek from where I will leave you to reach The Ancient One."*

CHAPTER TWENTY

R a Kor'el took a deep breath and sighed. It felt good to be back in the woodland. As much as he loved Oralia, the Tall Forest was his childhood home. As soon as he had bid his father farewell, the flora and fauna welcomed him like the long-lost friend he was. Ra smiled and began his journey under the mid-morning sky. He followed the path of youthful recollections to where Sani stood.

Though his mother and he had been exiled to the forest, his time there had been filled with adventures and exploration. As with most youngsters, Ra's curious nature had often placed him in some tomfoolery or other that he found difficult to extract himself from. He was thankful for a mother who understood the whimsy of youth, who had always tried to make the best of every situation.

When Ra grew older, he began to realize he was different. He had a difficult time accepting the fact that he would never be able to walk amongst the local Avalians or fly like other dragons. Above all, his deepest desire had been to feel the wind beneath a pair of his own wings.

Laliah had spent most of her time in her human guise while in exile within the forest. As a healer, Laliah had known enough to take note of his longing, thus she only adopted her dragon form when necessary or to delight her son with stories of his dragon heritage. The stories had made him laugh, which helped him reconcile his conflicting emotions.

When he left his childhood behind and became an adolescent, he became adept at leaving the nest on his own accord, to the chagrin of his poor mother. Off he would go, forgetting to advise her of his destination or how long he would be gone. His mother had found it exasperating. Since he was growing up in the wood, she had known the importance of learning the difference between prudence and folly. With her motherly directives, Laliah had known her son would come to that crucial understanding, as she delivered what she had called a "live demonstration," and it had only required one lesson. It consisted of a trip to the marshland where they had researched the many dangers of the fen and how to avoid them.

Ra had quickly become part of the research when he had found himself dangling by his dragon mother's claw over a smelly, stagnant bog pond. She had told him there was going to be a quiz after the demonstration, thus he needed to pay close attention.

The question: How long does it take to remove the smell of a bog pond off one's person when one does not listen to his mother?

Answer: Six baths and three days.

His course passed with flying colors, Ra was allowed to explore, with permission, and that had led to his interest in the affairs of the humans. He had come upon them often as a youngling traveling through the woodland, and he had become adept at hiding from their senses. Unable to control the impulse, he had often followed them. He had become so skillful at it that his subjects of curiosity were totally unaware of the young shadow who trailed them.

His mother had cautioned him against revealing his presence. He was a dragon, after all, and dragons led a clandestine existence, with the exception of a select few. So he had watched the humans from afar, reveling in their adventures and hunts in the wood. His beloved mother had indulged him and encouraged him to learn their history and behaviors. His life had been carefree and adventurous—until he came into his powers.

When Ra first demonstrated the most basic traits of his soothsaying gift, Laliah created games amongst the trees. She had combined education and play, requiring Ra to locate her—or specific hidden items—by applying his new abilities. Even more amazing was when he became so adept at his gifts that he could write down where she had intended to place the articles before she had decided where to hide them.

His gift erupted thereafter, and he started having prophetic dreams. Soon after, his soothsaying abilities grew in vast proportions, revealing themselves in his waking world. Intentionally or not, he somehow knew what would happen to the living beings he encountered in the forest, within the next hour, day, season, or calendar yearmark. It nearly drove him to madness. His mother had done her best to help him erect shields within his mind to restrain the ghostly, insistent presence of his powers. Nevertheless, these were powers she herself did not possess, and her training as a healer had its limits.

One particular occasion had proven unbearable. Unable to block the cerebral noise and the myriad images that assaulted him, Ra had hidden from his mother. He did not want to worry his beloved parent, for she had always ensured his wellbeing, and she would have been powerless to help him.

Ra had received an image so strong it blocked all others. Within a circle of brightly colored wagons, a copper-haired woman sang a haunting melody. Two men accompanied her with a wooden flute and tambourine while the image of a red rose appeared above the woman's head. It seemed so real that Ra had believed he could smell the perfume of the lovely blossom. Though the scene itself was serene, he had sensed danger lurking in the shadows.

Then his vision had blurred, and he suffered a horrible headache. He had fallen to his knees, then to his side, curling into a ball. With eyes closed, he had waited wearily for the din and spectacle to calm itself.

Young Ra's Woodland Adventure

A youthful Ra awoke to the darkness of the forest. He sat up and blinked, taking in his surroundings. He remembered he was overcome by a horrible headache and blurred vision and must have passed out or fallen into a deep sleep. The unintentional sleep must have done him good. Feeling better, Ra knew he needed to make his way home so his mother would not worry.

Along his journey, he heard someone singing. He changed direction to investigate and discovered a circle of horse-drawn wagons. He crept as close as he could and hid in the shadows to watch. Before his very eyes he saw a beautiful, copper-haired woman singing, accompanied by flute and tambourine. People sat around a campfire laughing, clapping, and singing gaily in time to the melody. Ra smiled at the knowledge that his vision had come to pass.

His mother had told him that these wanderers were known as Vahlarian Travelers. They traversed the countryside in groups they called "tribes" in brightly painted enclosed wagons that also served as their homes. For three seasons the Vahlarians knew no bounds, attending every marketplace or festival they came across during their travels. They were tinkers, repairmen, crafters and, to Ra's delight, wonderful entertainers.

When the arctic season came to pass, all Vahlarian tribes migrated home to Vahlar, a village located in southern Sunon where the weather was warm year-round. Vahlar magically bustled to life for the span of three moons. Then, at the appearance of the season of growth, they packed up their horse-drawn traveling homes, and the city of Vahlar sat void of life once more.

The entertainers had just finished one song and were asking for requests when one fellow shouted, "Rose, sing the song about Mala and Prince Adar!"

Rose? Suddenly it made sense. The perfect, twelve-petal flower in his vision was the name of the singer. Ra was elated with the discovery. As he watched Rose and her companions sing, his keen ears detected a twig snapping in the boughs overhead where the performers had established their makeshift stage on the ground. He could discern dark shapes hiding in the shadows, just out of view of the merrymakers. They were crouched around the camp's perimeter using hand signals to communicate. Dressed in dark attire, they blended well with the shadows. Ra watched warily as one fellow stealthily advanced upon the Vahlarians, wicked dagger in hand.

Ra suddenly remembered his dream and the terrible feeling of hidden danger. He felt his anger rising and his breath quickening. He knew he had to help, so he found himself dashing toward the threat, heedless of his mother's warnings, thinking of nothing but helping the Vahlarian Travelers.

In one gargantuan, effortless leap, Ra was behind the man with the dagger. He seized the scoundrel's tunic and yanked as hard as he could. The assailant soared through the air until he collided against a tree with an awkward crack. Then he slid to the ground, unmoving. Ra held his arms in front of him as if seeing them for the first time. He had not known until that very moment he had a dragon's strength locked inside his slender frame.

The assailants whirled to gape at Ra crouching in the shadows. One of the assailants pointed his finger at Ra and he said, "He is just a young lad!" They all began to laugh.

"It was nothing more than luck on the boy's part," one of the other attackers hissed as he walked toward Ra. "Should have stayed hidden, boy," he continued, and made a grab for Ra's arm.

With lightning reflexes Ra eluded the grab and, instead, the attacker found his own arm had been seized. Ra squeezed the man's arm until there was a resounding crack. The attacker yelped and tried to pull away. Ra's claws caught in the man's retreating flesh and left bloody trails down the man's forearm as the fellow howled in pain.

There was a flash in Ra's mind, and he understood another assailant was about to attack him from behind. Ra sidestepped and the attacker hurtled by, clutching at the space where the boy had once been. Ra's gift flared again, and he leapt accordingly— straight up into the branches of a tree—where he watched as the two attackers ran toward each other to where Ra had once stood. They collided with one another and fell together in a tangled heap. Ra sprang from the treetops, landed lightly on his feet, and he sprinted toward his attackers.

It was in that moment, the young boy's hair billowing in the wind, that the moonlight gave them all a glimpse of exactly who stood before them. Ra's eyes caught the glow of the moon and blazed a lavender-blue, and the scales on his forearms shimmered. He smiled coldly at the remaining attackers as they drank in his unusual appearance.

Standing ready to spring again if his gift insisted, Ra hoped that his show of strength and courage would dissuade the attackers from harming the caravan of travelers.

"Leave!" screamed Ra, yelling over the entertainers' singing. He stretched a hand before him with a clawed finger pointing at the nearest threat. A spark of blue light sprung from that fingertip and struck the assailant in the chest. The man flew far and fast beyond everyone's visual range.

Ra was shocked at his own display of strength, and he was startled to discover his draconic gift. His mother had tried to prepare him for the possibility of a gift presenting itself one day, but there was no time to think about that now. His mysterious demonstration proved too much for the assailants. Ra watched as they fled into the night, taking their wounded comrades with them. The Vahlarians music continued to play. They never knew what had transpired around them, and Ra was pleased they were safe.

Just then Ra heard someone in heavy boots coming toward him. A large fellow emerged from the shadows of the forest, one who seemed not at all disturbed by Ra's presence. He was tall, muscular, and carried a menacing axe.

"I will kill you for keeping me and my band from our booty!" shouted the assailant. Then he raced toward Ra with his axe raised high and roared, "You half-faced, ill-bred monster!"

Ra pivoted and ran. The large, pitted axe whizzed by his ear and struck the tree in front of him. The youngling made a sharp turn to the left, weaving his way through the trees. Gruesome scenes of what would happen if he was caught urged him faster. Since Ra had excellent night vision, he maneuvered easily through the trees, but his exceptional hearing told him that he had put little distance between himself and his quick-footed assailant.

Knowing his mother could make everything right, Ra desperately tried to reach out and locate her with his senses. But, in her stead, he felt another presence before him, one that was foreign but calming. He could hear the rustling of leaves in the trees around him.

A deep, timbered tone resounded in his head. *"Fear not, little one. Follow my directions, and we shall shelter you from danger. Lead not this assailant to your mother. She is a gentle creature, but like all protectors of their young, she will fight to ensure your safety."*

Following instructions, Ra soon found himself diving into the shelter of a honeysuckle bush next to a giant redwood tree. The boughs glowed momentarily with a pale green light and then faded to their shadow-dappled hues once he was safely within. Ra watched in bewilderment as the attacker thundered past without noticing him within his meager shelter.

Once the threat was out of sight, Ra let out the breath he was holding. He rested his head against the cool bark of the giant tree as he inhaled great gulping breaths. It took a moment for his breathing to slow.

"Humph! Half an ill . . . whatever monster," the youngling whispered. "It was the assailants themselves who were the monsters."

His intuition revealed no present danger. Truth be told, he felt an overall sense of comfort, as if in the gentle embrace of his mother's protective arms. He looked around and saw that the bush and the enormous tree were in the center of a circular clearing. He looked up and noted the tree's emerald branches were reaching endlessly toward the cosmos. He could also make out the twinkling stars through the tree's branches.

While staring into the starry night, a single point of light detached itself from its resting place within the heavens and floated down toward Ra. Once it was close enough to distinguish, he realized it was not a star, but the magical aura radiating from a tiny being.

From Ra's perspective, the curvy little form with a flowered crown atop wispy lavender tresses was definitely a she. The tiny being fluttered her wings in front of his nose. Stunned, Ra froze lest he scare the little nature spirit away.

She spun in the space before his eyes like a blossom caught in the wind. Then she motioned with her hand to the velvet sky above. Within moments Ra was joined by multitudes of her kind. Mayhap they had been there all along, just not ablaze.

Their gossamer wings were fluttering so quickly they blurred into a rainbow of multiple hues. As they flew, they left a trail of illuminating dust that faded in passing. Each possessed a tiny pair of antennae, and their hair and skin demonstrated dazzling displays of pastel colors. Males and females floated about gracefully, whirling together in a hypnotic movement before Ra's eyes. They danced in the wind, bobbing in time to music they alone could hear.

Stunned by the spectacle and unable to comprehend why these beings were unafraid of one large enough to crush them, Ra purposefully began breathing in shallow breaths, so he would not send them fluttering away.

The little one he had first glimpsed concluded her dance with a curtsy, holding the sides of her exquisitely designed dress outwards. Her countenance betrayed a shy expression on perfect, tiny features, with cheeks tinted a dainty scarlet.

Ra noticed her lips moving, but her voice was but a faint whisper. She then waved her hands in a rolling motion, and Ra felt the air move around them. The gentle breeze she created must have gathered her words, for her voice grew louder as her words were carried on the wind closer to Ra's ears. Her message was received in audible clarity:

> "Forest glade sublime
> Shelter here and rest, Milord
> Taught under the stars."

Ra smiled at the little one and said, "Alas, I fear I am unable to grasp your meaning. Are you the one who helped me?" In retrospect, that was unlikely, for the voice he had heard seemed masculine and timeless, as though he had touched upon an ancient power.

She placed her tiny hands on her hips in an expression of frustration, blew a lock of fallen hair from her eyes, and tried again:

"Ancient test of time
Jade needles and boughs reach outward
Magic is not far."

Ra considered the puzzle of her poetic, windborne words for a moment, and then he experienced an epiphany. He turned toward the tree he had sheltered beneath, dropped to his knees before its giant trunk, and placed a hand respectfully on its bark.

It was the tree that had offered him shelter.

"Aye, that is correct," the giant tree confirmed. *"I am known as Sani, The Ancient One, and the protector of the Tall Forest."*

Ra glanced back at the little one and saw that she was smiling and nodding. She reached out a glowing, petite hand and patted Ra's cheek like a mother indulging her child.

The rest of her companions dispersed, disappearing into the boughs of the tree, their lights bobbing amongst Sani's needles and branches. The little one who had communicated with him tugged on his claws and, fearful of hurting her with his talons, Ra dutifully opened his hand.

She landed and paced across his opened hand. Unafraid of her landing place, she walked to the edge of his palm and studied her dim reflection upon the scales of his wrist. Presumably satisfied, she preened her beautiful wings. They were radiant and resembled miniature shafts of moonlight converted to physical form.

Folding her wings back into place, she sat down. Displaying a little yawn and stretching daintily, she reclined, pillowed her head on her arm, and closed her diminutive eyes. The glow vacated her body entirely, and Ra was gratified that she felt secure enough to sleep. With one hand pressed against the tree bark and the other holding the nearly weightless being, Ra was uncertain what he should do next.

"She is a faerie known as Oona," the giant redwood explained. *"It is truly an honor to hold within one's palm the trust of this little one."*

Stunned, Ra could only stare at the faerie in wonder.

"This is one of the fen folk of the forest who are known as the Fenrie. She does appear to have taken a rather strong liking to you." As the words rang within his mind, an airy chuckle followed. The sound reminded Ra of how the wind glided through the caverns back home with its hollow, soothing tone.

Sani then continued his explanation. *"The females of the species are known as faeries, and the males are known as zephyrs. They are beings with elemental gifts. Thus, both males and females hold some control over the growth of vegetation and the manipulation of earth and water. They differ in this: The females possess the gift of fire, exclusive only to them, and the males' special talent provides guidance to the wind."*

Ra was amazed that so much power could be manipulated by such tiny beings.

"It is an extraordinary occasion to come across such a faerie as Oona. She was bestowed with all four elements—earth, water, air, and fire. This is a great rarity, exhibiting itself roughly thrice a millennium. She also manifested the gift of prophecy, an endowment that never existed within the species before."

"Is she their queen?" wondered Ra. "She wears a crown."

"Aye, she is. The Fenrie address their queen as Tiaré. Only the queen of the Fenrie wears the Tiaré crown, which is composed of tiny white flowers that grow in the fen," explained Sani.

"Te-ah-ray," articulated Ra, trying out the word. "She is so fragile and small," said Ra in a worried tone. "I do not want to crush her."

"You need not worry about that. Her control of all the elements is supreme and it seems nothing can spoil her. She could give the red dragons' breath of fire an excellent challenge with the blazes she can conjure and manipulate. She also harnesses the wind to carry her words to the ears of those who cannot commune with her tiny voice and mental whispers, and she can employ small gales to move objects many times her size. Many of her kind together are enough to extinguish forest fires, using dirt to smother the blaze or water from nearby sources to quench it."

Ra glanced up at the forest giant he was leaning against. He had learned many things from his mother and from observing nature, but he had never been taught anything about the life-force of the trees. Thus, he certainly had not been prepared for the tree's tutoring in woodland lore, but he had been enthralled by it.

"I sense your mind awash in memories of our first meeting, Land Guardian."

The earthy sound of The Ancient One's thoughts brought a grin to Ra, who had been caught in a state of idle and pleasant contemplation. His thoughts from the past had made his journey through the fen pass swiftly. Ra could not contain his broad smile.

"Sani, my grand old friend, what a privilege it is to be in your presence once more." It was good to be home.

CHAPTER TWENTY-ONE

A fter a few hours of friendly conversation and meditation with Sani, it was time for Ra to make his way south to the Lands of Marsh. He dug through the items he and his father had dropped off earlier and grabbed his favorite walking stick and proper clothing to wear while in the Tall Forest.

Ra dressed in his royal yet practical attire, donning a white, puff sleeved tunic that was slashed with blue horizontal insets down the arms. Atop his tunic he wore a short, close-fitting blue leather vest, tooled and painted with an elegant gold leaf design. Ra's high top boots and wrist cuffs were made of the same decorated blue leather, and his leggings were made of a heavy, beige brocade fabric with gold stitching. He completed his attire by wearing matching waist armor which wrapped around his back and belted in the front.

Leaving the Tall Forest behind, Ra entered the outskirts of the reed-choked marshlands. The shadows wrapped the land in obscurity, not wishing to whisper their secrets. Even though the ground looked solid, it could be nothing more than illusion with quicksand beneath, lying in wait for the unwary. Almost nothing moved in the fog, and sounds drifted uncannily and softly through the moist, heavy air. It was here the onyx dragon known as Xalcon Rhylock made his lair.

Before the soothsayer left Oralia for the Tall Forest, he recommended to his father that Xalcon join their ranks. Not only were these black-colored dragons formidable in battle, the red dragons were wary of them. It seemed a black dragon was resistant to fire, and their caustic weapon of spraying acid made most dragons flee from them on sight, especially in a one-on-one confrontation. Known in certain circles as "Death Dragons," the majority of these dark beasts were unapproachable and, with the exception of mated pairs, they were rarely seen in groups.

Ahead, beyond the mist-dampened trees, was a large lake. The area was swarming with biting insects, and Ra donned a black silk cloak he pulled from his rucksack to cover his exposed skin.

Ra reached a giant marsh oak tree with moss hanging from its branches like scarves over the arms of a merchant. He walked halfway around its thick trunk. He then stepped over a few gnarled roots and looked down a dark passageway at the trunk's base that led down to an underground hollow. Had Ra not visited this area before, he would never have found the entrance.

Ra stepped down into the deep shadows of the natural passageway, where burled roots rose and then dove to claw into the earth, forming handholds and places to step to make his way down into the earth. Soft, old leaves littered the area in almost every nook and cranny. The locale was one Ra knew his objective favored for hunting and relaxing. Xalcon was not expecting his presence and would not appreciate the intrusion.

The hollow was a ragged circle, large enough to house one full-grown dragon and, for once, Ra was comfortable with his smaller size. The center was cleared until there was naught but hardened dirt. The soil was pocked and charred, and the occasional stone looked to be scorched by flame, but Ra was cultured enough to know it was not a flame's mark, but acid. He saw a small pile of white bones thrown haphazardly in one area, speaking silently of unseen danger.

The place was empty, but the marsh oak warned it would not be so for long. Xalcon would soon know of a presence in his favorite haunt, arrive through the back entrance, and wreak havoc upon the intruder.

Once settled inside the hollow, Ra clapped two small starfire stones together to light them. He placed one in his cloak pocket for warmth and held the other aloft to illuminate the area. The starfire stone's light pierced the darkness, pushing a wreath of light to the perimeter of the loop of bark and interwoven branches. Ra noted a pair of angry, golden-yellow eyes glaring at him from the shadows. Xalcon's murky scales dripped with moisture. He must have been swimming in the lake when he sensed the intrusion.

Ra offered the onyx dragon greetings. "I bid you salutations and wellbeing, Xalcon. Indeed, it is an honor to be in your presence once more." Ra inclined his head in respect before the black-scaled form.

"Remove your hood so I may get a closer look at you," boomed the dragon's thoughts into Ra's mind. The ebon-scaled dragon slipped through the narrow opening and stared down with ill-concealed irritation. The rough black onyx upon his forehead glinted in the starfire stone's light.

Ra believed Xalcon would be considered a magnificent dragon amongst his peers, and that he would be more at ease if he were not so keen on his own isolation. But instead, Xalcon was distrustful and cold after having been exiled from his own mother's nest and family at an early age. This had left him angry, suspicious, and on edge. His sleek, dark scales blended perfectly with the shadows, the ideal camouflage for seeking prey in the darkness, unnoticed, until it was too late.

The soothsayer slid back his hood and Xalcon's giant head swung down to study him. Ra was leaning casually against the rough edges of a tree root inside the hollow, and he allowed the dark dragon to move closer. "Is this any way to treat a guest, Xalcon? Mayhap you have forgotten our pact?"

"Ra!" bellowed Xalcon, the name emerging in a roar. Xalcon's green-tipped talons slowly retracted. Plumes of green gas escaped from the corners of his maw.

The beast appeared to contemplate Ra's presence, and then he demanded, *"What is the reason for this intrusion?"*

Ra knew Xalcon did not like being caught unaware on his own turf, but the land guardian could tell that his aggravation was subsiding.

Then there was a swirling of shadows where the darkness seemed to swallow the light itself. When it finally coalesced, Xalcon stood before Ra in his altered guise, the very trait that had led to his exile. Onyx dragons believed the humans weak-willed and beneath their notice, and since Xalcon had the "misfortune" to be a shape shifter, he was brushed aside.

Laliah and Ra had stumbled upon Xalcon when he was but a nestling. He had crash-landed while trying unsuccessfully to teach himself to fly. After Laliah had healed Xalcon's cuts and bruises he had run away. Soon after, they noticed him following them, mirroring their two-legged forms, throughout the forest. It had appeared to be his preferred form when he was in their company. Laliah had explained to a much younger Ra that Xalcon had accepted her because she had no shame in her altered form. Likewise, he could relate to Ra because Ra himself was different, having dragon heritage while possessing human features. This shared commonality helped both the young dragons cope with their differences.

Ra wondered if that was the reason he and Xalcon had come to a unique understanding of each other; both had been exiled and mistrusted for their abilities and forms. Thus, they had always treated each other with a wary respect, if not exactly friendship. Any other dragon bold enough to intrude on Xalcon's domain would have been driven out.

Xalcon's situation saddened Ra. It was regrettable that Xalcon had refused the empire's invitation to join. Since Oralia consisted of many environmental options, Ra was certain Xalcon could have found a secluded home within its borders, but he was distrustful and savored his privacy.

Returning from his musings, Ra sat himself on one of the large roots. "I would like to discuss a proposition with you." Xalcon moved to sit across from Ra. His movements were graceful and purposeful, marking him as the skilled predator he was.

In his upright, two-legged form Xalcon had dark skin and long, curling black hair. His striking gold eyes still smoldered as he swept his hair away from his face in an irritated motion. Xalcon's clothes were a dark wine-red, a color he fancied, and Ra had to smile picturing the dragon's treasure trove that he knew to be awash in the hue.

Xalcon had transferred his onyx stone to a circular pendant on a dark chain around his neck. The black dragon had never been able to satisfactorily explain to a curious younger Ra how he controlled the feat, much to their mutual frustration. He now fingered said chain about his throat in a telltale sign of consideration.

"Speak, Ra. I must admit to being more than a little curious as to what takes you from your comfortable empire and brings you here to me." His tone projected annoyance, but there was an undercurrent of something else in his voice that the soothsayer did not miss. Ra guessed the black dragon was in grave need of contact with others, even if he did not realize it himself. Ra's mother was a healer, after all, who had taught her son that not every wound was physical, and the knitting of flesh could not heal all.

"The dragon empire would like your help and allegiance to prevent a battle we fear is swiftly forthcoming," said Ra. "I have it from the trees, and several other sources, that there is a red flight aiming to annihilate or enslave all mankind and—"

"Why should I care about the humans?" The black dragon

215

snorted, cutting Ra's words short. "It was my ability to don the appearance of a man that caused my exile. I would have thought that *you*, of all dragons, would understand that."

"—and try to take the Oralian Empire as their own," Ra continued, refusing to be sidetracked. "I understand perfectly your reluctance in some matters, Xalcon. Nevertheless, the ruby dragons are not only after the Avalians. What makes you think they will stop at the lands of Avala and Oralia? If all reds have banded together into one flight, as we fear, they will want all lands, including the Lands of Marsh. They are greedy and violent, and your domain and treasures will be fair game to them. Although you are formidable in battle, you could not hope to drive them all out if it came to a mass assault. Nay, we need to stop this before it increases in magnitude."

Xalcon growled. "I agree the reds are our vile enemy. They have harassed us before, as you are well aware." He held up his muscled right arm and clearly displayed the long, horrible scars that ringed his flesh like bracelets and spoke to Ra through clenched teeth. "That treacherous red tried to enslave us both, Ra. I would love nothing more than to drive them all from these lands with no amount of gentle persuasion." His long tapering fingers hooked into claws, and he slashed through the air as if he were performing the act. Then he relaxed, letting his breath out in a rush, and his hand returned to its human shape. "Yet, I do not see your need for my assistance. Verily, you have enough warriors in all of Oralia that my presence alone could not render the slightest difference."

Ra inwardly cringed at the memories. The old scars circling Xalcon's limb were there because the black dragon had saved Ra's life that fateful day. It took a moment for Ra to speak again. "I have great respect for you, Xalcon; you know that. You must understand we are planning on a small force at our encampment where Sani stands. The whole of the empire will be involved, but their responsibility will be to protect Avala's borders and keep the reds away from Sapphirus. If the Sapphirian people ever found out we existed outside of the pretty tales they spin, our clandestine and peaceful world would turn to chaos. This would pose a threat to all that is life." The starfire light painted Ra's features with a flickering intensity. "I believe you to be perfect for this incursion, for there is none better. I would not be here otherwise."

Ra could not suppress his look of anguish as he said, "Tarry not, for I have glimpsed what will happen if we were to fail. Will you at least consider my words?"

Xalcon stood and restlessly paced before Ra's seated form

before he replied. "You have always been gifted with such pretty speech, Ra. I have never believed myself exceptionally wise, although I do think I am clever. I need time to ponder your proposal. I would be putting myself on the line for humans who know naught of my existence and for a dragon empire I want no part of. I also run the risk of drawing the unwanted attention of those who exiled me. They believe I perished here, and I do not want them to think otherwise."

"I understand, and I am humbly grateful for your consideration, Xalcon. When you are clear of mind that my words hold truth, you will find our camp where Sani stands. Be swift with your answer, for our gathered force will meet where Sani stands upon the morrow."

Xalcon nodded, his mind elsewhere, and the soothsayer knew he was weighing his options. The onyx whirled abruptly and stalked from the clearing, calling in a tone of warning over his shoulder. "I am going to hunt. When next you visit, make a proper announcement of your presence, Ra. Or not even our history together will save your hide." The onyx dragon was blunt and annoyed, but there was no missing the fact that he was not opposed to Ra's visit. Were it otherwise, he would have tossed Ra from his lands and bid him never return.

"Point noted and, incidentally, Xalcon, I know now, beyond a shadow of a doubt, that the ruby who tried to enslave us was, indeed, Flayre. He is alive and is the instigator of this forthcoming attack."

Ra Kor'el observed Xalcon halt in his tracks after hearing his parting words, and he watched as Xalcon balled his hands tightly into fists.

Without a response, Xalcon was once again in his dragon form, and he disappeared into the murky blackness.

The soothsayer dipped the starfire stones in a shallow pond of water to douse their light. Ra knew if anything could persuade Xalcon Rhylock to join their ranks, it would be the news that Flayre, the one that had targeted them both in their youth, was alive.

He was glad for the season of the sun, for even though it was late, there was still enough daylight left to get back to Sani and the encampment before darkness engulfed the land. He made his way from the bog, letting the trees guide him carefully through the marshlands.

Ra reached the top of the hillock as the orange glow of the evening sun was dipping beyond the horizon. His gaze fell upon the last few rays of pale sunlight filtering through the leaves and branches of the trees in the forest. Down he went and around the bend to a stream with a tree-laden meadow, stopping a moment at the water's edge to quench his growing thirst. As he trod along the forest floor, the night slowly rose to greet the stars. A pale blue corona encircled the luminous moon like an ethereal midnight sun.

"I am not sure how you managed to convince Xalcon Rhylock to join your ranks, Land Guardian," mused Sani as Ra came into view. *"Yet, the smile upon your face is a good indication of a winning venture."*

"I am not ready to claim victory just yet," explained Ra. "Nevertheless, it seems a strong possibility, and it was good to see my old friend."

"I would wager it more along the lines of probability," Sani replied. *"I have heard it from the sentinel trees standing watch in the marshlands that Xalcon stands in his human guise dressed in his best armor. As we speak, he is preparing his greatsword for battle."*

"Ah, well then," proclaimed Ra, "I will accept your first declaration of a 'winning venture' and gloat with unbound enthusiasm."

Sani's needles shifted above Ra's head in a display of mirth. Several needles fell to the forest floor as a result, and the land guardian was pleased with his old friend's amusement. They then spoke of inconsequential topics, enjoying each other's company for a time and reliving their mutual past.

Later that eve, Sani updated Ra on the latest intelligence the trees had gathered. *"Flayre was spotted dropping a nobleman at an abandoned encampment. He must have been using an invisibility spell because, other than his abrupt appearance and disappearance at the encampment, they were unable to track him. His magic rendered him invisible to their senses. I advised my forest brethren to keep track of the nobleman. Last observed, he was heading in a southeasterly direction toward Terra Leone."*

"That is excellent news, Sani," replied Ra, knowing Sani was speaking of Danuvius, the former steward from Terra Leone who was in league with Flayre. "Father will be pleased with all the information you have gleaned. Your assistance has been most helpful."

Soon thereafter, they bid each other goodnight, and Ra took his leave, retreating drowsily to set up his bed. He readied his sleeping pallet and placed his cloak around him, and used one of his packs to pillow his head. He let the sounds of the nearby stream and the musical duet of a frog and a cricket lull him into a blissful sleep.

Awakening to the blush of early dawn, Ra stretched in greeting to the morning sky. Feeling a little stiff from yesterday's excursions, he rose to straighten his legs and decided to take a lazy stroll to wash at the stream. Through the leafy forest he strode, in tunic and drawstring underbreeches, with boots and royal attire in hand. The cool morning air was crisp and refreshing as he made his way through shafts of sunlight under moss-laden trees while birds sang gaily amid the branches. He grinned at the comical antics of a bushy-tailed fox chasing a rabbit through the willowy thickets.

Upon reaching the bank of the stream, Ra dipped his clawed fingers within and brought cupped palms of cool water to his lips. Following the stream to the sound of cascading waters where a small waterfall tumbled into a pond, he undressed and jumped into the brisk pool to help awaken his senses. He let the rush of the water wash over his body, and then he floated on his back in a patch of warm sun.

Clean, refreshed, and dressed in regal blue attire, he walked along the banks of the stream, taking note of various rocks, round and flat, lying within the stream. He made a mental note to later return for these smooth stones to build a hearth for the encampment. He smiled as he decided to make the stew his father enjoyed so much the last time they had visited the Tall Forest.

The thought of cooking made the land guardian's stomach rumble, beckoning him to forage for food and break his fast. He found some edible wild greens, mushrooms, and a lovely blackberry bush, ripe for the picking. Once sated, Ra headed back to get dressed and ready their encampment.

When Kullipthius and Ra had arrived at the clearing early yester-morn, they had dropped the pavilions, gear, ropes, and stakes from the air to where they would stand upon the forest floor. The tents were tall enough for humans to stand upright inside and designed to erect easily with one center and four corner poles.

This would not be a problem for the dragons who could alter their form while at the encampment. However, Ra's father had been uncertain if the encampment's accommodations would be suitable for Shayde. In all the times that the amethyst had been in their presence, Shayde had remained in dragon form. To assuage their concerns, Sani had advised them that they need not worry. A suitable cavern had recently been abandoned by a family of bears and was in close proximity.

Ra then began the task of readying the camp by advising the trees of his intent, and then by asking them to alert him of any who might trespass. The tall sentinels were more than pleased to have the land guardian in their midst and were happy to help. Ra thought it a pity that more folk could not tap into the unique channel of communication used by the trees around them. He found them to be accommodating, simple, and refreshingly direct.

Ra started unpacking the gear while he awaited the arrival of his father's force. Of a sudden, there came a flash of colorful lights careening around Ra at high velocity, pulsing in a vibrant spectrum. A host of Fenrie had descended upon him and, ever spontaneous, had apparently decided to lend their elemental help to his campground's construction.

Since the tents needed to be pitched on level ground, the Fenrie began the task of clearing the area of leaves and stones using their gifts of earth and air. Half the host of zephyrs left to clear out the nearby cave that would be reserved for Shayde's use.

After the camp's ground was smooth and litter free, the large pavilions went up swiftly under the Fenries' diligent organization. Despite the imposing size of the structures, the thick swaths of green and brown fabric rose up of their own volition and tumbled over the tall poles with ease, aided by the element of wind and a touch of enchantment. If a rogue dragon were to fly above the canopy of trees, the tents' colors blended so well that it would appear as if they were nothing more than a part the forest.

While the Fenrie were working diligently on the cave and encampment, the land guardian set about the task of collecting the smooth, water-polished rocks from the stream to build the stone hearth.

It was mid-morn when all the tents were in place, the stone hearth finished, and the area windswept of debris. Ra inclined his head in gratitude and offered vocal thanks to his tiny helpers. A host of companionable zephyrs summoned the starfire stones in the hearth to life, and they soon had Ra's special blend of tea filling the air with cinnamon and spice.

The female fairies were braiding his long hair with small, colorful feathers expertly woven throughout, adding little splashes of color to his otherwise pale strands. A smile tugged at Ra's lips as he spied the male zephyrs, swirling and dancing within the starfire light, their wings a dazzling sight, ever-changing from brilliant azure to emerald to a sparkling crimson.

As Ra lost himself to the impromptu fey gala, a flash of light erupted almost directly under his nose. All Fenrie ceased activity and bowed in respect. Momentarily startled and blinking spots from his vision, it took Ra little time to understand what he bore witness to. It was the unbridled joy of a most powerful faerie. The light show dancing before his eyes was slowly dissipating. He smiled widely as the little being came into focus before him.

"Tiaré Oona," greeted Ra, holding out his upturned palm. She settled upon his outstretched hand and doused her radiance. Little antenna bobbed as the petite faerie hopped up with glee on tiptoes. Her lavender tresses were much longer than he remembered, and he watched as her hair bounced and danced around her slender shoulders. She gave his clawed index finger a hug.

"I am honored by your presence," said Land Guardian Ra. Oona offered a stunningly gorgeous smile in response and added a tiny curtsy that led Ra to laugh good-naturedly. "I must offer you my humble gratitude for providing the vision within my dreams. The revelation that the approaching threat is not Sapphirian-born brought great clarity and prompted us to investigate further. With this news, we are now better able to prepare."

Oona dipped her head in acknowledgement.

"I am glad to have this time to speak with you, for we have an issue of import to discuss. Sani informed me the red dragons have gathered under Flayre's leadership, and we must make hearty plans if we are to have hopes of triumph with little loss. In the past, when these ruby dragons entered the forestlands, they cared naught for any destruction they caused. Sometime later, their Chief Elder Py'ro made a pact with Dra'khar to respect each other's homelands.

"With his son Flayre now at the helm and his arsenal of magic fueled by *The Dark Arts*, I fear the worst, for it will not only be selfish instinct guiding the reds' deadly breath; they will be under the direction of Flayre and his vile machinations. We need a foolproof plan to prevent them from destroying what we hold mutually dear—our beloved forest friends, families, and homes. I was hoping you would have an idea to help overcome this threat."

Subsequently, Oona's eyes narrowed and her hands balled into tiny fists. Ra knew she was worried about her home being ruined under the fiery might of the ruby flight. She pulled herself up to her full height, and a look that was easy to interpret as determination crossed her features. She summoned the wind to carry her echoing declaration:

"Flames are trouble naught.
Gentle forest friends are safe
with Fenrie on watch."

"To douse their fire,
Fenrie gifts will be employed
to smother their breath."

To demonstrate her words, she summoned a firestorm to her left fist and a tiny rainstorm to her right. Then she clapped her hands to extinguish the fiery flames that threatened violent intent. Ra knew this was but a fraction of her might. Individually, Fenrie could do much to alter the elements; as a swarm, a host of Fenrie—led by Oona—would be nearly unstoppable in their efforts to douse the threat of fire.

"That is excellent, Tiaré Oona. With you and the Fenrie taking care of the forest, we can better handle things on our end."

Sooner than anticipated, the sound and force of rushing wind from the downdraft of large wings stirred the newly constructed encampment. The ensuing current of air disrupted the festivity, and the Fenrie disappeared into the shadowy places between tree leaves and trunks, ever elusive to those they did not know. Oona granted a teeny curtsy and swiftly departed to join the others.

One by one the dragons descended in a swift dive, extending their wings to great lengths to land with grace in the clearing's center. In turn, the men slid from the backs of the dragons. Flashes of transformation followed, and the dragons walked on two legs toward the encampment, followed by their Sapphirian charges: King Lucian, Eralon Wellsbough who was the Captain of the Elite Guardsmen, Scout Jhain Velendris, and the Liltian named Treyven Fontacue. Lucian and Kullipthius were the first to greet Ra.

"Welcome and greetings, Imperial Father, King Lucian," greeted Ra. Royalty nodded in acknowledgement.

King Lucian then introduced Eralon, Treyven and Jhain to Ra, and the trio bowed to the Prince of Oralia to show their respect.

"I am astonished and delighted that you managed to construct the encampment in such a short time," said Kullipthius.

"Aye," commented King Lucian as he looked around the camp, "a most excellent job. However did you get it done so quickly?"

"Mother and I made many friends while living here," explained Ra. "They were eager to lend a hand."

"I have news from Sani. He has advised me that Flayre dropped Danuvius off at an abandoned encampment. The sentinel trees that are tracking Danuvius said he is moving in the direction of Terra Leone. Unfortunately, they were unable to follow Flayre's movements, for he used his magic to make himself invisible."

"Gramercy Ra, that is good to know," replied Lucian. "Eralon advised me that Danuvius had escaped from a secret passageway in Terra Leone to avoid capture. We need to send a message to Balderon asking him to guard any underground passageways in case he tries to return in the same fashion."

"We can send a dragon scout to Terra Leone to advise Knight Master Balderon of his whereabouts," said Kullipthius. The king nodded his agreement as Kullipthius continued. "Once he is caught, we can send an amber quartz and see what we might glean from an interrogation."

"Additionally," continued Ra, "I made my trek through the marshlands and asked Xalcon Rhylock to assist us. He was hesitant at first and told me he had to weigh his options. He must have decided he will be joining our ranks, for Sani advised me that he will be arriving here shortly."

"His acid gift and resistance to flame will prove a tremendous asset to our party," said Kullipthius, looking pleased.

"Agreed," said Ra. "Let us prepare everyone for the black dragon's arrival."

CHAPTER TWENTY-TWO

R a Kor'el watched as a lone figure strode from the forest shadows and into view. Xalcon Rhylock was at least a head taller than anyone else in their encampment. Dark and imposing, he studied his surroundings with sharp, golden eyes. Ra thought the human side of the onyx dragon was magnificent. His long, dark hair was loosely pulled back into a braid and secured at the bottom with a leather strap. He held a two-handed greatsword in one hand, daring anyone to test the irrefutable evidence of his resolve and might. Its use required special skill, thus few could wield it effectively in battle.

Xalcon's armor, decorated with embossed metal studs, was intimidating. He wore a one piece pauldron that protected his neck, shoulders, and upper arms, over a sleeveless, knee-length blood-red tunic. Cosseting his muscular torso was a finely crafted cuirass made from metal that was covered inside and out with soft leather. A tasset, that held hanging strips of polished steel, was connected to the bottom of his cuirass to protect his upper legs and thighs. His otherwise bare, massive arms displayed wide, leather guards to shield forearms and wrists. He walked upon leather, sandal-like footwear with thick, heavy soles. They were knee-high with a solid leather backing and strapped in the front.

Ra grinned at Xalcon's look of surprise upon noticing the amethyst dragon that was standing in the clearing near the encampment. Here was a fellow dragon that was shunned by others, just as he and Xalcon had always been. This gathering just might prove to be of interest to the black dragon after all.

Shayde met Xalcon's eyes and nodded to the onyx dragon in respect. Obviously not used to such regard, Ra was astonished to see Xalcon nod back. Xalcon caught Ra watching the exchange and glared at him. He stomped toward Ra with irritation plainly inscribed on his face, as if daring him to comment. He then turned and planted his greatsword in the ground next to Ra and stood silently adjacent the soothsayer while resting both hands on the hilt.

Three topaz dragon brothers, Scout Leader Talin, Scout Swift, and Scout Kayne approached Ra in their human forms. Talin stepped forward to speak with Ra, nodding his head in greeting to Xalcon before he spoke.

"We supplied the mercenaries with the starfire stones you gave us, Your Highness," said Talin. "We explained how the smoke from their wood fires would attract the attention of the Avalian King, disclosing their location. They used them immediately and stopped felling the smaller trees for firewood."

"Excellent," said Ra. He was pleased to hear that his plan had worked. He could no longer tolerate these invaders or their ignorance and naivety. They were turning the forest to ruin with their wanton collecting of timber.

It came time for the meeting, and Ra called for everyone to gather around. Talin stood at Ra's left side while Xalcon remained sentinel at the soothsayer's right. Ra bid one and all a hearty greeting. The soothsayer was introduced to Jhain, Treyven, and Eralon. Then after giving Xalcon Rhylock a formal introduction to his imperial father and the king, Ra presented the stone-faced warrior to the rest of their group: Chief Romus, Vahl Zayne, Blayz, Shayde, the king's companions, and the three Oralian scouts. With introductions out of the way, he began.

"I would like to present Talin, the leader of the dragon scouts. He is here to provide us with the information he and his brethren gathered when they joined the Liltian force that is marching through the Tall Forest."

"During our investigations," began Talin, "we confirmed that the Liltian mercenaries are under the misguided belief that they need to save their brethren from a great injustice. Though this massed army that came under our scrutiny is strong, we surmised it is not powerful enough to take on the forces of the king.

"It started when Danuvius spread a wicked falsehood. He claimed that King Lucian had established the institution of slavery by removing the Liltian people from their homes, stripping them of their rights, and forcing them into servitude. Believing the steward of Terra Leone's lies, the Liltians living along the northern borders of Sunon and southwestern borders of Avala gathered their brethren.

"They were en route through the Tall Forest to meet up with Danuvius at a predetermined location. However, under the guidance of King Lucian and Imperator Kullipthius, we presented them a legitimate missive, supplied by Treyven Fontacue, telling them he had arrived at the Terra Leone fortress and would meet them there with further instructions. When we left them this day, they were on their way to Terra Leone."

"Gramercy Talin," said Ra. "In truth, the foot soldiers are naught but a distraction. However, when put in place with Flayre's other stratagem and dark magic, he might have succeeded had we not ferreted out his systematic plan of attack—namely, a large faction of ruby dragons under Flayre's corruptive guidance."

"Since these red dragons typically keep to their desert realms across the Carillion Sea," voiced King Lucian, "it's naturally worrisome for us to think of wild, fire-breathing dragons in our flammable forestlands."

"I am of the same opinion, Your Majesty," agreed Ra. "Their blatant disregard for all that is life has the entire forest in an uproar over this threat. Being solitary creatures, we know that the reds had to have been coerced into cooperating on one objective. And *that* brings us to the most recent and important information we have gleaned. Chief Romus, would you care to explain?"

Romus made his way forward. "My eldest son, Dag, visited the Desertlands to gather information on the ruby dragons' motivations. While there, he used his gift of influence with what we like to call "forget me." It is not quite invisibility, but a suggestion that he used in order to safely listen to their plans without being noticed. Dag returned from his task this very morn with the red dragons' intentions. They are planning to leave the Desertlands upon the morrow before dawn, which would put them here at noontide."

"Flayre has instructed the red dragons to set the entire forest ablaze," continued Romus. "If this occurs the Avalians would have had a fight on three fronts: the disaster of the burning wood, the armed foot soldiers who had been tricked into fighting, and a battle with the red dragons.

"Two major dragon assaults are planned to occur simultaneously. While one large faction of rubies surround Moorwyn Castle—which I am sure would cause a mighty blood bath with the Avalians—another flight is to invade the inhabitants of Oralia in the mountains. These attacks would have been devastating for us all. Fortunately, we received Dag's forewarning and are prepared."

"Gramercy Chief Romus," acknowledged Ra. "It is clear that Treyven's armed countrymen were the distraction and the red dragons are the obvious threat. If these fires are set in the forest, the armsmen would have surely been trapped within the flames while on their way to Moorwyn Castle."

"Talin," said the imperator, "I think it best that you, Swift, and Kayne rejoin our Oralian scouts patrolling the coast of Avala. We need all eyes available scrutinizing the horizon for the ruby dragons. Then send word to us here, as well as to Var'ohk, advising us of their arrival and position."

"We shall leave immediately, Your Imperial Majesty," said Talin, and the three scouts made their way to the clearing.

"I spotted the position of the Liltian forces on my way to your encampment," reported Xalcon. "If they keep to their current pace, I would calculate their arrival at Terra Leone this night."

"Excellent, Xalcon," said Kullipthius. "That information serves us greatly. It helps us with our schedule of defenses."

"This would be a good time ta go ta the fortress an' prepare fer me misguided Liltian brethren," stated Treyven. "I shall tell 'em ta rest fer the night, an' when they rise upon the morn, me men an' I can genuinely tell them we discovered Danuvius' lies about slavery in Avala. The townsfolk o' Terra Leone will back me story regarding Danuvius' behavior."

"There should be enough room for them to set up their camps at the showgrounds in the fortress, Your Majesty," advised Eralon.

"Both excellent ideas," commended Lucian. "Treyven, I will give you a message bearing my seal that you may present to Knight Master Balderon explaining my orders."

Lucian excused himself for a moment to prepare the missive, while the imperator addressed the amethyst dragon.

"Shayde, the time has come to carry Treyven to Terra Leone. While the humans were getting familiar with riding dragonback, Scout Swift showed Treyven the most secure route to guide you to your location safely. When you arrive, you will notice that the hill where the grotto is located will afford you the perfect vantage to discern the exact moment the Liltians' arrive at Terra Leone. Are you comfortable with the plans we discussed?"

"Aye, Your Imperial Majesty," replied Shayde, who was standing at the edge of the encampment. *"The purpose of the concealment will be twofold: The cloak will prevent the prying*

eyes of the red dragons from finding their intended target, and those within the fortress and village of Terra Leone will see nothing but blue skies above."

"Gramercy, Shayde. Since the majority of the reds rarely, if ever, come to the country of Sapphirus, they are not familiar with the terrain. What the rubies cannot see, they cannot attack, and we do not want the people within to panic. The Oralian Champions will keep the red dragons away from the populated landscape and send them back to the Desertlands."

Ra explained Shayde's cloaking abilities to Eralon, Treyven and Jhain, and he elaborated on their plans for cloaking Terra Leone.

When the king returned to Kullipthius' side, he handed Treyven the missive he penned for the new steward, Redwald Balderon.

"Once the Liltian forces have arrived at Terra Leone," stated the king, "I will need you to make sure the fortress is locked down tight. For safety's sake, no one is to leave until this is over. Place only those men who can be trusted at the front gate and await my arrival."

"Aye, Yer Majesty," replied Treyven.

After conferring with their majesties, Ra said, "Before Treyven and Shayde leave for Terra Leone, I believe this to be a favorable time for us all to break for our midday meal."

KULLIPTHIUS searched the skies. Unbeknownst to the group of men and dragons resting in their pavilions, one of the most beautiful creatures ever to grace the dragon world hovered just above the edges of their perceptions. Kullipthius had been made aware of the magnificent beast's forthcoming visit when he received a private message announcing aforementioned beast's intentions. And he had been waiting for this day for a long time.

This gold dragon, known as Vinander, did not interfere with the balance of life unless a great, devastating force was at hand. With a vast knowledge of history, culture, and tradition at his fingertips and the ability to seek out glimpses of what was to come, he lent his wisdom to help others shape their destinies—but only when the time was right—and it seemed this was such a time.

Kullipthius watched as Vinander dropped from the heights. He flapped his great wings, and a great thunder of wind rushed through the canopy of trees. His huge claws pounded the ground as he landed. The jarring impact bought him the attention he sought, and the rest of the encampment's occupants streamed from their tents.

As was his custom—and before the others could misconstrue his unanticipated arrival—Vinander lifted shining wings high in the air. He offered a low bow, which displayed his three gilded horns that sat, crown-like, upon his head. His identifying marker, a rather large hunk of gold, sat splendidly in the triangle of his crown. It gleamed majestically in the sun's light.

He uttered the ancient call for peace:

"I seek Imperator Kullipthius, son of Dra'khar and benevolent ruler of the Great Dragon Empire of Oralia. I am the Golden One known as Vinander, and I call for an agreement of peace. I approach you now to offer my assistance."

Kullipthius stepped forward and smiled, for Vinander was a most welcomed sight. He wished he could change back into a dragon and reply in kind, but there was not enough room in the confines of the encampment. With a regal bow, the platinum dragon leader said, "I, Rex Imperator Kullipthius, son of Dra'khar and ruler of the Great Dragon Empire of Oralia, am in accord with your call for peace. I am honored by your offer of assistance. Prithee, Vinander, join us."

Kullipthius remembered Vinander's visits with his father in Oralia. Any assistance the Golden One offered would be appreciated, for they were seldom seen, and it was rare for them to offer aid.

A flash of light and a billow of smoke followed the imperator's request and Vinander transformed. The man left standing in the space the dragon had occupied only moments before drew shocked expressions from the king and his men.

Kullipthius knew the Sapphirians were struck speechless as their gazes fell upon Vinander. His altered guise showed him to be of medium build and height. He was garbed in a white tunic under a heavy blue vest with gold trim. His pants were a homespun brown and tucked into worn leather boots. His hair was a long, shining grey. Gold fastenings in his hair caught the light in much the same manner his scales had only moments earlier. His vibrant sienna eyes drew one's gaze away from his laugh lines.

The imperator smiled as King Lucian and his entourage gaped at the fellow who strode past. He was a famous participant at the festivals in Kaleidos City who sang verses in honor of gallant knights and told stories of dragons and brave champions from faraway lands. His name was Lore Keeper Windermere—and he was a dragon!

As Vinander approached Kullipthius he said, "Your Imperial Majesty. I apologize for not having visited sooner, as I had promised. I was called away to a distant empire to help with a plague that killed many dragons. I ministered to the sick for many seasons and helped their healer formulate a cure."

"No apology needed, Vinander," said the imperator. "You are always a welcomed sight."

"Now, as to the reason for my visit this day," continued Vinander. "If I may, I would like to talk to you in private. I am the bearer of information that I have wanted to share with you since last I saw you on Kaleidos Peak following your father's untimely death. And as I feel the presence of dark magic growing since having arrived for the festival, I feel compelled to speak with you."

"Come, Vinander. Let us retire to my pavilion where we might speak privately."

The private meeting had ended late in the afternoon and the time had come for Vinander to depart. As Kullipthius led Vinander to the pavilion's exit, he said, "Rest assured that we will handle all the details for a grand quincentennial celebration at the sanctuary in Eva'kohr."

"Gramercy, my friend," replied Vinander. "Your assistance with this matter is greatly appreciated." Then he added, "Incidentally, I recounted the story of Py'ro and Flayre at this season's festival. I look forward to following up with the tale of how Flayre's evil reign ceased."

"I anticipate that will be a gratifying performance," replied Kullipthius.

"Fare thee well in all of your endeavors," said Vinander.

"I wish you wellbeing and safe journey, my friend," replied Kullipthius.

Vinander strode to the clearing and gave a smile and a wave to the others in the encampment. There was a blinding flash as radiant gold scales caught the light when Vinander launched himself airborne.

A private message touched Kullipthius as the enigmatic dragon flew away, quickly turning to a small speck upon the skyline. *"When you do catch Flayre, Kullipthius, remind him of the Golden One who swore to help Py'ro eradicate the evil dark arts from his son and stop his reign of terror. Tell him my vow still stands and, although delayed, was never forgotten."*

Kullipthius' eyes reflected a mind far away. A gentle nudge from Ra's thoughts asking how his time with Vinander went stirred the imperator from his musings, and he noted Ra standing before him.

"My apologies, Ra, it was an intense meeting. Vinander revealed information that filled the large gaps and addressed the assumptions regarding my father's demise. You already know Vinander was there when the events of that fateful day played out, and my father was poisoned. This day, he told me the ruby chieftain named Py'ro found my father and remained with him until the end. It gave me great comfort to know that father was not alone."

"If memory serves me correctly, Chief Elder Py'ro was Flayre's father and the ruler of all ruby dragon clans during the time of your sire's reign."

Kullipthius nodded.

"To hear Vahl Zayne talk about the desert chieftain's known history, he was fair and diplomatic—unusual attributes to find in a ruby," said Ra.

"Indeed," replied Kullipthius. "Vinander also provided the exact details as to how Flayre came upon *The Dark Arts*. Though he had tried to explain all this information on the day of my father's death, I was young and grieving and unable to comprehend the full extent of the story. He had promised to return to discuss the matter, and this day he fulfilled that pledge. I will share all the details with you and your mother when we return home."

"I look forward to it."

"On a lighter note, Vinander has advised me that his quincentennial celebration will occur in just sixteen short yearmarks. As you know, there is a sanctuary in Eva'kohr on the east side of Kaleidos Peak that is solely devoted to such celebrations. Our imperial family and Vahl Zayne have been invited to the ceremony, and I told Vinander it would be an honor for us to attend."

"That is quite an honor," agreed Ra, "since a Golden One must live for five hundred yearmarks in order for their transformation to occur. With the exception of Vinander, I am unaware of any other dragon alive that has been privy to their rebirth into a Feathered One. According to Vahl Zayne, they had been chronicled as Firebirds in the native folklore and poetry of the Vahlarian Travelers."

"There has not been a sign of a Feathered On amongst us since

Vinander's grandsire," confirmed Kullipthius. "But, from what I understand, four other Golden Ones have already committed to being at the event. It is important for other Golden Ones to be present so they can pass along the procedures of the ritual for future generations.

"The gold dragon Eleazar will lead the ceremony. Soon, he and Vinander will take the journey to a second sanctuary in a province known as Takari. Once there, they will record the future transformation.

"As you know, gold dragons keep very thorough records. They return to the closest sanctuary every decade to maintain these record books and to learn of future events. These ledgers are invaluable, as they also contain the questions and answers to many mysteries of the world that the Golden Ones may encounter."

"I must confess," said Ra, "I am looking forward to seeing a Feathered One."

"From what my father had told me," replied Kullipthius, "they are amongst the most beauteous beings to grace the planet."

Kullipthius knew his next words would stir many questions. "We also spoke of Aeternus."

Ra's eyes widened in surprise, and he asked, "Does Vinander know something of this legend?"

"Aye," replied Kullipthius. "Vinander advised me it is not a myth, as it was once believed."

"Before we discuss Aeternus, Ra, there is something I need you to understand." Kullipthius paused for a moment of consideration before he continued. "Vinander has thoroughly searched the archives in Eva'kohr and Takari for information regarding the dark magic's powerful hold.

"Vinander was the dragon who discovered an elixir that could destroy the power in dark arts tomes. By pouring the elixir directly on the book, its protective power is held in a temporary and motionless state, allowing the obliteration of both the book and the dark magic. However, if the power transfers itself from the book into a living being, as it did in Flayre's case, you have to be careful not to destroy the living being when you are trying to extinguish the dark art's magic.

"The Golden One found only one account of a dark magic extraction, where the dark power was removed from the living being and resulted in a successful recovery. It was an arduous undertaking that had been performed on an emerald dragon that had only been under the dark magic's control for a period of a sennight. And from what I understand, that dragon has never been the same.

"Unfortunately, Vinander was unable to find any chronicles of a living being held under the influence of dark magic for the duration that Flayre has been exposed. Vinander said that Flayre has runes all over his body, and shows signs of the dark sickness. The ruby is also looking for the second book, and if he is successful in finding it, there will be no stopping his wicked machinations.

"That brings us to Aeternus. I have discussed this at length with Vinander, and he will converse with the alchemist who created it. Since we do not know if there is any chance of Flayre recovering from the dark magic's possession, I believe Aeternus to be the proper punishment for his crimes. It is a sentence long overdue."

CHAPTER TWENTY-THREE

V inander flew into the silence of the deepening twilight. He reveled in the touch of the wind on his face as the shadows darkened into night. Kaleidos winked to life below him as the city's inhabitants set their lanterns and starfire stones alight, and a sense of hearth and home settled over the city.

This night he was gladdened for the festival's completion, for many shop owners were out late packing up their booths beyond the city gates. With fewer people in the merchant district, he could bend the rules and fly lower with little fear of being spotted. The alleyways and streets rushed by as he skimmed above Kaleidos to the Jade Lady Shoppe.

The storefront was well lit, a telling sign that its proprietor was in residence. Vinander circled the shop, relishing the night air against his scales before he back-winged gracefully and let himself drop. A quick flash of light splashed against the sides of the buildings and the cobbled lane below. Now wrapped in his human guise known as Windermere, he descended to a crouch, landing within the shadows of a nearby alley. He left the cover of the backstreet and let the glow from the window of the Jade Lady Shoppe light the way to his destination.

The Jade Lady dealt in fine items of antiquity that rivaled Vinander's own, but its main draw was in gems, stones and precious metals. It was run by a master artisan named Arius Faylien who only crafted the most precious and sought-after merchandise, and thus he held a renowned reputation. Monarchs and nobles flocked to him with orders. If ever one was going to propose to a noble lady, they had better come knocking with a Faylien original as an offering!

The shop looked as exclusive on the outside as the jewelry within. The building was painted in a green apple hue with silver dust mixed in that sparkled when in the sunlight. The sign that hung above the window of the shop portrayed a beautiful, raven-haired woman holding a gemmed ring aloft. Her wrists were bedecked with three colored bangles of the actual stone the shop was named after in lavender, green, and apricot. While the image was dazzling during the day, her beauty was now aglow in the gleam of the shop's lights.

Vinander had two items of import to discuss with Arius this eve. One was regarding a diamond and ruby necklace named Lore that was tucked safely away in a velvet-lined pouch in his pocket and snugly secured to his belt. The other was a request from Imperator Kullipthius.

A bell jingled as he pushed open the door.

"A moment and I shall be with you!" announced a familiar yet muffled voice that called out pleasantly from the back area of the shop. Vinander smiled and looked about with a curious eye, noting how much the place had changed since his last visit.

The interior was luxurious and well-maintained. The walls, like giant canvases, displayed a variety of painted scenes. To his left, a bright scarlet tanager sang its song in the branches of a moss-laden tree that draped over a babbling brook. The connecting wall portrayed a lush garden filled with mimosa, trumpet vines, and honeysuckle, all bowing before a pair of hummingbirds. It was a display of opulence Vinander knew Arius' patrons fancied.

Long benches upholstered with red velvet cushions were positioned before highly-polished wooden display cases that were lined with black satin. Nearly any gem-encrusted ornament or bauble one could wish for could be glimpsed within one of these cases or commissioned—for the right price. Lush tapestries lay underfoot while, overhead, the painted ceiling held soft, white clouds against a sun-kissed sky. Lanterns and mirrors were arranged about the room to provide the best light.

Vinander strolled toward the back of the shop where an elaborate archway stood. The woodwork bordering it was carved in intricate scrollwork and painted in gold leaf. Pulling aside a red velvet curtain that served as a partition, he made his way through the shop's storage room and out the rear exit.

The small back yard held the goldsmith's forge. It was enclosed with an overhang and three walls bordered its brick hearth and chimney. One wall was lined with the tools of the craft—files, gavels, hammers, pliers, and the like. Beside the hearth sat the hand-operated bellows and an anvil. Atop the anvil lay Arius' leather apron, a slender hammer, and a pair of tongs. His furnace must have been vacated recently, as smoke was rising through the chimney.

Adjacent to the hearth was an opened door that led to Arius' workroom where he cut and polished his precious gems and stones. Predictably, that is where Vinander found him amongst his enamels, crystals, and colored glass pastes, a rabbit's foot in hand, polishing an emerald amulet.

Arius looked to be in his early thirties by human standards. His eyes, a vibrant and odd brown-red hue, were taking in all the minute details of his work. His lips were slightly full, turning upwards at the corners as if entranced by his own private amusements. His rich brown hair was collar length and playfully tossing in the wind that was slipping through a window. He was wearing a thin black tunic, the sleeves pushed to his elbows, which only served to highlight the thick, gold cuffs about his wrists, a telltale mark of his gold dragon heritage.

"I should have known it was you in the shop," said the goldsmith with a smile. He placed the amulet in a small, black velvet pouch, pulled the drawstrings, and placed the pouch on the table. He turned his head to face his guest and gave a warm smile. "I have been feeling the presence of Ak'na throughout the day. What a pleasant surprise, Father." When he stood, his height topped Vinander's by a few inches. They each grabbed one another's right wrist and affectionately slapped each other's backs with their left hands in greeting.

"It is good to see you, my son."

"Is this a business or social visit?"

"A bit of both," replied Vinander.

"Might I interest you in some tea?"

"Aye, indeed," responded Vinander. "I must admit I have grown rather fond of the strong drink."

"Let me lock up and I will meet you in the storage room."

To the people of Sapphirus, the artisan Arius Faylien was the master gem smith who ran the Jade Lady Shoppe. Conversely, to the dragons, Vinander's son was the gold dragon Eleazar, one of the last dragon practitioners of the ancient art of alchemy.

After locking the front door of the shop and extinguishing the lights, the goldsmith joined his father who was waiting for him near a large tool cabinet set into the wall out back. Vinander watched as his son worked a hidden latch. The cabinet front swung inward to reveal a passageway leading into the earth and his son's lair.

Eleazar's last guise was that of Lazar, a lapidary and archmage for King Feroz in the ancient city of Mozai over two centuries ago. After the king's death, he had decided to explore the intriguing beauty and many wonders of the world. During that time he had lived as a dragon in the wild, so he was able to fly freely throughout the skies. Now he maintained a fine balance between both his worlds. As the jeweler and goldsmith Arius Faylien, he had the freedom to work in his shop and travel for his craft. He enjoyed mining precious crystals and stones as well as excavating ancient artifacts.

A stairway made its way into the earth to a long, underground passageway. The only adornment in the corridor sat in the center of the path in a polished silver case atop a waist-high pedestal. The light shining from within was bright enough to light the way through the passage.

This radiant treasure had always held Vinander's fascination. It was a large, translucent, disk-shaped stone of purple, blue, and violet, and its rounded edges were veined in silver. Each time Vinander approached the stone; the colors swirled and danced in ever-changing patterns and hues. It was entrancing.

Vinander delicately removed the colorful piece from its case. Whenever he held the stone, it felt alive in his hands. He cradled it carefully in one hand, and ran his fingers across its smooth surface. The stone's light brightened at his touch.

"I have dubbed her Glimmer," said Eleazar. "I do believe she likes you."

"A fitting name," replied Vinander with a smile. He reluctantly placed her back in her holder and followed Eleazar through the archway. Passing through the corridor without touching her had always proven challenging for Vinander.

They entered a cavernous room with a stone ceiling of sufficient height and width to accommodate several shape-shifting dragons. Starfire stones were placed around the room in sconces for warmth and light. Ornate beams and tall, spiraling pillars stretched far overhead. A bed of sand covered a portion of the floor with an underground thermal spring large enough for a dragon to bathe. A four-poster bed, complete with canopy and curtains, graced a nook along one wall. A footed bathing tub sat across from the bed in front of a hearth.

These human conveniences had been an indulgence for his

son's mate, Maddelina. The thought of the beautiful dragoness caused Vinander a sudden pang of grief. He remembered the day she had disappeared, and he knew Eleazar missed her desperately.

Summoned by his son the morn Maddelina had gone missing, Vinander had helped Eleazar search for her. The last time his son had seen Maddelina, she had departed for a moonlit horseback ride. They tracked her horse to a large meadow where they found the mare grazing. Desperately searching for clues, they had discovered a lone tree on the other side of the grassy field. It was still standing, but its trunk had been nearly stripped of its bark, and most of the limbs on one side of the tree were twisted and broken. The plants that surrounded the area near the tree had been ripped from their roots, and the earth was pocked with signs of a struggle. They had concluded that someone—or some*thing*— had taken her by force or deception. As she was more than she appeared, it had to have been something fierce, or most clever indeed, to have subdued a dragoness of her capabilities.

Shortly after Maddelina's disappearance, Vinander had taken Eleazar on a quest to help keep his son's mind occupied. Since gold dragons were an ancient breed, and their numbers few, he had asked his son to join him on a search for unknown Golden Ones who were young and unaware of the sanctuaries. As the oldest living gold dragon, Vinander was in charge of keeping the record books up to date in both Eva'kohr and Takari. According to Vinander, there had not been a recorded search for their particular breed in well over one hundred yearmarks.

Eleazar had been especially pleased when his father had suggested a stop at the Oralian Empire before they left. They told Kullipthius of Maddelina's disappearance, and the imperator had promised to have his scouts continue the search throughout Sapphirus during their absence.

Vinander found their quest had kept his son busy, and he was pleased their efforts had proven fruitful. They had come across a young, mated pair on Shelle Island, which was located many leagues off the eastern seaboard of Oralia. This brought the grand total, including themselves, to five Golden Ones living in their region, and ten last recorded in the province of Takari. When Vinander had recounted the total to Eleazar, he had realized his mistake when his son passionately reminded his father that Maddelina had brought the grand total to sixteen.

Eleazar led them through a doorway in the far corner of the cavern and to a sitting room. As they entered, Vinander noted his son's most recent artwork decorating the smooth, stone walls.

They were detailed scenes dedicated to the four classical elements of earth, fire, water, and air.

The scene for earth featured painted mountains highlighted with flecks of smoky-brown topaz and bands of tiger's-eye. Amber quartz crystals were used for the dawning sun, cresting the sides of the highest peak. At the mountain's base, trees flourished with leaf-shaped green jade and flecks of emeralds and a lake sparkled with deep blue sapphires.

The element of fire offered the majesty of the mighty volcano that graced the next setting. These ruptures in the planet's surface were responsible for massive destruction, yet Eleazar's painting depicted an astounding and awe-striking landscape. Rich red rubies protruded from the painting's bubbling magma inside the volcano. Carnelians and garnets spewed out in a fountain of lava that flowed down the mountainside, leaving a path of actual igneous rocks that had been formed from cooled and solidified magma. Red ribbon obsidian was used as molten rock that blackened the earth in its path of destruction.

Opposing the fiery panorama, the element of water was displayed. The oceanic depths held flecks of turquoise for water while sea foam was represented by splatters of paint, tiny sea pearl accents, and bits of coral. Flecks of aquamarine stones swirled in the ebb and surge of the tides with tiny seashells and crabs half-buried in the sand along the shore.

They turned back to the final wall from whence they came, the entryway positioned in its lower corner. This wall exhibited the classical element of air and, at that moment, it became Vinander's personal delight. Upon the smooth space his son had elected to depict two soaring gold dragons. Beneath a blue topaz sky they frolicked upon the wind, playing and tumbling through the clouds under a sun that sparkled with diamond dust along the horizon. Each scale was painstakingly set in precious gold, pounded and polished to a gleam for which the dragon had been named. Eleazar was truly gifted.

"I see by the expression on your face that you are enjoying my artwork," said Eleazar.

"I am, indeed, Eleazar. They are exquisite," replied Vinander.

"You have yet to see my favorite," confided Eleazar. He led his father to a long, rectangular slab of stone. The slab served as a partition, creating a secluded triangular space in the corner of the room. The nook held a small square table tucked in the corner and flanked by two high-back chairs. As Vinander took his seat, he was facing the stone slab with a curtain hanging before it. His son pulled the fabric aside, tying it off with a length of braided rope.

The unveiled masterpiece that had been painted directly on the smooth slab of stone was spectacular!

Maddelina had been portrayed in exquisite detail as she sat in a garden upon a white marble bench adorned with plump pillows. Her beauty was flawless, and Eleazar had captured it at a precise moment. Her dark hair fell to her waist to form a midnight curtain, and her cheeks were flushed to a perfect shade of pink. One dainty finger touched her cherry-red lips, and her violet eyes were alight with surprise and pleasure. No doubt the painting had been created from a tender memory.

Maddelina was examining a ring upon her left hand. It was the ring Eleazar had given her when asking, in human custom, if she would be his lifelong mate.

Eleazar's understanding of Maddelina's tastes and style had inspired the ring's creation. Though her favorite ornamental stone was jade, she had always deliberated at length before deciding which color to choose from her eight favorites: violet (to match her eyes), dusty rose, lemon yellow, peacock blue, forest green, crimson, apricot and, finally, the purest white.

Thus, Eleazar had designed two slender rings of platinum that jacketed interchangeable, solid jade bands in Maddelina's eight favorite colors. The two platinum rings were connected at the top by two intertwined dragons fashioned in a fine, yellow gold filigree. The bottom of the ring was left open between the two platinum loops to slide her chosen jade band within.

The ring that graced Maddelina's outstretched painted finger was an exquisite representation of the ring. Peeking through its outer, delicate filigree was a band of violet jade. The artwork must have been painstakingly created with the highest quality oils because it included the minutest details.

Eleazar spoke softly as he pointed at the painting. "This painting holds a treasure hidden in plain sight."

The stone wall magically shimmered as his son's hand appeared to pass through the painting. The illusion Eleazar had created made the colors appear to undulate under his touch like water rippling on the surface of a pond. When he withdrew his hand and the image settled, there was something missing from the painted scene: Maddelina's ring.

Vinander glanced at Eleazar and noted he was holding the ring aloft in triumph. Taking a second look at the painting, Vinander noted Maddelina's features had changed. She had taken on an unsuspecting and curious countenance. She looked as if she were in anticipation of a gift to come. "By the wind and stars, Eleazar, how . . . and where did you find her ring?"

"I returned again and again to search for her. I could not stop myself, Father. My persistence paid off in one respect because I found the ring far beyond the original site. I almost missed it because it had been half-buried in the dirt. I restored the ring to its former glory. To look upon it now gives me great comfort. I know she's out there, Father. I will not give up hope."

"One day I am sure you will learn the truth."

"Indeed, I will," said Eleazar with conviction. Then he turned to face the wall again and said, "I must confess that the best part of my painting is being able to give her the ring over and over again and see her face alight with happiness. I never tire of it."

Vinander watched as Eleazar slipped the ring back into position in the painting. It was as though he had slipped his hand through glass and she was waiting on the other side. There was another ripple as the scene in the painting changed, and the ring was on her finger. Once again the painting transformed before their eyes, and her features lit with happiness and love for her gift.

As a sad yet satisfied smile broke free upon Eleazar's lips, Vinander laid his hand on his son's shoulder in a gesture of comfort. With a last, lingering gaze upon his mate's features, Eleazar turned from the slab of stone and its treasure.

"Let's have that tea, shall we?"

Two fine mugs were soon warming the hands of both dragons who remained wrapped in their human appearance. They relaxed in silence at the sitting room table, lost in their own musings. Knowing how to cheer his son, Vinander pulled the velvet pouch from his pocket and slid it across the table. "I have something for you."

Eleazar picked up the pouch and poured its contents into his hand. His features lit with recognition and pleasure. "Lore!" exclaimed Eleazar. He held it before him and stared at his creation. Hanging from a gilt chain accented with ruby cabochons was a large, rare, pink diamond encircled by red rubies. "This brings back many fond memories."

"Aye, I thought it might," responded Vinander. "She now belongs to her creator since Mala has passed from our world, many yearmarks ago, and can no longer enjoy her. I have the letter you wrote that accompanied her as well, but I did not want to see it ruined. I shall wrap it for travel and give it to you when next we meet."

"Gramercy, Father, for returning her to me," said an awestruck

Eleazar. "I thought Lore was lost. I owe you a great debt of gratitude."

"Nay, not at all, I enjoy searching for your precious works of art. I had Lore on display at the faires for a time. Adults and children alike sat charmed by Mala's story. I do, however, have a request, if you are interested," continued Vinander. "Would it be possible for you to craft a copy of Lore? It should be the same pretty affair, including this pink diamond I brought from my collection." Vinander reached into a pocket and handed him the diamond for the centerpiece. "I have a persistent merchant after your fine necklace, and since he means well, I had thought to make him happy with an Arius Faylien copy."

"I have no objection with making you a reproduction," said Eleazar, placing the diamond in his pants pocket. "When would you like it finished?"

Vinander handed over the gold coins he had received from the merchant. "I advised Merchant Coenwalh that I would request it by the Festival of the Blue Moon, giving you plenty of time if you had other pursuits or clients. He knows it will be a duplicate, though his wife will be none the wiser."

"That shall not be a problem," Eleazar replied. He placed the necklace back into the velvet pouch and stood. "Excuse me a moment while I put Lore away for safe keeping."

When he came back, he stood before his father and said, "I believe it only fitting to return a good deed in kind. I know how you like your history and artifacts." Like a magician, Glimmer appeared in his son's hand, shifting and whirling with color. "I will not take 'no' for an answer."

It was Vinander's turn to be stunned by his son's generosity. He knew how his son cherished the stone, for it was placed as a centerpiece in his prized collection. He was about to protest when his son interrupted his thoughts.

"She has always had a connection with you. I believe she will flourish in your care." He pushed the stone into Vinander's hand and took up his cup of tea, draining it completely.

"But what of the grand lighting she provided in your hallway?" asked Vinander. He examined the stone, unable to believe it was his.

"A few starfire stones strategically placed along the hall will provide an efficient light source," answered Eleazar, who then flashed a satisfied grin.

"Gramercy, my son," replied Vinander. "I will treasure her always."

"Think nothing of it. You have done me a great service by reuniting me with my long-lost treasure."

Vinander's smile was contagious as he placed the precious relic in his vest pocket. He held his hand over the pocket, relishing the happy moment.

"Now," said Vinander, moving to a matter of great import, "I have a commission for you, requested by Imperator Kullipthius."

"I am honored. What is the imperator's wish?"

He did not know how to respond, so he moved directly to the point. "The imperator is in need of Aeternus at your earliest convenience."

Vinander watched Eleazar pinch his eyebrows. "For whom is Aeternus intended?"

"It is intended for Flayre. You are aware of this ruby's transgressions and the evil influence that now possesses him from the use of dark magic. Flayre means to destroy the Oralian Empire, and I hate to think of what will happen to the inhabitants of Sapphirus if he is allowed to continue on his path of destruction." Vinander looked thoughtfully at his son as he continued. "I know that Aeternus was believed a legend, Eleazar, and I hope you are not disappointed that I revealed its true existence when asked by the imperator. Kullipthius said he would only ask, not demand it of you."

Eleazar's features smoothed. "I understand why the imperator would see it as a befitting sentence for Flayre. The ruby's shadow is lengthy and has darkened our world for far too long." He paused for a moment before he continued. "It will take me all of tonight and half of the morrow to forge the pieces," explained Eleazar. "Does the imperator know that, because it is my magic that goes into its creation, I must be present for the fitting?"

"Aye, I have explained its application," answered Vinander.

Vinander knew his son had only crafted Aeternus once before, and it was a long time ago. Composed of many metals, it looked harmless enough and was actually quite beautiful, yet within its beauty lurked magical peculiarities. The properties of the combined metals in the necklace would mystically drain the wearer of his draconic strength, rendering him unable to fly or use his gifts.

Red dragons were capable of changing form, but they thought it a curse rather than a gift to change into what they believed to be a wingless, bipedal inferior. Therefore, as would likely be the case with Flayre, the necklace would slowly force him to change into his human form, while the links of Aeternus shrink to accommodate his new size. Once in place, Aeternus would remain around Flayre's neck, willing or not, forever.

Vinander believed it would be a fate worse than death for any dragon to lose the ability to fly and to have its draconic gifts rescinded.

Eleazar broke into his father's thoughts. "Inform the imperator that I will start preparations for the collar at once."

CHAPTER TWENTY-FOUR

A urora Leigh awoke to the sound of a soft swish, as if a door were opening. She sat upright in bed blinking and trying to focus on her bedchamber's main entrance, but there was no one there. Still groggy, it took her a moment to gather her thoughts, for in her half-sleeping state she did not immediately recognize her surroundings. As awareness dawned, she sighed in relief, and her body began to relax. She and her parents were tucked safely within Kaleidos Keep's Family Tower at Moorwyn Castle.

Aurora Leigh heard the guards outside her door talking softly and concluded it must have been their movements that woke her. She was having trouble sleeping, and the disturbance did not help. She yawned and placed her head back on the feathered pillow and nestled beneath her coverlets.

Was that movement in the shadows? Normally this would trigger an alarm, but a sense of calm enveloped Aurora Leigh's inner being, and she only sighed. She felt so relaxed she could not even sit up. The scent of night-blossom flowers followed a figure slowly approaching from the corner of the room. The figure found its way to the end of Aurora Leigh's canopied bed.

"Nestling, are you sleeping?" whispered a soft voice from the shadows. Aurora Leigh immediately recognized the voice.

"Oh, Imperatrix Laliah," said a drowsy Aurora Leigh, followed by a big yawn. "Is something amiss?"

"Forgive me, nestling," Laliah whispered. "I used one of my healing talents to calm you during my approach so I would not frighten you."

Aurora Leigh felt the smoothness of Laliah's hand upon her forehead, and immediately she felt refreshed.

"There, you should now feel more alert. I am sorry for the intrusion, Aurora Leigh. I could not bear to wait until morning's light to speak with you. Prithee, come with me to Oralia, and we shall speak where we know it to be a private conversation."

It would be awkward to explain the imperatrix's sudden appearance to any of the castle's normal denizens. Aurora Leigh whispered so as not to be overheard. "Certainly, as you wish."

Wondering what could bring the dragoness to Moorwyn at this odd hour, Aurora Leigh pulled herself out of bed and headed toward the wardrobe to search for something warm to wear in the chilly caverns of the dragon empire. "In sooth, though I feel quite refreshed at this very moment, I had been tossing and turning this night and found little rest. I would verily take pleasure in your company." She smiled at the dragoness and, having selected an emerald green travel dress, slipped behind the dressing screen to change.

Once Aurora Leigh emerged fully clothed and prepared for travel, Laliah smiled and extended her arms, gave the princess a hug and softly said, "Firstly, we must have you tell the door guardians that your maids are not allowed entrance into your room until they are beckoned. That way, we will not have any time constraints."

Aurora Leigh nodded, opened the door, and peeked out from behind it so as not to expose her guest. The guardians turned toward her doorway and stood at attention.

"Tell anyone who approaches this door that I have been tossing and turning the night away and have barely had a wink of sleep. No one is to be allowed to enter this room. This includes my attendant, Murielle. I will let you know when I wish to receive her or any other."

"As you wish, Your Highness," said the two guards in unison.

Task complete, Laliah led Aurora Leigh back toward the intricately adorned marble pillar in the corner of the bedchamber. Carved flowers and vines met the touch of Laliah's questing palm and fingers. There was a hissing noise as the hidden trigger was activated and the column moved aside to expose a passage beyond. They stepped through, and the portal closed softly behind them.

Momentarily engulfed in utter darkness, Laliah led Aurora Leigh through the passage toward a dim light flickering softly in the distance. Laliah's graceful form and warm countenance appeared in the light. "I brought a torch, little one, as I did not wish you to stumble along the way."

"That was most kind, Your Imperial Majesty."

"Prithee, nestling, from this moment forward, you must call me Laliah."

"Gramercy, Laliah. You have a lovely name. I will do my best to remember."

Now arm in arm and with a torch lighting their way, the two females started down the dim length of the passage, and Laliah began an explanation of her unannounced appearance at the castle.

"I was unable to sleep and felt that something was amiss, so I needed desperately to talk with someone."

"I, too, have been restless this night. My thoughts have not strayed far from Kulli and Uncle Lucian. Mayhap we are feeling ill at ease from their absence?" Aurora Leigh guessed.

"I wish I could dismiss these sensations. Empathy is part of my gift as a healer, and it helps me identify others' feelings and difficulties. My healing gifts cry to be used, but there is no one about. I am feeling quite anxious."

Laliah took a steadying breath of air. "I deem it wise to consult the starfire globe. At least it will give us something tangible to work with. My son taught me its use, and though I am not as versed as he, it should respond to my needs. Ra told me you have been blessed with the gift of sight while viewing the globe, so I thought we could view it together."

"I am most grateful you wish me here with you." As Aurora Leigh spoke, she noticed Laliah had become very still. "Pray tell, what is it, Laliah?"

The imperatrix's violet-blue eyes were locked intently on the staylace of Aurora Leigh's travel dress.

The princess glanced down at the bodice of her dress to see it aglow. She wonderingly pulled the pendant Kullipthius had given her as a youth from under her dress.

Before their dazzled eyes, the blessing disk suddenly burned brighter, its soft white light illuminating the walls. Laliah could have doused the torch she carried and they still would have been able to see clearly in the amulet's radiance. For the moment, both were calmly gazing at the mysteriously shining pendant.

Then a notion was brought to the forefront of Aurora Leigh's thoughts. "Once a starfire stone has lost its light, it has never been known to glow again, so this radiance could very well signify divine intervention."

"I concur. I know not the reason it would be alight, nestling, although I cannot dismiss the prompting within that this proves we move in the right direction."

Laliah placed her torch in a sconce when they arrived at the fire globe's chamber. They both approached the natural standing stones that bore strange inscriptive marks. The symbols seemed merely dark slashes instead of brightly lit from within as when Aurora Leigh last visited with Kulli and Ra.

Suddenly, the room flashed to brilliance. Aurora Leigh put an arm up to shield her eyes. When she regained her vision, she saw a look of perplexity on Laliah's delicate features.

Laliah's voice sounded shocked and confused. "Verily, it is not the starfire globe as I had scarcely begun my meditations." Aurora Leigh moved to her side and clutched her outstretched hand, wondering what other surprises this night might reveal.

As one, their eyes locked upon the source of luminosity. Indeed, it was not the starfire globe. In the corner of the room there stood a tall column of nearly eye-blinding light. As the brightness dimmed, a winged, angelic figure of regal bearing stood before them in a corona. She shone as if made from the light of a star, ethereal and vaporous. Her eyes displayed the heavens in their glory in a way that defied explanation. She was timeless beauty and grace, eternal splendor personified.

Speechless, Aurora Leigh could only stare. The winged lady of the light shimmered like a reflection in a pool. Both Laliah and Aurora Leigh curtsied, their fingers entwined in unspoken support like little children before a parent.

"Though the path you walk now is a most precarious one," the lady of light relayed, *"you must draw upon your fortitude, for you have a task of great import."* The winged being smiled, and it was like clouds lifting to reveal the beauty of the heavens.

"The time to act draws nigh." Her voice echoed within Aurora Leigh's mind, deep and soft. *"A great evil stalks these lands. This dark one has emerged from hiding, poised to strike, threatening your peaceful life once more. Thy champions shall be called upon to place all back on the elusive path of balance. Strength and determination are needed as ne'er before. Behold!"*

She placed her arms above her head in the form of an arc and then spread them out shoulder width. A bright ball of light flashed over her head, and a fiery glow manifested itself from the conjured radiance.

Within the depths of the firelight a scene was playing itself out. Aurora Leigh felt as if the images were from long, long ago. Crystal-clear, it was like a painting come to life, a moment captured in time that would never lose its vibrancy nor ever be forgotten.

In the closing dusk a young, silvery dragon landed at a cave's entrance. As the dragon entered, he noted the cavern was marked with the signs of some horrific conflict. He then came to a figure lying motionless upon the ground. A mournful keening rose from the throat of the young dragon, haunting and beautiful.

The young one returned to the cave's entrance and fixed his gaze upon the heavens. The beauty of the velvet night sky did nothing to help the dragon quell his lamentation. The sight puzzled Aurora Leigh until she heard Laliah whisper, "Kullipthius." The dragoness appeared unaware that she had spoken.

Aurora Leigh was suddenly reminded of the childhood tales Kulli had told her. She watched transfixed. Young Kullipthius' eyes squeezed shut as he sang his dirge to the heavens. The keening dragon's song was suddenly cut short by his wordless sobs. The sorrow-driven cries continued until there was a disturbance in the air before the night-dappled behemoth. The air became misty and Aurora Leigh saw the dragon shiver.

Aurora Leigh watched as Kulli opened his eyes and started at the sight before him. A single shaft of pure light erupted before his eyes. Although the phenomenon startled Kulli, he did not take flight.

When the mist cleared and the light dimmed, Aurora Leigh noted that it was the same lady of the light who now stood before her and Laliah. Kullipthius' head bobbed low before the figure, his wings flourished and spread wide in what Aurora Leigh assumed was a draconic bow. He then looked up and met the lady's gaze.

"Young one," her words echoed through time to those present in the room of the starfire globe. She gestured to the stars—one constellation in particular—one Aurora Leigh recognized. *"Temper thy mourning with this. Thy imperial father's strength hath saved his flight and countless Sapphirian lives. For now he rests a guest within heaven's gentle embrace amongst the stars. Look upon the skies to know thou art truly never without him."*

Kullipthius locked a longing gaze upon the evening stars. Then a flicker of light from inside the cavern caught his attention. The young dragon changed to human form and seemed a teenager. With wind ruffling his hair, he moved to where the light was flickering to conduct a closer examination. It was his father's beloved blessing disk. Kulli bent down and gathered it in his palm.

The magnificent lady of light moved to enfold Kulli in a tender embrace of bright white light that took the shape of wings and encircled him somewhat like a dragoness would comfort her young.

Aurora Leigh's eyes filled with tears as she realized Kulli's story of the dragon in the heavens had been the tale of his own father. The scene began to fade, but Aurora Leigh could still hear the angel's voice. *"A time will come when the strength of Dra'khar shall be called upon again."*

A moment later the room stood empty but for the light from the amulet.

A final message touched Aurora Leigh's thoughts. With the silky voice resounding in her mind, it whispered, *"Aurora Leigh, do as your heart dictates."* And then there was silence.

Aurora Leigh stood in mute understanding. She knew what needed to be done.

"Laliah, my heart tells me that this pendant is the key. We must find Kullipthius."

"We?" inquired Laliah. "Youngling, I know how much you want to help, but it is not safe for you in the forestlands. If you will entrust the amulet to me, I will see it is delivered to Kulli."

"Do you not see, Laliah?" began Aurora Leigh. She was desperate to make Laliah understand. "A princess must be brave at all times and do what is best for her country. It is destined that I go. After all, Kulli gave the amulet to me."

"Aurora Leigh, a war is brewing," explained Laliah. "I can feel it. The situation is dangerous for one so vulnerable."

"I understand that the lady of light told us the path was precarious," admitted Aurora Leigh. "She also said, 'Aurora Leigh, do as your heart dictates.' And my heart tells me that I must go. She would not have said that if any harm would befall me. I must be the one who returns it. Prithee, Laliah, it means so much to me." Aurora Leigh knew in her heart it was important that she go. Even if Laliah did not offer her help, she would somehow find a way to make it to the Tall Forest on her own.

"We must speak with Var'ohk about the lady of light," replied Laliah, concern written on her features. "I will allow you to fly with me *if*, and *only if*, the major domus deems it safe."

CHAPTER TWENTY-FIVE

B layz had set out early, riding the first rays of the sun to the west. On the imperator's orders, he and Jhain had gone to check on Shayde at his newly-prepared grotto near the shores of the Carillion Sea. The grotto was located atop a hill overlooking both the Carillion Sea and the fortress.

Shayde had advised them that the Liltians had arrived at Terra Leone the previous night. Blayz could see that the cloaking was already in place to prevent the reds from finding the fortress and the people within from seeing anything but the blue skies above.

With task complete, Blayz and Jhain were on their way back to the encampment in the forest when Blayz was unexpectedly struck with a familial presence, a feeling that resonated throughout his bronze-hued scales. This innate sense, known as Ak'na, presented itself to a dragon when a blood relative was near. The strength of Ak'na varied, depending upon the line of descent; the closer the bloodline between the two dragons, the stronger the feeling of Ak'na.

It came in a flood of awareness that enveloped Blayz so completely, it left little room for anything else. Blayz's only known family was his mother, and she never left the safety of the Oralian borders. Blayz was so shocked at the revelation presenting itself, he nearly dropped Jhain from his perch as he angled sharply to hone into the heightened sensation.

"Stand ready and stay focused at all times, foolish youngling!" Blayz's thoughts boomed powerfully within Jhain's mind. The dragon had almost forgotten the young scout in his care. He

spiraled down to set his bewildered charge upon the ground.

Jhain slid down from the dragon's back and made his way to face Blayz. "Yer warm and sincere apology fer nearly killing me be accepted," Jhain quipped.

"You are marked a worthy scout," Blayz retorted. *"Make your way to the encampment. They are just over that hillock to the east. Communicate our undertakings to your captain and tell the imperator that Shayde stands ready at Terra Leone. Leave at once and complete your assignment."*

"What got ya so fired up?" questioned Jhain. "The flames, verily, be getting ta yer rock-hard head, 'cause we be staying together! I refuse ta let a foolhardy dragon beget dishonor ta a pledge made betwixt a scout an' his Cap'n."

It was obvious that Jhain clearly did not understand that Blayz was trying to protect him.

Blayz looked distractedly through the trees in the direction that held his interest. Meanwhile, smoke plumed from his nostrils in irritation. He had neither the time to tarry nor the inclination to extend a lengthy explanation to calm the impetuous scout's concerns. He turned narrowed eyes toward his traveling companion and expressed his frustration. *"It is for your own protection that I must—and WILL—carry on alone."*

"Yer intentions be foolhardy, not ta mention dangerous."

Jhain's blue gaze held the dragon's own unflinchingly, as if daring him to deny the obvious logic in his words. Blayz found it amusing that Jhain, who smelled of night wind, inks, and dye aimed to keep a dragon safe. The youngling had a fire to him, a curious trait for a human to display in a dragon's presence.

Blayz watched as the scout's expression changed.

Jhain quickly surveyed the wood and then used his mind to touch the dragon's own. *"I feel eyes upon us."*

"Ak'na, the keenest of dragon senses, is what attracts this presence to us," the dragon answered while staring into the distance. Then, in his booming mind voice he bellowed out his orders to Jhain, exclaiming, *"Enow, no more argument from you!"*

A leap and great pumping of bronze and black-veined wings took Blayz above the level of the trees. The down draft from his leathery appendages swirled bits of dirt and leaves and had nearly knocked Jhain off his feet, but the scout managed to keep his balance while protecting his face from flying debris.

Reading Jhain's thoughts, Blayz heard him question:

"What be Ak'na?"

The dragon understood that the scout had instinctively felt that the presence of Ak'na could pose a danger to those at the encampment, warranting their immediate attention.

"*Ya errant, motley-minded fool!*" Jhain's thoughts bellowed after him.

Blayz could tell the scout's frustration was mounting, but there was no time for the youngling's tantrums.

"Arrogant flap-dragon!" Jhain yelled, his voice carrying to Blayz's sharp ears.

From his position in the sky, Blayz spotted Jhain running east toward the encampment, all the while muttering a tirade of creative oaths at the dragon for being left behind.

Blayz found himself unable to escape the pull that drew him to the high cliffs of Bocca di Leone on the shores of the Carillion Sea. Even at the blustery heights at which he flew, his keen eyes could detect his shimmering reflection against the waters far below. Studying his reflection caused him to wonder exactly whom he would be encountering on this spontaneous voyage. Blayz held to an uncanny feeling that he would be displeased with the outcome soon to present itself, for surely if a red family member had allied against Avala in this mad crusade, they would not want to get to know him in any familial sense. No, he doubted there would be a happy reunion at the end of this meeting, yet he was still driven with a relentless need to unveil his past, even if the answers were less than agreeable.

And that is what brought him to thoughts of his young charge, Jhain. Blayz would never have disobeyed an order, but he could not have kept the scout with him, or the youngling surely would have been in harm's way. Per the Oralian code, humans left in a dragon's care were to be protected at all costs, and this was the reasoning for leaving him behind. The imperator would have approved of his decision.

Awareness of his surroundings jostled Blayz from his murky speculations. Below he could clearly see the beautiful Bocca di Leone, or Lion's Mouth harbor, which was once a part of the former country of Liltimer's northwest coast.

The seaside inlet's only access was through a solitary, narrow channel, and was only large enough for one small fishing vessel, which he could see was currently moored therein, as it rolled with the swell.

The fishermen who operated *Stormwalker* were fearless. They placed their complete trust in their craft, unerringly coaxing it through the restricted access and treacherous waters to and from its circular, sheltered home. While out at sea, they would work tirelessly, providing fresh seafood for open markets and faires.

Even the mooring system was a testament to the fisher folk's craft. It was ingeniously designed with the vessel fixed firmly in place in the middle of the harbor on an intricate system of weights and pulleys to prevent it from being crushed against the sides of the cliff in times of foul weather or strong, high tides.

A curving stairway carved into the cliff's rocky side was the only other way out of or into the cove, leading to a land that once had flown the Liltian banner. From high atop the cliffs, you could take a footpath to the roadway, and from there it was a day's ride on horseback to the fortress. The trip was much shorter, of course, if you happened to be a dragon in flight.

Blayz was immediately bombarded with fond memories. The imperator had brought him here when he was a youngling. He had taught him how to tread the land in his alternate two-footed form while navigating over tide pools of multihued sea stars, mussels, and limpets.

Blayz did not often leave Avala for pleasure, nevertheless, this locale drew him like a moth to a candle's flame. It had only been during those specific times when the tide was too low for the brave little boat to cast out to sea. Yet it had been the best of times for a youngling to learn the particulars of the wind currents without worry of being noticed. He glanced down upon the cliffs to where he had taken his first leap of faith and become skilled at using the forces of the wind above and below the span of his wings. Bocca di Leone had the perfect weather conditions to help young ones learn how to save energy from flapping their wings unnecessarily to regain height.

Blayz flew back out to the sea and circled toward land again, gliding in low along the water's edge and reveling in the misty sea spray that greeted him as the waves continued their relentless crash against the rocky walls. He used a rising current of air to carry him up the sides of the cliff's rocky face. He wanted to come upon the land and keep to the shadows under the cliff's overhang, using his half-caste heritage to his benefit. He took on more of a red tone in the shadows and wanted to use this to his advantage as he approached the familial call.

The pull of Ak'na brought Blayz to a lone red behemoth perched within an outcropping of jagged rock. It seemed the red was trying to keep the odds of any deadly attack to his advantage. From high in the sky Blayz could see the full-blooded red whip his head around, honing in on his awareness and the object of his own familial sensations. Blayz winged his way to land in close proximity, remaining out of sight in the shadows of some nearby trees at the edge of the Tall Forest.

Blayz's eyes were drawn to the red's infamously carved scales that were pulsing in a hypnotic rhythm. He shook his head, for he felt magic trying to penetrate his mind, and he did not want to lose himself to its spellbinding effects. He tried to focus, keep his senses heightened, and his mind under control.

Blayz cautiously approached on dragon claw with every fiber of his being warning him to remain on heightened alert. Not only could he feel the dark force of wickedness, but judging from the sight of the magic that wrapped this red dragon as neatly as an embrace, it could not be denied that Blayz was related to Oralia's most formidable evil . . . the red dragon Flayre.

KULLIPTHIUS was speaking to Lucian when he noted his son's approach. "Pray pardon, Your Majesties," interrupted Ra, his eyes skyward, "The Ancient One tells me three dragons approach. Two Oralian Champions are flanking my imperial mother and Princess Aurora Leigh."

Shock and alarm appeared on King Lucian's features. Kullipthius understood from his royal friend's thoughts that the apprehension he was feeling was not only for Aurora Leigh but for his brother as well. If Dryden knew Aurora Leigh was missing from the castle, he would be consumed with heartbreak.

"I wonder what possibly could have occurred that would bring them out this early in the morning and into the forest?" wondered Lucian aloud in an unsteady voice.

"I feel your concerns as well, Lucian," sympathized Kullipthius, "it must be important, as Laliah would not unduly subject the youngling to such danger otherwise."

"Agreed," replied Lucian, nodding his understanding.

"Oh, Uncle Lucian," cried Aurora Leigh. She ran from the clearing and into the king's outstretched arms.

Kullipthius watched as Laliah changed form and approached.

"I am sure Your Majesties are both aware I would never put

Aurora Leigh in harm's way," explained Laliah. "We checked with Var'ohk on the ruby dragons' location, and according to the Imperial Champions who escorted us here, there is time for us to return Aurora Leigh to safety before their arrival. You must understand that it was most essential that we come."

"I feel no threat to the princess, Lucian," advised Ra.

King Lucian nodded and Kullipthius observed his friend visibly relax upon hearing Ra's words.

Laliah shared her thoughts privately, with both monarchs. *"I have blocked Aurora Leigh's mind from hearing my thoughts. Though I doubt she could know The Ancient One's location, I knew she would be safer with me than left to her own devices. I read her thoughts, and she was determined to find a way on her own if I had not allowed her to come. The youngling was quite obstinate in her conviction."*

"I trust your judgment unequivocally, Laliah," responded Lucian.

"Of that we are all aware," responded Kullipthius. He smiled at his mate before he gently kissed her on the forehead.

His smile rapidly faded when the familial awareness of Ak'na consumed his senses.

"My Emperor," asked Laliah, "is something amiss?"

Kullipthius could not answer, and he turned his head to hone in on its location. Since both his mother and father had passed from this world and he was the last of his line, he found it puzzling. It was most unsettling to experience the sensation on the field of a forthcoming battle.

Bewildered by its presence, Kullipthius found his wandering gaze settle on a glowing amulet about Aurora Leigh's neck. It was the blessing disk he had given her when she was a small child.

Kullipthius watched as Aurora Leigh removed the blessing disk from around her neck and held it aloft. A spectrum of color and light swirled within the Allurealis crystal that hung in the center of the disk. As if taking on a life of its own, the light somehow separated itself from the crystal and made its way toward him.

The light grew in height and width as it headed toward Kullipthius. As it approached him, he could feel its warmth. He squinted against the light and found he could not tear his gaze away as he noticed a form taking shape within its multihued luminosity.

Dark leather boots were the first to appear within the hazy light. Each displayed a complex design of scrollwork that decorated their outer sides, with black woolen breeches tucked neatly within the boots' knee-high tops. Next, an upper torso came into view clad in a dark purple tunic underneath a golden metal cuirass with leather lacings. The left wrist displayed a gold cuff rimmed in platinum with a large diamond centered in the middle of the cuff.

A black velvet mantle of voluminous material was draped over one shoulder and flowed down to a length that ended at the tops of the boots. The mantle's hood flaunted an immense amount of embroidery, making the fabric almost indistinguishable for all the decorative needlework. A pair of black velvet gloves held the same artistic needlecraft as the mantle, and graced the back of each hand. A fitted skullcap crown of gold with a diamond studded platinum rim sat atop dark, lustrous, wavy brown hair.

As the pearly mist that surrounded the figure floated away upon the forenoon breeze, the luminous spirit form of Dra'khar, Oralia's unifier and First Dynasty Imperator, stood before Kullipthius.

"This day is as the stars have foretold, my son."

The long-absent touch of Dra'khar's mental voice was a shock to Kullipthius' senses. His disbelief was etched upon his face for all to see, and his voice was soft, halting and shaking.

"Father?" Kullipthius' misting blue eyes shone, and he reached out to his sire, though common sense told him he was viewing him in spirit only. Even so, the instinctive need and heartfelt desire to confirm his father's presence could not be ignored.

He watched the dragons of his court bow before their former imperator as the truth settled upon them. Lucian and his men followed suit, understanding they were witness to something profound. Kullipthius stumbled upon unsteady feet as he, too, fell to his knees.

Dra'khar smiled warmly and bid his son and the others to rise.

"It seems these past yearmarks have turned a young and impulsive crown prince into a fine imperator indeed. You are much like I was in your manner and humble nature as you rule the Oralian Empire. I was blessed to have you as my son."

It was such a pleasure to share his father's company once more.

Kullipthius saw Aurora Leigh leave the embrace of her uncle's arms and walk toward him. She grabbed Kulli's left hand and returned her beloved treasure to its rightful owner.

"Can you not see the reason we are here?" Aurora Leigh asked Kulli. "This very morn, the amulet began pulsing with radiance, and a lady of light appeared before our very eyes," explained Aurora Leigh. "I know the tale of the *Dragon in the Heavens* is true. The shining lady of light showed what happened. She confirmed your story that Dra'khar was the first leader of all the dragons who lived within Kaleidos Peak long and ago as well as the humans' great protector. Not only do I believe the presence of this blessing disk brought your imperial father to you this day, I also feel it will be significant for you in the forthcoming situation here in the wood. The lady of the light told me that the time has come when the strength of Dra'khar will be needed again."

"The princess speaks the truth," confirmed Dra'khar.

Kullipthius watched as his father tuned his eyes toward Aurora Leigh.

"You are very wise indeed, Aurora Leigh. This amulet was a sacred treasure bestowed upon me by the lady of light you speak of. It was given to me as a gift for protecting those who lived in and around Kaleidos Peak," explained Dra'khar. *"You have been a wondrous caretaker of the blessing disk, youngling, and bringing it to my son was, indeed, the proper course. For this, Oralia and Avala are in your debt."*

Aurora Leigh curtsied in respect to Kulli's father.

Hearing his father's words, Kullipthius readjusted the leather cord of the pendent to fit, and placed it around his neck. Bestowing a kiss upon Aurora Leigh's forehead he said, "Gramercy, youngling. You are so very brave to have brought the blessing disk to me this day." Aurora Leigh smiled up at her beloved friend as she slipped back into her uncle's open arms.

Dra'khar surveyed those before him. *"The time has come for me to depart."* He then looked back to Kullipthius and smiled. *"Know this, my son. I will never be farther from you than I am now, in your thoughts and heart."*

The once imperial ruler disappeared slowly from their sight, turning to vapors that were whisked away to destinations unknown.

With eyes glistening, Kullipthius watched his father fade away. His hand was clutched to the blessing disk about his neck as the last shimmer of his father's spiritual existence faded from sight. He felt the feelings of Ak'na weaken, and it tore at his heart.

"Fare thee well, Imperial Father."

Kullipthius could feel Lucian's comforting hand upon his shoulder. "You have been given a great gift, my friend. Would that I could see my own father once more, bid him a fond farewell, and know his contentment and wellness is found in love within the empyreal heavens."

Kullipthius knew Lucian was right, and he gave his friend a smile.

He glanced over and reached for Laliah. She brought his hand to her check and he cupped her face. He felt the effects of Laliah's healing gift upon him, and was thankful for its calming results. He felt content in her presence and comfort.

Lucian's voice broke the quiet. "You must return to the safety of Moorwyn Castle, Aurora Leigh."

"I could not agree more, youngling," added Kullipthius, supporting his friend. He gave Aurora Leigh a reassuring smile.

Aurora Leigh nodded.

Kullipthius looked toward his mate, and she turned her enticing violet eyes upon him as they held a private conversation. *"It is time to take the youngling back to Moorwyn Castle, My Empress, now that your duty with the amulet has been fulfilled."*

"As you wish," responded Laliah, and she moved to be held within his arms. *"Oh, how I wish I could kiss you again like I did the previous morn."* She left the warmth of Kullipthius' embrace and said, *"I need to take my leave before I can no longer resist."*

He watched her glide away to the clearing to change form.

Turning his attention toward Lucian, Kullipthius found that his friend was grinning at Eralon. It appeared the young captain was having a hard time concentrating on anything other than the princess, and his monarch had taken notice.

At Laliah's announcement that she was ready for departure, the princess could not prevent a sigh of disappointment.

Aurora Leigh's eyes welled up as she stepped forward and bid the two sovereigns a fond farewell. "I do love you both so very much. I could not bear it if anything were to happen to either of you." Her voice was barely audible as she pressed her face into each of their chests. Each took a turn to wish her a safe and swift journey.

The king called out to his captain. "Eralon, would you kindly see to my niece's departure as the imperator and I confer?"

"Aye, Your Majesty." Eralon approached and offered the princess his arm to escort her to the opal dragoness. Aurora Leigh accepted, and rewarded her escort with a beaming smile.

"I do believe my captain and niece have developed a fondness for one another," observed Lucian.

Kullipthius smiled and said, "Aye, my friend, I agree."

Both monarchs watched as Eralon helped the princess to find a safe and comfortable place to sit upon the dragoness. It was when Aurora Leigh beckoned Eralon forward, and the captain turned an ear her way, that Kullipthius observed Lucian raise a royal brow.

The sovereigns made their way toward Eralon, as the captain

watched the dragoness and her charge recede into the distance. It was obvious to Kullipthius that Eralon did not hear their approach.

"I do believe, Captain Wellsbough, I saw my niece whispering in your ear."

The imperator's keen eyes saw Eralon's muscles twitch in surprise. Kullipthius watched as King Lucian strode forward purposefully to Eralon's side, and Eralon turned toward his king.

The king's expression was undecipherable when he spoke. "It would seem, Captain Wellsbough, that mayhap you have recently been in the princess's company?"

Eralon schooled his features and managed a quiet and respectful nod. "Aye, Your Majesty. She was on the outskirts of Morning Star Palace without escort recently, and I saw her home safely."

The king appeared shocked at the news.

This news concerned Kullipthius and he caught Eralon's pondering thoughts. The captain contemplated telling his monarch about two brigands in the woods and their failed attempts at kidnapping the youngling. The captain decided that now was not the time or place to relay the news, and Kullipthius agreed.

"That explains her covert glances your way. She was undoubtedly concerned that you would expose her lack of good judgment." He gave Eralon a hearty slap on his back. "I am sure there is more to the tale," replied Lucian sagely. "We will talk about it at a more appropriate time."

Kullipthius smiled. It seemed the king had a penchant for knowing his loyal captain had more to say about the subject.

The king looked at Eralon, and with a smile he said, "It appears you have also captured her attentions, Eralon—the gallant captain coming to the aid of the fair princess and seeing her home safely."

"Aye, Sire," replied Eralon, and he bowed his head respectfully to his king. The two monarchs turned and strolled side-by-side back to the encampment.

The captain must have forgotten about a dragon's exceptional hearing. Kullipthius could not help but overhear Eralon's whispered response once the king was out of earshot.

"I believe, Your Majesty, it is *my* attentions that have been captured by the fair princess."

Kullipthius heard Jhain's rapid footfalls approaching even before he saw him. The scout burst into the encampment with such urgency that Eralon surged to his feet and unsheathed his steel to stand before King Lucian. Fortunately for Jhain, the breeze had been in his favor, and the dragons had caught his scent and relaxed their guard. As Jhain made his way over to his king, Kullipthius joined them.

Jhain nodded and spoke with Kullipthius first. "Yer Imperial Majesty, we met with Shayde at the grotto, an' he has cloaked Terra Leone. We could'na see a thing. It looked as though Terra Leone had never been."

"Your report is appreciated Jhain," replied Kullipthius. Then he pinched his eyebrows in concern and said, "I sense tension and apprehension within you. Where is Blayz?"

"Blayz up an' abandoned me once we finished our assignment. I even told him it be a bad idea ta leave, but he be having none o' it. He was completely troubled an' distracted. He flew off in a northwestern direction. An' pray tell, what be Ak'na? Beyond doubt, that be truly what got him all fired up." Jhain brushed an unruly lock of dyed hair from his eyes.

As soon as the word "Ak'na" left the scout's lips Kullipthius began to worry. "Ak'na? You are certain?"

"Aye, Your Imperial Majesty," replied Jhain. "I be certs o' what he claimed."

"Mayhap it was for your own safety, Jhain," replied King Lucian. "I do not think Blayz would have left you behind otherwise. Allegiance and honor are vital to the Oralians."

Lucian turned to speak with Kullipthius. "What of your missing captain, Kullipthius? Is there anything that can be done?"

"Gramercy, Lucian, for your concern. You are correct in thinking that Blayz had the scout's safety in mind. Ak'na is a dragon sense that we feel when a family member is near. If one of Blayz's relations happened to be a red dragon and has arrived in Sapphirus undetected, it could have posed a very real threat for Jhain. Moreover, Blayz would not want to lead any potential danger toward our encampment."

Jhain next looked upon his captain and his words tumbled out in a frustrated rush. "Pray pardon, Cap'n. I know yer orders be ta nay leave the dragon's side. Lo verily, what am I ta do when the beast takes wing an' flies off on his own?"

"Understandable, Jhain," responded Eralon.

A look of worry crossed the king's features as he spoke. "I think the time has come to make ready our armor and be prepared in the event we need to make a swift departure."

"Agreed, said Kullipthius, "and we must do everything in our power to consider Commander Blayz's safety as well. Many pardons while I discuss Jhain's news with the other dragons."

CHAPTER TWENTY-SIX

L aliah and Aurora Leigh were soaring high, under the protection of two Oralian Champions. The countryside below was spread out like a colorful tapestry, the colors ever-changing from forest greens to straw yellows to the earthen tones of sienna and brown. They followed the path of a meandering river that reflected the sunlight as it cut deep ravines through the valley.

Laliah's thoughts filled Aurora Leigh's mind as they flew, pointing out interesting landmarks as they traveled. *"We are flying above the caves at Willow Glen, youngling. It was where Ra and I made our home as he was growing up. It was a time when Ra found himself in quite a bit of mischief in one form or another."*

The opal dragoness continued to fill her thoughts with stories about the life she and Ra had shared in the caverns, and both possessed a brighter outlook by the time they landed at Kaleidos Peak. Certes, Laliah was a healer of the spirit as well as the body.

Upon arriving at Kaleidos Peak, the dragoness changed form, and she guided Aurora Leigh down the passageway to the princess's private bedchambers at Moorwyn.

When they arrived at their destination, Laliah smiled and said, "Aurora Leigh, you must realize Kulli and I love you dearly. I hope you know we consider you a part of our family. Though you are a mere youngling by dragon standards, I must remember my place and remind myself that, to the humans who are your true kin, you have reached your majority.

"Moreover, I feel the fondness and affection shared between

you and Eralon Wellsbough, and it does not take intuition to see the beginnings of a bond forming between you."

Blushing, Aurora Leigh lowered her head and bit her bottom lip at Laliah's words.

The dragoness flashed a charming smile while watching the youngling's behavior and could not help but gather Aurora Leigh to her heart in a warm embrace to ease her embarrassment. "Fear naught," said Laliah as she kissed the top of her head. "I broach the topic so we may talk forthrightly upon the matter."

At Aurora Leigh's shy glance and receptive nod, Laliah offered her a conspiratorial wink designed to raise the girl's spirits. "More to the point, I will teach you of all the cunning wiles I had to put in play to ensnare our beloved Kulli."

And that admission unleashed a round of surreptitious giggles.

Laliah had escorted the princess safely back to her chambers and found the guards had performed their duty in dissuading all servants and visitors. The imperatrix then followed the tunnels within Kaleidos that took her to the outskirts of the Crystal Palace.

Careful of her footfalls upon the slippery shores of the palace lake, Laliah stooped at the water's edge and dipped a hand into the glassy liquid, causing gentle waves to flow outward and ripple upon the surface of the lake. Simultaneously, she sent a feathery-soft mental query into the depths of the lake floor where Chief Elder Var'ohk made his lair.

The dragon council told her that Var'ohk had slipped away to research a few books on red dragons in his private home library. She could have called upon Var'ohk and requested his presence in the council chambers, yet respect for the major domus of the palace brought her to the shore instead. It was ever her way to request rather than command an audience, and she liked to think her approach was one her dragon lords appreciated.

From the far center of the lake the water stirred, and Laliah knew she had gained the emerald's notice. There was an explosion of water in a great column as the emerald water dragon shattered the surface. Great sheets of liquid flowed from Var'ohk's scales as he smoothly made his way toward Laliah, cutting through the water with ease. Laliah marveled anew at how unique the amphibious water dragons were in comparison to other dragons.

Fanlike wings ran from shoulder to hip, stirring the water as easily as any fish's fin, and they were equally as well-suited to pull Var'ohk airborne. His scales displayed many shades of green, nearly running the entire oceanic spectrum of the hue. A frothy sea green at his snout, the color gradually deepened to emerald green along his front and hindquarters before ending in shades reminiscent of dark seaweeds running the length of his tail.

The emerald water dragon's sleek body was long and sinewy. Each of his four graceful limbs featured five digits with curious webbing between them. Exclusive to his kind, he displayed frilled, membranous ears at the sides of his head, framing his face. He had thin flaps of skin on his snout that allowed him to completely close his nostrils while under water.

The large emerald upon his brow possessed the ability to illuminate the murky lake bottom, though he could turn the phenomenon off at will to hunt covertly in the dark, inky depths. The stone was smooth and flat like a polished river stone from all the time Var'ohk spent submerged in his natural elements of ocean, stream, and lake. This did nothing, however, to diminish the stone's beauty. Laliah smiled as she admired the splendor of the elder dragon.

"I am honored by your perceptions, Your Imperial Majesty, though if you keep this up, you will make an old dragon vain." Var'ohk's laughter was a gravelly rumble like thunder, and his smile was lit with amusement. *"Now, I doubt you came here just to fuel my vanity, so how might I be of assistance?"*

"It seems the red dragons have started their journey across the Carillion Sea. Kullipthius has tasked me with retrieving the Imperial Water Squadron. I am to lead them to the western shores of the Carillion Sea where they are to keep the ruby dragons from reaching the shoreline. He also wants the Imperial Champions' numbers split neatly into two flights. One flight will travel to the western shores as soon as they can be assembled. Their task will be to prevent any red dragon who may break through the Imperial Water Squadrons' defenses from causing havoc upon our lands. The remaining champions are to protect the Crystal Palace and Moorwyn Castle."

Var'ohk dipped his head to the imperatrix in a mark of respect.

"Worry not," Var'ohk replied. *"I shall communicate Imperator Kullipthius' requests to the squadron leaders as we make our way back to the Crystal Palace."*

As the elder dragon made his way up the shore, he shed his draconic identity. His dragon claw prints abruptly ended, and black leather boots then left their impressions in the sand. As he approached her in his altered guise, the only visible evidence that he had been in the water was his damp, greying hair. He offered the imperatrix his arm which she graciously accepted, and then they walked together toward the palace.

FLAYRE closed his eyes and finely tuned his senses, allowing the burning sensation of Ak'na to guide him. Feeling its intense pull coming from the edges of the forest, he snapped his eyes open to find a single red dragon staring at him within the shadows of the trees.

Flayre had no doubt the dragon before him was family, for the young dragon's features were undeniable. His massive size and distinctive wing and bone structure told the story clearly. Flayre sent a retrieval spell to compel the dragon forward and out of the protection of the trees.

"What is your name, red dragon?" boomed Flayre's commanding thoughts. He sensed no fear from the dragon in the shadows and noted he stood his ground, seemingly unaffected by his magic.

"I am called Blayz," he replied.

"Answer me this, Blayz," demanded the legendary red. *"How do you shake the effects of my magical runes?"*

Blayz stepped forward into the daylight, and Flayre found the action to be the answer to his question. The sun's glow that kissed the dragon's scales revealed a subtle bronze sheen. His mind flashed back to a slave he had caught building a nest.

"My, my, my . . . Et'opia lived to have a son, and I had thought your mother dead." The red dragon's face took on a shrewd countenance. *"This could surely work to our advantage. It's obvious you inherited the gift of resistance from your mother. Why, with you standing at my side, nothing could stop me."*

With the gift of resistance came the ability to defy the damaging effects of disease, infection, and magic. Flayre also knew Blayz had been unaware that he had his mother's gift. He could tell by the way his newfound son widened his eyes in surprise. It was the same thing Flayre's father, Py'ro, had done when trying to hide his ignorance.

Blayz snarled. *"The only way to make this day any better would be if you were not in it, progenitor."* Smoke curled from his maw. *"That is all you will ever be to me. I would rather be a fly* dining on solid waste than play a part in your madness."

"Well, that could be arranged, my son, but I have a more palatable proposition for you. With your mother's gift of resistance, and with my blood flowing through your veins, you could go far. I could use your knowledge of Oralia, for where else could you dwell that I could not have found you before? We could easily rule this world. After all, boy, you do owe me that consideration and respect as your sire. You must know ruby heritage surpasses all." Flayre was sure the red in Blayz would concede.

Blayz approached the menacing dragon and nodded, "Aye, I do believe you are correct. Consideration and respect . . . I shall afford you the same . . . the same you bestowed upon my mother!"

A bright inferno followed his last roaring words as Blayz called upon his gift of fire.

Flayre turned his head away just in time as the flame approached, for the runes upon his back and wings were those housing his shielding spells. He lifted his wings to cover his head and the more delicate runes. He was amused until a searing pain started to penetrate his shields.

Flash fire! Flayre realized Blayz's flame obviously matched his own powerful traits, for this fire was unlike any ordinary red he had encountered. It matched Py'ro's gift and cut cleanly through his protection. He threw back his head, and it took everything he had not to cry out in agony and outrage. The flames had blackened and ruined half his shielding spells and had burned through to his flesh on a small area around his neck.

Flayre sent a healing spell throughout his body that helped him preserve his equanimity and lessen the pain that soon turned to fury. He looked directly into the eyes of his attacker and, with great difficulty, regained his composure. "Not a creature of words, I see. Your head is, indeed, full of logic and cunning."

He offered a bitter smile and was sorely disappointed he did not have the time to tame the young dragon to his liking. "You may deny it all you want Blayz, but you could not have inherited your cunning approach and the gift of flash fire from any other."

Once again, Flayre saw the wide-eyed look of surprise in Blayz's eyes. He wondered how Blayz could have lived all these yearmarks without knowing about his dragon gifts.

"What a pity to waste such talent, half-breed," Flayre said in exasperation, shaking his head in disgust at his son's ignorance. "We could have ruled this world together."

Flayre took a deep breath while tapping into the magic of his most lethal glyphs before he added with a snarl, *"Ponder that as you are dying, Blayz."*

As he let those final words fill Blayz's mind, Flayre unleashed a stream of his hottest blue-violet flame, a mixture of black magic and flash fire, upon his newfound son.

LALIAH flew over Avala's uninhabited northern rocky coast, leading the Imperial Water Squadron who soared wingtip to wingtip in tight formation. They continued over the Carillion Sea's sparkling blue waters and out of view of any chance spectators. Their plan was to intercept the red dragons and thwart Flayre's plans of attack. Satisfied she had reached a safe distance from the shore, Laliah turned south, making her way toward Terra Leone.

"Stand ready," commanded Laliah, for the time had come to follow Their Imperial Majesties' tactical maneuvers and defend Avala's western seaboard. *"Begin!"* Two by two the water dragons departed in perfectly timed and spaced intervals, diving headfirst into the ocean.

The defenders chosen for this task were known as aquamarine dragons. These blue-green water dragons possessed long, sleek, serpentine bodies, an aquamarine stone upon their heads, and a pair of beautiful turquoise wings. Aquamarines' preferred element was water, yet they could effortlessly adapt to any environment. Their gift of water manipulation allowed them to wield any body of water, be it a waterfall, river, or ocean. They could hide themselves in columns of water under the disguise of hurricanes or fair weather waterspouts over the ocean. To take flight, the dragons used the water's force to help propel their sleek, legless bodies into the sky. Their mission this day was to lie in wait beneath the water, ambush Flayre's red dragons and prevent them from reaching Avala's shores.

Laliah watched as multiple sleek bodies moved expertly through the water in an undulating progression. Water gave them a vast concealment area and negated much of their weight factor, making them fast and maneuverable, giving them an edge in their confrontation with the reds.

Without warning, Laliah's healing gift awakened. She opened her dragon senses, trying to pinpoint the healing call's direction. Her gift impressed upon her to go, and go *now*. It was similar to her son's gift in that, once the calling came, it became almost impossible to ignore. In that moment, as if to reinforce her growing urge to help, an agonized, draconic cry reverberated through the air.

The remaining airborne defenders slowed their flight at the sound. The scream's direction and her gift's persistence told her that her patient was close by, and could be found along the coastline, in the direction of Bocca di Leone.

"What is your command, Imperatrix?" questioned the aquamarine's squadron leader who was now at her side.

"You have your orders," she answered. *"You must carry on as planned. I will continue alone and fulfill my responsibilities as healer."*

At the squadron leader's nod of acquiescence, Laliah followed her gift's calling, hoping she could be of assistance to whomever it was who needed her, before it was too late.

KULLIPTHIUS and those present in the encampment stopped what they were doing when they heard a wounded dragon cry out in the distance. They all whirled to the west in the direction of the jolting howl.

"That pigheaded dragon," said Jhain, shaking his head. His words cut the quiet, and he fisted his hands at his side. "I knew he'd be getting inta trouble."

Kullipthius felt pressure on his shoulder and found his son standing at his side. Ra's eyes were troubled, and Kullipthius knew the news was not good. Kullipthius noted that the queen of the Fenrie sat on Ra's shoulder and she, too, held a look of concern.

Ra nodded in Jhain's direction as he communicated with his father. *"The scout proves to be quite perceptive, Father, for it is as he fears. My own gifts have shown it to be so, and the trees have sent warning. The Fenrie followed Blayz and then spread the word as quickly as they could to get the information back to us. The presence of Ak'na has lured Blayz into a dangerous position.*

He has just discovered that Flayre is his sire. They are at Bocca di Leone."

"It is as you and I have always suspected. What does this mean for Blayz?" asked Kullipthius.

Then, the imperator continued aloud, "Does your vision show you the outcome?"

"Aye, if we do not reach Blayz soon, I fear for his fate." Ra's eyes glittered with intensity, leaving no room for debate.

Kullipthius took a deep breath, trying to retain his composure. Smoothing his features, he turned to address the others in the encampment. "The forest denizens have informed Ra that Flayre encountered Blayz while our commander was preoccupied with the call of Ak'na." He was intentionally careful with his speech, for he believed that Blayz's heritage was his own to disclose, if and when he chose.

As those present absorbed his shocking news, Kullipthius turned back to Ra and said, "If we leave immediately, will this course give us sufficient time to alter Blayz's fate?"

Ra shook his head and said, "As hard as I have tried, I know not the outcome. I cannot summon a clear vision."

Kullipthius nodded his understanding. He turned to address Romus and issued swift instructions. "Take Jhain and Eralon to the fortress as planned. We cannot afford the luxury of awaiting Laliah's return. She will find us."

Next, he spoke with Vahl Zayne. "Fly King Lucian to Terra Leone and then help the Fenrie with any rubies that make it through the aquamarine dragons' line of defense."

Kulli's nerves were taut as he watched the dragons and their charges depart one by one from the clearing.

Kullipthius then turned to speak with the tiny fluttering form with the lavender tresses hovering at Ra's side.

"Tiaré Oona, the time has come to protect our home. Gather your host and tell them to prepare to follow any red dragons that have made it into the forest. Advise the Fenrie to be prepared for the possibility of multiple fires. Vahl Zayne will join you in the Tall Forest to offer any help you might need."

The Queen of the Host bowed and zipped out of sight.

Kullipthius addressed the imposing warrior dressed in red. "Xalcon, the imperatrix was to lead a flight of water dragons out to sea along the west coast. I would like for you and Ra to find her location and make sure she is out of harm's way. Then I would consider it an honor to have you at my side in our upcoming encounter with Flayre."

"You can count on it, Imperator," responded Xalcon.

Ra turned to Xalcon and held his penetrating lavender-blues upon the fierce warrior's gaze and said, "I do believe it is time to take our due reckoning against Flayre. Are you ready?"

Xalcon Rhylock's response was immediate. In a flash he was in his draconic form. His dark claws cut deeply into the earth as he flexed his massive wings.

Ra took his seat upon the black dragon's back, and Xalcon looked over at Kullipthius to relay his unspoken thoughts. *"Let us fly."*

CHAPTER TWENTY-SEVEN

S cale stared in utter confusion. Uncertainty nibbled at his thoughts like tiny scavenger fish. Bewildered, Scale drew his horse to a halt and dismounted.

"What dark sorcery is this?" he asked aloud. He had ridden this road many times. He should have been viewing the back entrance to Lionholm Manor's stables, but the fortress was not there!

He knew the area intimately, thanks to Danuvius' stolen memories, yet there was nothing to be seen but wilderness. Not a single rock was out of place, and there were no ruins from some great razing. There was nothing to indicate that anything untoward had happened to the fortress in his short absence. He dismounted and slowly stepped forward until his hand hit resistance, a telltale sign that magic was the source of his vexation.

"Flayre!" To Scale's mind, this was the only reasonable answer to his conundrum. This had to be yet another punishment from the fire-breather, aimed at some perceived offense Scale had unknowingly committed. He moved off the path, anxiously hoping that a different perspective would, somehow, reveal his prize. But he seethed when there was no alteration to what his eyes were telling him. Why had the dragon rendered the whole city invisible? Scale came to the conclusion that it must have been to keep him out and focused on his mission.

Flayre had ordered him to meet with the troops gathering in the forest. While Scale had started out following those directives explicitly, he had seen the wisdom in a small detour. The deception had to run smoothly if all were to work as Flayre planned. "Danuvius" could not just show up at the designated area inappropriately attired. He would also need the gold he had hidden in Lionholm Manor. The Liltian army he was meeting would not have taken him seriously without it. Surely the spell-wielding beast could understand that.

With a frustrated sigh, Scale would now have to guess where the fortress' secret entrance should be. With luck, he could find the now "twice" hidden door and passageway that led into the manor.

ERALON and Jhain made their way through the skies to Terra Leone on dragonback. It was unlike anything the captain had ever experienced. The clouds were close enough to touch. Heaven itself appeared within one's grasp, and he envied the birds and dragons their access to the skies.

"Flying dragonback is most exhilarating," exclaimed Eralon to no one in particular. He decided the experience was somewhat akin to riding a horse. There was the same sense of being part of the great outdoors and the feel of the rushing wind in your face astride a powerful being with rider and beast in perfect partnership. But that was where the similarities ended. One's well-trained steed did not verbally respond to your decisions with alternate suggestions, nor did said steed offer its own words regarding your safety. Eralon understood that he was at Romus' behest and under the directives of two monarchs. While he did have a voice and was treated with respect, he was certainly not the one in control of this particular mode of transportation.

Eralon knew that Jhain's spirits were soaring along with his outstretched arms and jet-black hair that waved through the wind with reckless abandon.

"Truly, 'tis regrettable we canna fly on dragon back ta all our assignments, eh Cap'n?" the scout called back over his shoulder and into the wind. "The journeys would nay be half as long as they be on horseback." His grin was in profile as he spoke to his superior. "We would'na need fer any fighting either. The opposition would see our allies an' run."

Eralon was happy for times like these when Jhain could display his youthful exuberance. He was younger than Eralon by nine yearmarks, but the scout rarely had the chance to enjoy himself because he bore so many responsibilities.

"We be nearing the outskirts of where the fortress should be," Jhain continued, "an' 'tis as if it never existed. The amethyst's gift be amazing."

"I shall pass your sentiments on to Shayde." Romus sounded amused as he conveyed his thoughts to Eralon and Jhain.

As they arrived at the fortress, Romus advised them, *"Shayde will make the back doors of the fortress visible soon so we can make a safe landing. I have, however, asked him to hold off for a moment. It seems we have a stray and baffled Liltian soldier on our hands."*

Romus smoothly glided lower to give them a better look, and Eralon spotted the dark-haired fellow below. He was shocked by the identity of the man, and apparently Jhain recognized him as well, for his jovial mood vanished without a trace, and his voice emerged as a growl.

"That's no Liltian soldier," Jhain ground out. "That be Danuvius. I'd know that mongrel face anywhere."

"Can you set us down, Chief Romus, so that we might deal with this fellow?" requested Eralon. "He is the one in league with Flayre. I think it best that he not be left to traipse freely about."

"I spotted a clearing where we can land. Once there, we can observe Danuvius from the cover of the trees," replied Romus.

The chieftain was quiet for a moment before he relayed his next message. *"Vahl Zayne is close behind us, and I told him the situation. He advised me that he will be leaving King Lucian with us. The frost dragon has orders to assist the forest denizens in their fight against any forest fires. Hold on while we make our descent."*

Upon landing, Romus changed to his human guise, and they made their way through the trees, ducking low behind a dense thicket of shrubs and berry bushes. Eralon watched Danuvius pace and mutter incoherently. His dark hair was wildly tangled, and his ill-fitted garb was stained from travel. Danuvius gave no indication that he knew he was under scrutiny as he glowered at the area that should have been the outer walls of the fortress.

"Do you think he knows the fortress is still there?" asked Jhain, as he offered Eralon some of the wild blackberries from the bush they were crouched beside.

Shaking his head, the captain lifted a brow and grinned.

Jhain shrugged. "I be hungry," he replied, with a mouthful of the proffered fruit.

"Strange," said Romus. "I tried to read what Danuvius was thinking, but his mind is shielded from me. Flayre may have taught him how to mask his thoughts." Romus' ochre eyes were narrowed in keen interest.

Eralon and Jhain glanced at each other upon hearing Romus' statement.

"Masking our thoughts be possible?" asked Jhain in an incredulous voice, his eyebrows rising.

The blond, spiky-haired chief shrugged his wide shoulders impressively. "Aye, one needs only to learn the proper technique."

Eralon watched as Jhain crunched his brows. The scout's questioning look spoke volumes.

Romus chuckled. "Mayhap at a more appropriate time I could teach you." Suddenly distracted, Romus spun to stare in the opposite direction.

On alert, Eralon and Jhain also pivoted as their hands instinctively hovered above their weapons. There was naught to be seen, though Eralon saw Romus' wolf-like eyes track something beyond the tree line. Romus' nostrils flared as he sniffed the air, and then he visibly relaxed. A few moments later, a rustle of leaves brought King Lucian into Eralon's view as he made his way through the trees.

When King Lucian reached his companions, he said, "Vahl Zayne and I saw your position from the air." Lucian's gaze shifted to peer over their shoulders. "Who is that running about?"

Eralon turned back and saw Danuvius running back and forth, desperate in his search to find something that was not to be found. "That, Sire, would be Danuvius Doral."

King Lucian peered closely, and then he frowned and nodded, apparently recognizing him.

"Aye," responded Jhain, joining in the conversation, "though me thinks he has misjudged the distance. According ta me internal map, he be right upon the fortress . . ."

"Ooh!" Eralon and the others chorused Jhain's exclaimed sentiment as they watched Danuvius imprint his face into the concealed wall and fall backward to the forest floor in a daze.

"It appears he found the fortress," stated Jhain with a smirk.

King Lucian shook his head. "He needs to be apprehended. We can place him in the fortress prison until we return to Moorwyn." His eyes were glued to Danuvius as he spoke. "Chief Romus, are we safe in the open? Do you have any alternatives to offer regarding his capture?"

When the trio tore their gaze from the outlaw and looked at

Romus, they discovered that he was not with their party.

"Chief Romus?"

There was no reply, so Eralon looked to his monarch, but Lucian could only shrug. Then Eralon looked to Jhain, whose attention was skyward. Eralon and the king followed Jhain's line of vision.

The amber quartz was in flight above them. He then folded his wings to his sides and dove like a falcon toward the unsuspecting Liltian. With fierce talons extended, Romus snagged a startled Danuvius by the waist and rose to the skies, circling back toward the clearing with his prize dangling helplessly from his claws.

King Lucian smiled and said, "Certainly a swift alternative."

SHAYDE watched the tree branches as they bent to and fro in the wind. Since the walls were closing in on him in his stuffy grotto, he stepped outside for a breath of fresh air. As he did so, he decided to check for any anomalies in his cloaking magic. He perched atop the thick trunk of a fallen tree and gazed down upon the area of Terra Leone to observe his magical handiwork.

After Romus and the men who accompanied him grabbed the intruder and were safely inside the fortress walls, the amethyst dragon had reconstructed his invisibility shield over the fortress' back gate. Now, upon his second inspection, Shayde discovered that he would need to make a few repairs around the perimeter of his work. Instantly, his gift heeded his call. He lengthened and heightened his veil, deflecting the light around and above the settlement until naught appeared but the native vegetation. Satisfied, he let the coolness of the breeze that rustled the leaves and swayed the trees envelope him.

A flash of light brought Shayde's attention to the east. It was the sun's reflection off Talin's honey-brown scales as he winged his way toward him. The topaz dragon used Drahk to communicate his thoughts and warn the amethyst of the reds' approach, and Shayde sent out his own appreciative reply in kind.

Looking out upon the blue expanse of the sea, he modified his vision to take in more light and bring the images he spotted into focus. He was thoroughly surprised at the number of ruby dragons lining the horizon. He watched as they drew ever closer to Avala's shores. He knew the time was nigh, and he waited patiently for the aquamarines to attack.

Soon after, the sea began to surge and churn above the serpentines' emerging forms, sending tumultuous waves crashing against the shore. As each waterspout shot into the air, it trapped many reds within the spinning columnar vortex. After whirling dizzily in a column's grasp, the reds were sent flying through the air and then crashing into the sea in their disoriented state.

The red dragons that evaded the rotating water columns were met by the second line of defenders. These aquamarines shot up from the sea and wound their rope-like bodies around the reds and dragged the fire breathers deep into the ocean by using their combined weight. Shayde had seen the aquamarines at work before, and he knew the tussle and dousing would surely discourage many of these elementally opposed invaders. Bubbles and frothy ripples atop the water's surface showed that many of the reds had been unable to escape from the aquamarines' time-proven tactics.

Regrettably, not all of the rubies had been caught in the ambush. Many had made their way to what the reds believed to be the safety of the shore. This thought had Shayde's mouth curving into the draconic version of a grin. He knew from the plans outlined back at the encampment that Avala's shores and forest were no safer for the rubies than the ocean had been. They would learn their mistake quickly enough.

No sooner had the thought left his mind than the evidence proved the Fenrie had encountered the invaders in the forest. Though he could not see the actual clash of Fenrie versus red dragons from his vantage point, the Fenries' climatic havoc justified his deductions.

Clouds were forming at an unnatural speed, and hailstones fell from the sky. Thunder rumbled and lightning streaked in bright assault at the Fenries' behest. Howling winds whipped and shook the greenery like flailing arms ready to beat the enemy away with scratching limbs and cruel thorns. The forest's host of Fenrie may have been diminutive creatures, but they had great power at their disposal. With their combined might, Shayde was confident the Fenrie could control any forest fires caused by the desert dragons' fiery breath.

Shayde turned back to peer out over the water and noted that many of the injured rubies were fleeing back toward their desert homelands. He observed that several red, barrel-chested hulks had bullied their way past the water defenders and had garnered the attention of a flight of Oralian scouts who were making their way out over the water to confront them.

Farther up Avala's northwestern coastline, another flight of Imperial Champions were heading out to sea toward a second wave of rubies that were approaching from the Desertlands. If these defenders could not dissuade them from coming ashore, the aquamarines, who were once again hidden under the waves, surely would.

Shayde spotted movement directly in front of him on the boulder-strewn shoreline. Where the spray struck the rocks with intensity, a small red dragon heaved itself out of the sea, shedding water as a snake sheds its skin. The dragon shook its head and looked around as if searching for potential threats. Evidently satisfied, it pulled itself ashore, breathing heavily. Pausing on the beach to catch its breath, a gull cried somewhere nearby, and the dragon ducked its head as if fearful of the sound.

It was in that moment that Shayde realized the dragon before him was an adolescent. He had not, as yet, developed the deep red color of an adult. He looked like a pinkish blot against the white sand backdrop. The youngling was definitely on edge and out of its element. The young dragon turned in the amethyst's direction and surveyed its environment. Shayde froze, wondering if it had somehow sensed his vigil from the grotto. Without hesitation, it headed up the embankment, its wet wings dragging. Shayde then understood that the red had not seen him but had spied the mouth of the grotto. Contemplating his next move, Shayde slowly backed into the dark entrance, pulling the shadows to him like a lover's embrace. Then he waited.

The amethyst watched the young ruby drag his sodden frame up the slippery incline toward him. Not knowing an amethyst dragon was cloaked and waiting in the very grotto he sought, the ruby had his mind open and Shayde could read his thoughts easily.

"Cursed water beasts," thought the youngling, as he shook the mixture of sand and mud free that had squelched between his rose-colored talons. He lost his hold and slid backward down the slope. He bared his sharp teeth in frustration and looked again to his coveted prize above. *"The cavern should be dry, and that will give me a chance to recover from my long flight and near drowning."*

He looked down to double-check his footing, and Shayde smiled at the youngling's curses as he took note that his fine, sleek scales were dusted with bits of greenery and smudged with mud and wet clumps of sand. The young red screeched, *"This is totally unacceptable!"*

The ruby finally pulled himself past the last tangle of foreign vegetation, and then he collapsed against the shaded, cool rock floor at the entrance of the grotto, only a stone's throw away from Shayde.

A breeze had kicked up from the water and blew over the youngling's damp hide and scales, causing a shiver to wrack his body. The boy was ashamed of this involuntary display of weakness. His thoughts were of how Flayre had always told him he was a pathetic and useless dragon, and surely this was just another reminder of his many failures. But then a sense of pride overcame the youngling. He reminded himself that he had escaped from Flayre's guards that had stood watch over his home, and he had followed a flight of dragons all the way from the Desertlands to the land of forests and mountains. That would show Flayre that he was not pathetic and useless.

"How could Flayre possibly wish to rule this place?" wondered the youngling. *"It is so cold and damp compared to my nice hot and dry desert homelands. This shelter is not even a decent cavern! Once this stupid war is over, I am going to find a nice, warm place away from the wretched ocean. Then I will plan—in grand detail—how I will make every single water dragon in this alien land pay for my near drowning!"*

Loose pebbles clattered from within the hollow, jarring the young dragon from his thoughts, and he peeked inside. Shayde knew he would see nothing but shadows and darkness.

Cursing himself for his overactive imagination, the youngling crawled further into the grotto, curled up and closed his eyes. He was complaining about being ice cold, waterlogged, and bone-achingly tired from the long flight as he fell asleep.

Shayde observed the shivering nestling while he slept. In such close proximity, he came to realize that the youngling could be no more than twelve yearmarks. What was such a child doing flying with red dragons who were off to battle? Was his appearance mere happenstance? Shayde shook his head.

When the youngling had first emerged from the water, Shayde mistook his wet, pink-tinged scales for a young red dragon. Upon closer inspection, Shayde had realized he was viewing something much more exotic. The most outstanding evidence was the shining hunk of rose-colored gold on the youngling's forehead.

He was a Metallic dragon, and a rare breed in the Kingdom of

Draconalia known as a golden fire dragon, a variety of the gold dragon family. They differed in appearance from their bright, gold-scaled kindred, possessing scales of a pale rose hue that flashed a gold undertone when dry and viewed in the proper light. This young one was just sprouting a crown of curved horns atop his head and had one small, magenta spike that graced the tip of his snout. His elegant wings were wide set and looked soft to the touch.

After a time, the youngling awoke, sighed, and moved around frequently, as if trying to find a comfortable position. Shayde took the opportunity to pounce.

Appearing like an apparition from the shadows, he pinned the young dragon under his bulk. Shayde's wings stretched, obstructing the view of the grotto's entrance and, hopefully, any means of escape.

The young dragon yelped in surprise and squirmed, trying to extract himself from his crushing predicament. His wide eyes displayed a multihued spectrum of leaves in autumn. He stared at Shayde in a mixture of horror and awe.

"LET ME GO!" the hot, young mind brushed against Shayde's own, petulance and anger warring for dominance over his fear.

"What are you doing here?" Shayde demanded. *"Do you not see a battle raging over the sea?"*

A bright flash stung Shayde's light-sensitive eyes, and suddenly the amethyst was holding nothing but air. The youngling had transformed. Surprised for a brief moment, Shayde could only gawk, for the feat was not available to all dragons and then, normally, only mastered at an older age. The dragon-turned-boy sprinted for the presumed safety of the grotto's entrance, dodging around the wing of the amethyst.

The nestling's dash for freedom was cut short as Shayde quickly blocked the grotto's exit by fully expanding his wings to their widest stretch, and then using one winged appendage to scoop the boy to the back of the cavern. This time Shayde blocked the entrance to the outside world with his bulk. He would not be repeating his mistake.

In his human guise the boy's burgundy hair fell in a long braid to his waist. His plait was tied at the end with a leather band and adorned with red beads and a blue feather. His skin was a tawny gold, and he had a lean build. He wore an open vest with red beadwork and quillwork with no tunic beneath. Around his upper arm he wore a rosy-hued metal band etched with swirling designs that portrayed his dragon heritage. His leggings were made of some unknown animal hide and matched his soft moccasins. He was, indeed, a youngling of about twelve yearmarks and, by dragon ethics, would not normally be allowed to leave the nesting grounds unsupervised—so where were the boy's parents?

The boy picked himself up and flipped his long braid over one shoulder before glaring at Shayde.

"I do not answer to you," the boy declared, "and I am not staying here. If your plan is to imprison me here, I will fight. I am not afraid of you!" Despite the youthful bravado, there was an undercurrent of fear in his voice.

Shayde, recognizing this, altered his tactics and conveyed his thoughts, *"I am only trying to protect you because it is not safe outside. I have no intentions of harming you, if that is your worry."*

The youngling remained silent.

"Tell me: Why did you trail Flayre and his red dragon followers? Surely your mother is worried about you."

"You know nothing of my mother! You will not speak of her!"

Obviously, that was a tender subject. Shayde tried again. *"I am Shayde. What is your name, and from where do you hail?"*

The boy scrutinized the amethyst and said softly, "Ariazar."

"I beg your pardon?" Shayde had not expected an answer, and he had not quite heard the response.

"Aw-REE-ah-zar," the boy repeated loudly and a little rudely. "That is my name. I prefer Ari. I am from the Desertlands. I flew here all by myself." His last words were prideful.

Shayde knew he had performed the task from reading his mind earlier. It was quite an accomplishment for a dragon of this young age. *"You are very strong and talented for such a young golden fire."*

"Obviously."

Shayde smiled inwardly, knowing he had baited his information trap well. *"Why, exactly, have you come here? Are you here to fight with the ruby dragons?"*

"I care nothing of this stupid battle. I came here to find my mother. Flayre took her away from me, and I came here to get her back."

Shayde tried to suppress his shock. Mayhap there was more to this war than the imperator suspected.

Shayde took a small gamble and moved to uncover the grotto's exit. *"I understand. If it were my mother who had been taken from me, I would have done anything to get her back. You are free to go."*

The boy looked shocked. Eagerly eyeing the outlet, he kept a wary watch on Shayde and his back to the stone wall.

Shayde tracked him with his eyes as he inched toward the exit. *"It is a pity that you do not wish to stay,"* Shayde remarked casually, *"for I know of a Golden One that would be more than happy to help you find your mother."*

Ari's jaw dropped, and he stopped in his tracks.

CHAPTER TWENTY-EIGHT

T iaré Oona scowled in frustration. Two more ruby dragons breached the tree line of the Tall Forest and immediately began their demolition. Heedless of the forest's natural beauty, they showed little regard for the intricate balance of life around them. Fires broke out quickly from the dragons' sulfurous breath as brush, flowers, and trees were consumed in a violent appetite of flames. The wildlife that could do so ran for whatever safety they could find. Air that was once cool and pleasant with the smell of bluebells, pine, and wild roses quickly became hot, acrid, and choked with smoke and whirling ashes.

The queen of the Fenrie's eyes narrowed, and her orders were carried out with all haste as her armies splintered their forces by necessity to chase down the reds and halt the devastation. Some converged with their gifts of water and earth to smother the flames while others confronted the two ruby behemoths head on. Tiaré Oona saw a third dragon landing in the forest, and she made her way to him on a blurring set of shimmering, glittering wings.

The red's hide was the same shade as the poppies that grew in the fields. Under other circumstances, she thought she might have admired its color and the fan-shaped, armored scales. As she zoomed after the red dragon, she saw its scaly tail crash uncaringly through the underbrush. Neither the kiss of falling leaves nor the tickle of hanging moss gave the monster pause. The stench of smoke and sulfur permeated the air as Oona doused the flames of burning foliage that the beast had left in its wake. It was then she noticed with horror that they were dangerously close to her home in Mistwood Glen. She needed to end this. She could not allow these beasts to continue to befoul the forestlands!

Like a flag billowing in the wind, Oona's lavender tresses streamed behind her as she swooped before its eyes, trying to draw its attention. The beast she dubbed "Fire Starter" shook its head in irritation and snapped at her, thinking her nothing more than a simple annoyance. Finally, at the third attempt to garner the red's notice, he stopped in his tracks. Glowing twin embers stared down to take in her measure.

His gruff laughter filled her head at an almost unbearable level. *"Fly away, strange little bug,"* he threatened, *"lest you wish to be swatted."* His words filled her mind to capacity and were followed by a growl obviously meant to leave her quaking, but it did little more than strengthen her resolve.

Indignant, Oona pulled herself up to her full height. With the wind to aid her, she magnified her voice to echo through the trees at a level the red dragon could comprehend:

> "Dragon, cease your flames
> I will restore my forest
> YOU will know defeat!"

By way of demonstration, she conjured an orb of swirling water between her palms. It rapidly swelled to double her size and continued growing. Directing it one-handed, the water swirled and frothed in a spinning ball and floated over the singed vegetation, spraying it down with a fine mist. With her free hand she directed the life still clinging to the injured plants and trees and urged their growth. Oona watched, content in her power, as the damage reversed and the singed foliage shed its burned leaves and began to grow with new life.

Fire Starter grew still. Tiny flames danced in his nostrils and licked at his mouth as he watched his fiery work reverse. Wildflowers unfurled from their buds and grew in splendor before his very eyes. This was the only warning Oona would give him—a demonstration of the mighty powers that were hers to command as Tiaré, Queen of the Host.

The red beast issued a bellowing roar that shook the trees to their roots and lunged forward. Branches broke and leaves fluttered to the forest floor as he surged through the greenery. The water orb trailed in his wake and grew to enormous proportions at Oona's silent command.

As Fire Starter drew in the air to release his stream of flame, the orb flew forward and swallowed him. He blinked in dumbfounded surprise as the water held his weight in the air. Perhaps he thought his weight would cause the globe of water to fall harmlessly to the forest floor from his jostling and clawing at the bubbles' edges. Instead, the water held him within the center of its swirling vortex like a fly in amber resin. Oona hovered before one giant eye. Irritated, she sent her message in the wind:

"Dragon, you must yield,
Return to your desert home.
I will not play nice!"

Fire Starter nodded his giant head miserably. Satisfied, Oona ceased her attack. Red dragons were not used to being submerged in water. She could imagine that, to a creature ruled by the element of fire, it would feel as uncomfortable in the water as the Fenrie felt when trapped within a spider's web. She knew his air was limited to whatever was in his lungs before she had caught him with her skillful use of elemental powers. Oona scolded the dragon, shaking a delicate finger at him in warning:

"Behave, red dragon!
I trust you will leave this place,
Or suffer you will!"

As the bubble burst, the ruby dropped ungracefully to the forest floor amongst the fallen leaves and knobby roots. Gasping and spitting water from his lungs, Fire Starter plumed thin streamers of smoke as he tried to refuel his fiery breath. He shook his head, and water droplets rained everywhere. He sat for a moment and stared at Oona with angry eyes.

The beast drew himself up to his full height. *"You have obviously not dealt with a ruby before,"* stated Fire Starter, coolly. He took a deep breath, and his next words, though spoken calmly and quietly, were meant as an immediate threat. *"I will kill you for that humiliation, tiny bug."*

He whipped his head forward and shot sputtering flames at her. Surprised, but not caught off guard, Oona used her magic to call forth a large shielding disk of water. Where the deadly flames touched the shield, it hissed and sizzled, leaving steam and smoke to billow into the air. Licks of flame shot out around Oona's shield and restarted some of the surrounding greenery ablaze.

The air around Oona became thick and extremely hot, and she

began to perspire as she battled the dragon's gift with her own. The heat from the flames caused Oona's clothes to stick to her dampened skin. She could barely breathe, unused to such extreme temperatures. The dragon's devious attack was slowly draining her energy. She needed to stop this dragon's reckless behavior.

Her attention shifted to the thick vegetation that hung over the trees around Fire Starter. Mentally she directed three vines to grow in length and girth. The vines curled their way around the dragon, one creeper climbing up the right side of the dragon, two up the left. Quickly they tangled around Fire Starter's snout, closing his maw and snuffing his flames. The dragon gulped his fires and belched smoke between his teeth.

The temperature around her began to drop, providing a much-needed reprieve. Frost formed on the ground below her and traced intricate patterns up the rough trunks of nearby trees.

"Did you not hear Tiaré Oona's words?" boomed a voice in Drahk. Oona expelled a sigh of relief when she spied Vahl Zayne in his alternate two-legged, wingless guise step into the clearing. "I do believe she asked you to leave," he verbalized aloud while pointing a frosty fingertip at Fire Starter, "and I would suggest you follow her advice."

VAHL ZAYNE moved to stand at Oona's side and held out a hand covered with a fingerless glove. He knew by the way she fell into his palm that she was exhausted. Her tresses were mussed and damp, and her clothes were sticking to her skin. The frost dragon moved her to his shoulder, tucking her gently beneath the collar of his cloak for protection against the cold he would surely be generating in her defense.

Fire Starter strained to open his jaws and the vines snapped. As Vahl Zayne turned to face their adversary, Fire Starter displayed what Vahl Zayne knew to be a dragon smirk.

Taunting laughter filled Vahl Zayne's mind as the dragon launched his own invasive thoughts back at Vahl Zayne. *"I must admit, you are brave while in your pitiful human size and shape. Just what do you intend to do? I could cook you where you stand!"*

Vahl Zayne merely smiled and peered at the towering beast, but he made no move to attack. He knew the other dragon had taken in his spectacles and slender frame and had underestimated him. It would prove to be Fire Starter's downfall. "Kindly return to the Desertlands as Tiaré Oona requested and you will be spared," declared Vahl Zayne. "Displaying any further aggression will only force my hand."

You sound just like that annoying bug! Flayre was right— Oralians are pathetic. Let us come to blows, just you and me! I know from my own experience in battling others from your empire that your frail, alternate forms hold no power. Forgo that weak shell and fight me, dragon to dragon. I will boil your blood and watch you die."

Vahl Zayne lifted his face, letting light and shadow dance across his skin. "Is that what you think?" The temperature in the air dropped several degrees in reaction to Vahl Zayne's growing ire.

"It is what I know," stated Fire Starter. He drew closer to Vahl Zayne and raised his head to show his height. It was a tactic the reds used to intimidate, and it was one Vahl Zayne had hoped for. *"Flayre's teachings have only raised my awareness of your weaknesses. Show your true self!"*

Instead of compliance, Vahl Zayne walked forward, raised a single fingertip, touched it to a scale on Fire Starter's chest, and said simply, "I believe your information is incorrect."

Frost spread in icy fingers across Fire Starter's body and, within seconds, the smug dragon was encased in ice. Only his head remained free, and the red dragon roared in fury as he tried to extricate himself.

Vahl Zayne stepped back, stared up into the dragon's eyes, and smiled. "It seems you have been misinformed. I trust my little demonstration has shown you that I am in full control of all my gifts, no matter what appearance I take."

The red tried to ready a blast of fire to melt the ice, but it only made matters worse. Ice crystals crept up the sides of his neck and stopped just short of his snout. With a yelp of shocked surprise, the dragon ceased his attempts at violence and, instead, locked his eyes on the master of ice who stood before him.

"Let me share something with you that you might find fascinating. Pay attention and pray you live long enough to enjoy this tutelage." Though Vahl Zayne's voice was calm, his next words were frightening. "If you stay below your normal body temperature for too long, the response will be shivering, which I see has already begun. But if you are wet and cold, now that is a different story! Your body will lose heat five and twenty times faster in water than in air, and you happen to be surrounded by freezing water that is melting slowly on the inside, by the way. But worry not. The outer portion will remain frozen, keeping you confined. You will soon experience memory loss, and then you will lose consciousness. Finally, I am sorry to say, death will occur. This fact is a delicious mystery to me and one, I might add, quite intriguing as my body and temperature do not seem to be affected in that manner whatsoever.

"YOU, on the other hand, must keep moving in colder climates to stay warm, so your body keeps burning energy by shivering and shuddering until you start to sweat. This sounds great until that sweat cools and, before you know it, you're dragging your delicate body temperature lower and lower. Intriguing, is it not?"

Vahl Zayne watched as the dragon tried to struggle from his frozen prison. "Oh, come now, you do not like my lesson? That's gratitude for you. You would think you would be pleased to know what is going to happen. After all, it is your body that is encased in ice." Vahl Zayne smiled at Fire Starter, pushed his spectacles further up on his nose, clasped his hands behind his back, and bounced on his heels. He knew he looked as if he were waiting for the job to be done so he could continue his job of Protector of the Forest . . . with the touch of a finger.

Fire Starter squeezed his eyes shut. His sharp teeth chattered from the numbingly persistent cold pressing against his body. *"T-this is not right!"*

Vahl Zayne took a step forward.

Fire Starter flinched. *"N-no! Stay away!"*

Vahl Zayne's smile turned cold and stony. His eyes turned blue-white and glowed intensely around the pupils' centers. "I do believe you mentioned that you wished to boil my blood? Well, it looks like the tables have turned. Let us see if I can suck all the heat from your bones."

With that ominous statement, Vahl Zayne lifted his collar and Tiaré Oona came forward, looking none the worse for wear from her bout with the red dragon. She nodded to Vahl Zayne and flew into the leaves of a nearby tree.

The imperial advisor then transformed, showing his true face. His large dragon shadow fell heavily over the ruby. Vahl Zayne watched the red dragon's eyes widen in panic and terror at the frost dragon's size. The advisor's mental voice was much deeper. *"Is this not what you wished to see, red—my true power and form? Are you satisfied with all your power and my 'lack' thereof?"*

The ruby's breath was rapid and frosted before him. Tears of helpless terror streaked the planes of his face and immediately froze in their tracks.

"I should n-never have listened to F-Flayre," was Fire Starter's bitter thought as he closed his eyes and awaited his demise.

"Ah, could that mean you have learned your lesson?" asked Vahl Zayne.

Fire Starter nodded.

Vahl Zayne directed his gift to release its frozen hold.

The ice melted as quickly as it had formed, and Fire Starter stumbled backward. Startled from the sudden freedom from his icy confinement, he opened his eyes to find himself nearly snout to snout with the mighty frost dragon.

"Fly home little firefly, lest I change my mind."

CHAPTER TWENTY-NINE

K ullipthius raced on dragon wing to Bocca di Leone. A strong wind at his tail urged him onward at great speed. He was worried for Blayz, and hoped he could make it there in time to make a difference.

A column of rising smoke near the cove in Bocca di Leone where *Stormwalker* was anchored spoke of trouble. Kullipthius' nostrils took in the odor of blood and burning flesh. Within two flaps of his massive wings, he was over the area and caught sight of the red blight that was the terror of all dragondom. The vile ruby beast was pacing around Blayz's prone form on a space of flat, grassy terrain near the rocky bluff. Flayre's mind was wide open, and his agitation was clearly recognizable, giving Kullipthius unfettered access to Flayre's twisted pomposity. The imperator flew to the cover of the low clouds while he tried to devise a successful strategy.

"*I am sorry, Blayz, but I no longer have any time to play,*" apologized Flayre, sarcastically. "*I must fly down the shores of Avala and join my army of ruby dragons so we can destroy Terra Leone. But worry not, I have not left Oralia out of my plans—the empire will be next. And we cannot forget about the Avalians at Moorwyn Castle. Your pets would feel left out.*"

Flayre sighed and continued, "*Unfortunately, I cannot have you running back to your precious empire to let the imperator know my intentions. It is a pity you have turned out to be such a disappointment, Blayz.*"

Kullipthius watched Flayre draw in his breath, preparing to put an end to Blayz's life.

Thunder roared from the clouds and lightning cracked in the middle of Flayre's chest, hurtling him through the air and over the side of the bluff with a pained snarl. The subsequent splash into the ocean was a momentary victory for Kullipthius, having saved Blayz from certain death.

Flayre burst from the water with a bellowing cry that amplified to a deafening roar.

Kullipthius withdrew himself from the clouds and watched as the ruby rotated his wedge-shaped head in Kullipthius' direction and fixed his angry green eyes upon him. Knowing that, at least for the moment, he had drawn Flayre's attention away from Blayz, he quickly turned and flew eastward, and the fire-breather followed.

Alone, Kullipthius knew he was no match for the combination of Flayre's flash fire and black magic. With an idea in mind, Kullipthius dove through the trees. In a flash he was in his human form, he dropped and rolled upon the forest floor, and then he ran to conceal himself behind the thickness of a giant redwood. He knew Flayre reviled his own human form so much that he would not follow suit.

Flayre dove upon the covering of trees with extended claws, each as sharp and deadly as a longsword. He uprooted a massive oak tree in his attempt to expose Kullipthius' whereabouts.

"You can try to hide, but I will find and crush you, little imperator."

Kullipthius moved just in time as the oak's severed trunk sailed past his head and crashed heavily into a nearby tree, thrusting fragments and broken bits of branches down upon him. Kullipthius dove under a nearby patch of shrubs dense enough to conceal him.

Flayre's frantic search continued. He sent a thick, leafy branch sailing, which fell on Kullipthius, knocking the breath from him. Kullipthius drew his arms and legs inward and under the giant branch as Flayre hovered directly above him. The downdraft from the beating wings swept at his hair and his eyes burned from Flayre's sulfuric breath as he struggled to breathe under the weight of the massive tree limb.

LALIAH caught sight of the object of her healing gift's attention. She landed on the bluff, transformed, and ran to Blayz's side. She observed him breathing in short, ragged breaths. Besides being beaten and stomped on, various places on his scales were scorched black, and his underbelly was blistered and torn. Upon closer inspection, Laliah realized that Blayz must have inherited the gift of resistance from his mother's bloodline because many areas on his reddish-bronze scales were blackened and scorched but were not damaged underneath. She knew that any other dragon would have died from such an attack. She concluded it must have been Flayre who had attacked Blayz, for the injuries Blayz sustained had been the work of flash fire. Blayz tried to move, but it was apparent that even the smallest effort was agony.

Laliah loathed causing Blayz more pain, but if he shifted to human guise she could heal him faster. Also, it was dangerous to be as exposed as they were on the bluff. She had already spied a red-hued dragon flying away from the area. Later, she would devise a litter from her underskirt to move him.

"Blayz, I have come to heal you," explained Laliah. "If you shift to your human form it will be easier to assist you. Try not to move too much as some of your burns are quite grievous."

As Blayz altered his guise, his roar of anguish changed to an agonized human scream.

Laliah's gifts touched her charge with feather-soft insistence as she breathed cooling vapors down upon him. "Sleep now."

Laliah had just finished healing Blayz's most serious wound when the sound of an approaching dragon startled her. She stood over her charge protectively with her pulse thudding in her throat. She sighed in relief when she recognized the black dragon, Xalcon Rhylock, carrying her son upon his back. She quickly dropped her defensive posture and waited for them to land. The black dragon shifted, and they both ran to Laliah's side.

She embraced Xalcon. "It has been too long, Con," she said, calling him the nickname she had given him many yearmarks ago. "You have grown."

Xalcon's eyes softened, a slight smile graced his lips, and he nodded his head in respect to the imperatrix.

"Prithee, help me move Blayz to the cover of the trees," implored Laliah as she scanned the skies. "We need to conceal our position from an aerial view."

"How does he fare, mother?" queried Ra.

"I believe he inherited Et'opia's gift of resistance, and that is the reason he survived the attack. He is stable for now, and I have him sleeping. I have stopped the bleeding and will work on healing his burns after he has had some rest."

KULLIPTHIUS had struggled to pull himself from beneath the heavy tree limb. He positioned himself behind Flayre and waited for the best opportunity to attack. He watched as Flayre opened his maw to its widest stretch. A sweltering inferno of flash fire bathed the forest in a crimson and violet-blue firestorm. Ravenous flames explored their timbered world, dancing vehemently in the wind, rapidly gaining ground. Fire and smoke spread quickly, crackling and jumping from leaf to bough to mossy trunk.

Kulli knew that the trees would be transmitting their distress to the Fenrie and Ra. The tiny beings would make all haste to repair and heal the land, but it did little to assuage his guilt for leading Flayre into the forest.

He spied a large boulder behind Flayre's position, half covered in fallen leaves. Kullipthius marked it in his mind and summoned his gift. With the gathering of his power, his eyes turned to silver pools. With a great clap, bright power arced and struck the boulder. The massive stone exploded, throwing fragments of rock out in a violent burst. Hot shards assaulted the ruby's back and caused small tears in his left wing. As Flayre was reeling in pain, Kullipthius seized the moment and transformed, launching himself at the red dragon with claws at the ready to tear at Flayre's hide.

RA'S foresight told him something was amiss. His gift showed him a vision of his father in battle with a ruby dragon. A moment later, Xalcon growled low in his throat. Following Xalcon's gaze to the south, Laliah and Ra spotted a pair of combatants, silver and red, clashing in the sky above a raging fire.

Laliah gasped, horror plain on her features.

"Father!" Ra sprinted for the edge of the bluff. Palms facing together and set about a foot's length apart, Ra Kor'el called forth his gift. A blue light sparked to life, crackling like a bolt of lightning, reflecting brilliance off the scales of his forearms, causing his hair to stand on end.

Ra took aim and released a pulsing rope of blue fire. It streaked through the sky, one end still tethered in the land guardian's grasp as it flew the great distance. The jolting whip wrapped unerringly about Flayre's hind legs and tail, and the red dragon stiffened from the resulting shock. The power convulsed through both combatants but Ra knew it had little effect on Kullipthius who commanded the greater effects of true lightning. With little effort, Ra yanked the scarlet behemoth from his father.

The soothsayer's talent flashed his own fate before him, but it was too late for Ra to react. Flayre had sent his dark power down the fiery rope, shattering the connection. The resultant backlash snaked back to Ra with explosive force, blasting him into the trees that sheltered Blayz and Laliah. He crashed against an oak tree's thick trunk and fell in a limp tangle upon the ground.

Laliah screamed out Ra's name as she rushed to his side to heal him.

Ra could not move his legs. He felt as if his ribs had been crushed and found he could barely breathe. He watched through half-closed lids as Xalcon snarled out in a bellow of seething rage. The onyx's roiling fury encouraged his change to dragon. His body grew to vast proportions as black scales covered him in armor. Claws emerged from his fingertips while leathery wings erupted from his back. Fangs sprung from his maw, and a heavy tail swung out and thrashed at the ground. Great wings flapped as he took flight, crashing through the treetops. Ra saw Xalcon burst into a sky swirling with smoke and ash just before his world went black.

KULLIPTHIUS was engaged in battle with Flayre when he spied Xalcon winging his way toward them. Mustering all his strength, the imperator struck Flayre with his tail and knocked him in Xalcon's direction. Now within striking distance, Xalcon discharged his caustic gift with a thundering roar.

With Xalcon's acid flinging aimlessly through the air, Kullipthius found he could not join the mêlée. He watched as it rained down upon Flayre's back and hind legs. Smoke began rising off the dragon's crimson scales. The red beast bucked and yowled as the acid penetrated his hide. The red's giant claws raked the air as Xalcon's potent gift found the opened wounds Kullipthius had inflicted.

Xalcon then slammed into Flayre, sending them both tumbling through the sky. Flayre lashed out with harsh talons at the black beast that was clinging to him. Flayre bit down on the black dragon's right forelimb. Xalcon retaliated by lunging forward, jaws snapping for the ruby dragon's face and throat. The red dragon jerked wildly away in panic as acid dripped off Xalcon's fangs, falling inches away from Flayre's eyes.

The imperator watched as a carved rune pulsed on Flayre's hide, and Xalcon's wings appeared to be locked in place. Kullipthius knew Flayre was ill-matched in a contest of brute strength against Xalcon Rhylock, but the onyx would be helpless against this magical attack.

Flayre displayed a superior glint in his eyes before he spun and kicked, flinging Xalcon violently up into the air. The onyx dragon hurled high above his enemy before gravity took effect, and the black dragon began his descent through lightning-charged skies, with his wings dragging uselessly.

While Flayre was preoccupied watching Xalcon fall powerlessly through the skies, Kullipthius made his way toward Flayre's turned back.

"Position him beneath me!" came a private message from Xalcon, as he shifted to his human form.

Kullipthius readied a bolt of lightning and waited for the

appropriate moment to strike. He had only one opportunity to act before Xalcon would be dashed against the ground far below.

"NOW!" exclaimed Kullipthius, as he sent his bolt of lightning straight at Flayre's back. The strike thrust Flayre closer to Xalcon's position.

The red beast turned toward his attacker. The runes on Flayre's hide pulsed green, and Kullipthius found himself driven groundward by an assault of Flayre's dreadful wizardry.

Flayre's attack struck Kullipthius in the forehead. Blood was trickling down his face, he felt disoriented, and his heart was thudding in his chest. He did not have the luxury to tarry or wait for his equilibrium and heartbeat to steady with Xalcon plummeting groundward.

To try and remedy the situation, Kullipthius decided to send a small jolt of his lightning gift throughout his body. The sharp zap made his breath catch and his head throb in relentless pain. However, he felt its restorative effects, noting the strike had reduced his thundering heartbeat and had lessened the dark magic's dizzying effects. That would have to do.

He righted himself as best he could, flapped his giant wings, and sped toward Flayre, garnering his attention. He would do his best to keep the red beast distracted and provide aid to Xalcon when the need arose.

Kullipthius watched as Xalcon's human form was able to expertly ride the currents of the wind toward his target. The wind swept him through the sky at a tremendous speed for a collision course with the red dragon's back.

Xalcon crashed onto Flayre's body between his wings, and he slid forward from the impact. He clung determinedly to the bony spines running down Flayre's back.

The jolt of the impact caused Flayre to falter in his course. Flayre flailed, dropping until he found his balance. Just as he was righting himself and ready to take the first steadying flaps of his giant wings, Xalcon rose and drew his blade.

Sunlight glowed along the edge of Xalcon's greatsword, and the dark-haired warrior readied a mortal strike. Using both hands, he plunged the weapon downward.

Flayre altered his position at the last moment, causing the blade to miss its intended target. The sword sank deeply into the red dragon's shoulder. Flayre howled in excruciating pain as he rolled in an effort to dislodge steel and rider.

Kullipthius watched helplessly as Xalcon clutched at the hilt of his blade, dangling sideways.

"You vile, base-born, barbaric scum!" growled Flayre in a gravely demonic manner. The giant blade slipped from the beast's hide and Xalcon plunged groundward.

Kullipthius dove under Xalcon, catching his falling form against his back. Xalcon slipped backward but managed to catch the top of the platinum dragon's left wing. Kullipthius dipped left from Xalcon's sudden weight but righted himself as the warrior settled between his neck and back.

"Are you capable of flight?" inquired Kullipthius, as he looked back to see Flayre had used his magic to recover and was now in furious pursuit.

"I tried to make the change, but my wings are still magically frozen. I can feel the spell wearing off, albeit, rather slowly."

"I will drop you in the cover of the forest until then."

Kullipthius flew low, and Xalcon threw his greatsword to the forest floor while jumping from the imperator's back.

FLAYRE smiled in predatory delight as he flew straight for his prey with an anticipatory, unblinking gaze. He watched as Kullipthius banked sharply and circled to face him.

The red had drawn upon a potent spell that had healed his wounds fully and made him nigh invulnerable to any attack. So, when the imperator released his lightning gift at Flayre's right flank, it appeared as if an invisible shield had blocked the strike.

Flayre knew he would pay for its use later when he would become drained, collapsing into unconsciousness for a time. Yet, that was a trifling matter. He would have plenty of time to lead his ruby dragon clan and overthrow the Oralian Empire before seeking solitude for his recuperation. But for now, victory over Kullipthius was about to be his.

Smoke plumed thickly from the red dragon's nostrils as he prepared his strike. Flayre smiled, as another blast of lightning struck him, and it was equally as ineffective as the first. A sigil on the red beast's chest glowed as he unleashed his ultimate power. Like an explosion, a green and black projectile of the same poison Flayre had used on Dra'khar erupted from his foreclaw, and it streaked toward Kullipthius at high velocity.

The ruby's diabolical aim was true and Kullipthius' body jerked from the hit. As the glowing spear of dark magic plunged into Kullipthius it ripped a hole right through the left side of his body. The shrill, wailing cry that rang through the air spoke of the insurmountable pain that must have permeated the imperator's body. Kullipthius went limp as he tumbled through the air uncontrollably.

Instant gratification followed the strike as Flayre savored the cracking sound of breaking bones and branches while watching Kullipthius plunge to the ground. He knew Kullipthius would suffer a slow, painful death.

RA KOR'EL heard the agonizing cries of a dragon rip through the air. He watched as his mother shot to her feet while surveying the skies. He knew something was horribly wrong, for he could sense it, and it had to do with his father.

"Kullipthius!" shrieked Laliah, pointing to the east.

Ra searched the skies and caught sight of his father falling powerlessly groundward. Intense energy wreathed through Ra's clawed hands, when he saw Flayre in the vicinity, winging in the opposite direction. The charge in the air brought Laliah out of her shocked state, and she looked to her son.

"Go mother—now! The trees have advised me the Imperial Champions will arrive here shortly. Stay hidden in the cloud cover as you fly, for I witnessed Flayre in the area."

"What of you and Blayz?" inquired Laliah.

"Worry naught," exclaimed Ra, his eyes mirroring her worries, "My ribs are now healed, mother. I will protect Blayz."

Without further prompting, the dragoness raced toward the bluff and changed into a dragon as she leapt from the cliffs. Ra watched her lustrous pale form quickly leaving Bocca di Leone behind as she winged frantically toward her mate.

Ra had yet to regain feeling in his legs from the paralyzing spell Flayre had sent down his rope of blue light. He pulled himself to a sitting position, and leaned against an old oak tree who had offered him shelter. The oak had informed him that his father and Xalcon had been attacked with the same spell, and the paralysis would dissipate with time.

Lost in concern for his parents, Ra did not notice the six Imperial Champions circling overhead until the surrounding trees advised him of their arrival. The lead champion touched down on the grassy plateau while the others circled high above, keeping an eye out for any hidden intrigue. The dragon officer changed his guise and approached, giving a respectful bow. He summarized the current situation in the battle with the rubies.

"Your Imperial Highness, our latest reports show that the queen of the Fenrie and Vahl Zayne have the fires in the Tall Forest under control. Romus is currently at the king's side in Terra Leone. Var'ohk has sent a fresh flight of defenders to assist the aquamarines who are fighting a second wave of ruby dragons on the Carillion Sea. After they have things well in claw, the defenders will help rout out the remaining reds that may still be in the woodland."

The champion's leader had a troubled look on his face as he continued. "We have come here to assist you in any way we can. We were notified by the Oralian scouts that Blayz and you had been injured. We are prepared to take you both to the safety of the Crystal Palace, if that is your wish."

"Gramercy, Captain Skor, for the news. At the moment, Blayz is stable and resting peacefully, and time will heal the paralyzing spell placed on me," explained Ra. It took everything he had to remain calm. "However, there is a pressing matter that requires your immediate attention. The imperatrix needs your assistance immediately." Ra pointed to the smoke billowing in the south, rising like a hazy serpent. "Imperator Kullipthius was injured in a clash with Flayre, and the ruby dragon is still in the area. Go now and do whatever it takes to protect Their Imperial Majesties."

"As you command, Imperial Highness," replied Captain Skor, his grey eyes intense. He gave a silent command to his defenders, and they departed in the direction Ra had indicated.

"We brought along Truth Seeker Kaimi. The blue lace dragon should be able to track the criminal, if he is near." Captain Skor formally bowed to Ra, changed back into a dragon form, and took to the skies to catch up with his flight of warriors.

Ra was pleased with this revelation. Kaimi's gifts were potent. When her agate stone glowed, it gave her the ability to nullify any dragon's gift or magic. Her abilities would certainly come in handy when they encountered Flayre.

FLAYRE could not believe his good fortune. The delectable opal dragoness winging her way toward Kullipthius most certainly had to be Laliah. What a fortuitous day. Turning to covertly follow her, he stuck to the cloud cover as best he could. He would most assuredly enjoy the chase.

He was plotting Laliah's demise when a thundering explosion nearly tumbled him from the sky. Cries from multiple dragons trumpeted their intent to attack. Six Imperial Champions in a variety of hues swooped after him. Cursing, Flayre turned to confront his foes.

Three dove for him immediately, their shrieks tearing the air. They clawed at his scales and Flayre screamed in defiance. Expelling his flaming breath, he dropped and tumbled to try to shake his pursuers. Everywhere he gazed there were furious eyes, large fangs, and razor-sharp talons harassing him. He sent a spell to ground the closest pair and strained forward, trying to put distance between himself and the others. Another explosion detonated in the air next to Flayre, and he took evasive maneuvers.

Colossal wings pumping, Flayre summoned a powerful replication spell that sent a tingle down his body. His form blurred, and then fifteen duplicates of Flayre appeared all around him.

The copies all streaked in different directions. Flayre would use the confusion they caused to his advantage. For a time, Flayre thought he was clear from pursuit as the defenders chased after his lifelike reproductions. However, one sleek, blue and white speckled dragon broke from the commotion and zoomed toward him.

Twin indigo orbs locked upon Flayre, and her blue lace agate stone sat upon the dragoness' forehead between two slender, antler-like horns. Her scales were the perfect mixture of blue and white that looked like lace on her sleek body. Flayre had never seen the like. He bristled to think that she dared to tangle with the likes of him. The lissome female was certainly not the docile persona he expected most Oralian dragoness' to be in the face of his might, for she roared directly at him, vicious claws extended.

His fire peppered the air around her while her sinewy body dodged his magic with ease. She was not one to be easily deterred.

"What a delightful little morsel you are. Come to tangle with the hunter?" inquired Flayre, baring razor-sharp fangs.

"Which of us is the hunter?" she threw back, apparently not intimidated, her mental thoughts saucy. *"Just let me get my claws into your hide, and we will find out who the prey really is."*

Flayre rendered himself invisible and then repositioned himself, but her eyes continued to track him. She followed his course as if she were his mirror, wing beat for wing beat.

"Running away, coward?" taunted Kaimi as she crooked a talon in a beckoning motion. *"Come a little closer and I will show you exactly what my gift is all about."*

He did not know enough about this blue-hued enigma before him. She wanted to move within striking distance, so logic decreed he should stay away. Not wishing to waste his energy, he unfastened the invisibility spell that surrounded him and, at the same time, he heard her trumpeting her wrath.

Two Oralian Champions had noticed his reappearance and appeared eager to help. The blue lace dragon flung herself forward, claws stretching for his hide. Flayre slammed his magic into the approaching champions with great force, crashing them into the diving female. She gave a sharp yelp as the trio tumbled to the ground, crushing her foot beneath them.

"Get off me, defenders!" Kaimi screeched to Flayre's amusement as he stared upon the tangle of dragons below.

Flayre summoned his duplicates to crisscross around him as he recalled his invisibility spell and took the opportunity to flee. He then sent each duplicate away, flying in a different direction.

LALIAH caught sight of her mate's crumpled body within the thick cluster of trees, and her heart leapt in her throat. With sheer determination, she forced herself to look upon the scene with a healer's eye. Kullipthius had fallen into a tangled section of forest. A line of broken tree limbs clearly marked the path of descent where he now lay motionless upon the forest floor, bleeding heavily.

She changed from her draconic guise while hovering several feet above the forest floor. Her pearly plating of scales disappeared as she turned to human in a burst of light. She landed in a crouched position, stood and raced toward her beloved as fast as her two legs would carry her. She stumbled upon weak limbs toward Kullipthius, and she immediately sent her healing abilities to work, trying to stop the blood flow from the hole in his side.

As she worked, she noted some of Kullipthius silver scales had fused in the hit of Flayre's terrible magic, and others had disintegrated entirely. His wounds wept with blood. There were multiple broken bones throughout his body, and from the discoloration beneath his skin, Laliah understood with sickening clarity that he had been poisoned.

Struggling to regain some semblance of composure, Laliah summoned her strength and courage. She took a deep breath to steady her shaking limbs and drew closer to her mate to draw the poison from his body. With gentle pressure, she placed her hands upon his dragon chest, willing her gift throughout his body.

There was a flash of light, and a ragged breath escaped from Kullipthius as he changed his guise. She wondered if it had been an unconscious reaction to his wounds until a bloodstained human hand reached out for her tear-stained face. Her hard-sought calm shattered.

RA KOR'EL watched as an Imperial Champion lifted Blayz's human frame onto a rope stretcher and made his way to the Crystal Palace. Four others accompanied them. Kaimi was one of those returning to Oralia, as she needed to have her broken leg tended.

Before their departure, Blayz had been conscious long enough to inform them that Flayre had mentioned he was going to meet the reds at Terra Leone before moving inland toward Kaleidos Peak. Ra was now doubly grateful that Shayde had been posted to protect the area with his concealing magic.

"Imperatrix Laliah said that His Imperial Majesty could not be moved," advised the captain. "Therefore, we left two Imperial Champions to watch over Their Imperial Majesties. We also came across the onyx dragon, Xalcon Rhylock. He has nearly regained full use of his wings and said to inform you he would bring you to your imperial mother and father shortly. Would you like for me to wait here with you until his arrival?"

"Worry not, Captain Skor," said Ra. "The paralyzing spell is wearing off my legs. The trees have informed me that the black dragon has regained full use of his wings and is on his way back here to me now. Xalcon Rhylock is a fierce warrior. He will arrive soon, and the trees will notify me of any hidden dangers.

"You are needed to lead the remainder of your flight to locate the red menace. Send a message to the Imperial Scouts, Kayne, Swift, and Talin and have them assist Their Imperial Majesties back to the palace."

With a bow of his head to the prince, Captain Skor changed form and took to the skies.

FLAYRE was wrapped in an invisibility spell and clinging to the bluff face at Bocca di Leone. He was fortunate to have gained some valuable insight while eavesdropping on his enemies.

The red snarled, and clenched his jaw as he pondered how the imperial peons had caught wind of his plans. It had to have been the soothsayer. Seeing him alive made his teeth ache. He had thought his magical backlash had done away with Laliah's spawn.

He watched as the barbaric black dragon drew closer. If he remained invisible and left now, the trees would not be able to inform Ra of his whereabouts and the black dragon would not see him.

Flayre had an overwhelming urge to stay and do away with that acid spitting freak and the whelp Ra. Then he reminded himself that he would need to save his remaining strength, and he launched himself off the cliffs of Bocca di Leone.

Flayre believed it unfortunate that the Oralian Empire was on to his schemes, but that was not enough to stop him. He was a powerful magician and a master at stratagems.

The first thing he would need to do is devise a way to get rid of those two imperial watchdogs circling over Kullipthius. It was then that the perfect plan came to mind.

Arriving at his destination, he flew into the clouds for cover and conjured a single replicating spell. Flayre watched as Kullipthius' defenders took off after his replica like hungry dogs after a bone. A draconic smile spread across his maw. Now he can carry out his main objective—to make sure he put an end to Dra'khar's true bloodline.

CHAPTER THIRTY

L aliah was working her healing magic on her mate when a shimmer of light drew her attention to the blessing disk. She watched as Dra'khar's spirit form coalesced above the amulet's luminosity. This time the amulet radiated a warm, amber glow, and Dra'khar's incorporeal essence appeared to be in solid form. Though Laliah knew that Dra'khar was an apparition, this second manifestation was so real it was as if she could reach out and grasp his arm and feel warm skin beneath her fingertips.

Of a sudden, a dragon's bellowing rage shook the branches and leaves above them. Laliah shot to her feet. Dra'khar was by her side in a flash. Flayre suddenly materialized, hovering high above the trees with steam welling from his nostrils. His initial look of astonishment quickly transformed into an expression of white-hot rage as he surveyed the scene below.

Laliah knew the reason for Flayre's display of shock. Dra'khar truly did appear lifelike in the amber glow of the Allurealis crystal. The evil ruby believed Dra'khar had somehow managed to survive the poison from his fatal attack many yearmarks ago.

"NO! This cannot be! I killed you!" exclaimed Flayre, openly admitting his heinous crime.

Laliah could clearly see the ruby dragon's shock and fury as he roared his rage.

"You must stop this madness and treachery at once!" declared Dra'khar. *"This is your only warning, Flayre. You will not receive another chance to emerge from this unscathed if you do not heed my words."*

"How can you still live?" continued Flayre, ignoring Dra'khar's warning. *"I used the strongest of poisons to which there is no cure, and I watched as the arrow hit its mark. It is the same poison I used on your son."* His rage assaulted Laliah's mind and heart as he screamed out his fury. *"This time, there will be no escape! I will watch with pleasure as you and your family dies!"*

While Flayre was screaming his wrath, Laliah looked to Dra'khar and noticed his gaze on the blessing disk that lay upon Kullipthius' chest. His eyes were drawn to the Allurealis crystal and the platinum dragon delicately entwined around it.

"The time has come for you to fulfill your destiny, Allurealis!" proclaimed Dra'khar, in a voice that seemed to echo through the skies. *"It is once again your time to shine, My Lady Star."*

And so she did.

Allurealis' Ultimate Dance

At Flayre's release of flash fire, a pulse of the purest white light exploded from the Allurealis crystal and shot toward the red beast. Its radiance encompassed his menacing flames and snuffed them as if they had never been.

A glorious and sublime radiance then held Flayre within its luminosity, forcing his wings and forelimbs outward to their farthest reach and his lower body downward, long and rigid.

Like a candle lit within a lantern his body shone brighter and hotter. The sigils that had been painstakingly carved onto Flayre's scales grew as red-hot as glowing coals. The ruby roared with excruciating pain as the evil marks were seared from his hide.

There was a flash of blinding green brilliance and when it had dimmed, the beast could no longer be seen. In the dragon's place was a man's slumped and unconscious body. He floated through the canopy of trees and, by what appeared to be contrary to the laws of nature, managed to land gently on the leaf-littered ground below.

Allurealis released a second pulse. Multiple beams flew through the woodland, targeting the red dragon army that was influenced by Flayre's wicked ways.

The iridescent lights were indescribably beautiful and feverishly determined. They flew throughout the forest, targeting each red dragon that had been magically swayed and struck them all with great intensity. Those in the air were forced to join the other red behemoths on the ground. Their giant heads were thrown back, and they were all made to rise on hind legs with wings outstretched. As all the ruby dragons were held in place, Allurealis' white starlight did its work.

New twisting shafts of light appeared and they slammed into all the reds imprisoned by Flayre's sorcerous sway. Green spikes flared as it struck each dragon. Once the luminosity had scoured every trace of magical influence from their bodies, all the red dragons collapsed to the ground.

Immediately thereafter, Allurealis' lights gathered en masse and flew high above the trees. The twinkling beamss made their way past the Carillion shoreline and out to sea. The lights then made a grand eruption, detonating high in the heavens, sending some dazzling trails spiraling through the sky. Other lights blazed and tumbled down into the ocean in a crimson waterfall of flames.

A second explosion followed the first. It shattered into thousands of glittering sparkles that resembled iridescent rain that did more than just fall to the ground below. It spun and whirled, glowed and glimmered, until the last light twinkled out in a blink.

When the smoke cleared, a lone, brightly glowing ember appeared to have lingered. It was drifting, ever so slowly, downward. It hovered a sword's length above the ocean waves, but only for a twinkling, before it fell. It was held in the cradle of a wave, until it extinguished, and then disappeared into the water's shadowy blue depths.

Having recovered and no longer burdened with Flayre's influence, the red dragons stood and shook their heads. They flapped their wings, and took to the air with great resolve. The ruby beasts were heading west, in the direction of the Desertlands and back to their solitary lives. There is a delicate balance to all that is life, and the light had helped to restore things back to their natural order.

CHAPTER THIRTY-ONE

T reyven took the platform in Terra Leone's festival
showgrounds. He looked out at the Liltian mercenaries who
had filled every available seat and crammed into rapidly filling
standing room.

Dressed in his leathers with the Liltimer emblem upon his
chest, Treyven stopped center stage. Jhain Velendris flanked him
on his right and offered silent support as he surveyed the crowd
with shifting, watchful eyes. To his left, at crisp attention, was the
transformed dragon Romus, looking intimidating in the uniform
he wore as the human gate guardian for Oralia.

When the Liltian mercenaries began expressing their angry
words and desires to take their former country back by force,
Romus called out, "Let Treyven speak!" Stillness followed.

"Might I remind ye," Treyven stated with patience, "that those
very words be going against the queen o' Liltimer's last wishes. It
be Danuvius who caused all yer mental anguish an' confusion, nay
Avala's king. According ta archived documents I meself have been
privy ta view, Queen Mariselle specifically stated she be wanting
King Lucian ta rule in her stead. She believed His Majesty ta be
fair an' kind. The Avalian ruler more than proved the queen's
claims with his gift o' the fortress of Terra Leone upon our own
Valen Doral.

"I meself 'aves met with the king an' the citizens o' Terra Leone.
Their words proved that Danuvius be spouting falsehoods with his
claims of slavery." Treyven could not blame the mercenaries for
believing the worst, for it was not that long ago that he was also

caught in Danuvius' web of deceit.

Treyven knew King Lucian and Eralon stood ready at the back entrance of the showgrounds with Knight Master Balderon and the Elite Guardsmen under his command. They had stationed themselves in tactical positions in case Treyven's words fell on deaf ears.

Moreover, with the combined effort of Romus calming the crowd with his gift of influence, and the rapt attention the men in the showgrounds were giving him, Treyven believed they would soon have matters well in hand.

A sudden hush fell over the crowd, and all eyes were turned toward the steps of the showground's platform. As they had prearranged, Eralon had allowed the citizens of Terra Leone to enter the grounds, and they were climbing the steps of the stage to join him.

"Yer friends and family who live within the fortress walls o' Terra Leone have arrived. Talk ta 'em, an' listen carefully ta their words. They be the ones caught in Danuvius' mad schemes. They will tell ya the name o' the true villain."

Treyven turned to Jhain and Romus. "Now that the citizens 'aves arrived, we need ta walk amongst 'em as a reassuring presence. I think the armsmen be ready ta talk with the citizens an' hear the truth o' Danuvius' schemes."

"I will remain at your side in case of any altercations," said Romus. "My gift of influence may help to keep any problems at bay."

"Much appreciated, Romus," replied Treyven. "Let us away."

As Treyven walked amongst his brethren he could see that his words and those of the denizens of Terra Leone did not fall on deaf ears. The verbal exchanges around him exposed Danuvius' treachery for what it was. The ultimate proof of the tyrannical steward's lies came directly from the mouths of those living within the fortress walls.

KING LUCIAN and Eralon had watched Treyven from the stable area near the back entrance of the showgrounds.

"I believe Treyven has things well in hand here," remarked the king. "Come Eralon, we shall go to the jailhouse and speak with Danuvius to see if his demeanor has improved. Perhaps he will be ready to talk." Lucian turned to the new steward of Terra Leone, Redwald Balderon. "Steward Balderon, have your men remain here in case they are needed. You, however, shall accompany us."

"As you will it, Your Majesty." Redwald bowed before his monarch and issued orders to his first in command.

As the king and his entourage entered the fortress guardhouse, the guards snapped to attention, rising from their chairs and straightening their uniforms. When they recognized the King of Avala, their salutes quickly became scraping bows.

Eralon turned to the closest man and asked, "Which cell encases the prisoner Danuvius Doral? The king wishes an audience."

The guard stood straighter. "He be housed in the last cell in the back. We dinna have the room ta put him in his own cell, so we put him in with his cohort, Eldred."

Another guard continued the conversation. "A short while ago, Eldred started yelling an' screaming fer freedom. All's been quiet fer a time now. It seems he doesna like his cellmate anymore."

Eralon obtained the key from the prison guards and led his small group forward.

The cells were uncannily silent. It was as if no one was housed within. No matter how few occupants in a prison, Lucian thought it odd that there was not at least one cry for freedom, the clink of chains, or the sight of prisoners standing at the bars, hoping for release. Instead, the criminals were huddled in the furthest corners and did not even cast their eyes upward as the trio passed. The king could see Eralon himself was on edge because of the silence, for he pulled his weapon free of its bindings and motioned for the king to stand behind him. Steward Balderon took up the rear guard.

As they turned the corner and made their way to the last cell, they were met with a disturbing sight. The thick, steel-banded cell door was smashed to bits. Scraps of wood and twisted metal were strewn across the walkway.

"Wait here, Your Majesty," said Eralon, and he cautiously stepped inside the small room, blade ready, only to emerge a moment later to report, "There is no one inside." Looking vexed, he replaced his blade in its sheath. "The place is a bloody mess."

Lucian and Redwald moved to peer in, and Lucian shook his head. His captain was correct. Blood was streaked over the floor and speckled high on the walls and ceiling of the small cell. The pottery used to serve prisoners their meals was broken to shards, as if smashed underfoot. Deep gouges marred the floor and walls.

"Something foul has transpired here," remarked Steward Balderon as he straightened from the crouch he had been in while studying the scuffed floor. He pointed to some marks and said, "It's as if a mighty beast broke in and gobbled them up."

Eralon and King Lucian eyed each other. "Return topside and gather your men, Redwald," said Lucian. "Have them search the fortress for any unseen danger. On your way, question the guardsmen to see if there were any visitors here before us. Also, I want you to find the Oralian Romus and send him to me with all haste."

"Understood, Your Majesty." Redwald bowed before his king and saluted his captain before making a rapid retreat down the corridors of the jailhouse.

Once they were alone, Eralon puzzled silently for a moment and then said, "Do you think the reds came to tie up their loose ends?"

"I would loathe venturing a guess," Lucian remarked, and his eyes were serious and dark. "But I intend to find out."

LALIAH was alive though she could not find it in her heart to rejoice. She did not even have the strength to lift her head from her emperor's chest. Though she knew that Flayre was lying in his human form nearby, she could not rouse herself to care. Her energy was spent, and she felt in the depths of her broken heart that it was only a matter of moments before her beloved Kulli took his last breath.

As she held her emperor close, she felt growing warmth beside her arm. The Allurealis crystal was aglow. She looked up and saw the figure of Dra'khar next to her.

"I believe there is no hope," cried Laliah, her eyes red and swollen.

"When it is beyond your ability to believe, Laliah, faith can make all things possible," replied Dra'khar. "Prithee, place the blessing disk over Kullipthius' heart."

She did as she was bid, and Dra'khar placed his hands above hers. Laliah watched as he closed his eyes.

Dra'khar's spiritual form started to glimmer. Tiny motes of light pulsed and swirled around his hands. The twinkling elements that were once a part of Dra'khar's spiritual essence slowly descended into Kullipthius' chest, spread throughout his body, and shone beneath his skin.

Laliah could actually see the healing effects upon her mate's wounds. She watched enrapt as Kulli's wounds knitted together. His color started to return. She looked up; Though Dra'khar was fading, he beamed a warm smile, and she watched as all traces of his spiritual essence disappeared from sight. Dra'khar was gone.

The imperatrix felt the heat from the Allurealis amulet grow cold under her hand. It turned as clear as a perfect diamond. Laliah instinctively knew that it would shine no more. Then she looked down at Kullipthius. He was not breathing!

KULLIPTHIUS found himself wondering exactly where it was that he was standing. He was in his human guise, and the ground beneath his boots appeared to be the leaf-cloaked lands of the forest. Even his nose told him this was truth, for the scents in the air confirmed it—tree sap, wildflowers, small prey—yet even as he thought these things, he was forced to question his senses. He lifted his eyes and focused on the space; there was nothing but a dense, softly roiling mist, and faintly glowing scenery that held subtle movement. He spun slowly in a circle while confusion painted his mind with shades of uncertainty.

He felt oddly serene, as if he stood in his own private glade. Birds warbled a soft serenade, the temperature was perfect, and a hint of a breeze ruffled his hair. It was as if he was in a dream, but everything appeared so real, and he could not help but know something was very otherworldly about this place.

Then, with shocking clarity, his memories flooded to the forefront of his mind. His last recollection was of battling Oralia's nemesis in the skies above the Tall Forest, being poisoned and crashing rapidly downward through the trees. He scrutinized his arms and hands, and then his gaze traveled down his torso. He took mental stock of where injuries should have been. All of his wounds were healed, and he was pain free. He stood in his peaceful surroundings and stared into the mist as he tried to make sense of it all, but failed.

Before him, like a flower unfurling, the mist swirled into a near blinding tunnel of light. Kullipthius shaded his eyes with a hand and squinted against the brightness. A human figure stepped forward from within the luminance. Instinctively he knew, without a shred of doubt, that it was his father.

A warm smile lit Dra'khar's features as father and son moved to embrace and greet each other. Kullipthius pulled from his father's hold and expressed the thoughts weighing on his mind. "Father, my wounds are healed. I feel no pain, and in my heart there is so much peace. Have I joined you in the empyreal heavens?"

"We are in a place I call the 'in-between'," explained Dra'khar. "But you cannot stay here, Kullipthius; it is not your time. The Oralian Empire still has need of you as well as your mate and your sons. Even though the light has purged the dark magic and things are currently well in hand, you are destined to do great things."

"I have missed you, Father," replied Kullipthius.

Dra'khar placed his hand over his son's heart. "We shall always have each other here." He studied his son's face for a moment, then he placed his hands on the sides of Kullipthius' head, a gesture he had performed when his son had been a youngling, and he brought his son's head forward to touch his own.

Kullipthius felt a zap that resembled lightning surge through his entire body and take his breath away. His body jerked and then went rigid. He felt a tingling sensation throughout his being; his heart thudded in his chest, and then he had a sensation of falling backward. His vision went black.

Regaining consciousness, Kullipthius knew without opening his eyes that he had left the in-between and was back in the Tall Forest. As he lay there, he felt an ache in his heart as the presence of Ak'na slowly faded from his senses. He blinked his eyes into focus and saw a cascade of pale hair obscuring his view. Laliah was a slight but persistent weight upon his chest, and she was sobbing. Her face was pressed against him, and her hands were clutched tightly to his dirty, bloodstained clothes as if she were trying to physically anchor his soul to his body. He slowly reached out a comforting hand and placed it atop her glorious crown of hair.

Instantly her head jerked up, her face was bright red, and her violet eyes were shining with moisture. Her shock was easy to read upon her lovely features.

"Kullipthius!" Laliah threw herself forward to press her lips to his.

Her sobs then started anew, but this time, Kullipthius knew her tears were those of joy.

"You were poisoned and your heart had stopped!" exclaimed Laliah. "I thought you were taken from me! I could not bear a life without you, My Emperor!"

"Nor I without you," replied Kullipthius, and he meant it from the depths of his heart. He held her close, savoring the moment and feeling very happy to be alive.

"Prithee, My Empress, help me sit up against the tree." Once sitting and clear-headed, he continued. "It was in a place labeled the in-between that my father came to me. I felt such peace and contentment that I believed I had joined him in the heavens. I asked him if such were the case, and he told me it was not yet my time to depart our mortal world. His reply was, 'The Oralian Empire still has need of you as well as your mate and your *sons*.'" Kullipthius gazed at his mate with loving eyes and asked, "I wondered if there was something you wished to tell me, my love?"

Laliah's cheeks held a slight blush as she peeked at her mate through her lashes. "It is true, My Emperor; I am with child." She placed her cheek on her emperor's chest and said, "I am so very pleased your father was able to be the first to tell you." She then raised her face up to look in Kullipthius' eyes and smiled. They sealed their happiness with a kiss that spoke of ministration and relief and of love and contentment.

RA'S triumphant thoughts rang from the skies. *"The time has come to rejoice!"* He and Xalcon circled once around Ra's family and landed in the clearing.

Ra slid from Xalcon's back and approached his parents with quick steps. "I am thankful you are alive and well, Father. I had feared the worst."

His father was standing tall, as if his wounds had never been, and his mother smiled beside him. Their relief and joy was palpable, and the trio held each other for a moment in silence.

"How does Blayz fare?" Laliah asked at last.

"The Imperial Champions have returned him to the palace."

Kullipthius looked up to communicate with the towering black dragon. *"I wish to offer my gratitude for your assistance, Xalcon. Our empire is at your service, if you ever have need."*

"Your words and offer are unnecessary, Your Imperial Majesty," replied Xalcon. He looked over at Flayre's unconscious body lying on the ground nearby. *"I was more than pleased to assist you in putting an end to Flayre's reign of evil schemes."*

Xalcon then bid them all farewell. Ra knew he was anxious to check on the condition of his home in the marshlands.

After Xalcon departed, Ra and his parents walked to the supine form lying unconscious on the ground. "It is a true shame," Ra said, "that the ruby dragons revile their altered, indigenous appearance."

Ra took in Flayre's features. As a dragon, Flayre radiated danger, fire, blood, and anger. But seeing Flayre in his human form, he saw that his alter-ego was striking and regal. His skin tone was that of the Desertland's Red Mountains, and his long, black hair shone a reddish-violet in the sun's rays. High cheekbones and a strong nose sat above his full lips and square jawline. His closed, almond-shaped eyelids held long black lashes. Ra thought the race of those from the Desertlands quite exotic.

Three dragon scouts and two Oralian Champions circled overhead. Their wings stirred the air above those present, and three of them landed nearby. The trio's transformation revealed Swift, Talin, and Kayne, who gave their reports in an orderly fashion.

Talin began the account, his dark chocolate hair mussed beyond its usual artful display.

"The reds have turned tail and are returning to their Desertlands, Your Imperial Majesties. The Imperial Champions are patrolling the shoreline and will remain there as you ordered until they are called home."

Tufts of Kayne's sun-kissed hair were coming free of their normally meticulous plaits, and he had a bloodied cut under one coppery eye. He picked up the thread of information from his brother and continued the narrative, his smile still as bright as usual, even with his scuffed appearance. "I observed the light phenomenon that struck the ruby dragons and watched as it exploded into fluttering light motes and drifted away. The Liltians are unharmed and in accord with the wishes of King Lucian and Treyven for peace. According to Romus' testimony, he was at their side and only lent a helping claw when needed. Treyven and the Avalian King have things well in hand there. Shayde is still at the grotto awaiting your command to remove the cloak from the fortress."

Swift looked the least worse for wear of the siblings—aside from a visible bruise blossoming on his right cheek and a healing cut on his lip. "We took minimal casualties in our clash with the reds. Var'ohk had the practitioners ready to tend to the injured as soon as they arrived."

"Gramercy for your reports Talin, Kayne, and Swift," said the imperator. "Your good tidings are welcome indeed."

"Talin, return to the amethyst dragon. Have him uncloak the fortress and return home for the threat is, indeed, behind us.

"Kayne, fly to Terra Leone, inform the Avalian King that all is well, and be sure to answer any questions he may have. Direct Romus to accompany King Lucian and his men to Moorwyn. Advise His Majesty that as soon as our dragon affairs are in order, I will call upon him for a grand celebration.

"Swift, make your way to the Jade Lady Shoppe in Kaleidos. Advise Vinander and Eleazar that we have Flayre in our custody and have them meet us at the entrance to the Crystal Palace when they are ready. Also, have the two Imperial Champions who are circling overhead accompany us and carry Flayre back to the Crystal Palace.

"With Flayre in our custody, the Imperial Champions on patrol, and the reds heading back to their desert homelands, we can claim this conflict to have ended successfully."

CHAPTER THIRTY-TWO

K ullipthius shielded his eyes as he peered out over Serenity Bay. He saw glinting flecks of light flashing off the scales of Vinander and Eleazar heading his way. They soon landed on the summit at the dragon entrance of Oralia, and joined the imperial family in their altered forms.

"May fair greetings fall upon you and yours, Imperial Majesties," proclaimed Eleazar as he gave a bow.

Laliah nodded in acknowledgement to her guests as Kullipthius spoke. "Fair greetings upon you as well, Eleazar."

Their Majesties greeted Vinander and then Laliah said, "It is good to see you again, Vinander." She offered her hand, and Vinander took hers in his own hand as she continued. "It has been quite some time. I believe it was when you came to visit my Grandmother Haelan in Nirvana Kai when I was but a child."

"You were a beauty even then and cherished above all others in Haelan's eyes, as I recall," responded Vinander as he nodded in greeting to the imperatrix. His golden hair clips in his long, grey strands clicked together with the motion.

Ra was next to greet their guests, Then he led them all into the heart of the empire.

Deep inside the mountain, they came to Flayre's new home. It was a massive compartment, half of which was Flayre's prison. The cell had originally been designed to accommodate a dragon, however, new amenities and slender bars had to be outfitted to lodge its current occupant. These bars were yet to be installed and were lying to the side of the cell's entryway. Four amber quartzes were standing guard over the bed where Flayre's unconscious human body reclined.

A large stone table with a long bench stood against the back prison wall. Above the table was a small, barred window to the outside world. To the right, shelves had been carved into the wall, creating an enclosed bookcase. A metal wash basin and pitcher rested on the top shelf, linens on the center shelf, and a metal chamber pot on the bottom. Flayre's bed stood against the adjacent sidewall. In the center of the room lay a hearth with a pair of starfire stones for warmth and light. Though Flayre was provided with a vast compartment with all the amenities he would need to live out his life, it was most definitely a prison. They were just waiting for Aeternus to be placed around Flayre's neck before they fit the bars in place and closed him within.

Kullipthius watched as Eleazar removed a polished, wooden box from a drawstring pouch he had been holding. He lifted the lid and his nimble fingers produced Aeternus from its velvet-lined confines. The necklace itself looked harmless enough; it actually was a stunning piece.

While walking toward Flayre's cell, Eleazar explained where he had found the idea for the design. "I found a gold necklace with this same design during an excavation in Flayre's desert homelands over a hundred yearmarks ago. I thought it fitting to incorporate the motif into this latest creation of Aeternus."

All agreed it suited the red dragon.

"However do you manage such fine work, Eleazar?" inquired Kullipthius. "Its beauty belies its power."

"I agree it is an exquisite design," replied Eleazar.

"I can feel its magical properties from here," said Ra. "How does it work, exactly?"

"I combined various metals in the right formulation to create Aeternus' energy. The metal was then pounded into a thin, round sheet. After the metal had cooled, I drew the circular dragon outline on the metal plate. Then I went back and etched the intricate details of the dragon you see here with its tail in its mouth."

Eleazar traced the lines with his finger and continued his explanation.

"Using a small pair of shears I call 'snips,' I cut out the circular dragon's shape. Once that was done, I measured, cut, and separated the dragon into ten pieces. Natural pigments were used for the colors you see here; gold-tones, greens, purples, blue, and red for the ruby dragon, were used to make it esthetically pleasing.

I reassembled the dragon into this necklace by boring two holes on the top ends of each piece, riveting each segment to the next. The head holding the tail in its mouth is the largest and primary piece that will hang in the center. I used a ruby cabochon on the dragon's forehead and yellow sapphires for his eyes. Finally, I used an ancient formula that evokes the necklace's magical properties and makes the necklace indestructible.

"In essence, the magical properties, the combination of the metals, the ingredients in the paints, and separating the dragon pieces are what keep the dragon apart from the man. When the necklace is placed around the ruby's neck and the last metal rivet is attached, Flayre will never again be able to change into his natural dragon form."

"It seems a tremendous amount of work. I want to express my gratitude for making Aeternus, and on such short notice. I am genuinely impressed and appreciative, Eleazar," Kullipthius commended.

"Flayre has been under the influence of the dark sickness for over a century, and he would have been difficult to control. It is an appropriate solution," said Eleazar. He then moved into the chamber next to Flayre's unconscious form while the others looked on. He fit the necklace about Flayre's neck and attached the last metal rivet to the necklace. He produced a thin tool from an inner pocket of his garb and made a small adjustment. Everyone present watched in amazement as the necklace shrunk to a perfect fit around Flayre's neck.

Once his task was completed, he and the guardians retreated from the cell. Then the bars were fitted into place and sealed by the amber quartzes.

"That did not take as long to apply as I thought," remarked Laliah. "It certainly was not anything dreadful, and it was less dramatic than I imagined. I expected a lengthy incantation or the like. Perhaps that is fitting seeing as Flayre himself caused enough problems to last a lifetime."

Vinander smiled at the dragoness and said, "Eleazar did all the spagyrical work in its creation. There was nothing left but for the necklace to be fitted."

The amber quartz guardians left the cell area and the bars were tightly affixed in a puzzle like formation, enclosing Flayre within. Kullipthius gave a nod of his head, and all the guardians but one filed from the room. Laliah, Ra, Eleazar and Vinander followed close behind. The remaining guardian turned at Imperator Kullipthius' signal and spoke to the form lying on the bed:

"Awaken."

Flayre stirred from his place on the mattress. It took him a few minutes to fully awaken and take in his surroundings. He sat up woozily, blinking. His eyes widened as he looked down at his human hands. He examined the confining walls around him and scoffed. Then he set his yellow eyes on Kullipthius. "You think to trap me here, as a human? Make no mistake; I will soon be free." And he growled low in his throat.

Kullipthius shook his head sadly. "You will find it will not be as simple as you believe, Flayre. The beautiful collar you wear is a gift—courtesy of the Golden One who vowed to help your father, Py'ro, end your reign of terror. It is punishment for the crimes you have committed against the Oralian Empire and your use of dark magic. You will never again be able to change back into a dragon, use your gifts, or fly through the skies, Flayre. You wear Aeternus."

Flayre could not keep the shock from his indigenous features. He yanked at the metal collar, only to evoke its magic. The collar tightened around his neck until he was forced to remove his fingers from the links or suffocate himself.

He bared his teeth in frustration as the instrument of his punishment reset itself to the proper size once he calmed down.

"You cannot keep me like this, Kullipthius!" Flayre bellowed. "It is a sentence worse than death!"

"It is already done, Flayre." Kullipthius turned to leave, and Flayre's screams of outrage followed him from the chamber.

Kullipthius entered a lavish chamber where the others awaited him in the Crystal Palace proper. He felt as if a giant weight had been lifted from his shoulders. It was then he announced with pleasure, "My imperial father's work is finally done, and he can now rest in peace. This day will be my father's legacy, a day of celebration in my imperial father's honor."

Lounging on plush cushions, the imperial family made good on the promise of a proper visit with Vinander and Eleazar. The lore keeper had broken the stress of the day with a tale that had them all laughing.

Just then a guard approached and announced, "Your Imperial Majesty, the amethyst dragon, Shayde, and another guest have arrived. Shayde requests an audience with you. I informed him you were in the company of the Golden Ones, and he requested their presence as well. He said it was urgent."

"Where is he now, Rogar?"

"I was not sure if he was able to transform, so they are waiting for you outside the palace near the lake."

"Gramercy, Rogar." He turned to Vinander and said, "It must be vital if he has come to the palace and asks for you and Eleazar to join us."

"Then let us away and see to his needs," replied Vinander.

"Aye, I am pleased to have an invitation," said Eleazar as he stood to join them. "It would be a pleasure to meet an amethyst dragon."

As the three made their way down the halls toward the lake, Vinander and Eleazar stopped in their tracks.

"What is it, Vinander?" asked Kullipthius.

"It appears that Shayde's guest is a relation of ours. We are having a very strong connection of Ak'na as we approach the lake."

"Who could it be?" asked Eleazar. "I thought the two of us were the last of our bloodline. In truth, I was feeling the stirrings of Ak'na for the last hour as we sat here talking in the palace. I thought because we had not seen each other in a while our connection was growing stronger. It is now calling out to me, and I dare say, I am having a hard time containing myself. I have an urge to run to the lake."

"Aye, Eleazar. Its pull is strong indeed. It must be a direct descendant."

Vinander looked to Kullipthius and said, "I apologize; we have not felt these sensations in many yearmarks—much like what you told us you had gone through this very day regarding the appearance of Dra'khar."

"Aye, Vinander," agreed Kullipthius. "Let us see exactly who this mystery guest is."

When they reached the lake they saw Shayde, and then a small dragon slinked out from behind the amethyst's large draconic frame. When the youngling saw the others approach, there was a flash of light and there stood a child of about eleven or twelve yearmarks.

Kullipthius looked over at Vinander and Eleazar who had stopped and were staring at the boy in astonishment.

"What is it, Vinander?" asked Kullipthius. "Do you recognize the child?"

"The youngling is a rare golden fire," said Vinander. "The only other one I have ever seen was my grandfather, and he has passed from this life long and ago."

"I am sorry to interrupt your visit, imperator," apologized Shayde, *"but it was imperative that I speak with you."*

Shayde told them the story of how he came upon the youngling who had flown across the expanse of the Carillion Sea from the Desertlands by himself. He also explained how Flayre had held the boy and his mother captive for many yearmarks. The little one had come here out of pure determination to save her.

Vinander slowly approached the youngling. "You must have been through a great ordeal to get here."

Kullipthius watched as the young boy backed up. "You need not worry. I am the ruler of this empire. All of us here will make sure no harm comes to you."

"I can understand that you are feeling uncertain," added Vinander. He then pointed to his son and himself and said, "Eleazar and I are gold dragons, as you are. We will help you get your mother back. What is your name?"

"Ariazar," said the boy as he stared at Vinander and Eleazar in wonderment, "but you can call me Ari."

"What a fine name," praised Vinander. "In fact, it was my grandfather's name."

"Why did Flayre bring your mother to Sapphirus?" ask Kullipthius.

"Golden Ones are good at finding things. He had found records that mentioned a magical book he wanted my mother to find so he could rule over all of dragondom."

"Must have been another dark arts tome," Kullipthius murmured.

"That is right," Ari confirmed softly to Kullipthius.

He then turned his gaze back to the two adult gold dragons before him. "Though my mother is not present, I still feel the presence of Ak'na. I do not understand."

"We have the same feelings for you, little one," Vinander said, "which means we are family. Is that not correct, Eleazar?"

Eleazar nodded.

Kullipthius noted Eleazar appeared introspective and had not said a word since they had arrived at the lake.

The boy felt the pull of his mother as we were flying here, explained Shayde. *I did not want to bring the child into a situation where I was uncertain of the danger. I told Ari we would come here first for your assistance.*

"A wise course, Shayde," Vinander commended. Then he looked at Ari, gave him a smile, and added, "We will be more than pleased to take you to her."

"I would like to go now," said Ari, looking anxious. "She needs me, and I have not seen her in a long while."

"How much time has passed since you have seen your mother?" asked Kullipthius.

"I was eight yearmarks when Flayre took her away," replied Ari, "and I am twelve at present."

The imperator was shocked. "I vouchsafe you will not have to wait much longer. I will make all the arrangements so you will be able to see her very soon."

Kullipthius called out to Laliah to come to the lake and use her healing gifts to help the boy cope with the time it would take to make the proper preparations. There were many things to take into consideration if the boy's mother had been in Flayre's custody for so long, and safety was a priority.

The imperator noticed Eleazar was staring at the young boy and, just as enrapt, Ari was staring back.

"Ari," Eleazar said in a ragged near whisper, "what is your mother's name?"

"Her name is Maddelina."

CHAPTER THIRTY-THREE

I have a son! Eleazar's thoughts were dually introspective and turbulent. There was an immediate transformation in how he viewed the world around him in light of this new and startling revelation. The sense of who he was had changed dramatically in the span of a few heartbeats. It was when he had first beheld his young son's face and had seen his own eyes staring back. There was a sense of unconditional love that had accompanied Ak'na, and the connection with his son was more intense than anything he had ever experienced.

Ari was a rare golden fire like his great grandfather, Ariazar—or Ari, as they had both preferred to be called. It pleased Eleazar that his mate had named their son Ari, and it prompted another thought.

Maddelina lives! This second revelation was as wonderful as the first. His mate was coming home. The very fact that she was alive lifted an emotional weight he had thought would never vacate his heart. He could scarcely believe he had lived without her for more than thirteen devastatingly long yearmarks.

As Ari's Ak'na led their flight of dragons to rescue Maddelina, Eleazar worried for her health and wellbeing, wondering what Flayre had put her through. He wanted her to know that if she had any fears or challenges from the experience, they would work through them together.

"Worry not, Eleazar," Vinander's thoughts were a comforting balm that soothed Eleazar's overactive mind. *"Our family will soon be reunited."*

Eleazar fashioned a draconic smile and nodded, thankful for his father's presence and encouragement.

Ari was riding Shayde, and sitting behind Andro, the blond son of Chief Romus. Eleazar was glad for the imperator's forethought to send Andro along as it seemed to ease his newfound son's worries. The two young dragons had hit it off immediately, and Eleazar could hear their mental transferences as they discussed the differences between the Desertlands and Oralia. Ari had expressed curiosity about the Oralian Empire and how it functioned so smoothly in comparison to the erratic and sometimes violent interactions between the desert dragon clans. Ari had also expressed his surprise when he had learned the Desertlands had once been the home of Andro's ancestors.

Eleazar and his father were present when Kullipthius held a lengthy discussion with Ari, and they were all appalled to hear what the youngling had described as Flayre's demands and lifestyle choices. They concluded that not only would there be human and dragon slaves present, there was also a strong indication that ruby dragons would be guarding them. With this bit of information the imperatrix had graciously arranged for five of her best amber quartz healers to accompany them. Kullipthius had also decided to send Imperatrix Laliah, who would arrive later in the day to assist with any physical wounds.

Eleazar was happy for the imperator's precautions and plan of action. The amber quartzes would remain in their human appearance and use their gifts of influence to work with any slaves and guards they encountered in Flayre's lair. They surely would be needed to help reintegrate any captives back into their appropriate home environments. But first, these dragons would help to abate any fears by putting prisoners and guards they found on site into a blissful slumber. When they awakened, it would take time to fully mend any trauma or suffering Flayre undoubtedly would have caused.

By posing as Sapphirian healers, the amber quartz dragons would work with the distressed individuals and use their gifts of influence by removing any thoughts of "dragons" and helping them heal from the anguish of being held as prisoners. Finally, the amber quartz healers would alleviate their minds by invoking pleasant thoughts of family, friends, and returning home. Once the prisoners were found capable of maintaining an emotional balance, the dragons would accompany them on horseback to reunite them with their friends and families.

Their group was now flying over a densely wooded and

uninhabited landscape. Following the Ak'na trail, Shayde started a spiraling descent, and the flight of saviors followed suit.

Upon landing, Shayde and the amber quartzes remained in their dragon forms while the others shifted to their human guise. They trekked a short distance beneath the dense boughs of emerald green before coming upon an overhang of jagged rock near a dark cave with three upright standing stones resting before it. Vinander paused near the tall stones, frowning at the triangular grouping.

"I can feel an evil pulsing off of these stones," observed Shayde. *"It is most disturbing."*

"These stones have been used for nefarious purposes," replied Vinander. "We shall destroy them after our rescue so no further harm may be wrought from them."

Just then a scraping sound came from inside the cave, alerting the group that their approach had not gone undetected.

Peering at the cavern entrance, Eleazar spied a man staring at them with mouth agape. He could see the man was dressed in intricate armor and carried a wicked-looking spear. A large, carved stone pendant was dangling around the man's throat. When he stumbled toward them as if desperate for help, Eleazar was thankful that four amber quartz dragons slid protectively in front of the younglings. The armored guard dropped to his knees before their bulk, obviously unafraid of their presence.

"Thank the four winds!" exclaimed the man. "I am an amber quartz held captive by that wretched dragon Flayre! I pray thee, brothers, remove this cursed pendant and free me from the red beast's clutches!" And he threw down his spear to show he was not a threat.

Eleazar watched as the closest amber quartz dragoness shimmered and shifted to her human guise, rushing to the fellow's side. "We will not harm you," she soothed, obviously trying to calm the panicked man, "we have come here to help you." The blonde transformed dragoness raised her hands into the air, palms forward in a sign of peace. She then slowly brought her arms down and wrapped them about his shoulders in an obvious attempt to comfort him as she spoke. "What is your name, brother?"

"My name is Vin'jaune, and I have been entrusted with the duty of entrance guardian. Prithee, I only want to be free and feel the wind beneath my wings once more!" sobbed Flayre's servant.

"We will help you, Vin'jaune. Can you tell us how many guardians and prisoners Flayre has inside so we can better prepare?"

"C-certainly," he stammered, as he wiped at his red-rimmed eyes. "There are three male dragons and one dragoness that Flayre holds as slaves. Each dragon prisoner is being magically held in their two-legged form. He also has nine human prisoners locked in cages. Beware of Flayre's two dragon minions. Their breath of fire is menacing. They abuse and threaten us with it daily and force us to do Flayre's bidding."

"Gramercy, Vin'jaune, you have been most helpful," commended the dragoness. "Now, open your mind to me. I will help you relax and sleep. When you awaken, you will be safe."

At his relieved nod, she stared directly into his eyes and soothingly said, "Sleep."

The man slumped, and the dragoness helped lower Vin'jaune gently to the ground, as a mother would her newborn babe.

The lead healer issued orders to his team of assistants but left his mind open for Eleazar and the rest of the group to hear.

It seems the human captives have been distressed enough, and so I believe entering the cavern as their brethren will be the least threatening approach we can take. Our first priority will be to subdue the two ruby dragons.

Flashes followed his words, and the amber quartz dragons made their way into the cave's mouth, all marching steadily on two legs.

Shayde and Vinander remained outside with Eleazar, to watch over Vin'jaune and the younglings. Ari was pacing before the cave's mouth, angst obvious in his posture and features.

"My Mother is inside!" Ari implored as he gazed up at Eleazar with a determined expression. "I want to go in!"

"Understandable, Ari," said Eleazar, smiling reassuringly, "but we must remain here until our friends make sure all is safe for both you and your mother."

The boy must have realized the wisdom in Eleazar's words, for the youngling nodded and turned to maintain a vigilant eye on the cave's entrance.

Eleazar felt a moment of pride for his son. He was such a prudent, brave youngling—and so smart for his age. Such thoughts led Eleazar to wonder if Ari suspected that he was his father. He did not know how much Maddelina had told Ari, so he would wait for her guidance.

Eleazar realized it was not easy to follow his own advice; he wanted nothing more than to abandon caution and race inside to his mate's side. He ran a hand through his rich, brown hair. Now that they were so close to their goal, Eleazar could not help but fret.

Thankfully, they were beckoned inside by the lead healer before too much time passed. The amber quartz leader retrieved Vin'jaune and led everyone inside. Shayde volunteered to remain outside, hidden in the shadows, where he could serve as the lookout for any stray red dragons on the ground or overhead.

The cavern's opening flowed into a spacious hollow. The place was so wide and rose so high overhead that it could accommodate half a dozen large dragons comfortably. In addition, four large cages stood at odd intervals around the vast chamber.

A glinting pile of baubles, coins, and gold caught Eleazar's eye in one shallow nook. Above it was a jutting rock shelf that displayed a row of crumbling scrolls and tomes. Eleazar noticed Vinander could not seem to tear his eyes from the antiquated objects. He knew that, in any other circumstance, it would have been a find his father could not have resisted perusing.

Just then, footfalls echoed within the chamber as the amber quartz dragons moved between the cages. The amber quartz dragoness approached and delivered her report to Vinander.

"We subdued the two ruby dragons Vin'jaune spoke of, and they are currently sleeping soundly down the left passageway. We will send them back to the Desertlands as soon as we can, after the imperator speaks with them. The captives were happy to see us and are sleeping peacefully on the blankets and pillows we brought with us. We will begin working with them individually to learn what transpired under Flayre's evil rule. We also discovered another cell down that corridor to your right."

She smiled at Eleazar and nodded. Vinander patted his son on the back. Eleazar's heart leapt into his throat as he stared intently down the long, dark hallway the amber quartz had indicated. He could not wait to gather his mate in his arms, but he wanted their son to be the first to see his mother.

The dragoness handed Ari a key and with a sweeping gesture of her hand toward the passage said, "After you, Ari."

ARI did not hesitate. He sprinted forward as fast as his legs could safely carry him. As he went, he recalled his mother's last words, before she had been taken away:

"Listen Ari, we do not have much time." Her eyes and her tone had been serious and intense. "I have left a dagger hidden in the water pitcher. It will fit securely in the red-beaded vest I made for you. I fashioned a sheath in the lining under the beads and quillwork on the left side. At your earliest convenience, I beseech you, place that dagger in its sheath and wear that vest whenever you leave the safety of the cavern." At his nod of consent she had continued. "But I pray thee, Ari, whatever you do, DO NOT lead Flayre to the grimoire he has been trying to force us to search for. It will bring nothing but death and destruction."

It was then that two guards appeared and told her it was time to depart. She had sent her son a final message in Drahk, one that only he could hear.

"When your gifts present themselves, do not let anyone know." She had held him close as he cried, and she kissed his forehead. *"We will find a way to be together again soon, I promise you that."*

"I love you so much, mother," Ari had told her as the guards wrenched her from his small hands.

"And I love you, Ari." Her tears were streaking down her cheeks when the guards had whisked her away.

Ari's mother had never said anything negative to him about the grimoire before that day. He had always thought she was willing to find the book of dark arts for Flayre. The chieftain had spoken passionately of the grimoire often and had promised his ruby dragon clans that it would save them all and bring them their every desire.

A bronze dragon named Taliah had looked after Ari while his mother was gone. Taliah had been a captive of the desert chieftain for many years and had been on many tasks with Flayre and forced, as Maddelina and Ari had been, to do his bidding. Ari had known Taliah his whole life and had loved her like any youngling would love a grandmother.

Though Flayre had occasionally returned to the Desertlands, he had never brought Maddelina with him. Whenever Ari had asked Flayre about his mother, Flayre would tell him that she was on a treasure hunt to save their desert clans and would return as soon she could.

Ari remembered Flayre's most recent trip home. He had told Ari that his mother had recently finished her treasure hunt and was cataloging her finds. He had pledged he would bring her back to the Desertlands before the next full moon. Ari had believed

Flayre because his mother promised they would see each other again.

Even though Ari's draconic talents had manifested before Flayre's last visit, Ari had kept that news a secret from everyone, obediently following his mother's wishes. It was when Flayre was leaving that Ari understood why his mother had insisted he keep his gifts a secret.

Ari overheard the dragon chieftain talking to the guards outside his cavern entrance. He made his way over to the entryway to listen, as he heard Flayre speak his name. The chieftain was asking the guards stationed outside Ari's door if they had seen any signs of Ari's gifts manifesting. Even though they said they had not, Flayre did not believe it.

"Keep a close eye on him to make sure he is not hiding anything," Flayre had said. "I will kill his mother in front of him if he is trying to hide his talent from me, mark my words!"

Ari had known right then that if he did not try to find his mother, he might never see her again.

On the day he had escaped there was only one guard at the cave's entrance as the other guard had taken Taliah to perform a task for Flayre. All the other ruby dragons had been busy preparing for the war with Sapphirus. Ari had made his escape when the cavern's lone guardian had fallen asleep at his post, and then Ari had followed a flight of red dragons across the sea.

Ari's feet came to a halt. After four long yearmarks, here he was, standing in front of his mother's prison cell. Ari wiped away the tear that had slid unbidden down his cheek. He vowed he would be strong for his mother. He wanted her to see that he was not a nestling anymore, and that he had flown all the way across the expanse of the Carillion Sea to take care of her.

She was sitting on the bed with her head hung low. Her hair was longer than he remembered, and she was hiding her face from view. Ari was struck by her words.

"Why do I ache with the feelings of Ak'na?" She shook her head as if to clear it, and said, "I know you are here, Flayre. Is this one of your dark, twisted ruses designed to torture me? I have told you a million times—I do not know where The Dark Arts tome is, so you need not use your evil magic."

"But I really am here, mother," replied Ari aloud, tears once again, glistening in his eyes. They were tears of joy because he had found her, but also tears of sorrow for how horribly Flayre must have treated her. "I have come to save you."

"Stop, Flayre," replied Maddelina in a soft voice. She did not look up. "I cannot give you what I cannot find, no matter how much you try to torment me. As I told you before, it must have been destroyed, for I have never felt its power."

Ari turned the key in the lock and tugged the cell door open while it protested on stiff, creaky hinges. She flinched at the sound but never lifted her head as he slowly moved toward her.

The boy took in their surroundings: a four-poster bed with a lavishly designed blue quilt, starfire stones in front of a hearth for warmth and light, and a soft fur rug in front of the bed. An ornately carved table with a matching chair was to his right, and a privacy screen stood in front of a large bathing tub on the other side of the bed. He also noted the room was not big enough for her to change into a dragon. A gut-wrenching gasp escaped unbidden as he wondered when she last had been able to fly free as a dragon.

Ari stopped a few feet from Maddelina. He pulled a golden dagger out of its built-in sheath that had been sown to the inside of his vest. The dagger's hilt was laden with small emerald and ruby cabochons that glinted softly in the starfire light.

"I can prove it is me, mother. I have the dagger that you left for me. You told me to never leave the cavern without it."

Maddelina's head snapped up.

"Is it truly you?" she asked as tears streamed down her face.

She tried to stand, but Ari noticed she seemed weak and fell back to a seated position on the bed. Ari sheathed his dagger and closed the distance between them. She reached out tentatively to touch him, and she gasped when her fingertips touched his skin. They held each other and cried helplessly as they lamented the time that had been stolen from them as mother and son.

Suddenly, Ari felt his mother pull back from him, and her face reflected a different, harder countenance.

"Where is Flayre?" asked Maddelina. "Did he hurt you?" She examined him closely from head to toe.

"Nay mother, he did not bring me here. I escaped from our cavern and followed a flight of ruby dragons across the Carillion Sea. They were on their way to start a war with Sapphirus. When I arrived in Avala, I came across a real amethyst dragon. He brought me to Oralia, and I spoke with the imperator.

"They captured Flayre, mother, and he is safely locked away. They took away his dark magic and sent the red dragons back to the Desertlands. Then I led a flight of dragons here to save you."

"Flayre's dark magic is gone?" his mother asked in shocked astonishment.

"Aye," replied Ari.

His mother then fell as still as stone.

He was worried. "Mother, are you hurt?"

He noticed that she blinked a few times and appeared to regain her composure at his words.

"I am well now that you are here." She smiled weakly at him and said, "You were so very brave to fly all the way across the Carillion Sea to come and save me, Ari." She pushed a strand of hair from his face and placed it behind his ear. "You are so tall; you sound so grown up . . . and you look so much like your father."

Beyond the cell's iron door, Ari heard a shuffling of feet, and a voice that said, "I had rather thought that he took after you."

ELEAZAR heard Maddelina's breath catch in her throat at his words. He stood there, frozen, drinking in the sight of her.

Eleazar felt his father place a hand on his shoulder before joining his grandson. Maddelina looked up at Vinander and he gave her a warm smile.

"Ari, I believe we should allow your mother some time to rest. The Imperatrix Laliah is a healer, and she is on the way to tend to her."

Ari's gaze remained fixed on his mother, and Eleazar knew his son did not want to leave his mother's side.

Vinander bent down to his grandson's level. "Do you want to go outside with me and tear down those standing stones?"

Eleazar noted his son's uncertain look. He had yet to release his mother's hand.

"Can Andro help, too?" asked Ari.

"Certainly," replied Vinander. He is already there waiting for us."

"I will be right back, mother," said Ari. "I have an important task to undertake." He kissed her on the cheek and said, "Now you get some rest."

Eleazar neither remembered his father and son taking their leave, nor did he realize how he had come to stand in front of Maddelina. Tears were trailing down her face, and his heart went out to her.

He pledged that from that moment on, he would do whatever was needed to bring joy back into her heart.

Eleazar took in the sight of his beloved. Her midnight hair was in an uncontrollable, tangled mess, almost reaching the floor. Her eyes were red from crying, and she looked pale from lack of sunlight. Yet, to Eleazar she had never looked more beautiful.

"I have something for you," he heard himself say. And without thought of preamble, he fell to his knees in front of her and reached into his vest pocket. When he withdrew his hand, he held Maddelina's ring between thumb and forefinger. The two gold, intertwined dragons gleamed in the starfire light. The stark white jade band could be seen on the bottom inside of the ring.

She drew in a breath, and, just as she had done all those yearmarks past, she placed a fingertip to her lips and gasped in surprise. The memory of the first time he had given Maddelina the ring flashed through Eleazar's mind as he slipped it on her finger. The ring was loose and looked so large on her delicate hand that it made his heart ache. His tears mingled with hers upon the cavern floor.

"Your love left its fingerprint upon my soul," confessed Eleazar. "You were always a part of me wherever I went. Inside my heart, I held you in love's embrace. And my lips . . ."

He paused for a moment to compose himself before he began again, "and my lips are actually trembling for your kiss."

They fell into each other in a tangle of arms and lips, soothing one another in their amorous embrace, and Eleazar's heart rejoiced.

"Hush," cooed Eleazar. He rocked her in his arms as she cried. "Hush now, my love. The nightmare has ended. You are now in my arms that hold for you and our son the dreams of our future. Soon your eyes will be filled with tears of joy . . . and all will be right in our world, Maddelina. All will be right."

CHAPTER THIRTY-FOUR

"Aurora Leigh," sighed Prince Dryden in exasperation, "we have discussed this kind of behavior before. You cannot go traipsing about the countryside on your own without my permission, mind you . . ."

Aurora Leigh noted his temper began to rise when he saw her open her mouth to speak.

He held up a hand to forestall her attempt and continued, ". . . *and* expect to come away unscathed. Consider yourself fortunate that it is only the sting of my temper and not that of something far worse that could have happened to you. It would devastate your mother if she learned that you had slipped out of the castle without permission, or attendants, or—*Injuriae contumeliam addere!*"

Aurora Leigh did not believe that she had "added insult to injury" as her father had indicated with his quote from the ancient texts. She knew in her heart that she had done the right thing by bringing the amulet to Kullipthius. Even Kulli's imperial father had told her so. After all, it was the blessing disk that had saved the Kingdom of Avala and the Oralian Empire from an evil dragon.

"You left without consulting me," her father added hotly. "Then you had the audacity NOT to say anything about your departure when you returned, acting as if nothing had happened. Most regrettably, I had to hear of your escapade from the king himself! Not only did you willfully disregard our rules, you disobeyed King Lucian's direct command to stay within the safety of Moorwyn's walls!

"I have conferred with the king on this matter, and we have devised a proper solution. It is for your own good, Aurora Leigh. We are scheduled to meet your uncle in the throne room. I need not remind you that you will hold your tongue in the presence of the King of Avala, and you will not argue with his decision. Is that understood?"

Nodding in compliance, Aurora Leigh followed her father out the door of her bedchamber in Moorwyn Castle and down the stairs. Her heart was pounding furiously as she entered the doors of her uncle's throne room. She felt that she was being treated like a pickpocket or horse thief who had come to stand before the King of Avala for punishment. As the opulent doors closed behind her with a final click, Aurora Leigh felt trapped. She stopped dead in her tracks and found that she could not move. Her breath quickened, and she felt herself sway. Her father grasped her upper arm, and she was happy for the support. He pulled her forward to stand before the king.

Ashamed, she could not even meet her uncle's gaze. She loved Uncle Lucian dearly and hated that he was displeased with her.

"Aurora Leigh, look at me," commanded the king. At her compliance, he continued. "First, let me say that your foresight and decision that the amulet needed to be brought to Kullipthius in the forest was what saved Sapphirus from an all-out war. That is to be commended. However, you ran heedlessly into a dangerous situation despite knowing it was my will that my family remain safe. You could have simply given the amulet to the imperatrix with instructions and achieved the same outcome.

"Your father and I have discussed your recent actions and have determined that you are too willful for your own good. You cannot act on a dangerous situation without consulting your father who, by the way, was left at the castle in my stead and should have been consulted.

"I know this is not the first time you have disobeyed your family's wishes. Captain Wellsbough informed me that you had recently left Morning Star Palace unattended, and he had to rescue you from bandits in the woods! You could have been kidnapped— or worse!"

Aurora's Leigh's face burned crimson. Her father stiffened beside her, and his grip on her arm tightened at this news.

"It is my duty as king to inform you that we have decided it is time that you fulfill your duty as princess. You are to be wed, Aurora Leigh. We have chosen a man of noble lineage—a perfect match—to be your husband."

Aurora Leigh went pale. She had thought her punishment would be to have more attendants assigned to her personage or restrictions placed on her freedom, but not this! Her panic-stricken gaze fell on her father, then her uncle, but both revealed stern looks that seemed to unwaveringly seal her fate.

"Prithee, Uncle, I beg of you! I am not ready to wed!" exclaimed Aurora Leigh in a panic. How could they do this to her? She had been in love with Eralon her whole life and could never see herself loving another.

"The king and I have already discussed this, Aurora Leigh," explained Dryden with resolution and a warning tone, "and the decision has been made."

"As you will it, Father," whispered Aurora Leigh solemnly, dropping her head and staring listlessly at the floor.

"Come forward, my dear," beckoned Lucian, speaking in a gentle tone.

The princess made her way to the throne where her uncle sat. She knelt beside him as she had so often done as a small child, dropping her head in his lap. She felt the weight of his hand fall tenderly upon her head in a comforting gesture.

"I am not getting any younger, and I am without a son to be heir to my throne. As it stands now, your father will be my successor to the crown, and then it will be up to you to have a son to carry on the royal bloodline."

"Uncle, I have faith that you will marry and have many sons," replied Aurora Leigh with heartfelt conviction.

"If and until that day comes, I must prepare and do what is best for my family and my kingdom." He placed his forefinger under her chin and nudged her head upward to gaze into her eyes. "You were born to privilege, Princess Aurora Leigh, and with privilege comes great responsibility. You knew this day would come. You have been preparing for this since you were but a child."

Aurora Leigh nodded. Lucian stood and pulled her into a hug. Aurora Leigh drank in the warmth of his embrace and whispered in his ear, "But what of love, Uncle Lucian? What of love?"

"I am sure you will grow to love your new husband-to-be just as your mother truly loves your father. The noble I have chosen for you will make a wonderful husband and father for the future King of Avala. I am sure of it."

"Who is he, Uncle Lucian?"

"He is the Marquis of Sandesh, with lands inside the southern borders of Avala, just above the neighboring borders of Sunon and Vashires. His marquisate is about a day's ride to both Moorwyn

Castle and the Morning Star Palace, so you will be close to your family.

"His maternal grandfather has recently passed from this, our mortal realm. Since both his parents are deceased, he was next in line to inherit his grandfather's title and familial estates. Your betrothed also has royalty in his blood from his father's side. King Matthias of Vashires is the Marquis' grand uncle."

Aurora Leigh wracked her brain trying to remember her lineage lessons but came up blank. She cringed inwardly and scolded herself for not paying better attention to her tutors. "I am scared, Uncle," replied Aurora Leigh. "I do not know anything about being a wife."

"Your mother said those very words to me on the eve of her wedding. You can tell by your mother's and father's actions that, over time, they have grown to love each other very much. All will be well, Aurora Leigh," comforted Lucian. "I assure you."

Aurora Leigh looked up at the king and offered a weak smile. She knew she could not speak for fear of bursting into helpless tears. She felt as if her heart had been torn-asunder.

"We have arranged for your royal betrothal celebration, commencing this very eve," explained the king. "You will have a chance to greet your betrothed then. Your mother is waiting for you in your chambers. She has brought your personal attendants to dress you for this evening's festivities. Go to her, Aurora Leigh. You must prepare."

Aurora Leigh curtsied to her Uncle Lucian, turned and gave the same respect to her father. Then, with tears streaming, she ran toward the throne room's exit with all the haste she could muster. The doors were quickly opened at her approach. She could hear her father calling out to her, but she did not stop. She desperately needed the comfort of her mother's arms.

"You must admit, darling," said Isa Dora with tears welling, "you look absolutely stunning."

Aurora Leigh had to agree; the gown that had been designed especially for her betrothal celebration was beautiful. Her underdress was spun silk in the color of shimmering gold. What caught the eye were the sleeves that puffed elegantly over the shoulders and tightened to fit from above the elbows to the wrists.

A rich velvet fabric the color of amethysts created the front and back panels of the overdress. It was trimmed with golden lace and blue sapphires that ran across the square neckline, down the sides, and along the hemlines of both the front panel and the flowing train. The wide belt and velvet slipshoes completed the outfit, each trimmed elegantly in matching lace and gems.

Murielle had done her hair in ringlets down her back that were held back by her bejeweled and floral tiara, emblematic of her station.

"Do not cry, Aurora Leigh," begged her mother. "Your eyes are already red and swollen. Murielle, get my daughter a wet handkerchief."

Murielle hurried away to do as she was bid and soon brought back the dampened cloth.

Accepting the handkerchief, Isa Dora dabbed at her daughter's eyes and said, "You remind me of when I learned I was betrothed to your father. I felt just as you do now. I was frightened, unhappy, and my stomach felt as if it were tied in knots. I thought I was going to swoon at any moment while my mother readied me for the celebration."

"You did?" asked Aurora Leigh.

"I did, and later I acted like a complete fool. I even tried to run when my chamber doors were opened and the guards came to escort me. Of course, I did not get far. I ran right into my father while I was looking back to see if I was being pursued."

That evoked a smile from Aurora Leigh.

"He did not look pleased, to say the least, and helped me to straighten myself. When he was sure I was composed and loosened his grip, I slipped away once again. I ran down the stairs, eyes darting left and right. It turned out that I should have been looking straight ahead because, when I reached the bottom of the steps, I did it again and ran right into your father. He was waiting for me at the bottom of the steps."

That coaxed a giggle from the princess.

"He said, 'Fear not, I have you,' and then I looked up into the most handsome face I had ever seen. With my mouth agape, all I could do was stare at him, and I must have looked like a complete fool. Of course, I did not know at the time it was your father because I had never met him, and I thought, 'He is simply wonderful. Why could I not be betrothed to him instead?'

"My stomach was flipping and flopping, and I was just about to take his arm when my father came up behind me and said, 'I see you have met Prince Dryden.'

"Nay!" exclaimed Aurora Leigh.

"Aye, and that was when I swooned."

Aurora Leigh could not contain her laughter any longer, and her mother smiled.

"Come now, darling, it is not *that* funny," teased her mother. "I was quite overcome and out of breath from running."

That brought on another bout of laughter from mother and daughter that was interrupted by a knock upon Aurora Leigh's chamber door.

Aurora Leigh could see between the half-drawn curtains that Uncle Lucian and her father had entered her receiving room. Murielle slipped through the curtain to announce the arrival of the king and the prince. Aurora Leigh then turned toward her mother for support, anxiety quickly swallowing up her cheerful mood.

"Do not be nervous, darling," whispered Isa Dora out of earshot of the royals standing in her daughter's receiving room. "I will be right there with you. Frankly, I believe everything will turn out wonderfully. I have met your betrothed, and he is quite dashing and handsome. I am sure you will be pleased."

Aurora Leigh took a deep breath and released it slowly. She looked up at her mother and tried her best to look courageous and act the part of a dutiful daughter and princess. "I will try to be brave, mother." Aurora Leigh knew from the depths of her being that no one could ever take the place of her knight in shining armor. Captain Eralon Wellsbough would always have her heart.

The royal family was being escorted to the ballroom in Moorwyn Castle where the celebration was taking place. The announcement of their arrival was made, and all in attendance turned in their direction and bowed as they entered.

They were walking toward their thrones in the back of the room when, out of the corner of her eye, Aurora Leigh spotted Eralon. Her heart raced at the sight of him. He had not yet seen her and was in conversation with a stately nobleman she knew to be on the king's council. Her mother had said that the Marquis of Sandesh was handsome, but Aurora Leigh knew that no one could ever compare to Eralon. She turned her head away from him, for she knew she would start to cry and run, as her mother had, if she did not. As the royals continued to advance toward the back of the ballroom, she noted her uncle and father had stopped. Because she and her mother were behind them, she could not see who approached. She wondered if it might be the Marquis of Sandesh, and her pulse raced faster.

When the king stepped to the side in greeting, she saw that Eralon was amongst the group that was talking with her father and uncle. That only made matters worse. She could barely breathe as she ducked her head and tried to ignore him while he and her uncle were in deep conversation. Eyes on the floor, she watched as her uncle and father stepped aside and two freshly polished boots stopped in front of her. Her mother grabbed her hand, which gave her the courage to look up. She gasped and then turned red at her own reaction.

Eralon stood before her, not in his captain's uniform as she had always seen him, but in ceremonial accouterments. He was dressed in black from head to toe with an adornment of a white horse salient decorating the side of each boot. His cape was clasped with an ornamental gold horse pin. The material draped over his shoulders and down his back, leaving the front of his large, muscular chest at her eye level. He smelled of cloves and sea oats and was more handsome than ever—if that was possible.

Her Uncle Lucian's voice broke through her thoughts. "I can see by the look on your face, Aurora Leigh, you have noticed Eralon is not dressed in his usual captain's uniform.

"What you may not know," continued King Lucian, "is that, since the tragic death of his maternal grandfather, he is now dressed according to his station as the new Marquis and Lord of Sandesh—and your betrothed."

Aurora Leigh gasped. As she looked up, Eralon's eyes met hers.

His smile was breathtaking and he said, "You look lovely this evening, Princess Aurora Leigh."

It was then she realized she had offered Eralon her hand because he had bowed down to gently kiss her fingers.

And that is when Aurora Leigh swooned.

CHAPTER THIRTY-FIVE

A knock reverberated through the heavy wood door, and King Lucian called for his visitor to enter. Treyven Fontacue appeared at the threshold and greeted the King of Avala, bowing his head and placing fist over heart.

"Ya wished ta see me Yer Majesty?"

If the Liltian was nervous being alone in the company of a monarch, he did not reveal the fact in any way, and Lucian smiled his approval.

"Aye, Treyven, do come in," answered King Lucian. He gestured to a grouping of comfortable chairs. "Have a seat."

Lucian had purposefully chosen this receiving room for his talk with Treyven. Above the wide mantel hung the banners of Avala's allies, including that of the former country of Liltimer.

Lucian watched as Treyven chose his seat, allowing him the best view of the room and door. It was probably an unconscious decision on Treyven's part, but one the king could not help but mark, driving home the fact of the former Liltian's mercenary way of life.

Treyven respectfully waited to sit until Lucian was seated comfortably. After the two were settled, the king leaned forward. "When last we spoke, you expressed an interest in hearing the continuing saga that held regard to the fall of Liltimer."

Treyven nodded. "'Tis true, Sire. I remain most interested."

"It is my hope our conversation here will provide you with much insight and set the records straight about what transpired during those fateful days."

Another rap came upon the door, and Lucian smiled. "I hope you do not mind the intrusion," he said. "I invited another to join us."

Treyven rose to properly greet King Lucian's visitor.

The king's chamber room guards opened the door for Sedgwick, the castle's stable master. He entered, and the guards closed the doors behind them. "Ya called for me, Yer Majesty?" asked Sedgwick, and he bowed before his king.

"Aye, I did Sedgwick," responded Lucian, and he made introductions.

"Treyven Fontacue, this is Sedgwick, the castle's stable master. More important to our conversation, he is Lord Sedgwick Bromwell, Former Marshal of Liltimer for the Royal Liltian Court in charge of military affairs for King Tridan."

Treyven fell motionless a moment before a spark of great interest lit his features. It was the brave marshal who had cut the stinger off the chameleon's tail in Lucian's story of King Tridan. This was a pleasant addition to their meeting. "What an unexpected pleasure ta make yer acquaintance, good sir!" His enthusiasm was evident as he offered his hand to the bemused stable master.

Lord Bromwell shook his shaggy head, perhaps wondering what exactly was taking place and jested, "Aves I an admirer, Yer Majesty?" He grinned and clasped Treyven's hand in return.

"Aye indeed, Sedgwick," replied Lucian with a smile. "May I introduce Treyven Fontacue, the leader of the Liltian mercenaries who joined our forces in the fight against Flayre. He is well aware of the dragons in our midst and has been enlightened as to the unfortunate events surrounding Liltimer's downfall." He gestured to the chairs on his left. "Prithee, have a seat."

Lucian took his seat and waited until both men were seated comfortably before he spoke. "I believe you will find this meeting as interesting and informative as Treyven. He has many questions, and I wish to indulge him. As the leader of such a large force of Liltian soldiers, Treyven's alliance and understanding will be highly beneficial."

Sedgwick turned in his seat to better address Treyven and spread his hands, "Ask o' me what ya will, lad."

Treyven nodded, needing no further prompting. "Could ya tell me about King Tridan's true manner? Mostly one just hears about the unfortunate circumstances at the end o' his reign. I would like ta know more about him, if ya don't mind."

Sedgwick smiled indulgently. "Before the fall, nearly everyone in the kingdom o' Liltimer loved me sister an' our king. His Majesty be happy an' full o' life an' loved his family more than anything. I know he would'na hurt his queen or his children. He woulda protected them with his life."

King Lucian joined in. "During the anniversary of our four countries' alliances, we would hold council before our annual feast. He would always end our meetings with a laugh. More often than not, they would be stories about the amusing antics of his children."

That reminded Sedgwick of a few stories of his own, and the three were soon laughing from his tales. They talked for quite a while and drank spiced wine while relaxing in front of the fire. A few hours passed before the conversation began winding down.

"The moment King Tridan showed up at the castle gates, I knew something be amiss. It be something in his eyes," noted Sedgwick. "However, since he had arrived at the gates alone, I dismissed it at the time believing he be mad with grief o'er the loss o' his guards. Never would I'ves entertained the thought o' real monsters such as chameleons in our midst," Sedgwick emphasized. "If only I had the insights then that I hold now." Sedgwick's eyes stared into the distance in contemplation.

"You had no way of knowing the tragedy that befell him, Sedgwick," added Lucian. "Had not the dragons been our allies, many would have been killed by that treacherous beast. It would have ended in total mayhem."

"It sounds like King Tridan be a good an' just ruler, one who suffered a horrible tragedy," said Treyven sadly. "Verily, 'tis unfortunate that most will never know the truth o' his demise."

"Ah, but *we* know," said King Lucian, "and so did his queen shortly before she died, and that is what is most important."

Another rap was heard at the door. The three men rose and the king called to enter.

Standing upon the threshold was a slender and fair woman of middle age. Her dark hair was pulled back in an elegant knot and held in place with silver pins. Dressed in ankle length skirts dyed an emerald green, she wore practical leather boots for riding. A laced purple bodice over a green blouse of gauzy material completed her attire.

Her features were quite lovely for her age, and her green eyes were fixed upon the King of Avala.

She curtsied deeply and said, "I came as soon as I got yer message, Yer Majesty."

"Mother?" asked Treyven. His face displayed a quizzical look, and his mouth fell open.

Esmeralda's eyes were drawn past the king, and she caught sight of the other two men in the chamber.

Her eyes widened in surprise.

"Treyven!" She surged forward, forgetting she was in the presence of the king in her excitement, and she embraced her son.

Treyven disengaged from his mother's arms and said, "It surely be good ta see ya, but what brings ya here, mother? Where be Father an' Atticus?"

Esmeralda Fontacue looked up at Lucian. A flush came to her cheeks as she must have remembered she was in Moorwyn Castle and standing before the king.

"Pray pardon, Yer Majesty, fer me lack o' manners," beseeched Esmeralda, looking embarrassed.

The king smiled and nodded in understanding, quite accustomed to his own niece's exuberance.

His party now complete, Lucian smiled and spoke to Treyven before Esmeralda had a chance to answer. "I took the liberty of locating your mother and invited her to join us at this meeting. I thought it suitable. I wanted the two of you to have a pleasant reunion."

Treyven beamed and said, "I dare say, 'tis a most pleasant surprise, Yer Majesty. It be quite some time since last we saw one another."

"Two yearmarks too long, ta be exact, Yer Majesty," explained Esmeralda, displaying a side glance upon her son that said more than any words ever could.

However, she appeared to not be able to stay upset for long, and her pinched brows softened. She gave her son another hug and said, "I'm just glad ta sees ya alive an' looking so well."

A short time later, while Treyven and Bromwell were deep in conversation, Lucian looked upon Esmeralda as she sat in quiet contemplation. She must have felt eyes upon her, for she looked over at the king.

"Yer Majesty—," she began, but the king held up his hand to gently dissuade her from going any further.

"Perhaps now would be a good time for you to tell your story, Esmeralda," Lucian said, encouraging her to begin a difficult tale.

When she nodded her response, Lucian raised his voice to garner the attention of Treyven and Bromwell during a lull in their dialog.

"Sedgwick, pray pardon my oversight for not making proper introductions between you and Esmeralda Fontacue. I had assumed the two of you had met. She was just saying how she remembered you as Lionholm's Marshal. However, even after all the times she was in your presence with the queen you had never been formally introduced. She was Queen Mariselle's handmaid."

Sedgwick beamed at Esmeralda and exclaimed, "Aye, of course! Ya looked verra familiar, an' I be trying ta place where I'd seen ya."

"Mother, ya never told me this," said Treyven. At that moment he realized he knew little of her life prior to her being a beloved wife and mother. "Did Father know ya be the queen's attendant?"

"Aye, he most certainly did," responded Esmeralda. "That is where we met. Before yer father be a healer in our village, he be the queen's personal healer at the castle."

"Esmeralda was forbidden by her queen to tell anyone she had worked at the castle," explained Lucian, "and with good reason. I have given her permission to tell the two of you her tale."

Esmeralda sat in reflection a moment before she glanced at Lucian. He nodded his support, and she began her account, wringing her hands as she spoke.

"King Tridan be a wonderful ruler, father, an' husband, make no mistake. The castle staff felt fortunate ta 'aves him as our king fer he treated us with respect an' care.

"Certes 'twas when he returned alone to the castle that fateful day, he was nay the same. We knew not what ta make o' his horrible tirades. We worried fer our beloved king an' his family when the healers explained he suffered a blow ta the head. In addition, he had just lost his guards in a mysterious battle, which be a terrible loss fer us all, fer most were kin an' friends."

Lucian noted Esmeralda's hands trembled, and she shifted in her seat as if to hide her distress.

"I was tending ta me chores when a castle guard came an' told me the horrible fate o' the babe prince. He told me I be chosen by the queen ta retrieve the body. I was heartbroken at the news an' ran ta me queen's side ta comfort her.

"When they let me in her chamber door, I knew the queen was beyond consolation. She was sick, weak, an' on the floor rocking the poor child. She asked me ta stay with her as long as the guards would allow, fer she be wanting ta hold the babe a little longer. I had always hidden some food on me person whenever I came ta see her, but this time she refused ta eat. She had fallen into great despair.

"Whilst we both sat in mourning, the babe stirred! Though he moved he remained unconscious. We be delighted, but the queen's joy quickly sobered. She begged me ta take the child ta her personal healer, Arland."

She looked over at Treyven and said, "If anyone could'a saved him, yer father could. Even though I knew the babe would'na live, I did as she bade.

"She had heard news that her brother had gone ta Avala fer aid in our plight, an' she knew if the babe lived, King Lucian would help.

"I wrapped the child, except fer his face, held him to my bosom an' left out her chamber door. The child was so weak I believed in me heart when she handed him ta me that the prince would be dead before we even made it ta Arland. But I did it for me queen so she would'na need ta suffer more."

Sir Bromwell closed his eyes against his old grief and sighed.

Treyven was somber and asked, "How long did the babe live?"

Esmeralda looked at the king, and he nodded. She then peered at Sedgwick before her eyes meet Treyven's own. Lucian watched as she gazed down at her hands before she answered.

"He still lives."

Bromwell was instantly on his feet. His breath was suddenly ragged, and one could tell he was valiantly trying to keep his composure and not shout. "Where be me nephew, Esmeralda?" pleaded Sedgwick. "Where be the prince? I must know. I must see him!"

King Lucian placed a hand on Sedgwick's shoulder and said, "Give her time. It was her queen's orders, your sister's wish that she had to abide by all these passing yearmarks." Lucian could see Sedgwick's hands were shaking and that he was desperately trying to remain calm.

Esmeralda's eyes clouded over with tears, and then she began to cry. Treyven moved to put an arm around her shoulders. "Indeed, 'tis a heavy burden ya carried all this time, mother. Shush now—yer no ta blame."

Finally, Esmeralda managed to speak. "You must understand, Sir Bromwell. I swore me allegiance ta Her Majesty. I could'na break me oath. She be dying an' she knew it, an' she wanted ta keep her child safe! So she stuffed me pockets with fine glittering pieces from her jewel box. She told me I could sell 'em ta take care o' the prince. That is when Arland an' I left with the babe."

She then looked to her son for understanding. "I be repentant, Treyven. I should'na kept things from ya, but it nay be what ya think. I'ves nay seen ya fer two yearmarks." She then looked to Sedgwick. Lucian knew she needed his understanding. "I wanted me whole family around ta bring the prince ta the king. I was told specifically by Queen Mariselle ta take the heir ta King Lucian when he reaches his majority." Esmeralda looked back into Treyven's eyes. "I could'na find ya ta tell ya the truth o' things, or ta fulfill my long-kept promise ta my queen in a timely manner, so I remained silent."

"Aves mercy on me, Lord Sedgwick!" she sobbed. "I never meant ta cause anyone pain."

Lucian was happy for Sedgwick's silence. The king reached over and patted Esmeralda's hand in consolation.

"Worry naught over this matter, Esmeralda," counseled Lucian. "The timing is trivial when compared to the outcome. There is plenty of time, a whole lifetime in fact, to set things right."

Lucian glanced at Treyven, and he saw him shift in his seat.

Treyven's words were calm when next he spoke. "Where be me brother, Atticus, mother?"

Esmeralda's eyes darted to Lucian and Treyven. She put her hands to her face and started crying again.

"Where be Atticus, mother?" Treyven repeated with a look of confidence. "We *all* want ta see the Prince of Liltimer."

"Nay Treyven," Esmeralda continued. "Ya misunderstand." She took Treyven's face in her hands and said, "'Tis not Atticus, Treyven . . . 'tis you."

The king noted that Treyven was staring at his mother in what must have been sheer disbelief.

Treyven raised his head and his eyes shifted from the king's eyes to Bromwell's. Lucian watched as both men looked upon the other, each checking for similarities between them.

Lucian could see the resemblance plainly as he compared them side-by-side. They displayed the same russet hair and blue-grey eyes as well as the same slender build. Age differences could not disguise the telling similarities of nose and jaw line. Even when Lucian had spent time with Treyven in the Tall Forest he had found Treyven to have his mother's looks and even temperament and his father's influence and appeal. He was a natural-born leader.

Lord Bromwell looked to King Lucian as if he doubted his own eyes and senses. Lucian smiled. "You have my word that Esmeralda speaks the truth, Sedgwick," declared Lucian. "Mariselle would not tell me Treyven's whereabouts unless I gave my word to uphold her dying wish to keep his whereabouts unknown to everyone until he reached his majority. You only need look at Treyven, for it is plain to see."

As was his habit when in contemplation, Lucian watched as

Treyven's hand involuntarily traced the scar upon his face.

Bromwell's eyes caught the gesture. "That scar!" he gasped, staring at Treyven's chin. "I be holding the babe prince in me arms whilst atop me charger. We be trotting around the castle gardens an' the babe be laughing. Mariselle be delighted ta see him laugh so heartily.

"A gardener tripped over his tools in the queen's pleasure garden an' startled me horse. The charger reared an' the babe fell from me arms an' got that gash upon his . . . yer chin." Moisture clouded Lord Bromwell's eyes, and Lucian could plainly see that the last of his misgivings vanished as if they had never been.

"I' faith!" exclaimed Sedgwick. He grabbed Treyven by the shoulders and announced, "The prince lives!"

CHAPTER THIRTY-SIX

K ing Lucian looked out at the growing crowd. Many people lined the walls, gathered in small knots, and conversed while waiting for the ceremony to begin. Lionholm's great hall was strung with banners this day, the symbol of the lion boldly displayed for the Liltians. Sunbeams streamed through high, stained-glass windows, bathing those in attendance in blessed warmth. Rays of light glittered off bejeweled nobles who were dressed in their finery, and rainbows of colorful fabrics worn by gentry and commoners alike swirled throughout the room. Many of the noble houses had arrived for this special event including the reigning monarchs of Avala, Sunon, and Vashires.

The king saw his newly betrothed niece, Aurora Leigh, on the arm of her intended, Eralon, and he could not help but smile at the perfect union. They were trailed by Dryden, Isa Dora, and three of the Elite Guardsmen, each dressed in royal finery. Eralon escorted the royal family to their seats on the second floor platform that overlooked the great hall and then stood proudly at their side awaiting the beginning of the ceremony.

Horns blew a lively fanfare, and then came the announcement. "All rise for His Majesty, the King of Avala!"

Rousing cheers erupted throughout the great hall with chants for King Lucian. "Long live the king! Long live the king!"

Lucian made his way to stand before the cheering mass. Turning to those gathered, he raised a hand to hush the crowd. "Welcome, welcome to you all! I would like to bid a special salutation to our visiting reigning monarchs, King Matthias of

Vashires and King Doros of Sunon."

The crowd cheered in a warm welcome to their allies.

"This is an astonishing day for us all," began King Lucian. "We are gathered here to bear witness and proclaim Treyven Leone, known to many of you as Treyven Fontacue and born Tridan Treyven Leone II, as the true son of King Tridan and Queen Mariselle."

Lucian held aloft a fading document he was carrying in his gloved hand. "This parchment is a declaration and the sworn testament of the late Queen Mariselle, signed on her deathbed with me as her witness," announced Lucian. "It is additionally authorized by the late Ambassador Valen Doral. Also, the Fontacues' signatures are on the document. Arden was Their Majesties' healer and Esmeralda was the queen's attendant, both were surrogate parents to Treyven. All herein corroborate that Treyven is the true successor to the throne, being the true son of King Tridan and Queen Mariselle.

"To further identify Treyven as the heir to the throne, we have present Liltimer's former Marshal Sedgwick Bromwell, Treyven's uncle and the queen's brother. We also bring before you the former palace healers of Lionholm." King Lucian continued as the witnesses approached. "They have examined Treyven and found him to have several identifying marks that prove our testimony."

Each one responded to Lucian's testimony, stating their evidence, and promised by their faith that Treyven was a true prince and son of King Tridan and Queen Mariselle.

"Everything we have told you is in accordance with this affidavit in my hand," continued King Lucian, "and it shall be posted outside the walls of Lionholm for all to see. Included in these official declarations you will find Queen Mariselle's proclamation that forbade us to disclose the true identity of the prince until Treyven had reached his majority and was fit to become the true ruler of his country."

At Lucian's signal, Treyven came forward to the cheers of the crowd. Lucian smiled as he watched the multitude welcome the newfound prince.

Once the crowd was settled, the keepers of the royal wardrobe stepped forward and dressed Treyven in Prince Blaine's fine mantle of royal blue that was fastened with a ring brooch at one shoulder. They then handed Lucian the royal crown that had belonged to Crown Prince Hayden. Treyven had requested these items be used in the ceremony to pay homage to his departed siblings. Treyven then bowed and dropped to one knee before King

Lucian as the ceremony continued.

"We beseech the Divine Majesty in the heavens above to grant unto his servant, Tridan Treyven Leone II, Prince of Liltimer, his rightful place as Crown Prince of Liltimer."

The king then set the crown upon Treyven's head.

Lucian bid Treyven to rise and led him to a pedestal that held several pages of documents. "As the true guardian of the lands of the former country of Liltimer, I do hereby pass the titles and lands that have always belonged to the family Leone while held under guardianship of Avala." Lucian produced another paper, and he signed the document with a flourish before passing it to Treyven for his signature, officially transferring the lands back to Treyven's hands. "Crown Prince Tridan Treyven Leone II, you have now taken over the lands of your birth."

Applause and cheers erupted at the pronouncement.

Lore Keeper Windermere then stepped forward to give the crown prince a gift of a beautiful bound leather book. The lore keeper bowed before Treyven and was bid to speak.

"Your Royal Highness, around the time of your birth, I was commissioned by your royal father, the late King Tridan, to trace your family's ancestry and record the information into a fine leather-bound book. Your family's history is elegantly detailed upon the pages herein with room for several generations to come. You will also find a pedigree chart displaying hand-drawn pictorials of all your known relatives from the lineage of both your royal father and mother. It has been in my possession for quite some time, and now it has found its way home to you."

"Gra'mercy, Lore Keeper Windermere," said Treyven. "I shall treasure it always."

Lucian could see he was clearly touched by the offering. Windermere bowed to the crown prince and made his way off the stage.

"Now that the crown prince has claimed his birthright," explained King Lucian, "we can move forward with the coronation. All rise for King Doros of Sunon and King Matthias of Vashires."

The sitting nobles stood with the others in attendance to greet the foreign monarchs.

The two monarchs approached King Lucian and, together, the three kings strode toward Treyven to offer him a branch from Sani, the oldest tree in Avala. All three kings had received a branch in their turn, a symbol of their alliance for peace. Each bough had been polished and carved with their country's coat of arms. Treyven nodded his head and took up the branch, thereby rejoining his country to their peace treaty.

The room grew silent and still, all understanding they were bearing witness to something of profound importance, for it sealed their union and once again marked Liltimer as part of their grand alliance.

Next, the royal keepers of the wardrobe returned to gently remove Treyven's mantel and crown. These were reverently placed in a silk-lined box for safekeeping.

They then fastened a leather sword belt about his waist. The belt featured two angled straps that hung from a large ring. A beautifully embossed leather scabbard with a gold collar and fittings were attached to the suspending straps. A heavy royal purple mantle was draped down his back and attached at his shoulders. Then, a black fur stole was placed about Treyven's shoulders. A gold and emerald brooch fastened the stole below his neck.

His raiment was followed by two rings to be placed upon his fingers by King Matthias of Vashires. One gold ring bore the head of a lion; it was a heavy piece favored by his late royal father that King Matthias placed on Treyven's right hand. The other was a signet ring that displayed the insignia and royal seal of the crown, and that ring was placed on his left hand.

As King Matthias placed the signet ring on Treyven's finger he announced, "We have now placed the signet seal on his finger bearing the arms of the Leone family, the emblem of authenticity and authority."

The people chorused, "So be it."

King Doros of Sunon then gave Treyven the royal scepter saying aloud, "Now we shall place the ceremonial scepter in his hand, the emblem of his power."

The people chorused, "So be it."

The keepers of the wardrobe then brought out a fine sword and handed it to King Lucian. It featured an elaborate hilt of various polished metals set with a large emerald at the rounded top of the pommel. Lucian presented the sword to Treyven.

"This sword was commissioned for you by your royal father on the day you were born," explained Lucian in quiet tones. "He affectionately dubbed your sword Lion's Pride after a pet name he had for you. He was a fine man and a good friend."

Treyven smiled at Lucian's words and sheathed the sword. "It is a good name for a sword. I will use it in my father's memory." Then, with a nod of his head to the King of Avala, he slowly knelt on one knee.

The last item brought Sedgwick Bromwell and King Lucian together. Each holding one side, they placed a jewel-encrusted crown upon Treyven's head, the very same crown that King Tridan had worn.

"This royal crown is the symbol of sovereignty and supreme power," said King Lucian. "I hereby place this crown upon the head of the new sovereign, which serves as a symbol of royalty to the people of Liltimer. Let it be known from this day forward, the Crown Prince Tridan Treyven Leone II, shall be known as King Treyven, and serve as the leader of the people of the country of Liltimer. May the Divine Majesty bless this crowning of your new sovereign."

The people again chorused, loudly and with excitement in their voices, "So be it!"

"Let us bestow many blessings upon the new king. May King Treyven live long and prosper."

All present spoke in unison: "May King Treyven live long and prosper."

King Treyven then received the respect of his peers. The kiss of peace was placed upon each cheek by the kings of Vashires, Sunon, and Avala.

Treyven dipped his head in respect to his peers and then turned to address the crowd. "I, King Treyven of the family Leone, do so solemnly swear to govern justly and preserve all the ancient customs of Liltimer.

"Let it be known that I have chosen a new name for our country so that under my rule we shall have a new start. From this day forward, our country shall be known as Terra Leone, and her people Terra Leoneans."

King Lucian then led King Treyven to his splendid new throne. The throne was an exquisite piece and looked as if the new king was about to sit within the protective embrace of a fierce lion that would help defend the crown.

The top of the chair featured an exquisitely carved growling lion's head with mane, and above its crown was the country's coat of arms. The chair's back resembled the lion's chest, generously cushioned and upholstered in soft, light brown velvet and decorated around the edges in gold piping. The padded armrests ended in carved paws, and the chair's legs were fashioned to resemble a lion's crouched hindquarters.

"A gift from Kullipthius," said Lucian, in a hushed tone.

King Treyven smiled at the imperator's gift, and then he sat humbly upon his new throne for the first time.

King Lucian concluded the coronation, and in a formal and serious voice, he said, "I ask the people of Terra Leone and all present to bow before King Treyven Leone, and he shall be strengthened on his throne by this blessing."

All those present showed their respect, each in the way of their own country. Women curtsied, many dropped to their knees, others bowed their heads, while some displayed fist over heart, for the newly appointed monarch of the country of Terra Leone, King Treyven, and the fallen country of Liltimer was born anew.

Long live the king!

Preview

BLUE CHAMELEON

C oncealed in a darkened alcove of a great cavern's passageway, a pair of piercing, crystal blue eyes watched as an opulently dressed royal figure exited one of the cave's hollowed assembly chambers. The figure stood with regal bearing in a creamy white doublet heavily embroidered in threads of gold that fastened in the front with ten golden buttons. This exquisite garment was worn over a purple silk tunic with long, fitted sleeves. Dark brown breeches were stylishly tucked into knee-high sable boots of the finest leather. Upon his brow he wore a bejeweled crown holding back the length of his dark-brown hair.

The observer with the crystal blue eyes knew there were many extraordinary curiosities about this regal gentleman, some hidden yet displayed openly, but none the less kept secret from humankind—except for a privileged few. This was exemplified by the platinum ore that was a part of his forehead's structure and composition, which fit like a puzzle piece in the center of his diadem. A diamond cabochon was added to the platinum, as had been done to his father before him, when he was crowned Imperator of the Oralian Empire. And adding to the mystery of this imperator was his uncanny ability to alter his physical form from man to dragon.

He was Imperator Kullipthius of Oralia, and all the inhabitants of his clandestine empire were dragons.

"We all have our secrets," whispered the observer. A sudden

flash of light lit the alcove as a fair-haired nobleman emerged from the recesses where a sapphire dragon with crystal blue eyes had once stood in observation. Brilliantly attired in turquoise and grey and displaying a silken headband with a sapphire cabochon in its center, the man approached the sovereign from behind and fell into step beside him.

He pushed a pair of spectacles higher on his nose before asking, "You called for me, Imperator Kullipthius?"

"Aye, Advisor Vahl Zayne. I would like for you to accompany me to Flayre's prison cell. A dire circumstance has come to my attention. Because you are the official authority and keeper of Oralia's Ancient Transcripts and have knowledge of the information I seek, I need your invaluable contribution."

"I shall be more than happy to assist in any way I can," replied Vahl Zayne.

"Chief Romus came to the palace yestereve to report some disturbing news," explained the imperator. "While at Terra Leone, King Lucian of Avala had summoned him to the fortress prison. When Romus arrived, he found that a door to one of the cells had been splintered and wrenched from its hinges. That particular cell had housed two prisoners. The chieftain said the cell was empty when he arrived, but there was blood everywhere. What I find disturbing is that he scented a chameleon at the site."

The advisor was shocked at the news. "That is dreadful. He was sure it was a chameleon?"

Kullipthius nodded. "As you are aware, it was about twenty yearmarks ago when the human named Lord Bromwell had leapt to Chief Romus' aid when the chieftain was bit in the leg by a chameleon. Sword in hand, the marshal had severed the venomous tip of the chameleon's tail from its body just as it was about to strike Chief Romus. Unfortunately, his lordship had little time to react, so the barbed tip imbedded itself in Bromwell's shoulder, injecting him with venom.

"Eternally grateful for the field marshal's intervention, the chieftain had stayed by Bromwell's side until he was healed.

"This is what led Romus to the realization that the prisoners had been attacked by a chameleon. He said that the smell of the chameleon's venom seeping from Bromwell's injuries was distinct, and he recognized it immediately when he inspected the cell.

"It has been many yearmarks since our last encounter with a chameleon, and we had thought it to be the last of its kind. It seems we were mistaken.

"Although I do not like to judge an entire species by the actions of the few we have encountered, I believe we must remain alert. As dragons, we have the benefit of protecting ourselves with our size, our tough hides, and our draconic gifts. Regrettably, chameleons do pose a dangerous threat to the humans who live amongst us. We know that once chameleons consume their prey, they can alter their physique into an exact duplicate of their victim while also acquiring their memories and intelligence. This affords them a grim and deadly advantage over the general human populace that is unaware of their existence and ill-equipped to survive an encounter."

"I do understand your concerns, Your Majesty," said Vahl Zayne, "and I am curious as to why the chameleon targeted these prisoners. Who was in that cell?"

"We had believed it was a human, by the name of Danuvius Doral and one of his mercenaries," answered Kullipthius. "Danuvius was in league with Flayre, and at this time we are uncertain if Danuvius was a victim, set free, or quite possibly, the chameleon.

"Since Danuvius was Flayre's underling, it seems logical that the ruby dragon Flayre had his claws in these troubling events. With all the crimes he has committed, along with the fact that Flayre was a wielder of dark magic, I am wondering if he has something to do with the chameleons' reappearance.

"I would like to question him. If we do not get anywhere, I will have an amber quartz use his gift of influence on Flayre to persuade him to talk. It is imperative that we get to the bottom of this mystery."

As Advisor Vahl Zayne followed Kullipthius into the cavern that held Flayre's prison, they called out a greeting to the guardian stationed outside Flayre's cell. Vahl Zayne noticed the guardian seemed deep in thought as he stared fixedly at Flayre, who appeared to be sleeping. The cell guardian turned slowly from his watch and bowed his head in greeting.

As Vahl Zayne moved closer to the guard, the advisor's keen eyes caught splashes of blood on the guard's dark attire and boots. With quick reflexes, he yanked a startled imperator back by the shoulder and stepped before the Oralian ruler, putting himself eye to eye with the surprised prison guard.

"Is something amiss, Vahl Zayne?" questioned Kullipthius.

The advisor threw his hand back. "Stay behind me, My Imperator."

Vahl Zayne never took his keen blue eyes from the guard as he addressed him. "His Imperial Majesty's guards are always impeccably dressed. None would dare stand watch in attire that was stained, most certainly not splattered in blood. I know what you are, chameleon. You may as well drop your charade."

The guardian's facial features blurred and, upon transformation, a smirking noble, dressed in the old Liltian garb appeared. The man clapped his hands slowly in a display of sarcasm as his eyes narrowed. "What good senses ya 'aves. What a pity ya spoiled me surprise."

Flayre's laughter caught the attention of those present. He rose from the bed where he had been sleeping and walked toward the bars of his cell. "The chameleon Scale has always been loyal, Kullipthius. As you can see, he was the one that took Danuvius' place under my orders. I shall take much pleasure in watching you die."

Flayre smirked as he looked Kullipthius in the eyes. "Kill the imperator slowly, Scale; and do not forget to eliminate his betraying advisor."

Scale's voice took on a menacing purr. "Come now, Flayre. I know ya be stripped o' yer dark magic, because I'm no longer under yer control. The only one I'd planned ta rip ta shreds be ye, Flayre.

"Ya 'aves taken away me love, Sauria, me clutchmates, an' me unhatched offspring ta the Desertlands an' treated me like I be something ya found stuck ta the bottom o' yer hind foot. An' I shall 'aves me revenge."

Scale turned back to Vahl Zayne, who was slowly making his way toward him.

"If ya insist on getting in me way," threatened Scale, "I will make short work o' ya as well. I'd advise ya ta keep out o' me affairs."

"The Desertlands are an expansive place," interrupted Flayre, "and I am the only one who knows where your family resides. Kill me and you will never find them. Free me from this prison, Scale, and I promise you will never regret your actions.

"You did well posing as Danuvius Doral, and you will be appropriately rewarded. And I have knowledge of where to find the last known volume of *The Dark Arts*. We can restore the rest of your brethren. You can rule over your own clan. Why, I will pledge that—"

"Silence!" hissed Scale. "I think ye 'aves forgotten, Flayre: I be me own master. After I devour ya, I will 'aves all o' yer memories an' be able ta find me family meself, including yer dark arts book. An' I'ves eaten a rat. I will soon slip in through the bars 'o yer cage an' keep ya company."

Vahl Zayne watched as Flayre distanced himself from the menacing being and placed his back against the far wall of his prison chamber. His frightened eyes sought out Kullipthius.

"Scale, Flayre cannot harm you anymore," said Kullipthius. "He can neither change into his dragon form nor use dark magic now. He is of little threat. Let me help you find your family."

"Help? Ye would help me? Nay, yer pretty words aim ta veer me from me course," scoffed Scale. "I follow no one's rules but me own. An' stay out o' me way! Or ye too shall find yer fate ta be the same as Flayre's. Prepare ta die, Flayre!"

No sooner had the words passed Scale's lips than a wall of ice formed across the cell bars from floor to ceiling. Vahl Zayne had used his draconic gift of frost and ice to stop the chameleon's advances. It was so thick that Flayre's silhouette was but a blurred shadow on the other side.

"I think not," said Vahl Zayne coolly. "And I beg you to reconsider as you will have to get past me."

The chameleon shrugged. "As ya wish."

Scale then launched himself at the lean blond advisor, transforming to his true self mid-leap. The weight of the chameleon sent the three of them sliding across the polished stone floor. Vahl Zayne could barely hold the chameleon's snapping jaws from his throat.

"Do not let it touch you! Get back!" yelled Vahl Zayne, and the imperator leapt to his feet and backed away. The chameleon seized upon the imperial advisor's distraction, and its wedge-shaped head dove and bit Vahl Zayne's forearm.

Blood welled from between its multiple rows of razor-sharp teeth. Vahl Zayne unleashed a pained roar and smashed an ice-coated fist against the beast's ferocious face. The frozen water cracked and jagged shards flew into the chameleon's eyes. Scale yelped, released his prey and jumped back, shaking his head and pawing at his eyes. Vahl Zayne scrambled to his feet and, again, placed himself between his imperator and the monster. Red fluid from the rips in his skin coated the sleeve of the advisor's tunic, and dark blood dripped from his fingers.

"Leave, Imperator Kullipthius! Keep away and let no one else in!" shouted Vahl Zayne over his shoulder before shedding his humanity amid a dazzling light. He knew it would be better to fight off Scale's advances in his sapphire dragon form.

"No! I cannot abandon you!" countered Kullipthius.

The words rang out loud and clear through Vahl Zayne's mind.

The imperator was using a dragon form of communication called *Drahk*, sending his thoughts directly to Vahl Zayne without speaking aloud.

With the sapphire dragon and the chameleon in their true sizes, there was not enough room in the chamber for Kullipthius to transform into a dragon. Vahl Zayne knew this and used the knowledge to prevent his imperator from joining the fight. He would keep the imperator safe, no matter the cost to himself.

"Do not worry for me. Go!" Vahl Zayne was tracking his adversary's movements as he responded. The beast flowed up the side of the cavern as nimbly as a spider, trying to get at the imperator with his sharp-as-steel claws.

The sapphire dragon had to react quickly.

The chameleon found he was painfully thwarted, knocked from his perch as a column of ice—slick with frost—suddenly thrust itself up from the ground. He landed hard on his back on the cavern floor. Deadly spears of ice formed on the ceiling and then sliced down toward him. The chameleon was on the defensive; he was dodging, leaping, rolling back, and forced further from his targets by the frost dragon's assault.

Scale narrowed his yellow, reptilian eyes on Vahl Zayne's dragon form once he gained his footing.

"Impressive, but nay powerful enough ta stop me," hissed the chameleon. He licked at his wicked teeth. *"Ya be bleeding heavily from me first strike an' tiring. Soon I shall be done with ya an' aves me way with Flayre."*

Vahl Zayne did not answer and, instead, summoned the cold. A curling fog lifted from the floor, and snow began falling about the room in earnest.

"Vahl Zayne!" Kullipthius' mind called out from somewhere within the blinding snowstorm.

All sight was obscured by the frost dragon's gifts and his imperator would be masked from view. Now Vahl Zayne could concentrate on his combatant.

As predicted, the chameleon appeared like a ghost from the freezing mist and leapt for the sapphire dragon.

Vahl Zayne dodged the strike at the last instant, and the chameleon slid forward on its stomach. Scrambling for leverage on the ice, it crashed headfirst into the wall.

Vahl Zayne used the opportunity to pounce. He pressed his superior weight down upon Scale's back as he clawed at the nape of the chameleon's neck, ripping at the bony spines projecting from its hide.

Scale screamed in what sounded like a combination of fury and agony, yet Vahl Zayne would not relent. With a resounding crack, the frost dragon tugged with all his might and stripped the plating from the monster's collar to reveal vulnerable flesh and arteries.

The chameleon struck Vahl Zayne with his stinger-tipped tail again and again, trying to dislodge the sapphire dragon from its back. Venom dripped from the hollow point of its stinger before each strike.

The frost dragon threw his head back and screamed in anguish. His cavernous jaw gaped to its widest stretch, and exposed a mouthful of menacingly sharp teeth. Snarling, Vahl Zayne threw his head forward and chomped on the chameleon's exposed neck. He growled and shook his head, causing his fangs to grip tighter and sink deeper, before he tore his head away. Then there was silence.

The ice was slowly melting to reveal the horrors of the battle. Water dripped from the cave's ceiling like rain. Blood splattered the cavern, staining the remaining snow crimson. The only ice that remained was the frozen shield that had been erected along Flayre's cell bars.

The chameleon's corpse lay upon the ground, its head severed from its body. Close by, Vahl Zayne was lying on his side, now wrapped in his human form. His turquoise cloak was shredded and his spectacles were gone. Blood was streaked through his fair hair. He had multiple, seeping puncture wounds where he had been stung by the chameleon's lethal tail.

"No!" cried Kullipthius, sprinting through the mist toward him. Kullipthius helped him roll to his back and Vahl Zayne moaned.

"Do not move. I will summon Laliah to heal you," said Kullipthius.

Vahl Zayne could see the worried expression on his imperator's face while he was studying his seeping wounds.

"I beg of you, Your Imperial Majesty, do not call Imperatrix Laliah. I need to talk with you privately," requested Vahl Zayne. "Prithee, help me sit against the cavern wall."

Vahl Zayne was brought to a sitting position with Kullipthius' support.

"I have other gifts," revealed Vah Zayne. "I can heal myself. I only ask that you allow me to do so, and take a step back."

Kullipthius did as he was bid, though he appeared to be reluctant to leave his advisor's side.

"I wanted to tell you for so long, but I did not know how. Now there is no choice."

There was a blurring about Vahl Zayne's human guise, and in a blink and a flash he had transformed. He knew his imperator was expecting to see his sapphire dragon form, but in its stead, a sinewy and vivid blue creature had materialized.

At first, shock and confusion marred his imperator's features, then his mouth gaped open and his eyes widened as recognition dawned.

"This is my true form," explained Vahl Zayne. *"I was born a chameleon."*

ABOUT THE AUTHOR

Melissa G. Lewis would love to tell you that she lives in the Bahamas with her billionaire husband, drinks tropical drinks while sunning on the beach, and spends her time hobnobbing with famous people on her yacht. But instead . . . oh, never mind, she said she will just stick with her dreams. (After all, she is a fantasy writer.)

Please visit the author's website at:
www.melissaglewis.com

Legends of Sapphirus Series
Books by
Melissa G. Lewis
are available in
eBook and Paperback

Book 1 - **Guardians of Sapphirus**

Book 2 – **The Lore Keeper's Tale**
(Find out how Flayre discovered dark magic)

**NEW BOOKS
COMING SOON**

Legends of the Lore Keeper
&
Hallows of the Mist Moors

Proof

Made in the USA
Columbia, SC
19 September 2018